THE
Lady
OF THE
HALL

Also by Veronica Heley

Eden Hall

THE *Eden* HALL SERIES

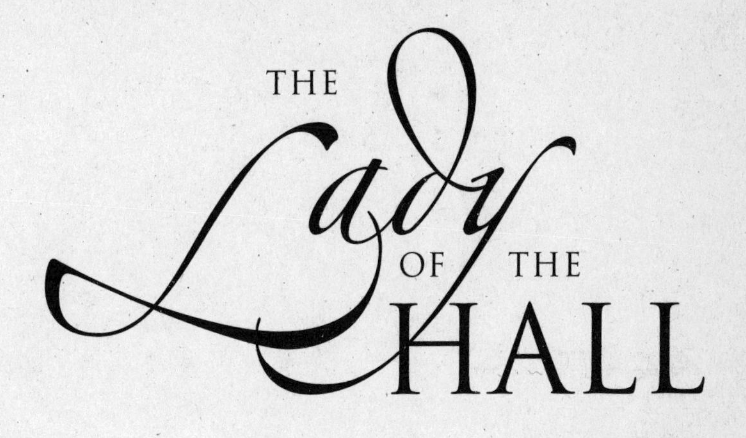

BOOK 2

VERONICA HELEY

ZONDERVAN™

GRAND RAPIDS, MICHIGAN 49530 USA

ZONDERVAN™

The Lady of the Hall

Requests for information should be addressed to:

Zondervan, *Grand Rapids, Michigan 49530*

Library of Congress Cataloging-in-Publication Data

Heley, Veronica
The lady of the hall / by Veronica Heley—1st ed.
p. cm.
ISBN 0-310-25079-X (softcover)
1. Young women—Fiction. 2. Inheritance and succession—Fiction. 3. Administration of estates—Fiction. 4. Home ownership—Fiction. 5. Villages—Fiction. 6. England—Fiction. I. Title.
PR6070.H6915L33 2005
823'.92—dc22

2004020699

Interior design by Michelle Espinoza

Printed in the United States of America

---

05 06 07 08 09 10 /❖ DCI/ 10 9 8 7 6 5 4 3 2 1

THE
Lady
OF THE
HALL

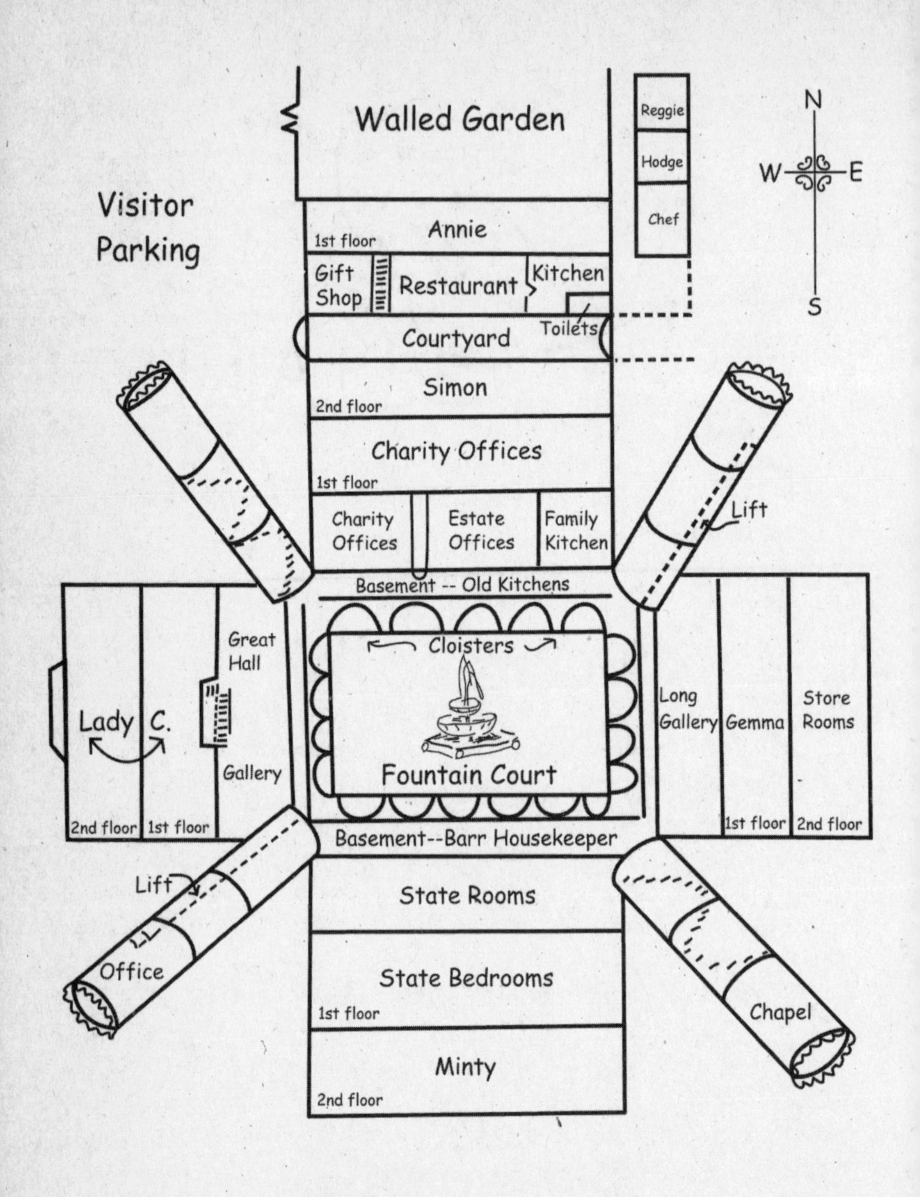
Walled Garden
Reggie
Hodge
Chef
N
W
E
S
Visitor Parking
Annie
1st floor
Gift Shop
Restaurant
Kitchen
Toilets
Courtyard
Simon
2nd floor
Charity Offices
1st floor
Lift
Charity Offices
Estate Offices
Family Kitchen
Basement -- Old Kitchens
Great Hall
Cloisters
Lady C.
Gallery
Fountain Court
Long Gallery
Gemma
Store Rooms
2nd floor
1st floor
1st floor
2nd floor
Basement--Barr Housekeeper
Lift
State Rooms
Office
State Bedrooms
1st floor
Chapel
Minty
2nd floor

Eden Hall

Chapter One

It was a cry for help. "Barr's in trouble. In the library. Oh, do come, quickly!"

The great house lay quiet about them. Waiting. Watchful.

Minty was fond of Barr, and couldn't refuse to help. "Of course I'll come."

The two girls passed swiftly back through the silent rooms, switching off lights as they went. When they reached the library, one girl stepped back to guard the door.

Shadows stole down from the ceiling and darkened the corners of the room.

It was a trap. Barr wasn't there. Instead there was the man Minty feared most in the world. He said, "At long, long last."

Minty balanced on her toes. "Do you really mean to rape me?"

"Who said anything about rape? You're going to come to me willingly, my lovely girl. I suppose you'll put up a token defence, but we both know that's just for show. Don't fight too hard, or I may well have to mark your face. I'm going to teach you enough so you won't want to marry anyone but me."

He lunged at her and she darted around the desk.

She felt her self-control slip and screamed. There was a listening silence. Nothing happened.

He laughed. He darted around the desk and caught her from behind as she fled. "Stop struggling, you little fool!"

He was holding her fast from behind, with both arms clamped to her sides.

She breathed rapidly, trying to snatch back her self-control. She was helpless. She couldn't do anything to save herself.

"There, now! You see, it's all going to be so easy."

Araminta Cardale—known as Minty—jumped out of bed and ran to throw back the curtains. Kneeling on the window seat, she lifted the thick, fair hair from her neck and tossed it back around her shoulders.

Two storeys below her window, a great swathe of lawn sloped down to a man-made lake. On this late September morning the water—and the Park beyond—shimmered through mist.

The sun tipped up over the horizon, bringing a flush of colour to the world. The mist over the lake thinned and parted. There hadn't been a hard frost yet, so only the topmost leaves of the trees in the Park were touched with gold.

The lawns sparkled as the first rays of the sun reached them. The sky was pale blue, washed clean by heavy dew, with not a cloud in sight.

Did all this really belong to her now? And her own true love Patrick, too? *Oh, Patrick! Are you out of bed yet? Is it too early to ring you?*

There was no photograph of him by her bedside. She grinned, thinking how he'd react if she wanted to take a photo of him.

He'd say, "Do you want to break the camera?"

Ah well; Patrick Sands wasn't anyone's idea of a pretty boy—his nose was too long for that—but he was tall, dark and elegant, and completely unaware how attractive he was to the opposite sex. He was a good man, though he'd have been embarrassed if anyone had said so, and Minty loved him as she'd never loved anyone before.

So many childhood sweethearts never find one another again. Thank You, Lord, for bringing us together again.

Yesterday she'd started the day as a poor relation and ended up as mistress of the vast Eden Hall, its surrounding acres of land and the village at its gates. Patrick had said she could do better than marry a poor country solicitor, but she'd refused to listen and now they were engaged.

She wanted to turn cartwheels. She shouted, "Yes!" and punched the air. She looked over her shoulder as if her aunt had scolded her for shouting. Then laughed aloud. Aunt Agnes belonged to the past and had no more power to hurt her.

Excitement made Minty restless. She longed to explore, and why shouldn't she? The Hall was now hers, at least till noon when it would be opened to the public and tourists would start to trickle through the State Rooms.

Well, there were certain parts which were off limits, occupied as they were for the time being by her father's second wife Lisa and her children, but she could avoid them. Below her the great house slept. Minty had the odd fancy that she could waken it to life again by visiting every room. Like Sleeping Beauty in reverse, she thought, smiling.

When Sir Micah's second wife Lisa had decided to open the Hall to the public, Sir Micah had reserved the top floor of the south wing for himself, bringing in a designer to furnish and decorate his suite. These were now Minty's own rooms. Unfortunately Minty's father had gone for the traditional-in-brocade look and the result—to Minty's mind—was a showpiece: stiff, dated and not particularly comfortable.

Her father had left Minty a great deal of money, so wouldn't it be possible to turn Eden Hall back again into a family home?

She glanced at the cheap watch she was wearing. She must keep an eye on the time, because she did have one important engagement that morning. Sir Micah Cardale had been an international financier who'd poured money into the Hall during his marriage to Minty's mother. That first marriage had led to tragedy, but Sir Micah had always been fond of Eden Hall and used it as his base in Britain, even during his later years when he'd been setting up a national charity for educational projects in deprived areas. In all his financial dealings Sir Micah had relied on a competent middle-aged woman called Annie Phillips.

Annie Phillips had been kind to the penniless Minty when she'd returned to the Hall a month ago. Annie had helped Minty to see her dying father, had found her a place to live in the village and a part-time job. Minty might now be mistress of the Hall, but she was grateful to the older woman and somewhat in awe of her. Ms Phillips had asked to see Minty at eleven, so she must keep an eye on the time. Until then she could do what she liked.

Minty pulled on a blue sweater, jeans and trainers. She didn't have many clothes and those she had were nearly all from charity shops. Autumn was coming and she'd need to buy some more. This time they would be brand new. Wowee!

Suddenly she felt hungry. There was no sign of her father's housekeeper, Serafina, who slept at the back of the suite, so Minty raided the kitchen for a chunk of bread and jam and a mug of coffee.

First things first. She would start her day and her new life with God in the Eden family chapel.

She slipped out of the door at the end of her father's suite into the tower . . . and came face-to-face with her stepbrother, Simon.

Despite herself, she recoiled. He was the last person she wanted to meet, especially in such an isolated place. He was Lisa's son from a previous marriage. And it was Lisa—previously Sir Micah's secretary—whose lies had led to the death of Minty's mother. In a shockingly short time Lisa had become his second wife and he'd adopted Simon.

Thoroughly spoilt, Simon was always in debt. He'd assumed he'd inherit everything, and had been furious when he'd learned the property was entailed on Minty. He hadn't given up; first he'd tried to seduce her, and then offered marriage. When that had failed, he'd organised attempts on her life.

Simon moved in close. "Dearest not-quite-sister, I was just coming to find you. We must talk, you and I."

His face was that of an angel, his eyes as blue as hers, his hair as fair. All the Edens were fair and blue-eyed but Simon was not an Eden, and there was a twist to his mind that came from his mother Lisa, and not from the straight-forward Edens.

Minty knew better than to trust him. Her heart was beating too fast. They were all alone in the tower. Even if she cried out for help, no one would hear. He was so close she could smell his aftershave and feel the warmth of his body.

He ran his fingertip down her cheek. "Loosen up."

She blurted out, "Patrick Sands has asked me to marry him and I've accepted."

His eyes deepened in colour and the lines of his mouth hardened. "You marry me, or no one. Understood?" He bent and kissed her, hard. He'd moved so quickly that she was taken by surprise. "There," he said, smiling again, very sure of himself. "Can your lukewarm lover match that?"

"How dare you!"

"Or else? There's no one here but . . ."

The door from the chapel clicked open and there stood her father's housekeeper, Serafina, in a quilted dressing gown, with her grey-streaked black hair in a long plait over her shoulder. Serafina folded her arms and looked at Simon as if he were a bottle of milk that had gone off.

Simon released Minty. "Another time." He ran lightly down the stairs.

"Thank you, Serafina." Minty drew in a deep breath. Despite her pretence of calmness, she was trembling. "Simon doesn't understand the meaning of the word 'no', does he?"

She went into the chapel and leaned against the door, telling herself that it was useless to get upset. Simon might think what he liked. It didn't mean it was going to happen.

Eden Hall had been built in a square around the Fountain Courtyard. To solve the problem of the wings having been built at different times and on different levels, a tower containing a staircase had been built at each corner. The top of this particular tower housed the chapel which had always been a place of refuge for the Eden women—not least for Minty's own mother through her short-lived marriage to Sir Micah. The chapel had windows on three sides and this morning was glowing with the light of the rising sun. It had a calming influence.

The white Michaelmas daisies Minty had placed there yesterday still looked fresh. She'd chosen daisies in memory of her unhappy mother and of the pact she and Patrick had made as children.

Patrick, aged ten, had been showing Minty how to make a daisy chain. She liked him better than anyone else in the whole world, except her mother and father. Patrick was an only child, like her. He'd taught her to read and write.

Minty, nearly five years old, announced, "I'm going to marry Patrick when I grow up."

Minty's mother and Patrick's father had laughed. But Patrick—six years older—had said, "I'll wait . . ."

Minty knelt on the cushion before the altar and discovered that she was still holding her mug of coffee and half a piece of bread. Oh dear! She hadn't meant any lack of reverence. She thought God might even be amused that she'd brought bread and a drink when she came to His place on her first morning as owner of the Hall.

She gave thanks. For everything she'd received. For friends, especially for Patrick, who was the best friend she could ever have. She thanked God for the understanding, the forgiveness and the love that had finally come about between her father and herself.

She asked for protection from Simon. She tried not to think about what he might have done if Serafina hadn't been there.

She prayed for guidance. Patrick had been a wise counsellor since her return to the village, but last night he refused to advise her any more, saying she was a lot stronger and wiser than she thought. Surely he was mistaken? She was only a green girl. He was older than she and surely it wasn't wrong to rely on him when he knew so much more about, well ... everything ... than she did?

The only advice he'd given her—and she ground her teeth remembering what the infuriating man had said—was "Have a look at the books." What on earth had he meant by that?

The morning sun was warm about her. She relaxed. *Dear Lord, give me wisdom and understanding. You know the problems I have to face, the difficulties in the family ... my stepmother Lisa ... Simon's greed and ambition. My poor half-sister drifting through life. Everything about the house and estate is run down, everyone is looking to me for work and money ...*

She remembered that Solomon had asked for wisdom when he succeeded his father David and felt comforted. Perhaps God would grant her a little wisdom, too.

She left the chapel cautiously, but there was no sign of Simon. For years he'd milked the estate to support his extravagant lifestyle, and when that crock of gold began to fail, he'd planned to lease the Hall to an American consortium to be run as a health farm, with himself as director of the company that was to run it.

Minty had to admit that she was afraid of Simon, not only because he thought she could still be his for the asking, but also because he was desperate for money and didn't care how he got it.

She pushed thoughts of Simon out of her head.

This was her first morning as Lady of the Hall, and she was going to make the most of it. Running down the stairs to the first floor, Minty opened the door into the room in which she'd been born. The four-poster bed stood against the inner wall, as it always had done. As a child she'd played on and in it with her mother. Even, sometimes, with her busy father.

The "bouncy" bed, they'd called it. This was not the great State Bed which the tourists would come to marvel at, but a lighter Victorian reproduction. The heavy cream curtains were not those embroidered by Eden women generations ago with green and blue flowers and fantastical birds on the important Jacobean bed, but were patterned in a William Morris design of willow leaves. When the curtains were let down, the bed made a private "house" in which to play.

Minty released the blinds at the windows which kept the room in shadow, and put her coffee mug down on the window-sill before unhooking the red rope which kept visitors away from the furniture. She smoothed the whitework counterpane only to discover it had been covered with a sheet of plastic.

She pulled the plastic off and climbed onto the bed to see if it still bounced. It didn't. It was unyielding and quite horrible. Yuk. She supposed it was historically correct to have a flock mattress on the bed, but it wouldn't be possible to sleep on it.

She wondered if Patrick would be amused by the idea of sleeping in the four poster—if she had a good mattress put on it—or if he would think it old-fashioned and inconvenient?

Patrick owned a red-brick, Virginia-creepered Georgian house in the village High Street nearby. His office and reception rooms were on the ground floor with his living quarters above. His furniture was antique but intended for daily use. You could flop into deeply cushioned chairs and put a mug of coffee on the floor without feeling like an intruder. Unlike life in her father's suite.

Minty had imagined she'd move into Patrick's home once they were married. Now she'd inherited the Hall, she didn't know what they'd do.

She looked at her watch. Half past eight. Was it still too early to ring him? She unhooked her mobile from her belt and at that moment he rang her.

"Minty . . . ?" No endearments, no enquiries after her well-being. "Have you any idea why the awe-inspiring Annie Phillips wants to see me this morning?" There was a clatter of cups in the background. "Your father's driver's just brought me a note, asking if I could spare her a few minutes at ten this morning. I'm quaking at the prospect."

He didn't sound as if he were quaking, but Patrick would crack a joke if he were facing a firing squad.

Minty pushed back her hair with one hand. "I've no idea. She asked me to meet her at eleven but she didn't say anything about seeing you. Can you fit her in?"

"With a bit of juggling. I've got an early bird in the office with me now—just making her a coffee. I'll ring when I'm finished, right?"

"Yes, but Patrick ... what did you mean about looking at the books?"

He laughed and disconnected. Infuriating man!

Minty glanced at her watch and hurriedly inspected the other rooms on that floor. Each was beautifully presented, but somehow lifeless. There was no trace of the Eden family, whose home it had been for centuries.

The last room had been her grandfather's study. She remembered that in her childhood it had retained the scent of his tobacco though he'd been dead for some years. She'd often played hide-and-seek there, crawling into the cubbyhole of his great desk. His study was now just another bedroom, and she couldn't spot his desk at all. Perhaps it had been put into storage? She knew there was a great jumble of family bits and pieces in the east wing.

She couldn't see Patrick living in these rooms. Or herself, for that matter.

She retraced her steps and took the stairs down to the ground floor and the Long Gallery. This was where she'd danced with Patrick in a charity shop dress at the Ball. She lifted her arms and waltzed around, imagining herself still in his arms. She sang, "I could have danced all night ..." Then laughed at herself.

In childhood this was where she'd run and played on rainy days. Could she still hear the echo of childish voices? Patrick had played with her, of course. Simon and his side-kick Miles had been the same age as Patrick, but they'd scorned to play with a little girl. There'd been other children? From the Manor?

Had they had a badminton net set up here? Had it been Patrick who'd taught her how to keep her eye on the racquet, never to take your eye off the shuttlecock? She grimaced. Hadn't Simon broken her racquet and lied that she'd done it herself? He'd been a nasty small boy even then, though so handsome that grown-ups never suspected what he was really like.

The sun had gone in and the oak floorboards looked dusty and neglected. She pulled up some of the window blinds and went to renew her friendship with the family portraits grouped over and around the two carved marble fireplaces.

Sir Ralph Eden had always been her favourite, swaggering away in his slashed doublet, the velvet cap on his head adorned with a fine red ostrich plume. Opposite him was the fair-haired heiress he'd married, in her stiff ruff and hooped skirt. Above the fireplace was her great-grandfather Edward Eden, who looked bad-tempered but apparently had been the gentlest of men. He'd been an Ambassador and died of typhoid in Constantinople.

She traced the family portraits down through the ages, as Eden followed Eden until at last the male line died out with her grandfather Ralph, who'd left the Hall to his only daughter, that pale butterfly Millicent Eden . . . who in turn had brought the wealthy financier Sir Micah Cardale into the family.

Millicent's portrait was not here. It had probably been banished to an attic, just as Minty had been banished to live with her uncle and aunt in the city. Sir Micah's portrait hung in the library opposite that of his second wife Lisa, but everyone else was here, including some relatives she didn't remember at all. But then, she'd only been five when she left.

The Edens were all fair of hair and blue of eye, with a strong chin—like Minty. None of them were spectacularly handsome or especially beautiful, but neither did they simper as sitters often did.

"You're terribly alike," said a voice behind Minty.

Minty whirled around. The girl behind her also jumped, blushing from high forehead to plump neck. She was more than a trifle overweight, had wispy fair hair inadequately held back with an elastic band and was dressed in a droopy black jumper and skirt. Her feet were encased in blue slip-ons and she was clutching a clipboard to her chest, which could have done with a better bra.

Minty held out her hand. "We met last night when I was introduced to everyone. You're in the Estate Office and your name is . . ."

"Tessa. Ms Phillips said you might need a personal assistant to help you with correspondence and would I report to you." She darted her eyes around. "You couldn't know, of course, but Mrs Kitchen—that's the housekeeper—will be furious that you've opened the blinds and let the light in. The cleaners are waiting to come in to make the place ready for opening time and Lady Cardale wants to see you, and Simon and your sister Gemma and oh, lots of people. And your father's housekeeper says you were expected for breakfast half an hour ago."

Minty knew which of those summons was important. She also decided that although she might need someone to help her, Tessa hardly looked bright enough for the job.

"I didn't realise it was so late." For a moment Minty was disorientated. "Which is the quickest way up to my father's rooms?"

Tessa led the way to the tower at the far end of the Gallery, where a modern lift had been installed beside the stairs for the benefit of disabled tourists. She pressed the button to summon the lift, her eyes twitching to Minty and away. "Everybody's afraid you're going to make a lot of changes, but you'll be guided by Simon, won't you? After all, he's been running the place for ever, and knows what's best."

So this was someone else who thought Simon was perfect. "Surely you don't want the Hall turned into a health farm?"

Tessa was beginning to relax. "The Hall is losing money, so why not? Someone said you were marrying Patrick Sands, but of course I didn't believe that."

"Why not?" The lift arrived, and they stepped inside.

"He's not at all good-looking or even rich, so you can't be serious about him."

Minty was amused. No, Patrick wasn't particularly good-looking, though she never thought of him in those terms. If you compared him to Simon, then Simon won in the looks department, but lost in any other.

"Patrick's my kind of man," said Minty, reducing Tessa to silence. "Well, Tessa, I've got a lot to learn and I'm sure you can be a great help. I need an office, a large diary, a telephone, a computer with access to the Internet. I need to make a list of all the people I ought to speak to . . ."

"Oh dear, I don't know if . . . I mean, I'm not sure how to . . ."

Minty gritted her teeth. Her first impulse was to blast this incompetent girl to smithereens but pity stayed her hand. Tessa couldn't help it. "I'm sorry, I shouldn't have asked you. May I borrow your clipboard with the list of everyone who wants to speak to me? Thanks."

They reached the top landing. "Simon's rooms," said Tessa, pointing to the oldest, Jacobean wing. "The Estate Office is on the ground floor and if you don't need me, I'd better get back or someone will get into a terrible state."

She pointed to a door on the opposite side of the tower. "That's the east wing, with the Long Gallery on the ground floor and your sister Gemma's rooms above it. There's nothing on this top floor except junk but if you follow the corridor, it'll lead you back to the chapel and from there you can get into your father's rooms."

Minty raced along the dusty corridor, glancing at the collection of Victorian silhouettes of past Edens that hung between the windows. Some hung askew and one had fallen to the floor. She picked it up to replace it on the wall but found the wire was broken. She propped portly Sir Piers against the wall and glanced down into the Fountain Court below. She thought it was typical of Simon's reign that the superb fountain, brought back from Rome by one of her forebears, no long worked.

Crossing the landing by the chapel, she slipped back into her father's rooms. Serafina was waiting for her in her daytime black, hair neatly pinned into a chignon, fingers tapping on crossed arms. The glass-topped dining table was elaborately laid for one person.

Minty's first reaction was to apologise for being late, like a naughty child. Then she straightened her back. Serafina, Annie Phillips and Minty had sat through long hours together, nursing Sir Micah when he was dying. Minty respected Serafina but didn't fear her. Come to think of it, she was actually very fond of her.

So instead of an apology, she gave Serafina a hug. "I forgot the time, and now I'm ravenous. How long have I got before Annie wants to see me?"

"Long enough to eat." Serafina poured orange juice and opened a hostess trolley to display a full English breakfast.

Minty gulped juice, talking through it. "That girl Tessa. Apparently Annie thought she could be my personal assistant, but . . ."

"You won't want that one. Simon only took her on to please her grandmother who's got money, and Tessa adores him. Mrs Kitchen does, too. She's the housekeeper. Says she's 'going to put you in your place'. Best get rid of both while you can."

Minty dived into scrambled eggs and bacon. "I must give them a chance. I do need somewhere to work, though. I need to make phone calls. I want to get hold of the brochures for the Hall, and oh, a dozen things."

"Micah's sick room used to be his office. I've had it put back for you."

Minty grabbed toast with one hand and a coffee with the other. "Serafina, I love you!" She kissed the older woman's cheek. "Oh, before I go … do you know why Annie Phillips went to see Patrick this morning?"

"She didn't say. I'll bring you some more coffee in a little while."

Chapter Two

Minty took the clipboard with its untidy sheaf of messages through the cool green sitting room into the room in which her father had died. Sir Micah had liked space around him, and apart from some comfortable chairs around a coffee table between the two windows, the only furniture was a couple of low bookcases and two desks with chairs behind them. The larger desk had two telephones on it, while another at the back supported a bank of computer equipment.

There were a number of files on the desk, presumably placed there by Ms Phillips for Minty's urgent attention. She riffled through them only to discover that they all dealt with the affairs of the charity her father had founded and not one referred to the Hall. Minty opened the drawers of the desk. The diary, the stationery, all were marked with the logo of the Foundation.

Annie Phillips had spent her life working for the Foundation. She'd been devoted to Sir Micah and would want his work to continue. Annie was making sure that Minty knew what was expected of her. Of course Minty wanted her father's work to continue and she wanted to please Annie.

But what of the Hall? Wasn't that equally important?

There were obviously going to be problems with the staff. How could she tell whether someone ought to be sacked or not? In the short time she'd returned, she'd seen that the restaurant at the Hall was serving poor food and looked shabby. The gift shop was stocked with shoddy goods. Both were probably losing money.

Patrick had cannily drawn her into caring about the village, which had too many shops vacant, no bank, no crèche, no community spirit. She'd had plans once to make a difference to the village. And now . . . ?

Please, Lord . . . tell me what to do. I want to serve You and the Hall and the village. I realise the work of the Foundation is important but . . . I feel so burdened.

This room wasn't easy to pray in, for some reason. Of course, when you prayed a lot in a certain place, it became easier.

There were winking lights on both telephones, indicating that messages were stacked up for her attention.

With a sense of shock she realised she was sitting at a desk where her father's bed had once stood. How she missed him! If only she could have him back for an hour, to ask his advice!

She had Patrick, instead. *Hold onto that thought.* The phone rang and the answerphone clicked in. Simon. "Minty, I know you're there. Pick up the phone."

She fled next door into the tower room. This was at the opposite end of Sir Micah's suite of rooms to the chapel, and had once been an office for her father's staff. Four chairs were still grouped around a coffee table near a window, and on the wall was a bank of clocks which told the time in different parts of the world. Two desks, computers and a clutch of telephones lay unattended. One door gave onto the top of the stairs and another onto Sir Micah's private lift—companion to the one on the opposite side of the Hall.

Now she could see out of three windows, to the lake, to the Park, and to the gravelled sweep of drive in front of the old Elizabethan entrance. Clouds had gathered, threatening rain.

She tried to think clearly. Her father had made his fortune before starting the Foundation. He'd married the last of the Edens and made the Hall his base till she died . . . when he'd turned the Hall over to Lisa . . . who had then turned it over to Simon.

If Sir Micah, with all his energy and talents, had decided he couldn't run both Foundation and Hall, then she couldn't, either.

What did she know of the Foundation? It assisted educational projects in inner cities, it was nationally renowned and both her stepmother and Annie Phillips were on the Board of Trustees. Lisa wanted to get Simon on the Board, and Sir Micah's executor had assumed that Minty would take her father's place.

Minty was no financial brain. Her uncle and aunt had shown her how a city parish was run, but what sort of training was that for work in the Foundation?

On the other hand—and here she smiled—she knew someone who could do it, if he wanted to. Patrick had a subtle, penetrating mind and he'd be an excellent trustee, besides acting as a check on Simon.

However, Patrick was not an ambitious man. Would he want to give up so much of his time? He'd made himself a comfortable, busy sort of life. Would he be willing to sit on committees and pore over balance sheets? Committee meetings bored him.

Perhaps Annie had gone to see Patrick to sound him out about joining the Foundation? As Minty's husband, he would be welcome and it would halve the load for her.

Surely Annie should be on her way back by now? Minty checked her mobile phone, intending to ring him. His phone was switched off, but he'd left a text message for her: "Proverbs 14:17". The nearest Bible was in her bedroom. She looked it up. "A quick-tempered man does foolish things."

Now what did he mean by that?

Serafina called out, "Annie's here. I'll bring coffee."

The two women met in Sir Micah's office. Annie was on time, of course. Fiftyish, conservatively dressed, she seated herself with knees and ankles together and proceeded to destroy Minty's happiness.

"There's no easy way to say this, my dear. I've just asked Patrick Sands to break off your engagement."

The shock was appalling. Minty slowly let herself down onto a chair.

Serafina placed coffee on the low table between the two women and withdrew. Annie leaned forward to depress the plunger on the cafetière.

"I do realise," said Annie, "that there was some sort of childhood pledge between you and Mr Sands, but that is not sufficient reason for you to marry."

Minty managed a tiny shake of her head. Patrick had said the same thing, and she'd agreed.

"Your father was extremely concerned that you might feel obliged to marry Mr Sands, to make up to him for what happened so long ago. Well, it was a shocking thing, of course, but you must understand that your stepmother really did believe that your mother and Mr Sands senior were having an affair. He was an old and valued family friend, but your mother relied on him far too much. It was understandable that gossip should link their names but highly regrettable that the ensuing scandal should have tragic consequences . . ."

Minty thought that was an understatement. Minty's mother had been killed in a car crash as she drove wildly away from the Hall after discovering her husband in bed with his secretary, Lisa. Minty's mother had been desperately seeking her friend's help, but the story had somehow got about that she was running away with her lover. The scandal had ruined Patrick's father and driven him and his family out of the village, while Minty had been sent away to live with people who cared nothing for her. Both of their lives had been altered for good. Yes, you could call that tragic!

". . . but sacrificing yourself to marry Patrick Sands would not be putting things right."

Minty reached for a cup of coffee. The sense of outrage was subsiding. Instead she felt her temper climb. "It wouldn't be a sacrifice, believe me. Do you really think that's all there is between us? Even if we'd never loved one another as children, once we'd met as adults, the result was bound to be the same."

Annie sniffed. "I'm told physical attraction soon wears off."

Minty set her teeth. *Oh yes, there was that, all right!* "Patrick's my best friend as well as my love. He knew I was going to inherit the Hall, though I didn't. Did he take advantage of me? No. He helped me, encouraged me, advised me and didn't speak of love till after my father's will was read. Why, I wasn't even sure that he really loved me till . . ." She cut the words off, seeing Annie's half smile.

Minty put iron into her voice. "You had no right to interfere."

"I would never have dreamed of it, but Micah most earnestly begged me to stop you making the biggest mistake of your life. Even he did not foresee that Patrick Sands would propose so quickly. To get engaged on the very day you inherited! You must admit he took advantage of you."

"If there was any entrapment," said Minty, with a snarl in her voice, "it was on my part. I'd have agreed to marry Patrick ages ago if he'd asked me. Before you go any further, Patrick has already brought up a number of objections to our marrying."

She counted them off on her fingers. "One: childhood promises aren't binding on adults. Two: he's only a poor country solicitor and I could do much better. Three: I've had no chance to meet any other eligible men."

"Your father's point exactly," said Annie. "All he's asking is that you give yourself a little time to look around and grow accustomed to your new position in life before you tie yourself down. Of course you like Patrick Sands. He's charming. Perhaps a little light-weight? But delightful company, I'm sure." Annie smiled, the forgiving, understanding smile of a big sister.

The word "light-weight" hurt, because there was some truth in it. Patrick seemed content to be a country solicitor, whereas Minty had been moved up the social scale whether she wanted to or no.

She pulled out her mobile phone, intending to speak to him, to get him to deny what Annie said. He'd turned his mobile off, but the text message he'd left earlier was still there. "A quick-tempered man does foolish things."

He'd known what Annie was going to say, and he hadn't wanted Minty to lose her temper. Lose her temper? She wanted to kill him and Annie and everyone within reach. She mustn't, of course. Tantrums never got you anywhere.

Well, she'd hold onto her temper and have it out with Patrick later. And try to forget that word "light-weight".

Annie put her empty cup down with a sigh. "Mr Sands appreciated your father's point of view. I must say I was surprised at how receptive he was to my arguments—" Annie poured herself some more coffee—"but then I remembered how impulsive you can be. If you made the running . . . ?" She shrugged. "I really don't think—forgive me, Araminta—he can love you very deeply. Why, when I told him what your father wanted, he laughed!"

Minty sprang up to wrestle the nearest window open. She breathed deeply, shaking her hair forward to hide her face.

He'd laughed?

Annie was still speaking, but Minty heard the words as a babble in the background. Patrick had betrayed her. Something tore deep inside her. *Lord, help me! I thought Patrick loved me.*

Without him, the years ahead looked grey.

She had the Hall and would have plenty of money, but without Patrick there would be no loving-kindness, no laughter, no joy.

The pain was so intense she gasped.

True, he'd held back during their courtship, but that had been to protect her, to give her time to grow up. Hadn't it?

He did love her. She'd got to believe that. He'd proved it over and over again. He loved her deeply, selflessly.

His message meant . . . what? It was the kind of message passed between good friends. "Don't lose your temper." He hadn't texted, "I'm not marrying you."

He knew her very well. Better than anyone else in the world.

Ten minutes ago she'd have sworn that she knew him.

True, he was not an easy man to know. He was many-layered, like an onion. Peel off the surface of the urbane, kindly solicitor and what did you get? Someone who worked selflessly and often without a fee for others. Someone who often forgot to eat. Someone who'd given up smoking for her. Someone who'd attracted many women, but never got deeply involved himself.

Underneath that, there was another layer, of someone who boiled with hate toward Lisa Cardale and her son Simon for what they'd done to him and his family. He'd cared deeply enough to show Minty the bad as well as the good in him.

She relaxed. She doubted him no longer. Patrick loved her, perhaps almost as much as she loved him. So why had he agreed with Annie . . . and then laughed?

Annie's proposition must have struck at him like a mugger's knife.

She'd thought he'd crack a joke if he were facing a firing squad. Faced with Annie's demand, he'd laughed.

He'd laughed because he'd been wounded almost to death. As Minty had been.

I can't laugh, thought Minty. *I'm not stoical, like Patrick. When you cut me, I bleed. But I can hide my wounds, just as he can. I'm not letting you go, Patrick. No. Even if you've given in, I haven't.*

She pushed her grief and anger down inside herself. She straightened up, tossed back her hair and snapped the window shut against the cold and the rain outside.

Returning to her seat she forced a bright smile. "So, Annie. You asked him to break off our engagement, and he was receptive to your arguments. Then what?"

A slight frown crossed Annie's forehead. "Well, he wouldn't agree to break off the engagement entirely, but he did say if you wished to be free, he wouldn't stand in your way."

Minty let out a long breath. The tightness at the back of her neck eased off. So in spite of everything Annie could throw at him, Patrick had not agreed to breaking off their engagement. Good.

"But—" Annie consulted her fingernails—"he agreed with me that there should be no public announcement of your engagement for the time being."

"I see." Yes, Minty did see. He'd come under attack and because he'd an over-active conscience and feared that he really had taken advantage of Minty, he'd given ground to a certain extent. She must keep calm. "What next?"

Annie smiled her approval of the way Minty was taking this. "I always said you were a little soldier. It was your father's dearest wish that you continue his interest in the Foundation. He fretted that he had so little time left to help you get settled. He wanted to give you a flat in London. He wanted you to meet men with the right sort of background, men of good character who could be trusted to look after you."

"Unlike Patrick," said Minty, with an edge to her voice. "He won't advise me any more. He says I'm capable of making my own decisions."

Annie blinked. Perhaps she'd expected Patrick to make himself indispensable to Minty. But Patrick wasn't like that.

Annie indicated the papers she'd picked out for Minty. "I dare say Mr Sands is at home on the Parish Council and could give you good advice there, but we are talking about a great national charity . . ."

"Oh, no," said Minty, with another barbed smile. "Patrick thinks sitting on committees is a waste of time. He was talking about the Hall."

"The Hall? That shouldn't take much time to settle. I know you don't approve of everything Simon did when he was running the Hall, but leasing the place to the Americans . . ."

"No way. This is my family's home, and I won't turn my back on it."

"Well, the house will shortly be closed to visitors for the winter. You have some sort of Houseman, I believe, who could be promoted into

Simon's place as Administrator and take over the day-to-day running of the place. Lady Cardale never liked him and neither did Simon but I dare say he'll do.

"You can re-appoint Mrs Kitchen as housekeeper, while the shop and restaurant will be closed till the spring. Perhaps you can ask your half-sister Gemma to look after what little business needs to be done here over winter? She used to help her mother with the social and charity events. If any problem arises that Gemma can't deal with, I suppose she could always email you.

"As to replacing Miles, the previous Estate Manager—" Minty felt a frisson of fear at this reminder of the attempts Simon's crony had made on her life—"I believe his assistant is competent enough, though young. Sir Micah set up a trust fund to cover all ongoing repairs to the fabric of the Hall. So that takes care of the Hall. Under the terms of Sir Micah's will, Lady Cardale has to leave the Hall very soon. She has chosen to remove to Sir Micah's own flat in Knightsbridge, but we can easily find you somewhere else suitable to live."

Minty felt the heat mount in her face, but bit her lips and managed to say nothing at all. Did Annie really think Minty would turn her back on the Hall so easily?

Apparently Annie did. With an air of getting down to the real business of the day, Annie produced a large, leather-bound book with the Foundation crest of a bird in flight on it. "I suggest you use your father's diary. On Monday I will take you into the bank in town to set up an account for you, arrange for credit cards and so on. You can't touch the money your father left you until probate is granted, but the bank will let you draw on them to keep you going meantime. I expect you'd like to buy a car for yourself, among other things. On Wednesday you will be in the thick of Foundation business . . ."

"I know nothing about finance."

Anne became almost animated. "Each trustee brings their own expertise to the table. No one's expecting you to be a financier. Nowadays there are so many charities struggling for a decreasing share of the public purse that the Foundation needs to fight for a higher profile in the media. Over the past ten years we have helped to fund many projects for youth in the inner cities, not just after-school clubs, but providing new buildings to replace outdated and outgrown schools.

"This is where you come in. Our public relations firm recommends focusing our publicity on you, Sir Micah's daughter, someone young and pretty, who has been brought up in the city and can talk with conviction about the problems of inner-city schools. We hope you're photogenic but with an experienced photographer, we can surely get some media coverage going.

"I suggest that Reggie, your father's driver, takes you up to London on Tuesday and I'll book you into a quiet hotel. Buy some clothes, have your hair done. On Wednesday morning there is a photo opportunity tailor-made for you; you are to cut the ribbon opening a brand-new school built by the Foundation. Then in the afternoon there will be a Board Meeting when Lord Asher—he's the executor of your father's will, remember?—will propose your name to the Board . . ."

"He's the grey man who read the will and didn't seem to like Simon?"

"Araminta, you must be more tactful. It is true that in the past Lord Asher has opposed Lady Cardale's wish to have Simon appointed to the Board, but Simon knows a great many people and will bring in a lot of sponsorship for the Foundation."

Minty could be stubborn. "What's in it for Simon?"

"No money, if that's what you're thinking, but there is considerable kudos." Annie was trying to be conciliatory. "Lord Asher and I will be there to look after you. And James, of course."

Minty held down panic. James. Someone her father had wanted her to meet? Annie took a photograph and a sheet of paper out of her briefcase and handed it over. James was possibly in his late thirties, handsome in a heavy-set, blonde way. The camera had caught him looking up as he descended an ornamental iron staircase. Casually but expensively dressed, he looked as if he enjoyed an executive lifestyle, expensive restaurants, Ascot and Henley, good wines. Minty disliked him on sight.

"He was supposed to come down this weekend to meet you," said Annie. "But your father's death . . . He inherited money and made more, mostly in the media. He's on the Board of the Foundation. He's heard a lot about you and is intrigued. Here's a resumé of his career. He'll meet us at the school and take you out for lunch afterwards."

Minty kept the lid on her temper. Just. "Marital status?"

"He married the daughter of an earl, who ran off with someone else after they'd only been married a short time. No children. Since then he's had several long-term relationships but avoided marriage. He recently inherited a title and a charming country house, so he is thinking seriously about settling down."

Minty wanted to scream, to tear the picture of James into tiny fragments and thrust them down Annie's throat. She did none of those things, but put the photograph carefully back on the table and stood up.

"I'll think over what you've said. Most of it sounds . . . sensible." She clutched at her temper and pushed it back down again. "Now, if you'll forgive me, I have a great many things to see to. You seem to think I can walk away from the Hall, but I can't. My most urgent problem is that I need someone to help me understand the workings of this place, arrange meetings, take notes of everything that's decided. Someone who can think for herself. *Not* that girl from the Estate Office. Someone I can trust to get things done."

Annie bridled. "Tessa came very highly recommended from Lady Silchester, who happens—in case you've forgotten—to be your godmother. But—" having gained most of her points that morning, Annie was in a conciliatory mood—"I suppose I see what you mean. Perhaps an agency girl from town might do? You can hardly need her for long."

Minty reminded herself that Annie had been very kind to her in the past, and was acting in what she thought were Minty's best interests now. "I need someone full-time who is accountable to me, not to the Foundation. I'll pay her wages. And, talking of the Foundation, why do they need such expensive offices in London? Why not continue to run the Foundation from the north wing of this place?"

Annie produced an indulgent smile. "That remark just shows how little you know of these things, Araminta. To compete in the world of charities, you must have a visible presence in the world of money. With the winding up of Micah's financial empire, the staff here will naturally relocate to the London office. As I am sure you will soon, too." Annie stood up.

Minty smiled that bright, new smile of hers and watched the woman leave. Her anger settled into a thick, heavy cloud deep inside her.

Chapter Three

There was no disturbance in the air behind her, but she was beginning to recognise the scent of lily of the valley that hung around Serafina. Minty wanted to lash out and hurt somebody, but it wouldn't be fair to lash out at Serafina. She made her voice gentle.

"Do you listen at doors, Serafina? Did you know what Annie was going to say?"

Serafina picked up the coffee tray. "Annie understands balance sheets, but she hasn't got your measure yet."

"Have you got my measure, Serafina? Were you going to tell me I mustn't enter your kitchen? I'd love you to stay on to look after me. I'll try to be considerate and tell you when I'm going to need meals, but would you arrange a shelf on the fridge so that if I'm hungry or thirsty, I can help myself without troubling you?"

"I don't go out much."

"I'm used to catering for myself."

Serafina backed down from the challenge. "I thought you'd lose your temper with Annie. Micah had a terrible temper but he used to hold onto it, sometimes for days, till he could let it all out."

"Would you have liked me to lose my temper with Annie?" Minty pushed back her hair with both hands and down the years came the sour echo of her aunt's voice. "Minty, you look like a tart with your hair loose."

She shook the memory away. "Help me to understand, Serafina. You're settled here. You don't want me leaving the Hall and running off to live in London. You want me to stay and marry a local man. It would suit you if I ran the Hall myself and relied on you for everything?"

"You're taking my measure now, are you?" As she took the tray out, Serafina said, "I don't think Annie's got the measure of that long man of yours, either. I expect you'll be out tonight. I'll put a casserole in the oven for your lunch, and you can have it when you want it. Simon's been up looking for you. I told him you were with Annie. He's afraid of her so he didn't intrude, but I wouldn't count on him leaving you in peace for long. Also the phone's been ringing non-stop, and you'd better pick up your keys from the top right-hand drawer of your father's desk."

Minty sat behind her father's desk to listen to the messages, taking notes as she did so. The number of people who wanted to speak to her was mounting. Her stepmother Lisa, and her children Simon and Gemma. Her loud-voiced uncle—though not her aunt, thank goodness—and her aunt's horrible nephew Lucas in the city. She shuddered at the thought of Lucas. At least she'd never again have to jam a chair under the doorknob to keep him out of her bedroom.

There was also a message from Carol, her best friend from college, who was about the only true friend she had in the city. Minty would return that call.

Then there were the friends she'd made since she arrived: the lovely people from the Manor who'd given her a part-time job in the bookshop, and the farming family who'd helped her settle in and whose daughter-in-law and granddaughter worked at the Hall.

There was a frantic, almost tearful call from the Assistant Estate Manager, worried about keeping his job. Some names she didn't recognise. Well, they could wait.

All of them wanting something from her . . . or rather, from the person who'd inherited the Hall and a sizeable fortune.

She couldn't think where to begin so roved around the office, looking at the contents of the bookcases, exploring the drawers in the second desk. She found a couple of files there which, for a wonder, dealt with the Hall. One contained notes on the negotiations Simon had started with the American company to lease the Hall. Simon must be livid that even that source of revenue had now been closed to him.

She tipped that file into the wastepaper basket. Then rescued it because she supposed she'd have to write to them formally saying she wasn't interested in their deal.

The other file made Minty laugh out loud for the first time that day. It dealt with the projected makeover of the restaurant, another of the projects Simon had started and not finished.

Slim & Fawcett advertised themselves as "A design team with a vision for exclusivity. We aim to create a stream-lined venue, expressing modernity with a flash of humour, reaching back into the psyche to create a daring and innovative womb-structure."

An artist's impression of the restaurant showed something out of a Star Wars movie. "Prunes and prisms!" went the blurb. "The dark maturity of damson paint and table linen is allied to the glittering integrity of metal furniture and cutlery. Crockery imported specially from Sweden will be in a variety of original patterns. Uniforms to be damson coloured, skin-tight tops and black trousers, with make-up to match, creating an all-over erotic effect."

Apparently the existing kitchen was to be torn out and replaced, walls would be rebuilt, ceilings lowered, new lighting, granite surfaces . . . slate floors . . . specially commissioned artwork from Italy . . . and the cost!

Minty had been thinking of coach parties who wanted bangers and mash, or steak and kidney pudding. The design team were into BMWs, champagne and truffles. She wrote a note to herself to cancel the makeover.

She desperately needed to speak to Patrick, to hear his voice.

She put out her hand to ring his land line. He'd be in his office and his secretary didn't work on Saturdays, so he'd have to take the call. Then she took her hand away. He wouldn't thank her for interrupting his work. As an afterthought, she checked the voicemail on her mobile, and there was—at last—a message from him. He had a deep, pleasant voice. A voice which said, "You can trust me."

"Annie's right. I did take advantage of you . . . but . . . oh, Minty!" He'd ended the call abruptly at that point.

She played the message over and over again. It wasn't what she wanted to hear from him but it went a long way to clear the confusion in her mind. He wasn't saying he didn't love her. He wasn't saying that they'd never marry. He was saying, "We have to be sure what we're doing."

When they met again, she'd reassure him . . . and bash his head in with a poker for giving her such a fright!

What next? The family could wait. First she must tell that poor man in the Estate Office that his job was safe. She collected a large bunch of keys from the desk, hooked them onto her belt and after a moment's thought, recollected that the Estate Offices were on the ground floor across the courtyard.

The first Edens of any note had made their money from sheep and built an L-shaped Hall in Elizabethan and Jacobean times. They'd diversified into coal in the eighteenth century, building on two more wings to complete the square. This enclosed what had once been the grand approach to the house and turned it into the Fountain Court.

Although they'd been built in the local golden stone, the Estate Offices in the north wing were rather dark since they retained the original wainscoting and mullion windows.

Simon's crony Miles had been the Estate Manager and danced to his master's tune until he'd attacked Minty and ended up in jail.

Miles' assistant was called Tim. He proved to be a lanky lad not long out of college, bespectacled and nervous. Minty tried to put him at his ease, but he stuttered and blushed so much that she had hard work not to be sharp with him. However, he did seem to have a grasp of what the job entailed.

Tessa hovered, plump and ineffectual. She was supposed to be doing some filing but in reality was listening to what was going on.

Minty said she would like Tim and Tessa to continue doing their best by the Hall and the Estate at least till the end of October when the house would close to visitors for the winter. And perhaps they'd think what they'd like to see happen at the Hall in the long-term . . . ?

Tessa said, "Better loos for a start."

Tim blushed and protested that Minty didn't want that sort of idea.

"Tessa's right," said Minty, who'd not been impressed by the public toilets at the Hall. "Thank you, Tessa. I look forward to our next meeting."

Her phone rang and it was Patrick, speaking live. Which made *four* calls interrupting his work schedule that morning. Unheard of for such a busy man!

"Minty, I'm running late. Catch up with you about five?" He was making more coffee, by the sound of it.

Without thinking, Minty said, "Is that before or after I disembowel you?"

Tim and Tessa both looked shocked. Minty was annoyed with herself. Hadn't she learned by now how gossip spread in a village?

Patrick sounded grim. "I know, we need to talk. Perhaps we can go for a walk in the Park and have supper afterwards? Today's been ... messy."

"Have you eaten today?"

"Ruby's bringing me something in. She's distressed. Can you find time to talk to her this weekend?" Ruby was the downtrodden little woman who ran the village charity shop and who had befriended Minty when she first arrived. She'd led a sad life, first looking after her father and then caring for a man who'd been left childlike after an accident. Minty had a fellow-feeling for her, one Cinderella to another.

Patrick said, "Ruby's worried that you haven't got enough warm clothing now the weather's changed. She didn't want to bother you at the Hall, but she's brought me some things she's picked out for you. Shall I bring them up with me?"

"Fine. Patrick, can you dig up something for me about the trustees of the Foundation?"

"What do you think I've been doing lately?" He rang off.

Ah-ha, thought Minty. *So Patrick's ahead of the game, is he?* Annie definitely didn't have the measure of this particular country solicitor.

She smiled at Tim and Tessa, whose mouths were still agape. "I'm afraid I was rather indiscreet there. Keep it to yourselves, will you?" Round-eyed, they gave her identical nods, and she didn't believe them for an instant.

"I must be moving. Where will I find the housekeeper, Mrs Kitchen, and the ... Houseman? Is that the right term?"

Tessa said, "Ms Kitchen doesn't work at weekends."

Minty was surprised. "Isn't she needed when the house is open to the public?"

Tessa exchanged looks with Tim, who said, "Simon arranges all that sort of thing. She v–visits relatives at w–weekends. I d–don't know where you'd find Barr—I mean, the Houseman. He could be anywhere."

Minty gave them a bright nod and left by the door to the outer courtyard. It was after one and tourists would have been in the house for an hour, so some should by now be heading for the restaurant and shop.

Minty checked, but neither the restaurant nor the shop was doing good business. She hadn't liked Simon's ideas for the restaurant but something did need to be done about it. And the shop.

She pushed her hair back out of her eyes. More trouble ahead . . . but first things first. If Mrs Kitchen was not available, she must find the Houseman.

She tracked him down to the library.

Over the fireplace hung a portrait of her father, Sir Micah Cardale. Minty had heard her father called both "a man of ferocious intelligence" and "a serial adulterer". The portrait reflected a complex character, a man of power and charisma. A great sinner, but he'd said he was sorry to God and to man before his end.

Next to it hung a companion picture of Sir Micah's second wife, Minty's hated stepmother Lisa. A man was standing on a ladder to take that down.

The man had very long arms and legs. He was about fifty and had a jaunty, capable air to him. He also had a rosy complexion which reminded Minty of one of her uncle's churchwardens, who'd been a secret drinker. Visitors moving through the rooms looked surprised as Minty legged it over the red rope keeping them away from the antiques.

"You're . . . Mr Houseman? Is that right?"

"*The* Houseman, that's right. Barrington, known as Barr." He descended to earth, carrying the picture. "And you're Miss Cardale." He folded up the ladder. "Lady Cardale wishes to take her portrait with her when she leaves. Do you want your mother's picture hung up here instead?"

Minty nodded.

Barr shouldered the ladder and picked up the picture. "Would you care for a little something in my den?"

Barr's "den" was in the basement under the library and the terrace outside. He stowed the ladder in a cupboard and deposited the picture on the floor. His office contained an up-to-date computer and filing cabinets, with detailed plans of the Hall and surrounding estate on the walls.

"Sherry? A glass of wine? Nothing? May I say how pleased we all are to welcome your mother's daughter back to the Hall. May I ask if you plan to hand the place over to the Americans?"

"No, this is my home now. How long have you worked here and exactly what is your job?"

Barr did an up and down trick with his eyebrows. He had very little hair left, and what there was formed a dark fringe around the back of his head. There were dark hairs on the backs of his hands, too. Minty's conjecture that he might be fond of drink was confirmed by the sight of a tray of bottles in a corner.

"I was born here in the village. Your grandfather caught me trespassing one day, should have given me a clout over the ear, but showed me round and told me some stories about the Hall. Got me hooked on old houses.

"I worked in the City after I got married but never liked it and got a job as Houseman at a National Trust Property before I was thirty-five. Your father appointed me Administrator when Lady Cardale opened the Hall to the public and I've been here nearly twenty years."

"So why are you only Houseman now?"

"Simon didn't want to pay for an Administrator *and* a Houseman. He thought he could do the job of Administrator himself but needed someone to carry out his orders, so he sacked our Houseman and offered me the lower job at a reduced salary. My wife died just before Simon took over and I lacked the incentive to move on. Like a fool, I've been both Houseman and Administrator for the last few years. But then, as Simon kept reminding me, I'd be unlikely to get another good job coming up to fifty-five years old. Plus my flat here is rent free."

"Mrs Kitchen—have I got her name right?—is the housekeeper. How does her job differ from yours?"

"Mrs Kitchen is in charge of the cleaning staff, putting the house under covers for winter, seeing to cleaning and renovating while we're closed, and getting everything ready for reopening in the spring. Her flat is here in the basement, next to mine. She's efficient—I'll give her that—but she worships the ground Simon walks upon, so she may not wish to stay once he goes.

"The Administrator is supposed to be in overall charge of everything, the estate, the properties in the village, the maintenance of the fabric of the buildings and all the staff employed at the Hall, inside and out. He employs any outside contractors that are needed from time to time—and there's always something that needs attending to in a house this old. Simon was supposed to do all that, but in practice . . ."

He spread his hands. "I acted on his instructions, some of them hasty and ill-conceived, but who was I to quibble? I was one of the co-signatories on all the accounts with Lady Cardale, and then with Simon. But the only account I've been allowed to handle these last few years is the General one for the day-to-day running of the Hall. Simon brought in an accountant, some friend of his, who dealt with everything else. Until last week, that is, when they had a blazing row and the man resigned because Simon wouldn't pay his bill."

He grinned. Minty grinned back.

"Another thing I don't do nowadays is to look after the special events: open days, musical evenings and so on. Lady Cardale arranges those, and her daughter Gemma is supposed to help, but . . ." He glanced at Minty, obviously wondering if it would be politic to speak his mind about her half-sister.

"Tell me about the Houseman's job," said Minty, registering his low opinion of Gemma but not prepared to discuss her with him.

"The Houseman works for the Administrator. He's a Jack of All Trades. A sort of super-caretaker. He helps out wherever there's a problem in the house and the buildings around it. He locks up at night and unlocks in the morning. You name a job around the place, and I've done it in my time. I'd like to apply for the job of Administrator if it's going. I've got years of work in me still, and I like to keep busy. Are you sure you wouldn't care for a small glass of sherry?"

"No, thank you," said Minty. "It's been suggested that I make your job back up to Administrator, but first I need to know how you'd react to my making some changes at the Hall."

"You're a true Eden. I'd work for you all right."

Minty thought he'd probably work for anyone who let him stay in his flat, but he had years of experience behind him and she needed to tap into that. His hand was straying to the sherry, and Minty wondered how far she could trust him.

"I suggest I give you a short-term contract initially—say for six months—and the same for Tim in the Estate Office? I'll get round to the others as quickly as I can."

"Forget Chef in the restaurant." Barr pulled a face. "He's a drinking companion of Simon's and has his own water-tight contract—same as Miles. I expect you can sack Miles after he attacked you, but Chef . . ." He shook his head.

That was bad news, because Minty didn't think Chef was up to the job. "Let me have a look at his contract. Presumably we need a new Houseman?"

"I'll ask around, see who might be available. Anything you want done from now on, you tell me and I'll see to it."

"I suggest we have weekly meetings. I have to be in London on Tuesday and Wednesday, so shall we have our first meeting on Friday at ten?"

"Simon didn't think that necessary."

"I do. I need to understand how the finances work for a start. I assume we're solvent?"

Barr grunted. "I'm thinking the finances will take some disentangling. Simon's accountant had an office next to Miles. Drinking cronies, of course. I'll see if I can get hold of the books, have a look at them. Don't hope for too much."

The books. Patrick had suggested she look at the books. Was it these books he meant?

"Let me know what you find. And I suppose I ought to see Mrs Kitchen next, but . . ."

"She doesn't work weekends. Maybe she'll have cooled down by Monday. Someone told her about your opening blinds and leaving coffee cups around. She went ballistic."

Minty was torn between telling him that she'd open what blinds she wanted in her own house, and apologising for having done so.

Barr explained. "You let in the daylight, you see. There's nothing rots fabric and bleaches wood like daylight. Unless it's the heating, playing havoc with the glues in the old furniture. And the dust." He sighed. "You'll soon get used to the rules. We've had it drummed into us so much, we take it for granted."

She nodded. She had a lot to learn.

He said, "There's just one other thing. There's stuff coming in all the time, ordered by her ladyship and Simon. Things we couldn't possibly want for the Hall, but which Simon's accountant paid for out of income. Like Simon's latest car. I'll make sure nothing gets accepted for delivery in future without my signature. Anything I'm not sure about, I'll query with you. Right?"

He grinned, and lifted Lady Cardale's portrait onto the desk. "Talking of which, this portrait was paid for by the estate. I was there when your father's will was read and it said Lady C can't take anything out of the Hall which was bought for the Hall. That would include her portrait, wouldn't it?"

Both of them ironed out smiles. Minty said, "Lady Cardale must have forgotten that when she asked you to collect her portrait. Perhaps I'd better take it with me for safe keeping?"

"Burn the old witch," suggested Barr.

Minty's smile faded. The three-quarter length portrait had been done by the same master who'd painted Sir Micah. It showed an elegant, handsome, hard-faced woman with a close-cut helmet of hair against a background of the Hall. Lady C wore her favourite black, with good pearls and diamonds. The concept was a trifle old-fashioned, stressing that this was the Mistress of Eden Hall, rather than a secretary who'd climbed into her boss' bed.

"Every time she looks at that portrait," observed Barr, filling a schooner with sherry, "it must remind her she's a woman of importance. You know something? I almost feel sorry for her. She dotes on Simon but he only sees money-bags when he looks at her, and she's never to my knowledge spoken kindly to Gemma in her life. Lady C's worked hard at her charities these last few years, but will they still want to know her when she can't host their events for free?"

"What! For free?"

"Mark my words, she'll expect you to let her continue. You won't want to keep that portrait, but you could screw a fair amount out of her for it." He took a gulp of sherry and shuddered with pleasure. "Ah, that's better."

Minty gave him one of her clear-eyed looks. "I could also put a clause in our agreement that you don't drink when you're on duty." She put her hand on his arm and looked up at him. "Please, Barr. I need you sober."

He hesitated. "Never drunk on duty. Trust me."

"I hope I can trust you. I need all the help I can get. You've had a difficult few years but now we've got to look forward, not back. So—just to please me—would you leave the drink till you go off duty in the evening?"

"They say you got Patrick Sands to stop smoking. Is that right?"

Minty thought it best not to reply. There were many channels between village and Hall, and something said in confidence here might well be in the village shop before nightfall.

So she smiled, and eased her way out.

Chapter Four

Carrying the portrait, she crossed the Fountain Court and made her way into the Great Hall, now respectably filling up with visitors. She paused there only long enough to introduce herself to the stewards on duty and pick up some brochures.

Taking the lift back up to her father's rooms on the top floor, she thought her office still seemed more like her father's than hers. There were more messages on the answerphone, including a second one from her uncle in the city, saying it was urgent. She didn't want to speak to him or to her aunt ever again. Gone was the drudgery of looking after them in that grim vicarage, and the hours of unpaid labour in the parish office. Gone was the constant sniping which had almost broken her spirit.

Her stepmother, Lady Cardale, had also called. Minty didn't reply to that call, either.

But she did speak to Venetia and Hugh Wootton at the Manor, who'd given her a job at the bookshop when she'd first returned to the village. They were genuinely thrilled about her inheritance and invited her for lunch the next day.

Then there was a message from Alice Mount, a single parent who lived in the village, and who'd befriended Minty when they'd been cleaning holiday cottages together at weekends. Alice was after Minty's old job at the bookshop; would Minty put in a good word for her? Minty rang back, suggesting she call in on Alice after her lunch at the Woottons.

Would Alice be suitable as a secretary to Minty? Alice had a business degree, but she also had a delightful but demanding toddler to look after, which was partly why she hadn't been able to get any better job than cleaning in the daytime and working in the pub in the evenings.

Minty ate Serafina's chicken casserole in the office while making notes of what she'd done that morning, and what she planned to do. She flicked through a drab, badly written brochure on the Hall. Not a good advertisement!

The phone rang again. It was Simon, telling her to pick up the phone. She ignored it. The problem with men like him was that they could be charming right up to the point a girl said no, and then . . .

She'd been told Simon never did his own dirty work, and Miles was in prison. Simon couldn't do anything now, could he? Apart from making a nuisance of himself, or waylaying her in quiet places. Luckily Serafina had been on hand that morning, but suppose she hadn't been there?

Minty turned to the top file on the Foundation, but her concentration had gone and she found herself reading the same sentence over and over.

She realised why. Someone had come up by the lift and was opening the door to her office.

It was Simon. "Minty, so you are here, after all. Did I frighten you this morning? I didn't mean to, honest."

Was he sorry? He looked it, but . . . probably Serafina was within call.

"You should have returned my calls and let me explain." He took a chair beside the window and said, "Come over here where I can see you."

Against her better judgement she obeyed, taking a chair opposite him. He crossed one leg over the other, smoothing back his fair hair, a faint flush on his cheek-bones, his aftershave tantalising her senses. She knew he lived and drank hard, but there was as yet no sign of it on his good looks and incredible tan.

"Where have you been all morning?" He didn't wait for a reply, but swung around to look out of the window. "What a view! These rooms should be mine by rights. They led me to believe I would get everything, but . . ." He checked himself, turning on Minty with a hard, white smile.

"You're looking pale, my almost-sister. Have they been getting at you, Annie and that drunken Houseman and the rest? My dear sister Gemma too? Well, we all want something from you, but I suppose you've worked that out already."

Now that he'd got past his apology, there was a spiky edge to his words. He exuded impatience and a forcefulness which made Minty wary.

He shot out of his seat and went to sit in Minty's chair behind her father's desk. He'd outmanoeuvred her, reversing their previous positions. Minty bit her lip. She went to the inner door and called out to Serafina, asking if there was any coffee on the go.

Simon's eyelids flickered, acknowledging that she was calling for back up. He turned on the charm. "Do you know something? You look out of place here. A little girl playing at being grown up. I think I prefer you in a dress, showing your ankles. You've got good ankles. Will you wear a dress to the Grand Opening of the school in London on Wednesday? Something showing a little cleavage for the photographers? I dare say the whole affair frightens you a little.

"Suppose I take you up to London in my car? I could show you around, introduce you to some of my friends, take you to the theatre and supper afterwards. I promise to be very, very good and not give you even the slightest reason to be frightened of me. Because you are frightened of me, a little, aren't you?"

She had tried not to show it. "What do you want, Simon?"

He sighed deeply. "Understanding, my dear. Don't look at your watch. We have all afternoon. I gather you've promoted that wimp Tim at the Estate Office. A bad choice; he stutters and cringes whenever he sees me coming. And that drunken sod of a Houseman is to be Administrator? Tut, my dear. You should have asked me for advice. Neither of them will be the slightest use to you."

Minty leaned against the wall and folded her arms. "What would you have advised me?"

"You don't need them—either of them. They'll only bring you a mountain of trouble and cost you money in the long run. Why not walk away from it all? Enjoy yourself while you're still young and pretty. Let the Americans have the Hall."

"This is my family's home, Simon. I know there'll be problems but I'm prepared to deal with them. You'll be leaving the Hall at the same time as your mother, won't you? Let me have your address when you're settled, so that I can forward any bills that might come in afterwards."

"She bites, does she?" His smile slipped. "Oh, come on, Minty. You know how it is with me. I've been dumped in the mire and need your help. Be an obliging girl and meet the Americans; let them explain everything to you."

"You got five million pounds in the will. Isn't that enough?"

"It doesn't even cover my debts. Even if I sell my cars and the aeroplane, I'll have nothing left to live on. I know your soft heart. You won't turn me out of the Hall, but . . ."

She clenched her hands into fists. "You're wrong there, Simon. I want you out as soon as possible. You can always live with your mother in London till you find a place of your own."

"I want to be here. I've a right to be here."

She shook her head. She could understand how a doting mother and besotted nurse had turned a handsome boy into a spoilt, handsome man. He'd been brought up to believe the world was his for the taking, but his innate dishonesty had caused him to throw away all the golden opportunities that had come his way. Sir Micah had given him a start in business, only to dispense with his services after a couple of years. He'd cultivated friends who led a spectacular life-style and got into debt trying to emulate them. He'd taken on the Hall and driven that into the ground. His final scheme to turn the Hall into a health farm was failing because Minty refused to agree to it. He'd once had everything, and now he had nothing. She was almost sorry for him . . . until she remembered how badly he treated everybody.

"Simon, neither of us expected this and we need time to come to terms with it. But now, if you don't mind, I've some work to do . . ."

His mouth twisted. "You can't brush me off like that. You forget that I know things. I know you're not a virgin, for a start. You were engaged to your cousin Lucas and used to let him into your bedroom night after night, didn't you? Would you like your precious Patrick to hear about that? And the other directors of the Foundation? How would they feel about you then, eh?"

Minty regarded him with horror. It was true that for a short time she'd been engaged to Lucas, her aunt's bullying nephew. Her aunt had encouraged him, and even now talked as if they would one day be married. It was true that Lucas had tried to get into her bedroom at the vicarage, but she'd never let him in.

"How dare you!"

He smiled, sure of himself. "Touched a nerve, did I? Who would have guessed it! Was it all true, then?"

She calmed herself with an effort. "No, it's not true. Now, would you please go?" She held the door open for him to leave.

He didn't move. "Come on, now. We're only just beginning to understand one another . . ."

Lily of the valley scented the air. Serafina stood four square in the doorway, her arms folded.

Simon held up his hands in mock surrender. "I go, I go. See how I go. I nearly forgot. My mother wants to see you . . . now!" He held out his hand with a knowing smile. "I'll take you down, shall I?"

Minty stared back, thinking that Simon had cleverly manipulated her. He'd flattered, pleaded and finally threatened. She'd lost the initiative in the conversation early on and now, when he'd reduced her to a shaking wreck, he wanted her to face his mother.

"In a minute."

Serafina marched to the outer door and held it open for him. He hesitated, shrugged and disappeared.

Minty sank onto the window seat and covered her eyes with her hands.

Serafina said, "Adders bite, and so does he. I thought he might be harmless once his toady Miles was out of the way, but it seems he still has some venom in him. You'd best tell Patrick straight away."

Good advice but she didn't think she could follow it. If Patrick were to hear the story, he might believe it. She couldn't bear that. She was shaking. Her mobile rang, and it was Patrick himself.

"I've got five seconds between clients. Are you all right?"

"Yes, of course." She tried to make her voice sound natural. "Why shouldn't I be all right?"

"I don't know. I just thought . . . Anyway, I'll be free in an hour. Where will you be?"

She got her voice under control. "The Hall's open today. Come up to my rooms."

He disconnected.

Serafina patted her on her shoulder. "Go and sit in the chapel for a while. That'll calm you."

It was good advice but she couldn't keep on avoiding her stepmother.

She stood up, attempting to smooth back her unruly hair. "I'd better see what Lady Cardale wants first."

"Whatever it is, tell her you'll think about it and let her know."

Minty nodded, hardly hearing the words. She went through to the tower office expecting to find a door in the wall opposite which would lead into the Elizabethan wing where Lady Cardale had her rooms. There was no such door, only a smooth plastered wall.

So where was the entrance to her suite? Minty went down one flight of stairs to the gallery above the Great Hall and there, sure enough, was a door into the old wing. Marked "Private".

Lady Cardale herself opened the door, looking for all the world like Cruella de Vil. Her skin had a pallid lustre, and she was all in black.

She struck the first blow. "Not wearing mourning for your father, I see."

Minty flinched. She'd worn black for the funeral and the reading of the will on the previous day. That had felt right. But jeans and a sweater had seemed more appropriate for scrambling round the house. She missed her father terribly but maybe in other people's eyes it wasn't enough to say so, and she ought to have continued wearing black for a while.

The part of her mind which stood apart told her that Lady C's show of mourning was a laugh, seeing that she hadn't seemed concerned about her husband when he was dying.

Lisa Cardale led the way into a long, panelled sitting room, hung with old tapestries. The wide floorboards glinted with light reflected from mullion windows, while here and there faded rugs were spread before enormous settees, heaped with cushions. Occasional tables and display cabinets were crowded with delicate pieces of china. Stands of lilies and roses had been arranged on side tables, and bowls of sweet-smelling pot-pourri were on each of the window-sills.

It ought to have been a welcoming, comfortable room, and Minty couldn't work out why it wasn't. Was it because she feared the woman whose territory it was?

Lady C didn't invite Minty to sit down and remained standing herself.

"I should have thought," she said, in her hard voice, "that you would have had the courtesy to return my calls instead of gossiping with the servants."

"Perhaps I ought," agreed Minty. Unasked, she took a seat and tried to appear at her ease.

Lady C lifted exquisite eyebrows and allowed herself a sigh, to show her tolerance of Minty's poor manners. "We have to remember that you've been brought up in very different circumstances. I dread to think what solecisms you'll commit in London. We must all make excuses for you, for the time being. No doubt you'll learn soon enough how to behave."

Minty didn't reply. Aunt Agnes used to scold her in exactly the same tone of voice. The words might be different, but the intention was the same. To cow Minty into obedience.

Lady C produced a file and held it out to Minty, who had to get out of her chair to take it. Another point to Lady C, that she'd made Minty go to her.

"These are the charity events which have been booked for the next six months. I expect you to absent yourself on those dates, as I will of course be returning to act as hostess and stay here in my own rooms. Gemma will fill you in on anything else you wish to know."

Minty blinked. Whatever she'd expected, it hadn't been this.

"On Monday I've asked my dear friend Guy Hertz down to meet you. He's the international fine arts dealer who buys antiques for the Hall. No one expects you to recognise a good piece of furniture from junk but if you're guided by him, I don't suppose you'll make too many costly mistakes."

She implied by her tone that she thought Minty would probably make a great many costly mistakes, but that that was none of her business.

Minty took a deep breath. "I have appointments out with Annie on Monday."

"I think meeting with Mr Hertz should take precedence, don't you?"

Minty shook her head, wondering why the room repelled her. It was quite perfect in its own way, wasn't it?

As was Lady Cardale. Polished, superbly gowned and shod.

"Well, what is it?" The hard voice became harsh. "I assure you I'll be out of here by the end of next month. As you can see, I've already started putting stickers on those pieces of furniture which I intend to take with me."

Minty saw that twinkling yellow labels festooned the handles and knobs of most of the furniture in the room. Was her stepmother planning to take all those things? It would leave the room empty.

Did it matter? Shouldn't Minty let her go, with whatever she wanted to take?

Perhaps.

But echoes of good advice floated through her mind. Patrick had talked about looking at the books—query, did he mean the accounts?—Barr had mentioned Lady C making the Hall pay for her luxuries, and Serafina had suggested Minty shouldn't automatically agree to anything her stepmother wanted.

Minty steeled herself. "I'll think over what you've said and let you know."

Lady Cardale recoiled and then struck. "What a dear, sweet, naive little girl you are. Not at all sweet or naive underneath, I understand. I'd the most enlightening conversation with your dear aunt after the funeral yesterday. Like me, she has your best interests at heart. And her charming nephew, so devoted? You were engaged to him once, I believe? And allowed him certain privileges?"

She grasped Minty's arms and drew her close, dropping her voice to a purr. "So like your dear mother. So very, very fond of the men!"

She kissed Minty, then let her go with a pretty laugh. "But we're such good friends we can keep that to ourselves, can't we? Can't have dear little Patrick upset like his father was."

Lady C opened the door, indicating that Minty should now leave. She did so in a state of shock.

Minty found herself in the tower office without a clue as to how she'd climbed the stairs.

That was a Judas kiss!

She passed through into her father's office and dumped the file on his desk.

This is exactly what that woman did to my mother. Lady C fed Simon that lie about me and Lucas.

The only things Minty liked about the cool green sitting room were the pictures on the walls. All the furniture was placed just so, defying you to move it. As in a hotel room.

I understand now how my mother felt. Helpless. Desperate.

The dining room was no better. Fancy having a glass-topped dining table!

I can't fight that lie. No one would believe me.

The bedroom. Hers, now. Everything in its place, and a place for everything.

I want to cry.

The spare bedroom, pink. Yuk.

The chapel, at last. *I can cry now.*

The chapel was cool and quiet. Someone—probably Serafina—had filled the vase at the side of the altar with brilliant red dahlias. Minty sank onto her knees before the altar and stared at the cross with eyes that ached to weep, yet could not.

Dear Lord above. My mother knelt here and prayed for help. Now it's my turn. You didn't help her. So why should You help me?

She replayed the scene with her stepmother. She closed her eyes in despair. From somewhere she dragged up the words. *Lord, hear my prayer. Lord, hear my prayer. Please. Help. I'm lost.*

Patrick's father couldn't help my poor mother. Patrick can't help me. I can't tell him. Impossible. Too shameful.

Dear Lord in heaven, why?

Lord God! For pity's sake!

In the end, some measure of peace returned. She still didn't know what words to use, what she ought to pray for, but at last she realised He was trying to reach her through her wild screaming. He enfolded her in His love, reassuring her. He knew everything that had happened to her, and He loved her so much.

More than she deserved. For who could deserve God's love? She could make mistakes—everyone could make mistakes—but He was always there, waiting for her to open herself up to Him again, to accept His love.

And then came another thought.

Patrick's father had been a kindly, gentle character, and her mother had been a naive child—just as Lady Cardale had said.

Patrick was not naive, and he'd been through a harsh schooling. She herself had been hardened in a war of attrition with her aunt.

Even so, how could they fight the scandal that threatened to destroy them?

Chapter Five

She thought she heard voices, and a door slam. It would be Patrick. How could she face him, tell him what had been said about her? Patrick might seem easy-going, but he was bedrock Christian underneath. He understood and forgave other people's foibles, but he'd put her on a pedestal. She knew nothing had happened between her and Lucas, but gossip could destroy Patrick's peace of mind, never mind hers.

She tossed back her hair, straightened her shoulders and returned to the flat.

She found Patrick in the sitting room, pulling armfuls of clothing out of plastic bags under Annie Phillips' disbelieving eye. He was wearing a thick Arran sweater and cords, plus a leather jacket. Though he could never be described as handsome, he had an attraction stronger than mere good looks and that hit her almost physically as their eyes met across the room.

Annie was ruffled. "Mr Sands, I thought we had reached an agreement this morning . . ."

"So we did. Hi, Minty. Fancy this?" He held up a feather-light pink jacket. "We aren't formally engaged at the moment, are we?"

She met his eye.

Do you still love me, Patrick?

You know I do.

She wanted to run to him and be held tightly. She loved the look of him, the tall, rangy, elegant length of him. The steadiness of far-seeing grey eyes that held hers and invited her to follow his lead. Which she did.

"That's right, we're not formally engaged at the moment," said Minty, trying to match his lightness of touch. "Look, Annie. No ring!" She held up her left hand to prove it.

Patrick touched the right-hand pocket of his trousers and tossed her the jacket. "Try it on."

Annie was annoyed. "You are breaking our contract . . ."

"Not at all," said Patrick. "I'm obeying it to the very letter. Yes, Minty; that looks good on you."

Annie set her teeth. "Is this setting Araminta free to make her own choices? Anyway, she's going up to Town to buy clothes on Tuesday. She doesn't need any more second-hand clothing from the charity shop."

Patrick treated her to a bland smile. "The weather has turned colder and she needs something for the next few days, doesn't she? Minty, there's this blue knitted cap with a scarf to match. What do you think?"

Minty pulled the cap down over her curls and flung the scarf around her neck. "How do I look?"

"More important, are you going to be warm enough? Have you got any strong outdoor shoes? Yes, those might do, I suppose. I think Ruby put some knitted gloves in for you . . . ah, there they are. Look, no holes!"

Patrick was putting on a good front but Minty knew him well, and could spot tension around his eyes and jaw.

She managed a light laugh. "Let's run before the sun goes in." Seizing Patrick's hand, she was out of the door and running down the stairs before Annie could make any further objections.

Patrick was right; it was chilly outside though the sun was still up. There were a few clouds in the sky but they were flying high. There'd probably be a frost that night. They walked down towards the lake where a family of ducks ducked and dabbled.

Patrick said, "Did we both walk into walls today? You look tired."

"Your wall was called Annie Phillips and mine was . . . well, never mind that now."

They tramped on in silence. A pair of swans came flying in low, and landed on the lake, sending ripples across the glittering surface.

Patrick looked at the swans and not at her. "Are you very angry with me?"

"Why did you let Annie push you around, Patrick?"

"She was right. I ought not to have asked you to marry me so soon, before you'd had a chance to look around you. I did take advantage of you. I was aware of it even as I proposed to you, but I've dreamed of you for so many years . . ." His voice hardened. "You must be able to withdraw, any time you want."

"You, too?"

"No, not me. My offer stands, but . . ." He tried to laugh. "I'm going to need some convincing that you ought to accept it."

They stood still to watch the swans circle the lake. They were fully grown. If one of them caught you a blow with a wing, you'd end up in hospital. They were beautiful to look at, but dangerous. Like Simon. She wouldn't think about Simon now.

"What's wrong, Minty?"

She couldn't tell him what Simon had said. "Nothing. My stepmother. Simon. I think I'm afraid of him."

"He can't do much harm with Miles in prison. Simon never does his own dirty work."

She wasn't so sure about that.

He turned to face her. "There's a way out of this. Would you consider turning the Hall over to the National Trust? Would you be satisfied to marry a country solicitor and live in the village?"

She looked back at the splendid house, golden in the late afternoon sun. She shook her head. "I used to dream of marrying you and living in your house, but I can't leave the Hall now. It's not that I love it more than you. It's my job, a job that may be too big for me. There's so many problems. I made a lot of decisions today and I think they're probably all bad ones." She shook herself. "I don't want to think about that now. Did you daydream that I'd marry you and live in your house?"

"In the evenings I'd sit and imagine you in the house with me. Sometimes I'd talk to you, going along in the car. First sign of mental instability. Tell you one thing, though. I never dreamed of walking in the Park with you."

He pulled her cap further down over her head and touched the tip of her nose with his forefinger.

She felt a little comforted. "All right. We're not officially engaged. I don't wear your ring . . ." Here his hand went to his trouser pocket . . . and away again. *Ah-ha. You've got an engagement ring in there, haven't you? But we won't mention it, yet.* ". . .but we're to continue to see one another. For how long?"

"Until we both feel comfortable about it?"

Frowning, she took his arm and they continued their walk around the lake. She felt frustrated. How could he be so calm? She would prod him into a reaction.

"Annie has fixed up a date for me in London. A suitable man with a title and a country house, someone with money in the City, someone who's already on the Board of Trustees and who wants to meet me. He's called James. He's fair of hair and reasonably good-looking."

His arm jerked within hers. "That's not very clever of them. Now if I'd been arranging things, I'd have found you a quiet, dark man—because that's the kind you like. Attraction of opposites."

Minty giggled. "A quiet man like you? You're not all that quiet, are you, Patrick? You're deceptive, that's what you are." She broke free of him and started to run. "Race you to the oak tree!"

They ran together, he complaining that she was bound to beat him, since he never took any exercise . . . but they reached the tree at the same time.

He said, "Shall I carve your initials in the oak?" He laughed at himself. "Hark at me. As maudlin as any teenager, mooning after a rock star."

"I don't suppose you've got as much as a pen-knife on you."

She wondered if he'd pull out his pockets to show he hadn't . . . and then a ring might tumble out . . . ?

The sun was hovering low in the sky, a bright red ball.

"Shall we walk further? You're not getting cold?"

Minty shook her head. "I don't want to go back yet. I want to walk to the world's end. Walk away from all my problems. Let's carry on for a bit. I don't even know how big the Park is. Tell me, could I rent a bit of the Park to the village for a playground? Or perhaps open the Park free to everyone? I hate the thought of there being no playground in the village."

Now it was his turn to frown. "Don't do anything in a hurry."

She flashed out. "Now why did I think you'd be against it?"

"Because it might not be the right answer. You might offer to install some play equipment on part of the Green at the top of the village, but first you'd have to make sure the Council would look after it.

"As to the Park, yes, you could throw it open at weekends, say. But not for every day of the year, because then it would become common land, and you'd lose all your rights on it."

"Yes, Daddy," said Minty, turning sulky. "Anything else I mustn't do?"

"Tell me what else you've done today." He lifted his arm, and she tucked her hand firmly inside it.

"Well," she said, as they walked along, "I made Tim up to Estate Manager and Barr to Administrator. Temporary appointments only. I pinched Lisa's portrait, which she'd planned to make off with, and tucked it away out of sight behind the dressing table in my bedroom. I had a horrid interview with Simon, who still wants me to meet the Americans; and another with Lisa, who wants to come back here to host all the charity events she's arranged for months . . . and she's tagged almost all the furniture in her room with stickers, planning to take them away with her."

She couldn't bring herself to mention what her stepmother and Simon had said about her cousin Lucas. It was too shame-making. Especially as Patrick was now smiling down at her.

She said, "I'm going to have to watch Barr, of course. And Tim, too, I suppose. Oh, and Annie briefed me on my future with the Foundation. They want me to act the bimbo for them."

Patrick shouted with laughter. She went pink. "Do you think I'm pretty, Patrick?"

He took time to consider her question. "I don't think about you in those terms. You're just . . . you. I suppose 'lovely' is a better word, but every now and then you light up and blaze—yes, 'blaze' is the right word—you blaze into beauty. 'Pretty' doesn't do you justice."

"Lady Cardale said I was 'pretty, like my mother'."

He frowned. "You're no naive child like your mother and I'm certainly not as trusting as my father."

She nodded. She'd worked that out, too.

They reached a boundary wall of the Park and turned. The Hall glowed red and gold in the setting sun, a magnificent sight. The sky behind it was streaked with red and orange.

"No," said Patrick. "Of course you can't leave the Hall."

She was silent. Was that fantastic pile of stone really hers? It seemed impossible. She felt dizzy. How could she ever be worthy of it? Of course it wasn't really hers, but lent to her for a while, to pass on to her heirs. Which was where Patrick came in—if he could be brought to agree.

A complicated man, Patrick. He loved her, but he was letting her go free if that was what she wanted. They were not formally engaged, but he could go on telling her how much he loved her. He was perhaps the only person in the world she could trust to tell her the truth about herself.

He said, "Let's get moving. I left the car at the Hall. Let's pick it up and think about food. Or do you want to go back and change first?"

The thought of going back into the Hall filled her with gloom. "I'll come as I am, if that's all right with you?"

He'd left his ancient but much loved Rover in the visitors' car park. Minty got in, and relaxed. "I didn't make one appointment which Annie suggested. She thought a girl called Tessa, who works in the Estate Office, would be OK as my personal assistant, but I fobbed her off even though I desperately need someone."

"Ah," said Patrick, driving along the avenue, "Tessa. I'm not one of her favourite people, I'm afraid. But maybe I know someone who might do as your personal assistant. I'll make some enquiries."

Minty said, "I've talked only about myself. You said your day had been messy. So what went wrong—apart from the visitation from Annie?"

He took his time to reply, turning onto the busy main road. He was a good driver. "Last night we told Annie and Serafina that we were engaged but no one else, right? This morning everyone in the village knew. Someone talked. Probably Florence Thornby, who was just packing up in the kitchen when she spotted me leaving. She asked me why I was grinning, and I said, 'Wait and see', which was tantamount to telling the Town Crier."

He negotiated the hump-backed bridge over the river where Minty's mother had crashed her car and died so long ago, and took the back lane which brought him to the parking space at the end of his garden.

"You know what the village is like. Sneeze in a five-acre field with not a soul in sight and by the time you get home, you'll be asked where you caught that dreadful cold. By the time I unlocked my front door this morning, everyone hereabouts seemed to know that I was your Flavour of the Month. Before the day's out, the news will probably be in the national gossip columns."

The sun had almost disappeared but the air was so still it promised to be a fine evening, with a blush in the sky which foretold another good day on the morrow. The house martins had left for their winter habitats, but a blackbird sang on the roof of his tall house, and hawthorn berries blazed in his garden. They were in another world, far removed from the Hall. This was the world of the village, of professional people, small shops and the ancient church. A world on which the surrounding farms and the Manor house depended. A world that she had grown to love—and regretted leaving in a way.

Next door reared the back of the bookshop where Minty had worked till recently. Now Mr Lightowler had taken over the shop, and single parent Alice Mount wanted Minty's job there.

Patrick opened the car door for her, and led the way into the cool black and white tiled hall of his house. "You've no idea how many people rang to make appointments to see me, or actually arrived on the doorstep, wanting to tell me how they felt about my consorting with the Lady of the Hall. The villagers are all for it, but the County give it the thumbs down. Lady Silchester was most forthright. 'What makes you think you could marry an Eden of Eden Hall?' She told me three times that she was your godmother and as such, and with her granddaughter Tessa working for you, she wished to make it clear that, etc., etc."

"How dare she!"

"That's rather what I thought. Especially since she was conspicuous by her absence in your life when you could have done with a helping hand."

"I can't remember her though I've come across her granddaughter, of course. Why doesn't Tessa like you?"

"Her grandfather left a great deal of money in trust for her, to be released when she was twenty-five. He hadn't a great opinion of her financial ability and thought she might fritter it away if she had it earlier. There's a discretionary clause, but so far I've not seen fit to release the money for any of the wild-cat schemes Tessa has thought up. Naturally I'm the wicked ogre to her."

"Right. Now what was all that about Ruby this morning?"

"I found her sitting in the hallway, mid-morning. She said she didn't want to come in, that it had been a mistake and she wasn't going to waste my time. She was holding a bag of clothes for you, but then she said you wouldn't want her rubbish and she was going to take it away again. It's all about her lodger, of course. Poor, damaged, child-like Jonah Wootton. I can remember when he was a respected teacher . . . ah well."

Many years ago Jonah had been caught playing around with Ruby behind his wife's back, had fallen out of a window and hurt his head. His wife Hannah had refused to have anything more to do with him, so Ruby had taken him in and looked after him ever since.

Patrick sighed. "Jonah's tried hard enough to get his wife to forgive him, but she won't. Now she's decided to go to live with her sister, and Jonah wants a divorce. Legally he's got grounds since Hannah's never let him back in, but Ruby's in a real muddle. One minute she says she doesn't believe in divorce and the next she wants to know if he could get one and if so, would I act for him. I said I would, even though I don't believe in divorce, either. It might help if you could find time to talk to her. Minty, you do understand that if we ever marry, it will be . . ."

". . . till death do us part. Yes. And if I ever catch you with another woman, as Hannah did with Ruby, you wouldn't get off as lightly as Jonah did."

"Now I can sue you for using threatening language. Damages to be arranged." He touched her cheek. "I used to dream of you sitting at my side in the car, coming home after a day's work, talking over what had happened that day. Some dreams do come true, it seems."

"I dreamed of being your wife and living here . . . and yes, it would have been good."

He sighed. "Back to reality. Let's freshen up and get something to eat."

Chapter Six

While she waited for Patrick, Minty wandered around his sitting room. She checked for dust on the mantelpiece; there was none. She rather regretted her decision not to change when he came down again, for he was looking elegant in a silky polo-neck grey jumper and charcoal trousers. He shrugged on a matching charcoal jacket and said, "I've managed to get the last table at the Chinese restaurant. All right?"

Minty had hoped for something more substantial tonight. Steak and kidney pudding, or pork with dumplings, perhaps. "Not the pub?"

"I've a reason for going Chinese. Bear with me?"

Patrick often ate at the Chinese restaurant across the High Street, and was friendly with Mr Willy, the proprietor, and his wife. The restaurant was full, as it usually was on a Saturday night, but they were shown up the stairs into the flat above.

A table was being laid for them there by an exquisite woman in her early thirties, who surely must be Willy's daughter. She was dressed in an expensive black trouser suit over a white T-shirt. She was nobody's idea of a waitress, but would have looked at home in any boardroom in the land.

"Iris!" Patrick kissed her on both cheeks. "I was just thinking about you. Iris, this is Araminta Cardale. Minty, I don't suppose you remember Iris but she was at school with me. We lost touch for a while but met up again when she was studying in London."

Iris shook Minty's hand, her mouth smiling while her eyes tried to take Minty's measure . . . exactly as Minty was doing to her.

Iris said, "What Patrick hasn't said was that after I did a Fine Arts degree I worked for Lady Cardale at the Hall, first in the Estate Office and then helping to organise special events. I loved the Hall and only left after a bad experience with her son."

Patrick said, "You can tell her, Iris."

Iris lifted her chin. "Simon wouldn't take no for an answer. He raped me. I didn't go to the police because he said it would be my word against his and my father rents this place from the estate. So I went to work in my uncle's import business in the East End of London."

Patrick said, "Her parents—all of us—have missed her very much."

Iris said, "My uncle appreciated my skills, but he has growing sons who should be learning my job. It is uncomfortable. So here I am back on a short visit."

Patrick pulled out a chair for Minty. "I was going to ask your father if you might think of returning now."

"Not so fast, Patrick." Iris smiled at Minty. "My father has a special menu in mind for you, unless there is some dish you particularly wish for?"

Iris vanished, and Minty took a deep breath. "Patrick, is she a past girl-friend of yours?"

He looked grim. "No, never. She did love someone else but he broke it off after she was raped. We did go around together for a while but only as friends. She's had offers of marriage since, but she's fastidious and still bears the scars of what happened to her."

"You thought that as Simon is leaving, Iris might become my personal assistant? Will you invite her to join us?"

"It's up to you to invite her, not me."

He was right, as usual. Infuriating man!

She put her elbows on the table and leaned her chin on her hands. "You've never kissed me on both cheeks like that."

He snarled at her. "You know very well that if I did, it wouldn't stop there. And nice girls don't tempt their boy-friends."

So he was her "boy-friend" now, was he? Was this progress? He was fiddling with the metal bracelet of his watch. She'd noticed it chafed him from time to time and wondered if he wouldn't be more comfortable with a leather strap. When Iris brought a platter of delicious titbits, Minty asked her to join them. Iris shook her head. "When you've finished eating, perhaps."

Minty watched Patrick attack the food. "Have you eaten anything at all today?"

"Ruby brought me in a sandwich and stood over me while I ate it."

"Wasn't she supposed to be working in the charity shop?"

"They have a roster of Ladies Who Help. Some of them don't help much, but today Ruby insisted. They must have felt as if a pet mouse had turned on them."

"Hugh and Venetia Wootton have asked me to lunch tomorrow at the Manor. Will you be there? I wonder what they think about poor Jonah wanting a divorce. I know they've asked him to move in with them at the Manor, but he seems to prefer life as Ruby's lodger."

"Closer to the pub," said Patrick. "Also, Ruby doesn't fuss over him, which Venetia would. Don't forget that Venetia is an inveterate gossip, and since she organises the stewards at the Hall, anything you say at the Manor will echo round the Hall and village within an hour. No, I won't be there. I'm standing godfather to my partner's daughter in Town. She's a poppet, worth all the anxiety she gave them when she was born. I'll stay overnight because I'm working there Monday to Wednesday. You do remember I split my week in Town and here? I'm on my own in the office here but in partnership there."

He'd make an excellent godfather. She wished he'd at least expressed disappointment that he couldn't see her on the morrow. Didn't he mind not seeing her for three—no, four days?

She could ask him to ring her. No, she wouldn't beg. "I'm off to London myself on Tuesday morning, back late Wednesday. You'll be in the village again on Thursday?"

Bowls of soup were wafted onto the table, and their first plates removed. Patrick concentrated on tasting the soup, which was delicious. "You won't keep me in suspense, will you? If you find Sir James to your liking, you'll tell me straight away?"

Minty hid a smile. She hadn't told him what James' title was, but Patrick knew, which proved that even he could slip up now and then. "You were going to give me some information about the Foundation."

He took an envelope out of his pocket and slid it over. "You'll be glad to hear I couldn't find anything much against Sir James. His business methods seem to be fairly ethical, and he's not been involved in any scandal." He frowned, wrestling with himself. "He's a good bit older than you, but I think maybe you'd like a father figure, having been without one yourself for so long."

Minty fired up. "You think that's why I love you? As a father figure? If that's so, I'm having a full-scale adolescent rebellion."

Another course appeared. Patrick tasted it, and said, "Mmmm. Did you ever rebel against your uncle and aunt?"

"Too tired, too disheartened. Cooking and cleaning for them, working in the parish office. Nothing I did was ever enough. I kept on trying because I wanted them to love me. I think now that Aunt Agnes hated me. As for him, he allowed her to snipe at me non-stop, even after she'd stopped hitting me."

He drew in his breath. "She used to hit you? And when I came to see how you were doing in the city, I let her drive me away!"

Snap! she thought. *And you gave ground too easily when Annie wanted you to break our engagement. So what's going on here? I don't have you down for a weakling.*

Something that sizzled was placed in front of her, and this time it was she who said, "Mmmm." She straightened her shoulders. "It taught me that there's lots of evil in the world—not that my uncle's evil, just weak. Not sure about her. I survived. Now let's ask Iris to join us, shall we?"

She liked Iris and Iris seemed to like her. Iris' qualifications were beyond reproach and she said she could start work on Monday if that's what Minty wanted. She would stay with her parents for the time being, while looking around for a flat or house to rent . . . or possibly there might be a room for her at the Hall?

"I need to look at the accommodation at the Hall," said Minty. "But first . . . Patrick, will you make yourself scarce for ten minutes?"

"Are you going to talk about me?"

"Of course we are," said Iris, smiling. "Off you go."

Patrick threatened to get into a state and start smoking again but the women merely laughed, so he disappeared.

Iris said, "You want to know if Patrick and I were ever an item and if I could be a threat to you as Lisa was to your mother. The answer is no. We didn't meet again for years after he left the village, not till we were both students. I bumped into him at the National Gallery one day and we recognised one another. Yes, of course I liked his looks though he's not really my type.

"He'd been looking at a pre-Raphaelite portrait of a woman with masses of fair hair and piercing eyes. I said, 'Why, that looks like little Minty, grown up.' He nodded, and I understood that he still loved you. After that we kept in touch, seeing one another perhaps two or three times a year.

"I was still at university doing an MA when he came back to the village. By the time I returned and started to work at the Hall, I was going out with another man. When Simon—when it happened—Patrick was away on holiday. I fled to London before he came back but he followed me—which was more than my other friend did. Patrick wanted me to press charges against Simon, but I was too ashamed."

"I'm so sorry," said Minty. "I know you're not the only one Simon's attacked. He frightens me, too. Do you feel safe enough to come back to the Hall?"

"Simon's going, isn't he? I loved my job at the Hall and it was cowardly of me to run away. If you'll have me, I'd love to work for you."

Minty warned, "There's lots of problems . . ."

"Good. I like a challenge. Nine o'clock Monday morning all right with you?"

Patrick resumed his seat. "Finished tearing my character to pieces?"

Minty grinned. "We can continue doing that any time. Iris is coming to work for me."

It was a beautiful night, so Patrick walked her back to the Hall. Half way down the avenue she put a hand on his arm and stood still.

The moon had risen, looking pale. The Park and its ancient stands of trees were clad in black and silver. The upper windows of the two oldest wings were glowing with light to show that Lady Cardale and Simon were both at home.

Patrick said, "Looks like a stage set. You're shivering. Do up your jacket."

"I'm scared, Patrick. That great house, lived in by generations of my family . . . all those antiques . . . the visitors . . . the estate! This morning when I woke up, I gloried in the thought that I'd inherited such a beautiful place. Now, I'm beginning to sense what a burden it's going to be."

He put his arms around her from behind. "You'll manage. Especially with Iris to help you."

She leaned back against him. "You're not going to help me, are you?"

"The Hall's your problem, not mine."

"And the Foundation?"

He didn't reply and she wondered again if sometime he might take on that part of her burden. She made herself comfortable against him, relishing his warmth against her back, the strength of his arms around her. The smell of him: a hint of Chinese cookery, good soap, no trace of cigarettes . . .

Could she tell him what Simon had threatened to do? She tried to get the words out, but couldn't. It was too embarrassing. Suppose he believed them? Would it matter? So few people were virgins when they married nowadays, but she was and she was proud of it. It hurt something inside her to think that Simon could spread such rumours.

She said, "Simon frightens me."

He was indulgent. "If it makes you feel any better I'll check every few days that they haven't let Miles out."

"You think it was his mother who made Simon what he is, but it goes back further. You know my old nanny, who still lives in the village?"

"Dreadful old woman. I do try to pray for her, but it's hard going."

"My stepmother grew up next door to Nanny Proud, and it was she who encouraged Lisa to fly high. Lisa's first marriage failed, leaving her with a baby just as she landed a job with the Foundation. So Nanny Proud offered to bring him up."

"And spoiled him?"

"Of course. Lisa set her sights on my father but he married my mother instead and produced me. It took Lisa another four years to get into my father's bed and drive my mother to her death, but in the meantime she'd arranged that Nanny—plus Simon—should come to the Hall to look after me. When the car bringing them to their new life reached this point in the avenue, Nanny Proud showed Simon the Hall and told him it was his for the taking. He grew up believing that. Still believes it."

Patrick's arms tightened around her. "I know Sir Micah gave him chance after chance in business and that Simon screwed them all up.

He doesn't seem able to learn from his mistakes. It's always someone else's fault. I'm glad he's going."

He walked her to the door in the courtyard marked "Private" and made sure she could get in. She hoped he'd take her in his arms and kiss her, but instead he touched the tip of her nose and said, "Take care of yourself, won't you?"

He put his hands in his pockets and walked away down the avenue of trees, till he was lost in the darkness . . . leaving her feeling desolate.

Sunday morning. Minty woke to find the sun sidling into her bedroom. She didn't feel sunny herself. She wouldn't see Patrick again for four days.

She told herself to forget him if he couldn't be bothered to fight for her.

Only, she couldn't. He was too much part of her.

Serafina had left out some croissants, orange juice, cereal and coffee. Minty helped herself and went through into her office. Both telephones seemed to be full of messages again. She played them back, making notes and trying to decide who she could talk to before she left for church.

She must see her half-sister Gemma as soon as possible. She sighed. Gemma was something of an enigma. Red-headed, beautiful, spoilt in some ways but neglected by her mother, she seemed poised between good and evil. Sometimes she seemed prepared to accept Minty, and sometimes she sided with Simon. She'd got herself engaged to Simon's crony Miles though she'd never seemed to be that fond of him. Perhaps Simon had pushed her into it as a reward for Miles' services. How would she react now Miles had been carted off to gaol?

And what about the busy Mrs Collins, who ran the village single-handed when she wasn't quarrelling with her rival, stately Mrs Chickward? Who had also rung.

Her uncle had rung again from the city. Why?

A strange American voice requested a word with her about the projected hand-over of the Hall. Why couldn't they take no for an answer? But . . . had they actually been told she wasn't going to play their game?

Maybe not. She must ring them . . . but not yet, not early on a Sunday morning.

Barr, the new Administrator, bleating about the state of the accounts . . . nothing properly recorded either on disc or in the ledgers . . . oh dear, Patrick had been right to warn her about the books.

Minty threw her papers in the air, swallowed the last bit of croissant and took her mug of coffee through into the chapel.

Lord, You know everything. You want us to keep Sunday a special day, and here I am rushing around. I'll stop. See? I've stopped. No work today. Except I must see Gemma, poor thing. Please be with me.

She hadn't opened her Bible-reading notes for a couple of days, but now did so, and read them. She followed that up with the recommended readings from the big Bible in front of her . . . her mother's Bible, which had been handed down from *her* mother, and *her* mother before her.

The thought for the day stayed with her. "Fear not . . ."

She tapped on the door that led to her half-sister's flat. No reply. There was a dead feeling to the silence beyond that door. Gemma probably hadn't got up yet. Gemma played hard, and worked as little as she could.

Minty went on down the stairs to the Long Gallery. The blinds were all down as they should be, turning the great room into a place of shadows. Even the portraits on the walls seemed insubstantial in this light. Swashbuckling Sir Ralph Eden alone seemed to glow in his frame, looking at her . . . perhaps waiting for her to bring this great house back to life again.

She saluted him. Laughed at herself for being fanciful.

Down the stairs again to the lower ground floor where Barr had his flat. There was no reply to her knock on his door, either, but another door further along the corridor opened, to reveal a fiftyish woman with stout legs, glaring at her.

Minty put on her best smile. "Mrs Kitchen? I was hoping to see you."

"As you may have heard, I do not work at weekends." No attempt at being conciliatory. Rather the reverse. Minty remembered that Mrs Kitchen had expressed a desire to "put her in her place".

"I heard. But if you could spare a moment?"

With a shrug the woman led the way back into an airless apartment, overcrowded with a collection of . . . teapots! Teapots in all shapes and sizes, some imitating animals and one in the shape of a fish. They were everywhere: on high ledges just under the ceiling, in display cabinets and on the top of an upright piano.

"Amazing!" said Minty. "Did you collect all these yourself?"

Mrs Kitchen gave a stiff nod. "I heard you were around, making extra work for my staff. Please see that all blinds are left in the down position if you have to disturb them at any time."

"I've a lot to learn," said Minty, hoping to turn away wrath with a soft answer. "Tell me, how long have you worked here?"

The woman flexed her neck. "I've worked for her ladyship nearly twelve years. Naturally when Mr Simon took over, he asked me to stay. 'How would I manage without you?' he said. I'd do anything for him, and so would my three lady cleaners. He said I only had to give him a month's notice if I ever got fed up with him. As if I would!"

"So you're on a monthly contract, are you?"

"Oh, we didn't need a formal contract, Mr Simon and I," said Mrs Kitchen.

Then, not being a fool, she tucked in her lips and gave Minty a look of alarm. "You don't mean you want to give me notice, do you? How could you manage this great place without someone who knows . . ."

"I wouldn't know where to begin," said Minty, being frank. "But I don't want people working for me without a proper contract. I've asked Barr and Tim to stay on for the time being. I'd very much like you to stay too, but I'd understand if you felt it was too much for you at your age."

"My age?" gasped Mrs Kitchen. "I'll have you know I'm still in my prime."

"So, would you like to stay?"

The woman looked as if she'd swallowed lemon juice. She looked around her, at the treasures collected over so many years. Minty could read her thoughts. The job was not difficult and the flat was free. Where would she go if she left the Hall? And at her age, what other job would she be likely to get?

"I'll stay," said Mrs Kitchen. "For the time being, at any rate. See how we get on."

"I'm delighted to hear it," said Minty, not at all sure that she was. "I've a new secretary starting on Monday—Iris, who used to work here some time ago? Will you see that she has keys to get in with? She'll be working up in the tower office."

Mrs Kitchen nodded. She knew when she was beaten.

There would be no Patrick today. Or tomorrow, or the next day.

She must try not to think of him.

She took the stairs two at a time and knocked on Gemma's door again. This time there was a mumble from within.

"Gemma? It's me, Minty. Let me in!"

After some fumbling around, the door opened a crack. Minty pushed, sending Gemma stumbling back into the room, sliding down to the floor. Minty knelt beside her.

Gemma's red hair was in a tangle and there was a nasty bruise on the side of her face. She was wearing a minimal halter-neck top and very tight trousers in jade green. She was no longer wearing the fabulous emerald engagement ring which her ex-fiancé Miles had given her. She stank of drink.

Nineteen years of age and educated to do nothing, Gemma had a model's face and figure, had got pregnant at sixteen and had an abortion under circumstances which meant she couldn't conceive again, and seemed to have become engaged to her brother's crony out of despair rather than love.

Minty tried to lift Gemma onto a chair and failed. There were cigarette stubs, empty bottles and glasses everywhere.

"Is there anyone there?" No reply. Minty hastily explored the other rooms in the suite which were expensively furnished, but looked neglected. Fabulous clothes draped chairs or lay in heaps on the floor, the bathroom was a tip and the kitchen looked as if it was used only to make coffee. There was no one else there.

Florence Thornby came down from Old Oak Farm daily to cook for Lady Cardale and her two children, but it didn't look as if anyone cleaned for Gemma. The bed had been lain on, but not slept in. The blinds were down and the windows closed, leaving the rooms in a dusky, smoky fug.

Gemma moaned, trying to sit up. "Need . . . bathroom!"

With some difficulty Minty got her half-sister to the bathroom. "I'll make some coffee, shall I?"

Gemma staggered back into her sitting room holding her head.

Minty found some aspirin and gave Gemma two with some coffee. Gemma could hardly open one eye.

"Who hit you?"

"Who'd . . . think?"

Not Miles. He was in jail. A horrible thought. "Simon?"

Gemma nodded, held her head. "Took . . . ring."

"You should have given it back to Miles before now."

"Simon took . . . for himself. What . . . do?"

"The police? No? Shall I call the doctor?"

Gemma shook her head, and then groaned again. "Leave . . . alone."

Minty sighed. Got a cool cloth with some ice in it to lay on Gemma's face. Gemma grabbed her hand and held it fast. Wept, silently.

Time passed. Minty tried not to be impatient, but soon she must be leaving for church . . . only perhaps this was more important? What would Patrick advise, if he were here? *Oh, Patrick, I miss you so.*

At last Gemma let go of Minty's hand and tried to sit up. "Help me? The house Simon was buying us? Putting it back on . . . market. You turn me out, what . . . do?"

"Shush. I won't turn you out."

Gemma didn't seem to be listening. She lurched over to the table and picked up a folder with hands so shaky that the contents spilled onto the floor.

"Whoops! Dream bites . . . dust!" Gemma kicked at the cascading designs for wedding dresses, pictures of wedding bouquets . . . all the notes she'd made for her wedding to Miles, which would now never take place. As Minty began to pick up the papers, Gemma lunged for a second folder and pulled out the contents, leafing through them till she found the estate agent's colour picture of a large early Georgian house, pillared and porticoed, with extensive outbuildings.

"See? Pretty!" Gemma stumbled to a chair, holding onto the picture. "Could . . . been happy there. Promise . . . not turn me out, Minty?"

Minty didn't want to take responsibility for someone who didn't seem to know the difference between good and evil. She wanted to be out of there, running wild in the Park, running to Patrick, to be caught up in his arms and . . .

But she *was* sitting there, with her half-sister. She grimaced, reminding herself that Jesus said we should love one another, care for one another, help one another. Patrick dropped everything to help people in trouble. Part of Minty did want to help Gemma, even though the rest of her didn't.

"Gemma, you still have a job looking after the charity events," she said. "Your mother has given me a file on them, though I haven't had a chance to look at it properly yet. We'll talk about that when you're feeling better."

Gemma tried to sit upright. "All Mother wants . . . call from Downing Street . . . New Year's Honour's list. Doesn't care . . . me . . . anything! Not proper job. Had to pay . . . dresses from allowance. Suppose that's gone, too."

"Father did leave you a lot of money."

"Simon went on and on at me . . . all of us drinking . . . seemed right thing . . . give him the money. I signed, they witnessed. Watertight! Whoops, there goes money! Nothing left, Minty!" She began to weep. "Simon took . . . ring! Didn't want him to! Beautiful ring. He hit me! Going to be ill . . . !"

Minty steered Gemma through to the bathroom again. She thought Gemma was exaggerating. Simon couldn't just whisk his half-sister's money away like that. The ring had certainly disappeared, but Simon had probably taken it to give back to Miles. If anyone needed money now it must be Miles, who'd lost his freedom, his job and his fiancée.

Gemma had lied about things in the past. On the other hand, she was in distress and ought not to be left. Who would be willing to look after her?

Lady C? From what Gemma had said, Lisa wouldn't bother.

"Gemma, I've got to go out in a minute. Would you like to sleep it off in my bedroom? Then Serafina would be within call if you needed anything."

Gemma reacted badly. "What do I need . . . that old cow?"

So Minty got her half-sister into bed and left her, saying she'd call back later.

Chapter Seven

Minty thought, *Patrick will know what to do about Simon and Gemma.*

Patrick wasn't around to talk to.

Best get ready for church. She must wear her black outfit, of course.

She didn't take her father's car but walked through the Park and up the village street to the golden church at the top. Most of her ancestors were buried there, and soon a tablet to her father's memory would be placed on the wall beside the one to her mother.

She felt draggingly tired—nothing to do with the fact that she couldn't see Patrick today, of course. A Porsche passed her with Simon at the wheel and his mother at his side. Neither acknowledged her.

Minty bit her lip. Lady C and Simon would occupy the front pew on the left as they'd always done. Minty would like nothing better than to hide in a back row and join in the service as best she might. She didn't want to challenge their right to sit at the front of the church, though some might think she should. She didn't feel up to confrontations. What's more, Lady C was wearing an expensive hat, and Minty didn't possess anything but the knitted woollen cap Ruby had sent her.

Minty told herself God didn't care what she wore. Unfortunately that fact failed to boost her confidence.

She stepped into the deep porch of the church, to be met with a clamour of children led by their leader, the ten-year-old thug, Becky.

"We want you to take the junior church, like you did before . . ."

"We're not stopping if you don't . . ."

Minty blinked. She picked up one of the twins, who was hugging her leg. "Darlings, you have your own teacher."

"She's rubbish!"

"We told her we weren't stopping if you wouldn't do it."

"The Rev says it's OK . . ."

The other twin was now trying to climb up her. Minty hefted that one up, too. A child of about three was pushed forward by Becky. She stared up at Minty with enormous blue eyes, a dummy stuck firmly in her mouth. Surely she was too old for a dummy? Becky nudged the little girl. "Go on!"

The three-year-old took the dummy out of her mouth and said, "Say 'please'."

Becky turned to face the others. "All together, now . . . PLEASE!"

Minty laughed. She kissed the twins and put them down. "Darlings, I haven't got anything prepared and you can't just hijack anyone you like and get them to take you for Sunday School."

People were pushing past them into the church, with smiles or glares of annoyance. The Reverend Cecil Scott, who'd once been curate to Minty's uncle, came out to see what was holding up the traffic.

"Minty! Lovely to see you. We wondered if you'd make it today."

"She's teaching us," announced Becky, arms akimbo. "Or we all go out and play on the Green, and you know we've been told not to do that because of the traffic."

Cecil, pink and perspiring, gave Minty an imploring look. "Would you? Just for once? I'll square it with their teacher."

Surrounded by children, Minty was swept into the front pew on the right, where the twins sat one on either side of her, the three-year-old climbed on her lap, and Becky organised the distribution of hymn books. Minty hardly dared look across at Lady C, but when she did, she saw that her stepmother kept her eyes resolutely forward. Minty felt a giggle build up inside her.

Was this how God had responded to her feelings of embarrassment at attending church that day? There she was, all dressed up in her best black, and it would have been far more practical to wear jeans and a sweater if she was going to work with the children. And what on earth was she going to do with them?

There were twelve of them. No, two more were piling into the pew behind her, breathing down her neck . . . and another three tumbling down the aisle, only just ahead of Cecil processing to the altar.

When the time came, Minty felt as if she were the Pied Piper of Hamelin, taking the children out to the side room in which the children's church met. Almost, she panicked. She had a mental vision of Patrick holding his friend's baby in his arms . . . what a marvellous father he'd be, so patient but firm. Loving.

What story could she tell the children? The word "fear" popped into her mind.

"Whose name begins with a *G*? You're George? Right. You're named after a very special saint, but today I'm thinking about another man whose name also began with a *G*. Any guesses?"

A thin boy picked his nose. "My uncle's called Gidget. Dunno why." Becky thumped him.

Minty ignored this. "A long long time ago God's special people turned away from Him and began to worship idols, so He allowed their land to be invaded by enemies. These strangers had masses of weapons and if anyone argued, they got knocked down. The bad men took all the Israelites' food so no one ever had enough to eat. Can you imagine that?

"The people of Israel cried out to God to rescue them. God listened to their prayers and sent one of His angels down to earth to the man He'd chosen to be their new leader. God didn't choose the strongest, like Becky. He didn't choose the one who was the oldest, or the one whose father had the most money. No, He chose a man from a small family farm—like one of those on the hill-tops around here."

The thin boy gave Becky a triumphant look and she scowled.

Minty went on, "The angel found a young man hiding in a wine press. Can you guess what he was doing there? No, he wasn't treading grapes down to make wine. He was threshing wheat because the wine press had high sides, and he didn't want the baddies to see him and take the food. Clever, eh? His name began with a *G*. *G* for Gideon.

"The angel said to Gideon, 'The Lord is with you, mighty warrior!'

"Gideon couldn't believe his eyes and ears, because he was no warrior. He'd been so frightened of the enemy he'd been working inside a wine press, remember? He knew he'd no chance against the armies of the invaders—by himself. But if God was going to be on his side . . . ? Well, that might tip the odds in his favour.

"So he asked God to give him a sign. He said, 'Look, I'll leave a sheep's fleece on the threshing floor. If there's dew on the fleece tomorrow while all the ground around it is dry, then I'll believe You're going to help me save Israel.' That's what happened."

"Can't be done," said a quiet boy, sitting at the back.

Minty smiled. "With God, anything's possible. Next morning Gideon picked up the sodden fleece and wrung a bowl of water out of it . . . yet the ground around it was dry."

"You mean, it was a miracle?" asked Becky.

"Yes. But Gideon was still afraid. So he tested God again. 'This time make the fleece dry, and the ground wet.' God did, so Gideon realised he'd been chosen to drive out the invaders.

"He began to collect men around him. One by one and two by two, then in their dozens, men came to join him in the hills. Very soon, he had an army of his own, but that wasn't quite what God had in mind.

"'You have too many men,' He said to Gideon. 'I want everyone to realise that you won because I was with you, and not because you've a big army. Tell everyone who's frightened, to go home.'

"Most of them did go home. They knew how terrible the enemy was. They knew how many of their friends and families had suffered already. You can't really blame them for going, can you? That left only ten thousand men.

"God said, 'Gideon, you've still got too many. They're all thirsty now. Tell them they're going into battle today. Take them down to the stream below. Most will kneel down to drink. Send them home. Only keep the ones who scoop up water in their hands and continue on their way.'

"That left only three hundred men. Only three hundred, against the enormous army of the invaders! It was impossible to count how many there were. They'd arrived with their camels and their tents and their livestock and settled on the land like a cloud of flies, devouring everything in their path. What could Gideon and his three hundred men do against so many?

"Gideon himself didn't think he'd got any chance. He was near despair. He'd had thousands of men to attack the enemy with and *he'd sent them home*! He must have been out of his mind! There he was sitting up in the hills, and the enemy occupied the plain below as far as the eye could see.

"God knew Gideon's courage was failing him. He said, 'If you're scared to attack, go down quietly to the edge of the enemy's camp and listen to what they're saying.' Gideon took one servant and crept down the hill towards the enemy outposts. It was a still night, and he could hear people talking from a long way off."

Minty dropped her voice, and the children crowded in even closer. "Gideon heard one man telling another of a bad dream he'd had. 'A round loaf of bread came tumbling into our camp. It struck our tent with such force that it overturned and collapsed.' His friend said, 'This means Gideon will smash our camp and defeat us!'

"Gideon crept back up the hill, feeling a lot better. God now put a brilliant plan into his head. He divided his men into three companies of one hundred and gave them all trumpets, and torches which were first lit and then hidden in empty jars. He said, 'Watch me and do as I do. Encircle the camp, keeping your torches hidden in the jars. When I and those with me blow our trumpets, then everyone else must do the same, and shout out—'" and here Minty raised her voice—"'A SWORD FOR THE LORD AND FOR GIDEON!'

"When everyone was in place around the camp, Gideon and his men blew their trumpets and broke the jars that held the torches. They shouted out, 'A SWORD FOR THE LORD AND FOR GIDEON!' The enemy panicked, unable to tell who was who in the dark, knowing they were under attack, turning on each other with their swords . . . fighting one another . . . thinking they were caught in a trap by an enormous army, far greater than their own . . . and then they turned to run . . . and run . . . with Gideon and his men after them . . . chasing them . . . running them down . . . till there were none left in the land of Israel!"

"Phew!" said Becky.

"That wasn't the end of it," said Minty, "because the Israelites turned to Gideon and asked him to be their ruler. He said, 'No. God will be our ruler. For it was He who gave us the victory.'"

There was a thinking, absorbing silence.

"Yes," said Minty. "It needs thinking about, doesn't it? When we face big challenges, we get scared. We can't imagine how we're going to cope. But if we ask God to help us, He will."

Becky said softly, "A sword for Gideon and the Lord. I like that bit."

Minty said, "Yes, Becky, you're brave and a good soldier. But not everyone is as brave as you."

"You're brave," said Becky.

Minty smiled and shook her head. She knew she wasn't always brave or resourceful. That story reminded her that it was normal to be afraid when faced with so many problems. She'd been relying on Patrick to help her out of her difficulties and that was wrong, too. Patrick knew a lot of the answers, but he didn't know all of them, and at the moment he seemed afraid to accept her love.

She braced her shoulders. She'd asked God to help her, and she was sure He would. She mustn't rely on human beings. That had been silly of her. Only God knew everything, and knew what she ought to do. *Trust in the Lord.*

It was time to join the rest of the congregation for coffee, juice and biscuits. All the children except Becky rushed out, while Minty tried to brush herself down. That was the trouble with black; it showed every speck. Becky helped her.

"I must look a wreck," said Minty, thinking of the scornful look Lisa would turn on her if she turned up in a crumpled state.

"You look lovely," said Becky, firmly.

Minty thought of Patrick and automatically checked for messages on her mobile. There was just one.

Becky said, "Ringing Patrick? You're going to marry him, aren't you? My mum said you wouldn't now, but I said you knew a good thing when you saw it."

"Yes," said Minty, grateful for Becky's approval.

Becky vanished, and Minty listened to the message from Patrick.

"Minty, when you go to the bank, check that Simon can't continue as a signatory for the Hall accounts. Also, look at the direct debits."

What, pray, had she expected? Lover's language? Common sense, instead. She went out to face her family and see if she could snatch a word with Ruby.

Downtrodden Ruby was behind the tea urn as usual, but Minty found it difficult to work her way through the congregation to reach her. Everyone wanted to congratulate the heiress at the Hall, and either hinted they'd like her to do something for them, or issued invitations to her to visit them.

The Woottons—dear Hugh and Venetia—did their best to protect her, making sure she wasn't monopolised by anyone too long. Lady C and Simon looked through her and disappeared.

Finally, when Hugh was beginning to look at his watch and declare that they really must be off, Minty managed to catch Ruby, who by that time was washing up. And who had certainly been crying to judge by her reddened eyes.

"Ruby, dear, thank you for sending me those clothes. I don't know what I'd have done without them. May I come to see you later this afternoon? I have to see Alice about the holiday lets in the village at four, so . . . a little after that?"

"There's no need, really there isn't."

"I'll shake you in a minute. Patrick said something was wrong, and I want to hear all about it. Five o'clock?"

Ruby nodded, and Minty allowed herself to be inserted into the Woottons' car and borne away up the hill for lunch at the Manor house.

"Champagne!" cried Hugh. "We must celebrate!"

Minty didn't like champagne but didn't say so since he was already pouring it out. Venetia served up English lamb with roast potatoes, roast parsnips and leeks. Hugh carved with rapid efficiency.

"All our own produce," said Hugh, who had taken to gardening after retiring from the Army. "Our own red currants and mint for the sauces. Our own potatoes, parsnips and leeks. Saves us a packet, I can tell you, growing our own, and tastes twice as good as the stuff you get in the shops. You used to grow your own vegetables and fruit up at the Hall, I remember. Finest apricots and nectarines I ever did see. South-facing walled garden of course."

Venetia lifted her glass in a toast. "To the Lady of the Hall!"

Hugh echoed her. "To Minty. All the very best, my dear!"

Minty said, "I must give you a toast in return. To Hugh and Venetia, the friends who gave me so much help and encouragement—not to mention a job when I was desperate." She sipped her champagne and set it down to change the subject. "So tell me, how is Mr Lightowler coping at the bookshop in my absence?"

Venetia said, "He's got rid of a lot of old stock, replaced it with paperbacks, is advertising for people to join a reading circle and talking about starting a music appreciation class. You know that girl Alice Mount, who cleans some of the holiday lets? She's angling to take your place at the bookshop but the season's nearly over, so Mr Lightowler's put her on hold, together with his plans for opening up a café in the back garden."

Venetia pushed her water glass to Hugh, who poured for her and Minty. "Minty, you had some fine plans for the village once. Are you going to forget all about them now you're at the Hall?"

Minty grinned. "I have more ideas in my head than I can cope with, and probably half of them are no good. I'm going to need a lot of advice. For a start: Hugh, how do we proceed with turning those derelict farm buildings by the station into affordable housing?"

Venetia picked up on that. "What do you mean, 'we'? It was Patrick's idea to buy the site and develop it; he and Hugh and Norman Thornby found the money for it, but of course it's been held up for ages by Simon demanding a king's ransom for access. Fifteen feet of stony land, useless for farming, and he wanted . . . what? Three million for it?"

Hugh patted his wife's hand. "Calm down, my dear. Sir Micah put a codicil in his will proposing that access be granted the developers for a peppercorn rent, leaving Simon out in the cold."

Minty said, "I don't know if it makes any difference, but Patrick gave me his shares in the development as a twenty-fifth birthday present. He thought I might be left the Hall without any money to run it."

Consternation from Venetia. "But Minty, Patrick could have made a good profit from his shares."

Hugh rubbed his chin. "Well, my dear, I don't think Patrick's at a loss for a bob or two. Minty, I'll arrange a meeting with the others and we'll discuss what needs to be done. A site visit for a start, and then we must consider what architect to employ. What else have you in mind?"

Minty remembered Patrick's caveat on her plans to open the Park and give the village a playground. He'd warned her about Venetia gossiping, but surely it wouldn't do any harm to talk in general terms about her plans?

"I do want to do something for the village, but it gets complicated. My father left money to put into the Hall, but it's in a trust fund and everything has to get the trustees' approval. At the moment Annie wants me to hand over running the Hall to others and concentrate on the Foundation. I don't agree, but I do respect Annie's opinion and want to be guided by her. So I'm really torn."

"Think Blue Sky," suggested Hugh, as Venetia took away the dirty plates and brought in a blackberry and apple tart. "Imagine the sky's the limit, and you have unlimited funds. What would you like to see done?"

Minty ladled cream onto her tart. "Can I ask you to treat this in confidence, then? First, I want to open the Park to the public now and then, perhaps at weekends."

"Bravo," said Hugh.

Minty was encouraged by his approval. "Next I want to give the village some play equipment—possibly on part of the Green . . . ?"

Hugh laughed and slapped the table. "The Cricket Club will object!"

"Yes, but do they really need all of the Green all of the time? What about that funny-shaped bit at the top? Couldn't we fence that off and make it into a playground?"

"Splendid idea," said Hugh. "I'll bring it up at the next Parish Council meeting and ask them to co-opt you onto it."

"Please, don't do anything yet. There may be all sorts of legal reasons why I can't do it. But if we're thinking Blue Sky and what would benefit the village most, what I'd really like to do is to keep the Hall open for nine months of the year, say from March till Christmas. That would have a knock-on effect on everything in the village, wouldn't it? More trade, more jobs?"

"You can't keep it open in the winter," said Venetia promptly. "There's always repairs to be done and special cleaning and oh, a host of things. The Hall has to close completely for six months of the year."

"I realise that we have to close for at least three months and that sometimes individual rooms or even a whole wing might be out of operation. But I wondered whether we could have a Christmas tree season."

Silence. "Christmas trees?" said Venetia, bewildered.

Minty blushed. Was the idea really so stupid? "I know it sounds silly and it's a long-term project, of course. I thought I might ask a couple of the local Flower Clubs to decorate a room each as if for a Christmas party, with trees and lights and suitable flower arrangements. I thought people might come specially to see that.

"Of course it's impossible to do it this year—we're in late September now and all the organisations who might be interested in coming to see it will have filled their diaries already. But if we could only get a couple of rooms dressed this autumn, we could get a photographer round to take pictures and produce a brochure, perhaps even set up a Web site? I wouldn't expect to cover costs this year, but if we got full colour brochures out ready for next season . . . do you think it would work?"

Hugh was gaping at her, Virginia frowning.

With even less confidence Minty went on. "It would mean the Hall staying open till Christmas. The restaurant would serve special Christmas food, and the shop would sell Christmas trinkets. It would mean the stewards staying on till Christmas. Am I out of my mind even to dream of such a thing?"

"My dear . . . I'm speechless!"

Hugh smiled at Minty. "A rare occurrence. Make the most of it. Minty, that's a splendid idea."

Venetia recovered her voice. "The stewards are called in anyway during the winter when Lady Cardale does musical evenings and special events for her charities and . . ." Her voice tailed away. "Can she still go on doing them?"

Minty scraped her plate clean. "She's given me a file of charitable events which I've only had time to skim through. As far as I can see, not one of her charities pays to hold their functions at the Hall, while the Hall pays for heating, lighting, catering and stewarding. That can't be right."

Hugh pushed back his chair. "Of course you must charge a proper amount for hire of the Hall, and for the catering. Let's have coffee in the other room."

Venetia threw up her hands. "Toby! You need someone to organise everything for you. Photography. Web site. Leaflets. Mail-shot to organisations. Our son Toby's the man you want. He's been working all over the world in IT. He's in London now, looking for another job.

He'd jump at the chance to do this, and he can move back in with us, which would be a . . ."

Hugh said, "Steady on. Minty's not going to do anything overnight."

Minty realised this was how the grapevine worked. Patrick had produced Iris, and now the Woottons were finding the very man to make her dreams for the Hall come true.

"Perhaps he could come down for a chat? First I must sound out the two redoubtable ladies who run everything around here. Mrs Chickward and Mrs Collins could organise the Olympic Games if they put their minds to it, but would they be interested? And could I get them to work together since they're always at one another's throats . . . in the politest way possible, of course?"

"You'll manage it, dear," said Venetia. "As for my stewards, most of them would love to keep going till Christmas, and so would dear Doris in the gift shop, though she might need some assistance. Who do I know who might help her out? And . . . let me get my diary."

Minty realised that things were getting out of hand. "Hold on, Venetia. I must speak to both Mrs Collins and Mrs Chickward before any word of this gets out. If either of them were to hear it from anyone but me . . . disaster!"

Venetia was scrabbling in her handbag for her diary. "Suppose we all meet here on Thursday afternoon . . ."

"Venetia, please! I've hardly got time to turn round at the moment, and I don't know when I can get round to speaking to the ladies . . ."

"I'll pencil it in for Thursday, and—"

"The meeting must be at the Hall. Not here. And if one word of this gets out before then, the whole thing's off."

"Of course, my dear. But I'll ring Toby and sound him out, just in case. Oh, I'm so happy, I could fly!" She ran out of the room, leaving Minty feeling limp.

Hugh pushed back his chair. "Minty, I'm planting spring bulbs in the lawn this afternoon. You promised to help me, remember?"

"With pleasure, if you'll lend me some old gardening shoes."

It was a relief to shrug into some old gardening boots and get out of doors. Hugh was always restful to be with. Silently he ushered her into his favourite place, a walled garden with an amazing herbaceous border.

No frosts had as yet touched this part of the garden, patchworked with Michaelmas daisies, dahlias, rudbeckias and a riot of other autumn flowers. Strident yellows vied with royal purple. A sight to delight.

"I praise God here," said Hugh.

The Manor had a long sloping lawn down to the river, and Hugh had bought a thousand daffodil bulbs for it.

Minty had never planted bulbs in such quantities before. The vicarage garden had been a barren affair of grass surrounded by old trees, and all she'd been able to do there was plant up a few tubs with annuals.

The scale of Hugh's project daunted her. "How on earth do we get them to look natural? Plant in clumps?"

"See these two big trays? You pile them with bulbs, stand at the top of the slope and toss them up into the air. If you plant them where they fall, they'll look as if they've been there for years."

She did as she was bid, dug down into the turf and sank the bulbs into it. The air was crisp, her borrowed boots were waterproof and life was good, except . . .

"Hugh, Venetia isn't going to keep her mouth shut, is she?"

"She'll be on the phone this minute."

Oops! Patrick had warned her, too.

Chapter Eight

At four o'clock Minty raced down the hill to keep her appointment with Alice. Stumbling over an uneven paving stone outside the Chinese restaurant, she leant against an empty shop window to rub her ankle. *More haste, less speed.* There were three arcaded properties in this terrace, with iron-work supports in fantastical ivy shapes, the paint work now sadly peeling. One unit was occupied by the Chinese restaurant run by Iris' parents. Spacious and even gracious, the other two were empty but for dust and some butterflies which had spreadeagled themselves on the wide wooden floor boards inside.

If only she could find someone to occupy these shops! Did she know anyone in the city who might be interested? Mm, a name did come to mind. She must check it out.

She tested her ankle and resumed her journey down the street, sorting out what she should say to Alice. The two girls had become friends when Minty had been living in one of the estate's run-down holiday cottages and overseeing the others. Alice was bright, but her dreams of a business career had faded after she became pregnant and her boyfriend abandoned her.

When Minty moved up to the Hall, Alice—who'd been living in one room in her mother's council house—moved into Spring Cottage with her toddler. Alice couldn't afford to pay the rent of the cottage unless she got a full-time job, and she couldn't get a full-time job since there were no crèche facilities in the village.

It didn't particularly surprise Minty that Alice's new boy-friend Dwayne should be sitting in one of the big armchairs before the fireplace, with little Marie playing at his feet. Dwayne was big-boned and dark-skinned, a capable electrician who'd been hovering around Alice for a while. Minty worried that Alice's history might be about to repeat itself.

Everything in the living room had been washed and polished: brass lamps, curtains, chair covers, tables. Ornaments glistened, fringes swung from lampshades. There was a tea tray ready with home-made biscuits on it and a smell of baking hung in the air.

"Miss Cardale . . ." Dwayne vacated his chair for her.

Minty wanted to giggle. Dwayne was treating her as if she was somebody really important. She looked at Alice to see if she shared her amusement, but Alice was looking embarrassed, her fresh colour even higher than usual.

Oh dear, thought Minty, *they expect me to act the part of Lady of the Manor. Can I carry it off?*

She took the seat offered her while Dwayne took Marie upstairs to the bedroom.

Alice produced a teapot and handed home-made biscuits. Minty said how beautifully kept the cottage was, and did Alice like it here? Alice said, "Yes."

Minty said, "Come off it, Alice. You and I cleaned houses together. I've got a different job now but it doesn't mean we're no longer friends, does it?"

"Yes, it does," said Alice. "You're at the Hall now, and I'm still cleaning and working evenings in the pub. I thought I might apply for a part-time job at the bookshop, but Mr Lightowler says he can't afford to take anyone on till the spring. So I'm stuck and unless Dwayne helps me out, I can't afford the rent here."

Minty put her tea cup down with a snap. "That's what I wanted to talk to you about. You know my father left some money in trust for the Hall and estate? I've got to get the approval of the trustees first, but I want to get the holiday cottages put in good order and I need someone to manage them for me. You know what's needed. A building survey covering roofs, gutters, drains, electrics . . . everything. Refurbishing where necessary. Some cottages need new bathrooms and kitchens. Others just need redecorating. I need to find out how much it will cost, and then I'll need someone to oversee it. It'll be a full-time job. If I can get permission, will you take the job?"

Alice smiled for the first time. "I'd be lying if I said I hadn't hoped for it. Yes, of course I will. What about Marie? Will you start a crèche to help us young mothers?"

"You'll have a contract and draw a proper salary from the moment the job starts, and you can continue to live here while you do the job. It's up to you to sort out Marie's life. Does that sound harsh?"

Alice looked Minty in the eye for the first time. "I thought . . ."

". . . I'd do everything for you? No, Alice. Marie is your child and your responsibility."

Alice nodded, looking thoughtful. "You never were as green as you looked, were you? All right. So, what about Dwayne? Are you going to say he mustn't move in with me?"

Minty hesitated. "I can't decide that for you."

"I didn't think you'd approve."

Minty thought of Patrick, and how nearly they'd once lost control and tumbled into lust . . . and how satisfying that would have been . . . and how it had been Patrick who had managed to draw back . . . and how in a way she'd regretted that ever since . . . although realising of course that it was for the best, and respecting him all the more for it.

Patrick would be at the christening party now, perhaps dandling his godchild. Smiling, at ease with himself and his friends. She wished she were with him. She wished he were with her. But . . .

"I know what it's like to love someone, Alice, and to feel so lonely that you'd do almost anything to keep them with you. If Dwayne is serious about you . . ."

"It's too early to say. We just fell into it. It's so easy."

Minty sighed. "Yes, but . . . is it the best thing for you?"

Alice gave a short, hard laugh. "I can't be choosy, can I? If Dwayne likes me, how can I send him away?"

"My dear, you're a terrific girl, and a brilliant mother. You're smart, and a hard worker. You deserve nothing but the best. Have a little faith in yourself."

Alice flushed. "Faith? I thought you'd get round to religion in the end."

Minty blinked. "I suppose I could but since you don't go to church or know God's loving rules, I won't—unless you want me to. I really care about you, Alice, and I don't want to see you hurt all over again."

Dwayne came back into the room carrying Marie, asleep, over his shoulder. He addressed himself to Minty. "You've no right to interfere. This is between me and Alice."

Minty got to her feet. "Of course. Thank you for giving me tea, Alice. We'll talk later about the job."

Minty stepped out onto the pavement, feeling as if she'd made a fool of herself. Dwayne was right. She'd no business interfering.

She put her hands over her cheeks to cool them as she walked slowly up the street. Dear Ruby lived next to the charity shop in which she normally worked—on a voluntary basis—six days a week. Her tiny house was no bigger than Spring Cottage, but instead of being built of stone, it was a late Victorian red brick building, sandwiched between larger premises.

Once more Minty lifted a door knocker, and stepped straight from the street into a living room. This time the furniture and furnishings were all in shades of brown, with glints of gold here and there. The air carried the memory of a thousand past meals, because the windows were stuck fast in their frames.

Ruby looked more like a dun-coloured sparrow than ever but instead of throwing herself into Minty's arms and weeping, Ruby took one look at Minty's creased and dirtied black outfit and started scolding.

"Whatever have you been doing to your best black? Here, let me have the jacket and I'll brush it down for you, though goodness knows, it'll have to be cleaned before it'll look anything like!"

Minty meekly let her take the jacket. "I was working with the children this morning, and planting bulbs with Mr Wootton this afternoon."

"You had ought to know better, you really had. You really are hard on your clothes."

Minty looked around for Jonah, Ruby's lodger, but he was nowhere to be seen.

"What's more," said Ruby, brushing away at Minty's jacket, "you've upset Patrick. He was all fingers and thumbs yesterday and him usually so neat-handed. So what have you got to say for yourself, eh?" She glared at Minty.

Minty didn't know whether to laugh or cry. She'd come prepared to comfort Ruby, and instead found herself under attack. "It was Patrick who decided to . . . oh, I can't talk about that. Tell me what's upset you."

Ruby sat with her feet and knees tightly together, smoothing out Minty's jacket. "I don't know as there's anything to say. Jonah's wife's gone to live with her sister and Jonah wants a divorce. I can't believe he really wants it, not after all these years."

"Dear Ruby . . ." Minty put her arm round Ruby's thin shoulders. "Give it time."

"I don't believe in divorce. It's in the Bible. I can hardly bear to look at him. He's happy as a sand boy, too bright, if you know what I mean."

"I know what you mean."

"I can't think straight. I tried to open the shop, but I couldn't get the key into the lock and then I stood there, crying . . . silly old me." Still she stroked Minty's jacket.

Minty had an idea. "Ruby, could you leave Jonah on his own for a few days? Let him think things over quietly? The thing is, I've got to buy a whole new wardrobe and I don't know where to start. Almost everything I've got came from your charity shop, and you know how little that is. I have to open a new school in London on Wednesday, and go to a board meeting afterwards. I'm scared. Suppose I get something unsuitable and they're ashamed of me? Do you think you could come up to London to help me? We could stay in a hotel, perhaps go to a theatre together. What do you say?"

Ruby was no fool. She knew Minty could manage by herself if she had to, but she also knew that Minty was unsure of herself at times.

"I suppose I could if you really needed me. Jonah can get his meals at the pub." She sniffed and felt for a handkerchief. Blew her nose. "You might need a pinch of material taken up on the shoulders here and there. I could do that for you, if you liked. No need to pay shop prices to have things altered."

"I'll pick you up early on Tuesday morning. Bring an overnight bag."

Minty walked back to the Hall. The late afternoon sun sent long streaks of darkness across the avenue through the trees. The Park looked like one of Turner's sketches, all blue distances and golden-leaved trees. Last night she'd walked this way with Patrick, and it was at this point they'd stopped and looked at the Hall, with lights shining out from Lisa's and Simon's rooms.

Patrick had stood behind her and folded his arms about her. She'd felt safe and known herself loved.

And then he'd walked away from her.

Desolation.

Car tyres whispered behind her. She moved to one side to let the car pass but it idled, keeping pace with her. It was Simon in his Porsche, fair-haired, sun-tanned and leather clad. He looked good enough to eat, if you forgot his poisonous nature.

"Hop in, Minty. We need to talk."

She shook her head. "I'm walking, thanks." She quickened her pace, and he accelerated, arm resting on the back of the passenger seat, at ease.

"Anyone would think you're afraid of me. Get in. You can't put me off for ever, you know."

Again she shook her head. They were alone in the avenue at the moment, but the house was open to visitors today. Surely someone would come along soon? If she got in the car, he might well turn round and drive off to some place where he would have her at a disadvantage. At his mercy.

She slowed down, hoping he'd go ahead, but he copied her. Smiling. Her heart was thudding, her colour had risen. He was playing with her, as a cat plays with a sparrow.

Suddenly she remembered Gemma and stopped. "Simon, will you come with me to see Gemma? I'm worried about her. She's distressed, told me some rambling tale about your taking her money and her engagement ring. You didn't, of course. Did you?"

Until that moment she hadn't been sure Gemma had spoken the truth, but now Minty realised that she had. Simon laughed and accelerated in the direction of the Hall. He was out of sight when she got there and let herself in.

She longed to shuck off her crumpled black and dive into a shower, but first she must see to Gemma.

She knocked on Gemma's door. No reply. She looked at her watch, but it had stopped. It had never been reliable, being a cheap hand-me-down from a friend who'd been given a better one for her birthday. Bother.

She tapped the door again. "Gemma, open up. It's me, Minty."

Still no reply. Gemma might well be sleeping it off.

Minty went up to her own rooms and threw off her creased black clothes to get into the shower. Ah, that was better. She pulled on a pink jumper and blue jeans that Ruby had sent her over from the charity shop. They weren't new, but they were comfortably worn in and suited her well enough.

Her head buzzed with everything that had happened that day. With everything that needed doing. She worried that she'd been indiscreet over lunch. Venetia had promised to keep her mouth shut, but Minty was pretty sure she wouldn't. How to stop her? Perhaps if she rang Mrs Collins and Mrs Chickward, she might forestall Venetia . . . ?

She tried phoning, but both were out. Of course, there was a choral evensong this evening, and they'd be there. She didn't want to leave messages on their answerphones. Too complicated.

She was jittery. Serafina was nowhere to be seen, but Minty could hear the noise from a radio or television coming from rooms at the back of the suite. Serafina might be off duty but she'd left a meal of soup, chicken korma and rice ready to put in the microwave, with a fresh salad and a lemon cheesecake for afters.

Minty took the food into the sitting room but couldn't settle. She tried to eat, walking around with the plate in her hands, taking a mouthful now and then. She found a huge television set behind cupboard doors, but couldn't be bothered to watch. She kicked a piece of expensive reproduction furniture by accident, and kicked it again because she didn't like it, and because she loved Patrick so badly it hurt.

It wasn't just that she wanted to tell him what had been happening and ask his advice. Yes, she did want to know what he'd think about things, but more than that, she just wanted him. Now. Here. With that slightly crooked smile of his warming his cool grey eyes and deepening the vertical line down his cheek. She wanted his fine long-fingered hands touching her nose with the lightest of caresses. She wanted the warmth of his presence, his unconditional love.

And more. She wanted it all.

She flopped into an armchair and discovered that the coffee table was just too far away to reach. She hooked it nearer with her foot. It was lonely in that beautiful but too-quiet and too-formal room. A couple of pieces of furniture were old, selected by Serafina from the store-rooms to complement the designer's expensive pseudo-traditional taste. The mirror over the mantelpiece, for instance, had been Minty's mother's, and an elegant side-table shone like a peacock among pigeons.

She couldn't get comfortable in the armchair which was too long in the seat for her legs. She decided that the place would look better with flowers or plants. Perhaps with a table on which to make notes?

She took her plate through into her office. Too formal, again. Too full of space. There were more messages on the answerphone. Her uncle. That American again. She didn't attempt to ring them back. She was too wound up to sit down.

She tried to relax the muscles at the back of her neck. The tower office was better. That still had some sunlight coming through the west window. She sat at the bigger of the two desks and made notes of what she wanted Iris to do on the morrow. Annie was going to take Minty off to the nearby town first thing, so she might not have a chance to brief Iris before she went.

She needed a big map of the estate. Another of the house and its outbuildings. A list of the staff, and who had the right to live in the house and outbuildings. She dug out the folder for the restaurant and amended the note she'd made earlier, so that Iris could write to the designers, declining their proposal. Ditto for the Americans.

Annie. Minty ought to tell Annie about Iris starting tomorrow.

She started another list, of things she needed to buy. A laptop to replace the ancient one which Annie had lent her when she first arrived. A new, smaller mobile phone, ditto. A better watch, one that kept good time. Walking shoes. Casual clothes. Presentable clothes. A handbag. She abandoned the list half way.

Gemma. Minty had promised to see how Gemma was getting on. Suppose Gemma had fallen and hurt herself? Who would know? Who would have the keys to Gemma's suite? Lisa and Simon, presumably. Minty didn't fancy asking either of them . . . although perhaps if Lisa went to look after her daughter . . . ?

One of her phones was marked up for internal use. She pressed the keys for Gemma's phone and let it ring. Still no one answered.

Well, there was nothing for it. She pressed keys for Lisa, and eventually her stepmother picked up the phone. "I'm sorry to bother you, but I'm a bit worried about Gemma. She's not answering the phone, and she didn't come to the door when I knocked."

"You rang me for *that*? She's gone out, I suppose. Please don't disturb me again." The phone went dead. The snub cut into Minty's self-confidence, as it was designed to do.

Minty fled back through the silent rooms to the security of the chapel. She dropped onto the kneeler in front of the altar and buried her head in folded arms.

It was all too much.

She might even have slept awhile, for when she lifted her head again, the room seemed darker. But not lonely. No.

Words ran through her head.

I know you're surrounded by troubles . . . but are you right with Me, Minty?

Was she right with God? Yes, she thought so. She hoped so. Was there something she'd left undone? Well, plenty. But what in particular?

The answer came: *Your uncle*. She grimaced. She did not, repeat did not, want to speak to him.

She sighed. Relaxed. Scrubbed her face dry on the sleeve of her jumper. She'd better wash her face. Because if Lisa wouldn't help Gemma, then someone else must and obviously that someone had got to be her. She would try every single one of the keys on her bunch until she found one to fit the lock to Gemma's rooms. And if she couldn't find one, she'd rout out Mrs Kitchen and get her to help.

She knocked on Gemma's door. Again no reply. At the sixth try, one of her keys turned in the lock.

Gemma was up. She'd been in the shower and her hair was still wet. She was wearing a towelling robe and lying on a settee, using a remote control to change channels on television. There was a glass of wine beside her and she was smoking. Had been smoking for some time. The ashtray nearby was full of stubs.

"Gemma, I was worried about you. Are you all right?"

"No thanks to you." Gemma's mouth looked puffy, and there was a raw patch beside it which Minty hadn't noticed before. "I might have died for all you cared."

"I did care. I told you I had to go out. As soon as I came back, I tried your door and the phone, but . . ."

"You don't really care. Why should you?" Gemma began to weep, hard difficult tears which distorted her once perfect face. "If you really cared, you'd do something to help me instead of yelling at me."

Minty brought her voice down with an effort. "I do care. I will help you. I need you to help me run the events and it will be a proper paid job, I promise you, not . . ."

Gemma flung her glass at Minty. It fell short, but the contents spattered Minty's jeans.

"I don't want a job! I want what's mine by rights, and that's half of everything my father left. Simon says I can sue you for it, and I will!"

Minty walked back out of the room and very carefully closed the door behind her. She was shaking. Her hand was sticky. She licked it. A sweet wine.

Oh, dear Lord, what am I suppose to do about Gemma?

She went back to her own rooms, collected the dirty plates from her supper, took them to the kitchen, washed them up, dried them and put them away. She'd had enough. She wouldn't let herself think or feel. Not anything.

She would ring Annie on the internal phone and tell her about Iris, she would pray for everybody she'd met that day. She would pray for all their problems. She would read her Bible and go to bed. And not allow herself to worry about anybody . . .

. . . Except that she might let herself think about Patrick, just for a few minutes before she went to sleep.

Chapter Nine

Monday morning. Iris came, took possession of the larger desk in the tower office, said she understood Minty's notes and got down to work. Reggie, the bulky man who'd been Sir Micah's driver, inserted Annie and Minty into the back of the limousine and drove them off to the nearest town.

The bank manager received them in person. Various formalities had to be gone through, of course, but he was delighted, etcetera, and anything that Miss Cardale needed . . . naturally a platinum card, and sign here and here . . .

Minty signed. They were treating her like a child, but she really was a child in these matters, wasn't she? At least there were some sensible steps she could take.

"We need to arrange new signatories for the various Hall accounts."

"Of course. Yourself and Simon Cardale, perhaps?"

"Not Simon, no. Our new Administrator and myself. I'd like a set of up-to-date statements as well."

"Naturally. All the accounts were, of course, frozen on your father's death." He called up paperwork and handed it over. "A few hundreds only in the day-to-day General Account, and the Building and Maintenance . . ." He frowned. "It appears to have only a few pounds in it. I don't understand it. The Building and Maintenance Fund is fed by the other accounts throughout the year to pay for maintenance work in the wintertime, but . . . a large sum left the account recently."

Minty knew that the north wing was due to be re-wired and partially re-roofed that winter. "How much has gone, and how much is left?"

"Er, nearly three million pounds went, four weeks ago. Twenty-five pounds is all that's left."

Minty held out her hand for a copy of the balance sheet. Did this mean there were no funds left to run the Hall?

Annie was shocked. "You let Simon withdraw all that money?"

He sought to exonerate the bank. "We acted correctly. The cheque was presented and cleared a good four weeks before Sir Micah died, while Simon Cardale was the official signatory for the Buildings and Maintenance Fund, as indeed he has been for some years."

Minty was dazed. How was she to pay the staff wages at the end of the month?

The bank manager said he'd be happy to arrange facilities for her ... by which he meant she could have an overdraft, though it would be wise, perhaps, for her to prepare a business plan for the Hall ...

Of course he was happy; he'd charge her interest for every pound borrowed, and she'd no way of paying it back till probate was granted. She cringed at the thought of borrowing money. If her uncle and aunt had drummed anything into her, it had been that you never went into debt!

Badly shaken, Annie took Minty to a quiet restaurant to eat. "Three million!" said Annie. "How could Simon do that!"

Minty ran her hands back through her hair. "Would it be possible to start a civil action to recover the money?"

"Throw good money after bad? Simon's heavily in debt. That's where the money's gone, take my word for it."

Minty nodded. She suspected Annie was right. She looked around her. Might Patrick be eating here today? Was his office close by? She needed him. Patrick had given her some shares, thinking she might be left the Hall without any money to run it. It looked as if she'd have to cash them in to keep the Hall going.

She spoke her thought aloud. "Patrick will know what to do."

Annie sighed. "My dear Minty, you mustn't think your father and I came to a decision about Mr Sands lightly. We realised you were fond of him and in many respects he is quite admirable, but every time we went over his file we came to the same conclusion: Patrick Sands is a man without ambition. He has a 'glass ceiling', a barrier inhibiting him from rising to the top. Granted, he has brains and charm; but there's no drive. We believed that sooner or later you'd crave somebody, well, more exciting. Do you understand what I'm saying, Minty?"

For ten seconds Minty wavered in her love for Patrick. But then the bond between them reasserted itself. If Patrick were indeed a light-weight, if he had no ambition, it made no difference. Well, it did make a little difference, but not enough to count.

Annie said sternly, "I trust you to keep to your bargain, Minty. You will meet Sir James without prejudice, won't you?"

"Yes, of course," said Minty, smiling that bright new smile of hers. "I'm sure I'll like him if you think so much of him. But as to love . . . that's another matter. Now I know you planned to take me shopping this afternoon, but in view of the position at the bank . . ."

"I see no reason to change our plans. You need a new laptop, mobile and some good clothes, all legitimate expenses which I daresay the Foundation will recoup. You can't possibly represent them wearing cast-offs from the charity shop. I'll speak to Lord Asher later on today. He's not only your executor but also a trustee with me for the fund your father set up for the upkeep of the Hall. We'd better arrange a meeting to discuss your finances and prepare a business plan as soon as possible."

So Minty bought an up-to-date laptop computer, a better mobile phone, a pretty wrist-watch, some shoes, some light-weight luggage. They looked at cars, but Minty couldn't bring herself to buy any of the sleek models Annie seemed to think appropriate.

On the way home Minty automatically checked her new mobile phone for messages from Patrick—and realised that Annie had out-manoeuvred her, because her old mobile had been left behind in the shop, and she now had no idea what Patrick's mobile number might be. Frustration.

Partly to take her mind off Patrick, who might even now—perhaps—be trying to contact her, Minty mentioned the problem of Gemma to Annie. "Can Gemma sue?"

"No, my dear. There's a clause in the will which says that if any party mentioned in the will tries to sue, they automatically lose whatever amount they had been put down to receive."

Minty nodded. Gemma's behaviour made sense. Simon was short of money. The three million must have passed through him to his debtors faster than the speed of sound. He'd said that even the five million Sir Micah had left him wouldn't clear his debts, so presumably he still owed another two, possibly even three! He wasn't going to get a job with the Americans, he'd no income, so he'd persuaded Gemma to sign away her inheritance and taken her ring.

When Minty had tackled Simon about Gemma in the avenue, he must have rushed to neutralise her. Perhaps he'd shoved her in the shower, perhaps she'd already been in it. He'd hit her again—that fresh mark on her mouth—and then primed her to demand more money from Minty.

Wherever he went, he left a trail of slime behind him.

The immediate problem was what to tell the staff about the money situation. Would it be best to keep quiet, not spread alarm and despondency but borrow money or sell the shares to pay the wages? She hated the thought of going into debt, but didn't see any other way out.

Iris had been busy. A large plan of the Hall and outbuildings was now up on one wall of Minty's office, and an equally large map of the estate in the tower. There were neat files on her desk containing lists of all personnel employed at the Hall, plus various letters for Minty to sign, including ones to the Americans and to the design team which had proposed the fanciful restaurant makeover.

There was also a copy of Chef's contract, which ensured him free accommodation and long periods of paid leave every year; it made Minty wonder whether Simon had been drunk when he signed it.

There was also a pile of notes relating to phone calls, which Minty pushed to one side.

Minty realised that Iris was worth her weight in gold. Was it right to keep her in ignorance of the financial position? Minty couldn't decide.

She handed Iris her new mobile. "Would you key in Patrick's mobile phone number?"

Iris keyed it in. Iris had a cat-like smile.

Minty said, "If Patrick rings you, perhaps you could let him know my new number?"

Iris nodded.

Minty fiddled with the mobile, which had lots of features she didn't yet know how to use. "You may think I should ring him first, but . . . it's complicated."

She met Iris' eyes defiantly, expecting that the older woman would put in a word for Patrick. Iris nodded and said nothing.

"Thank you for being discreet," said Minty, reddening.

Serafina appeared as if summoned by remote control, bringing in tea and biscuits. Minty was too wound up to relax, but strode around the room nursing a cup of tea. She tossed up a coin in her mind and decided it would be wrong to keep Iris in the dark.

"Iris, we had a terrible shock at the bank. Simon's left us with under five hundred pounds in the bank. Three million has disappeared into the blue. I've used a new credit card to buy this mobile phone, a laptop and some clothes—as if they were important. I could kick myself for spending so much, but Annie seemed to think the Foundation might cover the cost and I suppose I follow her reasoning.

"Now it seems the bank will advance the Hall enough to keep us afloat if we provide them with a business plan, but of course that means paying them a high rate of interest on what we borrow. I've some shares I might be able to sell, but . . . the thing is, Iris, I offered you a job and it turns out I can't afford it."

She ran her hands back through her hair. "What a mess! I don't even know what our outgoings are. Simon had an accountant who resigned. Can you find out who he was? I'd better contact him, see if he'll come back . . . but no, anyone who's worked with Simon will be tarred with his brush.

"I don't know what to do. We can't afford to hire another accountant, but can we manage without? Will the money we're taking from visitors pay our current wages bill? If it doesn't, then should I close the Hall to the public earlier in the season than usual?"

She answered her own question. "No, I can't do that because it would have a knock-on effect on the village in terms of jobs and trade."

Iris' cool common sense brought Minty back to earth. "I've nearly three months of holiday pay coming to me from my uncle, so I can afford to wait for my salary. I'll stay. As for the Hall, surely this is only a temporary embarrassment which will disappear when probate is granted? Borrow as little as you can, and plan for the future."

Minty rubbed her forehead. Drank her tea. Ate a biscuit. Paced around the office. "Yes, you're right. I panicked, didn't I? Thank you, Iris. I accept your offer."

Iris inclined her head in acknowledgement. "What are your plans for the future?"

"Everything's been so neglected. I don't know where to start." She threw herself down into a chair and stretched out her legs.

"I did have some ideas, but . . . well, to begin with . . . you've probably been wondering why I haven't asked you to take over the charity events again. Of course you'd do it superbly, but first I have to do battle with Lady C about costs, and anyway, Gemma's been doing that job and I promised she may continue with it. Then I wanted to get a Christmas decoration season going, and I was going to bring in someone to arrange all that, mastermind the brochure and so on. I know you could do that, too. But . . ." Here she took a deep breath.

"Iris, what I really wanted was for you to help me make the Hall more interesting to visitors. Personalise it. Make it less like a museum. I want flowers in the rooms, knickknacks around and perhaps items of personal clothing. I want people to feel that they're looking at living history. I want the stewards to emphasise the human interest when they talk about my ancestors. It means a radical re-think of every item on show and a new brochure. Lady C said she wanted me to meet with some expert who supplies the Hall with pieces . . ."

"He came today while you were out. He wasn't best pleased."

"I told her I'd be out today, but she didn't want to hear. Oh, and I was stupid enough to talk to Venetia Wootton about my dreams for the Hall yesterday. I talked to her in confidence, but I'm afraid she may jump the gun and tell Mrs Chickward and Mrs Collins and . . . oh, I'm in such a tangle, Iris. Can you sort me out?"

Iris looked up from her notes. "Mrs Chickward and Mrs Collins both rang while you were out. Both said they'd make the Thursday afternoon meeting here."

Minty started to laugh. "Oh, Iris! Venetia's told them! Were they very cross?"

Iris smiled. "Slightly offended that you hadn't seen fit to consult them beforehand, but determined not to miss out on anything."

"They're incredible! Between them they could organise the entire Welfare State! That is, if they weren't always at loggerheads with one another. Oh well, I'll just have to ring and apologise. But for now, go home, Iris. You look as tired as I feel, and I've got to look over some notes for tomorrow and make some phone calls before I go to bed."

The sun hovered low in the sky, a bright red ball. It would be frosty tonight.

Serafina switched lights on. "You don't want to work in here, do you? Your desk next door is much bigger."

Obediently Minty took her notes through to her father's desk. Before she tackled her messages, there was one call she must make to Barr. She told him the bad news from the bank first, and then reassured him by saying she'd find enough money somehow to keep the Hall going. He didn't seem surprised, saying that Simon had probably bought himself a yacht with the money! He said he'd started trying to make sense of the accounts but it was an uphill job.

She shuffled through the notes Iris had left. So many people had called. Some of them she didn't know from Adam. Her uncle had rung yet again. She supposed she'd better return his call.

Minty forced herself to be calm before picking up the phone. She was no longer her aunt's maid-of-all-work, but mistress of Eden Hall.

"Uncle? It's me, Minty."

"You've taken your time ringing me, I must say." He had a loud voice which had frightened Minty almost as much as Aunt Agnes' belt in the past. Minty straightened her back and said, "Sorry, Uncle." What else could she say? That she was drowning in problems with which he'd have no sympathy? That she'd delayed phoning because even the thought of him made her feel nervous and insecure?

"I suppose you've got a swollen head now you've come into all that money, and we have to allow you time to glory in your good fortune before you remember what God has put you on earth for—which is *not* to indulge yourself at the expense of your relatives.

"I thought I'd made it clear that I needed to speak to you urgently. The fact is that your aunt's knee replacement has been put off yet again, and Lucas suggests that she go private. We couldn't possibly afford it, but since you've come into so much money . . . far too much for a girl of your age and experience . . . but there, my brother was always head-strong and—"

"Yes, of course," said Minty, without thinking. "Send the bills to me and I'll pay them. When do you move to your retirement home?"

"That's another problem. Apparently there isn't a vacancy at the moment. We know your stepmother will be moving out of the Hall soon, so it seems God's dispensation that we move into her rooms, especially as Micah had a lift put in. Most convenient."

"But . . . !"

"Lucas will come with us, of course. He's been trying to get you on the phone. The very least you can do is to respond to our calls. As your aunt says, if anyone has a right to your time now it's Lucas, considering how close you two have always been."

"It's true we were engaged for a few weeks, but . . ."

"You two really must get together again. Lucas will bring us over to look at the rooms at the Hall later this week or early next. I expect you'll need to put in various aids for older people, ramps to cover steps, and so on. I'll let you know when your aunt goes into hospital. You will, of course, want to visit her every day. I think that's all. I'll tell Lucas you'll be calling him this evening."

"You're assuming too much . . ." The phone went dead.

Minty kept her temper with difficulty. But succeeded. Just. Should she ring him back and say they'd be moving in over her dead body? No, she'd better calm down. And she would not speak to Lucas. No.

She punched in more numbers. Old friends—acquaintances, rather—from the vicarage days, had been ringing to congratulate her and suggest a meeting soon. All very bright and chirpy. It would have been nice if they'd befriended Minty when she was the parish dogsbody. She treated all but one of these old "friends" with a cool friendliness. Of course they must meet soon, when she'd got her diary sorted out . . .

One old friend from college was different. Carol Tinderman was Minty's opposite in many ways, being extrovert—almost flamboyant—whereas Minty was reserved. Carol had invited Minty into her chaotic but warm-hearted family whenever she'd been able to escape her duties at the vicarage. It was Carol who'd helped Minty buy the "best black" outfit she'd worn at the funeral. Carol sincerely rejoiced in Minty's good fortune.

"Come over, Carol. Some time next week? I need a friendly face in these ultra posh surroundings. It's a bit like living in the Ritz. Or shall I escape for a day and come to see you?"

Minty worked her way down the list.

Mrs Collins was next. A fairly recent newcomer to the village, Mrs Collins was a bustling, busty widow of uncertain age with the administrative capability of a sergeant major. She looked rather like one, too. Mrs Collins had the Women's Institute and the Parish Council under her thumb, and waged a war of attrition with Mrs Chickward, who was of old county stock.

The two ladies vied with one another to assist Lady Cardale with her charity work, and both had left messages asking Minty to dine.

"Mrs Collins? I'm so pleased I've managed to catch you. I'd love to come to supper soon, but before that I wanted to talk to you privately, ask your advice . . ."

"Mrs Chickward? I'm so glad to have caught you. I tried to ring you earlier to ask your advice, but I gather Venetia . . . yes . . . there's a problem with finance, but . . . yes, if you really think it's worth while . . . Thursday afternoon."

Venetia had left a message to say that she'd managed to contact her son Toby in London. He was on a short-term contract working all hours that week, but would come back to the village as soon as he finished—possibly in a week's time—and would Minty not fill the position till he was free?

As if she could.

Wearily Minty crossed through another name on her list, and stretched. The rest must wait. What had she forgotten? She couldn't think straight. She picked up her mobile to ring Patrick, and dropped it again. The phone on the desk rang and she snatched it up, thinking it might be Patrick. It wasn't. It was Simon.

"So you're back, are you? Shall I come up now, or are you already in bed . . . or perhaps I'd better come up and help you to bed."

"Simon! What have you done with all that money?"

A measuring silence. Perhaps he hadn't expected her to find out about it so quickly? "Gone with the wind. Debts, my dearest." He broke the connection.

Well, no good worrying about it.

What else must she do before she went to bed? Ah, yes. She wanted to see Hodge the gardener as soon as possible. The gardens at the Hall were a disgrace, but that probably wasn't Hodge's fault. If she knew anything about it, his budget had probably been cut to disappearing point. She could probably fit him in tomorrow morning early, before she went to London. She reached him via the internal phone and agreed on a time and place to meet.

She ate in the dining room because Serafina expected her to do so. Minty hated the stiff, mirror-surfaced dining table with its impractical glass top. She wished she could have had her supper on her lap in the sitting room—where Serafina had re-arranged the furniture back into its formal positions. Bother.

She took some coffee back to the sitting room, put the disc Patrick had given her into her new laptop and settled down to study his file on the Foundation trustees . . . and found herself waking two hours later. Cold. Tired. Cramped. Stretched out on that uncomfortable settee. The laptop had slid onto the floor.

She went to bed.

Early next morning Minty grabbed a piece of bread, took some time out in the chapel and went for a prowl around before anyone else was up and about.

She let herself into the deserted restaurant. She checked for cleanliness—mm, not as good as it might be. She looked at Chef's list of menus and saw he served the same dull food week after week. She investigated his store-room and peered into his freezer. He seemed to be buying in a lot of food which could have been cooked from fresh. She counted tables and chairs. Inspected cutlery and glassware. Made notes.

A glance at her new watch sent her hurrying to meet the head gardener.

Gabriel Hodge had mismatched eyes, one blue and one brown. The blue eye looked serene, but the brown had a roving glint. According to the estate records, he'd worked at the Hall since he left school at fifteen, was a widower, and occupied the head gardener's quarters in one of the stable blocks.

It was a sunless, chilly morning. The tall hedges which surrounded the formal garden looked ragged and the geometric design of the box hedges had gaps in it. Minty was not surprised that visitors failed to linger here, or on the neglected terrace above, whose outsize urns were filled with a straggle of dead and dying annuals.

The wind whipped around the corner of the house and Minty huddled into her pink jacket, but Hodge didn't seem to feel the cold. He wore clothing that might have started out life in different colours, but which was now of an indeterminate grey-brown hue. Like camouflage. Minty fancied that if he stood still long enough in the autumnal garden, he'd blend in.

He was looking at his watch as she ran down the steps into the garden. She was perhaps a minute late and made the mistake of apologising for it. This seemed to lower her in his eyes, for his mouth turned down and he turned his shoulder on her.

He sounded angry. "You've no need to tell me the garden's not up to scratch. Do you think I don't know? Raggedy hedges, weedy terraces, hardly a flower in the urns. But there's only been me to do everything for years. Trim, weed and mow. That's all I can manage. And half the time the mower's broke. It's lucky you've got money to spend, because you need to replace that first thing."

Yet another expense. "We'll have to talk about a budget. I want to see the garden bloom again as much as you do. I suppose the hedges around the outside just need clipping, but what about the box edgings?"

He sucked on his teeth, relishing the fact that he was about to impart more bad news. "That's a wicked virus, that is. Came in from Europe. The box is all diseased, every bit of it. We'll have to have it all out and burn it. Then we'll have to cart the earth away and bring in fresh. Maybe not plant again for a couple of years. It'll cost you, that."

She tugged on a nearby box plant, and it came away in her hand. Dying or dead. "Is it only the box plants which are affected? Couldn't we plant a new design with something else?"

He shrugged. "There's always been a box garden here."

"I saw some greenhouses on the estate map. Have you anything in them which might replace the box?"

"Greenhouses?" He screeched. "D'ye think I can look after greenhouses and raise exotic plants with all I've to do around the place?"

"All right. What have you got growing in the walled garden? Some wallflowers, perhaps? I was thinking perhaps we could plant wallflowers and bulbs in the urns on the terrace for winter."

"There's nothing been grown in the walled garden for years. If you want to throw good money after bad, I suppose I could buy some wallflower plants in the market, set them out for you. It'll cost you, mind."

"Let's have a look at the walled garden, then. Mr Wootton remembers it as being a splendid place, with apricots and nectarines growing against the walls."

She tried to remember how to get to the walled garden, but became disorientated when he led her in a different direction from the one she'd expected. Round the corner from the restaurant, he pointed out a solid wooden door with a large padlock on it, in the middle of a high brick wall. Weeds were growing up around the doorway, and it was clear no one had opened the door for months, if not years. "I've got a key somewhere in my den. I'll look it out for you sometime, and oil the lock so's you can see for yourself what needs doing there. Meantime, you'd best let me order a new mower, and get some help in to start clearing the box garden."

She sighed. Why was everything so difficult? "Find out how much a new mower will be and let me know."

Was there anything at the Hall that didn't need money spent on it?

Chapter Ten

She'd visited London before, of course. But not like this. On previous occasions she'd gone by coach, taking groups of Brownies to Madame Tussaud's waxworks, to the Science Museum and the London Eye. A couple of times she'd gone window shopping with Carol in Oxford Street and ridden on the top of a sight-seeing bus round Trafalgar Square and Buckingham Palace.

She'd never dreamed of being driven there in a limousine with Ruby perched beside Reggie in front, and Annie sitting composedly at her side. Minty accessed the information Patrick had provided on her new laptop. She'd tried to memorise some of it last night, but fallen asleep. Perhaps now she'd be able to work out who was who.

"What's that?" asked Annie.

"Patrick gave me a Who's Who of the trustees, because I don't know any of them except Lord Asher. First their companies and directorships. Then he's cross-referenced so that I can see who belongs to the same clubs, went to the same school or university. And last of all, who's connected by marriage."

Annie pinched in her lips. "May I ask how Mr Sands came by this information?"

Minty shrugged. "Friends from university? The Internet?" She concentrated.

On her previous trips Minty had stared at the outside of great hotels like the Savoy, the Dorchester and the Ritz and never imagined she'd dare cross their thresholds. Now she was checking herself and Ruby into a splendid old hotel, admittedly quieter and less expensive than the big three. There was a platinum credit card in her purse and the day ahead of her in which to buy clothes and not feel guilty about it. Annie was staying with friends and Reggie was making his own arrangements, so she and Ruby were on their own.

"I'm dreaming!" cried Ruby, half laughing and half crying as she ran from her bathroom to their shared sitting room and then back into her bedroom. "But come along, no time to waste," said Ruby, frowning at her shopping list. "How do we get hold of a taxi?"

"Reggie says we ask the doorman to get us one, but he didn't tell me how much we should tip." She thought, *Patrick would know. If he were here, he'd make the day into an amusing adventure whereas I'm really a bit daunted by everything.*

They took a taxi to Oxford Street and soon Minty was lost in a whirl, picking up a sweater here and a soft wool shirt there. She found boots and high-heeled shoes that fitted her and bought those. She bought some things for Ruby, too.

She bought a jacket and a good winter coat but couldn't decide which of the more formal clothes she should buy. She began to flag. Half vexed with herself, she wailed, "Ruby, there's too much choice."

Ruby took charge. "Now, Minty, what you really mean is that you need something to eat."

During lunch Minty's mobile rang and it was Annie, ringing from the Foundation offices. "Araminta, they would like you to say a few words tomorrow at the opening. Could you manage something short and amusing, about three minutes long? Thank you, dear." She rang off before Minty could protest.

"Ruby, they want me to make a speech, just as if I was someone important."

"So you are, dear. Eat up your pudding and we'll be on our way. We've lots to do yet. What you've bought so far is fine for everyday but we need to think about formal occasions. I think we should ask for a personal shopper . . ."

Minty let Ruby's voice wash over her. She had to make a speech in front of everyone? There'd be a photographer there, and the headmaster and the teachers and the children? She couldn't do it.

She pushed her pudding aside and refused a coffee. How to start? "Ladies and gentlemen"?

Ruby was acquiring the bossiness of a good nanny. She conveyed Minty to the next big department store on their list, summoned a personal shopper and told her what they needed. Colours, sizes . . . clothes came and went. Minty agreed with Ruby that nothing was quite right. Neither of them knew why; they just weren't.

"Unaccustomed as I am to public speaking . . ." That was true, but so corny Minty was angry with herself for letting the words form in her mind.

"I know," said Ruby. "The ladies at the charity shop are always talking about an exclusive boutique where they buy their clothes, so we'll go there." The taxi stopped outside a building which looked more like a private house than a shop. They stepped into a pleasant reception room. Minty sat down, and got out pen and paper. "I thought I'd seen my last of school . . ."

That might do.

Ruby's conference with a saleswoman produced clothes which felt like silk even when they were made of wool. A palette of pale colours, the clothes unusually well cut. Even the day dresses seemed to melt onto Minty's figure.

Minty woke up to find herself clad in a clinging pale grey-blue dress with a floating scarf over one shoulder, dropping down in folds almost to her heels at the back. It was so plain it hurt. It was a fabulous dress, which needed—perhaps—just one piece of good jewellery to set it off. But something was still not right.

"I have it!" cried the saleswoman. She tied Minty's hair back from her face with a ribbon. At once Minty's eyes seemed larger, her cheekbones shot up, and her neck elongated.

Minty was startled. She looked different. Older?

Ruby was nodding. "A style of her own."

The saleswoman nodded back. "An unusual look. Distinctive. Hardly any makeup needed. Perhaps a touch around the eyes? With that wild rose colour in her cheeks and speedwell blue eyes, she doesn't need it. High heels, of course."

"But . . . ," said Minty.

"She should try the others again," said Ruby. "They all need lifting on the shoulders, but I can do that . . . and a word with you . . ."

Minty thought, *But . . . !* She looked at herself in the mirror and saw a stranger. She'd worn her hair pinned securely back in a French plait when she'd lived in the vicarage, because her aunt had said she looked like a loose woman with her hair round her shoulders. She'd worn her hair loose when she'd escaped from the city, because it really was her best feature. She'd always thought her eyebrows and lashes were too pale for true beauty. If she tied her hair back like this, she'd look . . .

. . . like a grown-up . . . like the Lady of the Hall.

Looking like this, she looked capable of dealing with anything, but she didn't look like herself. She looked like "Araminta", instead of "Minty".

She tried the other things on again, and both Ruby and the saleswoman were pleased. Minty knew with one part of her mind that they were right, but with the other she had an urge to scream and declare she was going to live the rest of her life in jeans and running shoes, so there!

"Just this last one," said Ruby, deftly helping Minty into something long and silky.

"Diamonds, I think," said the saleswoman. "Not pearls."

Minty gaped.

It was a long dress with a suggestion of a stiffened mandarin collar around a high neckline. Long sleeves. It was made of a very heavy, off-white damask, cut to follow every line of the figure but never to be too revealing. A separate sleeveless coat fell in graceful folds to a small train at the back. The dress was plain, but the coat was embroidered all over with silver thread. It was a dress for an Ice Queen. It was a wedding dress.

Ruby had tears in her eyes. "Oh, Araminta! How beautiful you look!"

Minty was stunned. "I don't know whether Patrick . . . we haven't got as far as a formal engagement, and maybe he won't . . ."

"Of course he will. What a beautiful bride you'll make."

"Silk net for a short veil," said the saleswoman. "A diamond tiara, perhaps? And earrings. Possibly a diamond bracelet?"

Ruby got out her handkerchief and collapsed on a chair. Careless of her finery, Minty knelt beside her. "There, there!"

"To think I might once have had a wedding and worn white, if only I hadn't let Jonah in that night."

"I know." Minty stroked Ruby's age-freckled hands, and kissed her cheek.

"You only get one chance at a white wedding, so don't you let yours slip. You take that dress and wear it, do you hear?"

Minty smiled and nodded. It was possible she might never get Patrick to the altar, but she knew that she would never marry anyone else. Perhaps the dress would sit in a wardrobe for ever, swathed in tissue paper. But she had fallen in love with it, too. If she never married, if she only took it out once a year to look at it and sigh over it, then it would be worth it. And hang the expense.

"We'll take it and the others that Ruby likes," said Minty.

Ruby hit her eyes with her hanky, and gulped. "Thank goodness that's settled. Now off you go to have your hair done, and I'll walk back to the hotel and have a little rest before we go on to the theatre. What a day!"

The hairdressers was a disaster. They wanted to cut Minty's hair short and "shape" it into a modern style. They wanted to "add a touch of colour". She refused to let them do that, which didn't endear her to the temperamental artist who said he'd set aside his precious time to bring out the best in her.

She told him she wanted to wear her hair either loose about her shoulders, or back in a chignon. He said flatly that he didn't think either style would suit her, and she should have her eyelashes dyed. Minty refused, but let him do as he thought best with her hair while she worked on her speech. When he'd teased out her hair into his idea of a modern coiffure, she was appalled. He'd half hidden one eye with a fall of hair, tied the rest back and spread it out into a sort of fan which looked—and felt—artificial.

Minty gritted her teeth, paid his bill and summoned a taxi. On the way back to the hotel she undid the coiffure and brushed her hair back into an approximation of her usual style, vowing never to go to a hairdresser again.

There were two floral arrangements waiting for Minty in her suite at the hotel. One was from Lord Asher, and the other from James, who was apparently looking forward to meeting her the next day.

"Nothing from Patrick?" asked Ruby.

Minty shook her head. She wasn't disappointed. He was leaving her free to make her own choices. Blast him! She went to wash the stiff gel out of her hair, and use plenty of conditioner to make it more manageable.

They had an early supper at the hotel and enjoyed their visit to a light-hearted musical, but when they retired to bed at the hotel, neither could sleep. Minty wandered around, alternately practising her speech, worrying about money and about Patrick, until Ruby came out to say she couldn't sleep either and suggested they have a cup of tea to soothe them.

Minty tried to turn her mind from her problems. "How did you meet Jonah?"

Ruby shook her head, smiling. "Do you remember the nursery rhyme, 'Georgie Porgie, pudding and pie, kissed the girls and made them cry'? Except Jonah made us laugh. He kissed everyone, especially me. He wasn't serious, of course. I was the head gardener's daughter while Jonah was a teacher and came from the Manor. Then one day Jonah kissed Hannah and that was different because she was the daughter of a doctor and managed the bookshop. Everyone said how suitable it was, so they got married.

"I didn't care, did I? Gabriel Hodge, who was under gardener at the Hall, asked me to walk out with him. Maybe something would have come of that if Jonah hadn't started making eyes at me again. But there, it was my fault as much as his. Father cuffed me senseless, but I couldn't seem to stop. Jonah followed me into the house one afternoon and though I told him to leave, he wouldn't. I didn't really want him to. He chased me up to my little room and I tried to shut the door on him, but I didn't try hard enough, for he got in and . . . what with me laughing and shrieking to him to stop . . . we didn't hear Father coming back. So Jonah jumped out of the window."

"And hurt his head."

"Father beat me and locked me in my room. He had a stroke and died. No one expected Jonah to live, but he did. Just. I felt so guilty! Hannah came to see me. She said it was all my fault, that she was finished with Jonah, never wanted to see him again. I went up to the hospital and they said all Jonah's family were abroad and he needed someone to feed him, to teach him to speak and walk again.

"With my father dead, Gabriel Hodge was getting promotion at the Hall. He said he'd forgive me and we could be wed, if I promised never to see Jonah again. I could see in his eyes that he'd always hold it against me. Jonah had no one. When he was well enough, I took him home with me and I've looked after him ever since. Marriage is for life, so I've never stopped telling Jonah to make it up with Hannah."

"And Gabriel Hodge?"

"Married a shrew from over Chipping Norton way. She died two years back. Sometimes he looks at me across the road or in the market. I know what he's thinking. If I hadn't been so foolish, we'd have been wed with me in a white dress all those long years ago."

"You couldn't have married Gabriel if you loved Jonah."

Ruby's face twisted. "God said that, too. Many's the night I've spent on my knees, asking His forgiveness for my sin. He's forgiven me. I'm quiet in my mind about that."

"If you'd turned your back on Jonah, what would have happened to the poor creature?"

Ruby wailed, "But it's so hard! I thought I'd got it settled in my mind, but now Jonah wants to divorce Hannah and expects me to marry him! He can't really love me. He just wants to get even with Hannah. Or maybe he thinks, in his muddled way, that he'll be making it up to me by marrying me. Of course I'm very fond of him but . . . I can't get round it; marriage is for life."

Minty was silent. She had her own anxieties to take to God. "Ruby, will you pray with me?"

They prayed, and presently Minty felt the pressures on her ease. Ruby poured out more tea for both of them; they drank it in silence and went back to bed.

First thing in the morning, Annie phoned through a request from the photographer. Would Minty please not wear black to the Opening Ceremony, and did she have a coloured blouse . . . ? She had no coloured blouse so wore her new blue wool suit with its swishy skirt, a soft white blouse and her new boots. She coaxed her hair to lie smoothly, tying it back with ribbon. She added just a touch of lipstick, all the time wondering if her nervous stomach would betray her in front of all these important people.

Ruby had always longed to visit the Tower of London, and so would spend the day there.

Reggie arrived with the car, dropped Ruby off at an Underground station and took Minty on into a suburb of narrow streets of small houses and shops.

"Give me a bell when you need me," said Reggie, helping Minty out of the car. Minty shook out her skirt and tossed back her hair. The new school was situated behind high brick walls with iron railings on top and there were secure gate systems in place. Another chauffeured BMW drew up and out stepped grey-haired Lord Asher, executor of her father's will, and trustee of the Foundation.

He had a delightful smile, and good manners. "Miss Cardale . . ."

"Minty, please."

He ushered her through the main gate into a tarmacked courtyard, with the new school ahead. The building had been completed at the end of the summer holidays and the children had already moved in, but this was the official opening.

Shake hands. Smile. Try to remember names. Through the front entrance. Shake hands again. She began to identify a certain look among the trustees: a hungry, predatory look. The look of a successful businessman? Quite different from the teachers, who looked alert but not predatory.

"A glass of something? Cold for the time of the year, isn't it? This way . . ."

Minty stopped short, looking up at the high roof above her. Then at the open classrooms on either side. "Great space . . . flexibility," someone was saying.

All the classrooms were open to the central area *without a wall between*. She opened her mouth to say that the builders surely hadn't finished yet, but Lord Asher was urging her on. "We'll have a chance to look around later."

"Our photographer . . ."

Shake hands, accept a glass of wine, isn't there any coffee? No. Oh well. Lord Asher had vanished. His place was taken by a smiling, plump, sharp-nosed man. If she knew anything about men, this one would be a bottom pincher . . . ouch. Yes.

She said in a conversational tone, "If you do that again, I'll have an accident with my glass and spill it all over you."

He looked amazed and then roared with laughter.

She remembered his name now. Ugh. Patrick had said this man was a successful entrepreneur, much valued as a trustee, a friend of Lady C's, with interests in several large multi-nationals.

Lady C swept in with Simon in tow. Lady C was all in scarlet which made Minty grin, thinking of the Scarlet Woman, which Lady C had undoubtedly been in her time. Simon was enjoying a laugh with the bottom pincher, who must be one of those voting for Simon's election to the Board of Trustees. They both looked at Minty and away. And laughed again. Minty's colour rose. Had Simon told the bottom pincher that Minty allowed her cousin into her bedroom?

Annie arrived, but was corralled by two earnest-looking men in a corner. Discussing the election that was to be held that afternoon?

The level of conversation became deafening. She was introduced to the headmistress, the school governors. The photographer kept walking around her, eyeing her from different angles. Embarrassed, her colour rose.

"You really are as beautiful as they said." A pleasant baritone voice. She looked up to meet the amused gaze of a tall, well-built man. Sir James. He wasn't the type she normally admired, but she was so pleased to meet a friendly face that she relaxed.

The photographer cried, "Hold that!" And there was a flash.

"It's time," someone said, and there was a general movement towards some chairs. The children had all been drawn up in rows, the smallest sitting on the floor in front, biggest ones on benches at the back. The teachers lined the sides. Everyone was smiling, pleased with themselves and the new building.

Minty risked a glance around. Surely not everyone there was happy with the building? No, one or two of the teachers were looking stony-faced. Older teachers, who'd experienced different working conditions in their time. One of the governors—an older woman who looked like a magistrate—was also looking sour. But maybe she'd got a stomach upset.

Minty's own stomach wasn't behaving too well, either.

"Could you just drop your jacket off . . . for your speech . . . ? That's right. And undo a couple of buttons . . ."

Minty took off her jacket and undid the top button of her blouse, but no more.

"One more?"

Minty gave him a sharp look and shook her head. Did they want her to look like a wanton? She was led to the front and given a chair. A broad white ribbon had been stretched from one side to the other of the hallway. Presumably that was the ribbon she was meant to cut at the right moment.

She looked up and around her as the hum of conversation died away, and the Chair of the Board of Trustees brought out a sheaf of papers to make the first speech.

The building was a disaster. She knew it. Some of the teachers knew it. It didn't seem to have occurred to any of the trustees or to the headmistress, who was smiling broadly. Or to the prize-winning architect, who now took his place at the mike. How boring they were. The children were yawning, scratching. In a moment they'd start shoving one another. The teachers' eyes were on one or two children already.

Now it was Minty's turn. What could she say? The truth?

Wouldn't that bring the roof down on them! And she wasn't even a member of the Board of Trustees yet, not till the afternoon.

The school had been built. Finished. She couldn't alter that. Maybe she could do something about it once she was on the Board of Trustees.

She smiled at the children, at the teachers, the governors, the Board of Trustees. Perhaps, if she could only make them laugh, it might help to make the occasion less boring. She knew how to talk to small groups of children. Hadn't she done it often enough at church? She could put a touch of humour into her voice. If she could only keep her nerves under control!

"Ladies and gentlemen, I thought my schooldays were over for good, and now look at me! Back where I started, sitting in the front row of the Reception Class . . ."

There was a low giggle from someone, and then the rest of the audience got the joke and laughed. Minty paused to let them laugh. The photographer flashed his camera, and so did some others.

She got through her speech without referring to her notes, and asked for a small child to help her cut the ribbon. They loved that. What a photo opportunity! Would she sit on this high table here, with a couple of children around her? She would? *Flash, flash!* The skirt a little higher? No? Oh well.

The trustees were pleased with her. They loved her and they loved her speech. And it was all dust and ashes in her mouth.

Chapter Eleven

It was six o'clock before Minty and Ruby were driven out of London, with their purchases safely stowed in the boot of the car. Annie had stayed on to have a meal with a friend and would be returning to the Hall by train later that evening. Ruby dozed off, but Minty got out her new mobile phone and made some phone calls.

The first was to Barr. "Barr, have you traced the missing millions?"

"Sort of. Does 'F & F' mean anything to you? Two and a half million went to them, about twenty-five hundred to a Mr Purvey and the rest to various credit cards, clubs, motoring organisations and the airfield where he keeps his plane. Debts, just as we thought."

Next she rang Iris. The last call was to Patrick.

"Patrick, I want you to take me out to supper tonight. Somewhere smart, where it's difficult to get a table and the menu's hard to read. Reggie'll drop Ruby off and drive me there, returning for me later."

Patrick was sharp. "What are you up to? I was planning to emigrate, tell you the truth."

Now what did he mean by that? That he was planning to move away? "Don't buy your ticket yet."

"Seven o'clock, The Clock Tower in West Street. But Minty . . ."

She cut him off. He'd made her suffer. Let him wait to hear her decision.

Reggie dropped her in the market place, a triangular cobbled area adjacent to the stuccoed early Victorian Town Hall. Wriggling streets ran downhill in every direction. Houses and shops were of all shapes and sizes, old and older, red-brick and Cotswold stone.

The Clock Tower was exactly right. Cool, with pale wooden floors and furniture. As Minty entered, she caught sight of a tall, dark, elegant man in the mirror over the bar and experienced a moment of dislocation. For a moment she thought she'd been wrong about not finding anyone she could love as she loved Patrick, for there stood someone who might have stepped out of her dreams, with the hungry, almost predatory look which she was learning to recognise in the modern businessman.

Then she realised she was looking at Patrick himself, and that he did indeed look as if he knew how to handle himself in a fight.

He caught her eye in the mirror and held it. His look was a challenge, not a plea. She liked that, too.

"A drink?" he said. "No? I'll take my Perrier water in with me, then. This way."

Close to, she could see that he hadn't slept well, though it would take a sharp eye to notice it. He was wearing another of his grey suits, this one with a silky sheen to it. A white shirt, pale grey tie, platinum cuff-links.

The restaurant was bright and cheerful, the tables almost all occupied. She waited till they'd been seated in a good position, and then asked Patrick if they could change tables as this one didn't suit her. He looked around, saw no particular reason why they should change, lifted one eyebrow at Minty, considered her bland expression and did as she asked.

"What would you like to drink?" A wine waiter, suitably snobbish.

Minty hesitated. "I'm not sure . . ."

Patrick looked down the wine list. "I'll stick with my Perrier water. Minty, you look as if you've had a long day. Something long and cold? How about a fruit cordial, or a shandy?"

She nodded. She pushed the menu aside. "Tell me what I'd like to eat."

"Have you eaten anything today?"

"Not much, no." He made a couple of suggestions, and she chose one at random. He looked at her over his glass. "What's going on, Minty?"

"Well . . . the school building's a disaster . . ."

He nearly spilt his drink. "What!"

"Who's got the prettiest legs in the room, Patrick?"

He looked around, half annoyed, half puzzled. "Apart from you, you mean? Well, the girl in the far corner, I suppose, though your ankles are finer."

"Go on looking at her legs. The school has been badly designed. I know because—don't look at me, Patrick; look at her legs—I know because when our own church hall back in the city was closed for repairs, we used to meet in a new school nearby. Just like this one.

"That school hall was known as the railway station because the classrooms all gave on to it without any dividing walls between. The sound was appalling. There were panic-stricken plans to put sound-proof walls in to divide the space up. The temperature rose into the eighties in summer, but the children and teachers froze in the winter because of the lack of insulation. Oh yes, and the classrooms had sky-lights in the roof which leaked. Guess what! This building's exactly the same. You could see where the rain had come in through the roof already, and the building's only been finished a couple of months."

His eyes had switched to her as soon as she started talking about the school. "Is that how Sir James behaved today? Getting a table changed with the maximum of fuss, telling you what you wanted to drink and eat, and then looking at other girls' legs instead of listening to what you were saying?"

She nodded. How could she have doubted Patrick? He'd always treated her as an equal.

"The man's an idiot!"

She twitched a smile. "Exit Sir James. He was pleasant enough, I suppose. He and the other trustees treated me as if I were a pretty girl hired for a photo shoot. Sir James took me for lunch and behaved exactly as you've described, while I tried desperately to tell him what was wrong with the school and how worried I was that its problems would rebound on the Foundation. Sir James didn't want to know. He was oh, so kind and superior and condescending. I could have kicked him.

"We went on to the meeting where both Simon and I were duly elected trustees. I heard Lord Asher say that this was his last year on the Board, so I hijacked him, took him out for tea and told him what I thought."

Her drink came. She discovered she'd been thirsty. Patrick was still very tense, but it was interesting to see him overlay that dangerous edge with his usual urbanity.

Patrick said, "Lord Asher listened to you?"

"At first. Then he became sceptical. He didn't want to believe me because if he did he'd have to do something about it. He's known the other members of the Board for ages and he's only just met me. He said, Did I realise what I was saying? Did I realise the architect had won prizes for his buildings, and that's why he'd been chosen? He became . . . patronising."

Patrick stroked his chin. "The architect is the nephew of the managing director of the building firm."

"I checked back on your notes and yes, he was. The managing director of the building firm is also one of the trustees. And a bottom pincher."

Patrick laughed, short and sharp. "My, what a busy little girl you've been."

"I suggested to Lord Asher that we might run a check on the work the Foundation has been doing over the last ten years to see if we're giving value for money. He said that perhaps I hadn't quite understood how things were done, that I was completely new to this kind of thing, that I ought to wait awhile before jumping to conclusions. He said that in theory I had the right to put a motion to the Board, asking for the sort of check I was suggesting, but that he personally didn't think it would be at all wise to do so and that he would have to think very hard about supporting me.

"He was kind enough to say that I wasn't just a pretty face, but would actually be an asset in due course, when I'd seen a bit more of the world. I'm afraid I mentioned your name, told him I'd acted on the information you'd given me. He wanted to know all about you, and even said it might not be a bad idea to have a solicitor on the Board."

"What did you say to that?" Patrick frowned.

She gave him a bland, angry smile. "I said I couldn't answer for you. Then I asked him not to resign in a year's time, but to see that the Board was properly run before he retired. He said he'd think about it and—" through gritted teeth—"he complimented me on the outfit I was wearing. So my first venture into the great big world ended in failure."

Their first course arrived. An olive and tomato quiche for her, and soup for him.

He took a mouthful. "I wouldn't say you failed. You blew the whistle on corruption and whistle-blowers always have to take flak. They may try to act as if nothing has happened, they may try to make you feel as if you've made a stupid mistake, but nevertheless you'll have made them sit up and take notice."

"I handled it badly. What would you have done in my place?"

He thought about it. "Probably I'd have waited awhile, done a bit of digging around, collected a few facts to back up what I said."

"Of course that's what I ought to have done! I jumped in without thinking. Aunt Agnes always said it was one of my worst faults. I'm angry with myself."

Patrick lifted his glass in a toast to her. "Minty, you're growing up. I like the new look, by the way."

"Do you like it enough to put your ring on my finger? Patrick, I accept that there may somewhere in the world be another man who'd match my father's idea of a suitable husband for me, but I may never meet him. The truth is that you've spoilt me for anyone else."

He looked troubled. "Part of me wants to grab you by the hair and drag you off to my cave, but the rest keeps reminding me that I did take advantage of you. Mind you, by Sunday evening I'd got to the point of thinking it served me right if you went off with Sir James . . . a hundred times I've started to phone you. I've bitten my fingernails to the bone, taken to drink . . ."

His fingernails were, of course, immaculate. She translated, "You worked all hours, drank too much coffee, forgot to eat and started smoking again."

"I got up to thirty cigarettes today," he said, with guilty pride. "This morning I did actually try to phone you, only to discover that the line no longer worked. I thought that meant you'd cut me out of your life."

"New mobile. Why didn't you ring Iris? She would have given you the number."

"Never thought of it." The waiter removed their plates.

She leaned back in her chair. "I've sent the notice of our engagement to *The Times*."

It was a masterstroke and they both knew it.

"What!" He shook his head as if he hadn't heard her correctly.

"I asked Iris to do it for me, on my way back from London."

"You haven't considered . . ."

"Do you remember once when we were children, I wanted to walk across a tree that had fallen over a gully?"

"Little Miss Hot Head. The gully was filled with broken glass and brambles. If you'd fallen, you'd have hurt yourself badly."

"So you said, Mr Cautious. I insisted, so you went down into the gully and tried to remove anything that could have hurt me. Then you said, 'Keep your eyes fixed on the other side and don't look down.' And I walked over it as calm as anything."

He grimaced. "And you think that's what I've been doing? Looking down at all the problems we face instead of keeping an eye on the prize?"

"Oh, it's not a bad thing for you to be cautious, because I'm far too inclined to dash into things. We'll make a good team."

Their main course was delivered, but neither of them were interested in food. He put his hand over hers, stroking it with his thumb. "But Minty . . ."

"Do you or don't you want to marry me?"

"You're quite mad. You know that."

"Is it infectious?"

He fiddled with his watch strap and pushed his plate away. "Yes." He closed his fingers over her hand. He was still very tense, but now he was no longer shutting her out. His hand was warm over hers. His eyes were telling her everything she had ever wanted to know about love. There was some pain there, too. He'd suffered while he'd held back, but that only made his commitment now more valuable. She found herself short of breath.

The waiter hovered, indicating their untouched plates. "Is there something wrong?"

Patrick shook himself back to an acknowledgement of their surroundings. "Not a thing." He picked up his fork but continued to hold her hand.

"It looks delicious," said Minty, though in truth she had no idea what she had before her. "Patrick, there's one other thing. Can you be my fiancé *and* my solicitor? Simon's cleaned out the kitty so I'll have to sell those shares you gave me, to keep the Hall going."

"One thing at a time, woman. At the moment I can't cope with anything more than just thinking that you and I are actually going to ... just let me look at you ..."

She laughed. She heard herself chattering from nerves, from relief. For love of him. "You must eat, you're far too thin." She didn't touch the food herself.

He laughed, smiled. He put a forkful of food in his mouth but still didn't let go of her hand.

She said, "Tell me all about your work, I want to know everything about you—where's your office, do they keep you busy, where do you live when you're working in town? With your partner?"

He said, "In the next street. We're busy. I found a quiet place to stay on the edge of town. My partner would like me to give up my two and a half days' work in the village and be here all week."

"Which is what you meant by emigrating?"

She imagined him in a bed-and-breakfast place, with good food laid on. She knew he needed to be quiet by himself now and then, to pray and to listen to what God was telling him.

He said, "Don't look now, but we've been spotted by one of the County Court Officers and his wife, and they're coming over to see why I'm holding hands with a beautiful woman in a public place."

Patrick made the introductions and Minty blushed when he said, "My fiancée."

Patrick and Minty accepted congratulations and fended off enquiries as to when they were getting married, but when they were alone again Patrick said, "I know we've got to talk about these things and there are problems to solve, but don't let's look down yet. Let's give ourselves time to enjoy being engaged. I'll be free about seven tomorrow. Come to supper?"

"I'll cook for you, and then you'll give me my ring." She fell to worrying because she had meetings all the next day, and for all her wealth and possessions, she didn't have a kitchen she could call her own. Would he agree to living in her father's suite at the Hall? It wasn't what you might call homely. Perhaps he might have some ideas ...

The next day, Minty didn't just walk into a wall. It fell on her.

"I hope you're feeling strong." That was Iris' greeting when Minty walked into the tower office. "Ms Phillips is with Lady Cardale in her rooms, and they want to see you straight away."

An alliance between those two powerful women could only mean trouble. Minty took the stairs down to the first floor and knocked on the door. Lady Cardale's rooms seemed dark because the sky had clouded over.

Both of the older women wore black. Minty knew better than to wait for an invitation to be seated, so chose a chair opposite Annie.

"I suppose you know why you're here," said Lady Cardale, using the opening gambit of Authority about to Pulverise Naughty Little Girl. "The disgrace! Your father spent his life building up a charity which benefits thousands of children every year, and you destroy it in one afternoon." Lady C looked like a cobra about to strike.

Minty blinked. She'd acted for the best, hadn't she?

Annie was looking at her in a sorrowful, thoughtful way. That was understandable. The Foundation had been Annie's life, and Minty had attacked its worth.

"We realised," said Lisa, "we were taking a risk in electing you to the Board of Trustees. You've hardly any education, certainly no common sense or discretion. We believed you'd recognise your deficiencies and learn on the job. Hah!"

Minty could feel herself going pale, but held onto her chair seat with both hands and kept her head up. "I know a badly designed school when I see one and . . ."

"You know nothing! When the press gets hold of this, they'll slaughter us!"

Minty was puzzled. What did the press have to do with it?

Annie explained. "Simon thought the press should know, as a matter of public interest. He's meeting with a journalist from one of the tabloids this afternoon."

So she would be pilloried in the daily papers and made out to be a bungling fool. She remembered Patrick saying that whistle-blowers always suffered. "What I said to Sir James and to Lord Asher was in confidence."

Lisa swept that away with a magnificent gesture. "On a matter of such importance? Nonsense. The rest of the Board are extremely perturbed. There have already been calls for you to resign, and I think you'd better do just that."

Minty stood, holding on to the back of the chair in case she fell down. "I won't resign. If Simon wishes to wash your dirty linen in public, then so be it. I stand by what I said. And now, if you'll excuse me . . ."

"Just a minute!" Lisa hadn't finished yet. "In view of your inability to handle business matters, Ms Phillips and I have decided . . ."

Minty looked at Annie, who looked away. Annie wasn't altogether happy about this. Minty listened with dread.

". . . that you simply can't be trusted to handle large sums of money. Ms Phillips has reluctantly decided not to back any business plan you may see fit to put before the bank, which means they will allow you the bare minimum to live on till probate is granted, and it will have to be repaid at a high rate of interest. There will be no more money for extravagant outfits and trips to London. Or extra staff. I believe you've taken on a girl who told lies about my son. Get rid of her."

So much, thought Minty, *for Lisa's opinion of Iris.*

"Plus I understand you're planning to upset all my careful arrangements for the Hall, keeping it open when it should be closed for maintenance, re-stocking a gift shop nobody will visit and paying out wages for an empty restaurant."

Minty decided to have a word with Venetia, soonest.

"I suppose you thought to pay for these quite unnecessary expenses out of the trust fund your father left for the Hall, but Ms Phillips agrees with me that that money is for capital projects only, for maintenance, re-wiring and so on. The trustees will scrutinise very carefully every project you put before them and unless it falls into the essential category, they will refuse permission for you to draw on the trust—and that includes re-developing the holiday cottages. That's all. You may go."

Minty looked at Annie, who still kept her gaze averted. Annie wasn't going to contradict Lisa, even if she wasn't entirely happy about this turn of events. Minty stiffened her back. If all her plans were in ruin, she would not give Lisa the satisfaction of showing how soundly she'd been thrashed.

Minty looked around her at the costly furnishings, most of which boasted yellow stickers. It was probable that many of these pieces had been bought for the Hall with money from the Hall's accounts. She must make a list and present her stepmother with the bill for them . . . or insist they remained where they were.

Revenge would be sweet. And there was Lisa's portrait, too, which Minty could hang on to if she wished.

Lisa said, contemptuously, "I said, you may go! As for what the papers may see fit to print tomorrow, all I can say is that you brought it on yourself."

Minty remembered Simon's threat to spread a rumour about Minty and her cousin. Yes, Simon would take pleasure in doing that now. Tomorrow would see her character traduced, and she'd not even have the pleasure of Iris' support, or of making plans for the future of the Hall. But she would survive. She might have to wait six months for probate, and would Patrick still want to know her when he heard? Probably, but . . . doubt remained.

She said, softly, "You're an evil woman, Lisa. But time is on my side."

She saw Lisa wince. Only then did Minty leave.

Once onto the stairs, Minty leaned against the wall and covered her face with her hands. *Dear Lord, help me . . . what am I to do? Don't they realise that if Simon goes to the press, the Foundation is finished? How can I stop them? And Patrick. I must warn him, give him the chance to break off our engagement.*

She ran up the stairs and burst into the outer office, where Iris was sitting at her computer.

"Iris, I need to speak to Patrick at his office. Straight away."

Iris pressed numbers and was put on hold. Patrick was on another line. Minty paced the floor, thinking hard. If only she could get Simon to hold back, not spread those rumours about her—or what she'd said about the Foundation. Did she have anything to use against him?

Not really, no. Annie said he'd been within his rights to withdraw that money, and she couldn't prove she'd never let Lucas into her bedroom at the vicarage.

Where was Simon, anyway? She supposed he'd remained in London, to see a journalist this afternoon. How can one man do so much harm!

Iris handed over the phone.

"Patrick? Can I see you—now? It's important."

Patrick was quick on the uptake. "Come straight in."

Minty dropped the phone, Gulped, head down, wanting to lie down and cry.

Iris said, "Minty?"

Minty straightened up. "Simon's planning to smear my reputation all over the press. Every minute counts. I'm going to try to stop him, but if I can't then . . ."

Iris lifted the internal phone with one of her cat-like smiles. "Is that you, Reggie? Miss Cardale needs you to take her up to Mr Sands' office immediately. She'll be down in the courtyard in five minutes."

Minty discovered she was shaking. "Patrick's in the village today, isn't he? I can walk."

"No, you can't," said Iris. "Every minute counts, remember." She accompanied Minty down in the lift and put her in the car. "Take her to Mr Sands' back entrance and wait for her."

"Trouble, miss?" said Reggie, looking worried.

Minty meant to say, "Nothing I can't handle." It came out as, "Nothing Mr Sands can't handle."

"Ah," said Reggie. "That's about the size of it."

Chapter Twelve

Patrick's office was on the ground floor of his house. His secretary swept Minty through the wide hall with its black and white tiled floor, past a woman waiting on a chair and into a panelled office which wouldn't have been out of place in a Dickens' novel. The room was furnished with break-fronted bookcases, an enormous desk, deep swivel chairs and an Adam fireplace.

Patrick stood as she entered.

She gulped. "Patrick, we need to break off our engagement."

He didn't argue but took her in his arms and kissed her. Hard. And again. She tried to resist but he went on kissing her.

Her arms went up about his neck and she kissed him back. He held her tightly, smothering any protest she might be tempted to make, but after the first few kisses she didn't want to protest anyway.

Eventually he disentangled himself and, holding her at arm's length, said, "Try telling me that again and you'll get more of the same."

"Yes, please." Then remembered why she'd come. "You don't understand. Simon is going to tell the tabloid press that I've rubbished the work of the Foundation. Oh, and he'll probably also say that I used to let Lucas into my room at the vicarage."

"That old story!"

She was surprised. "You knew? Why didn't you say?"

"Why didn't you?"

"It made me feel dirty, just to think of him saying that. I couldn't bear you to hear it."

"Two people told me and I didn't believe either of them." He put her in the chair by his desk. "Start at the beginning."

So she did. She gave him the facts as quickly as she could. As he listened, the lines of his face sharpened. "What was that you said last night about Simon cleaning out the kitty?"

She shook her head. "It was before I came back, when he thought he was going to inherit the Hall. I suppose he was entitled to do what he wanted with the money then."

"Have you enough to pay the wages bill this month?"

She threw out her hands. "I don't think so. I'll have to ask the bank for a loan or sell the shares you gave me."

"Don't do anything in a hurry." He called up a file on his laptop. "I may have to exert some pressure to get Lord Asher on the line."

It was an exquisite relief to leave the problem in his hands. Like Reggie, she had faith in this man. He was murmuring something into the phone, reading from his screen.

He put the phone down. "Lord Asher will ring me back in ten to fifteen minutes. Give me your cousin's phone number."

She controlled her shaking hands long enough to write it down for him.

He punched numbers. "Is that Lucas? Patrick Sands here, solicitor for Miss Cardale. I'm ringing to warn you that one of the tabloids is about to run a story damaging your reputation. Miss Cardale's step-brother is saying you tried to force your cousin to have sex with you at the vicarage . . ."

He held the phone away from his ear for a moment. "I know it's ridiculous! Exactly! As if you could have done anything with your aunt and uncle aware of every footstep! It's not much use threatening to sue Simon as he's more debts than assets . . . Your indignation does you credit. I'm sure your cousin will be very happy to have your support. Yes, I'm trying to have it stopped, naturally. I'll ring you back the moment I hear anything. Have a nice day." He put the phone down.

Minty said, "He did try to force his way into my bedroom, but I suppose he won't want that spread around."

Patrick's phone rang. "Lord Asher? Apologies for dragging you away from your meeting. My name is Patrick Sands, of Sands and Sands, solicitors. I represent Miss Cardale of Eden Hall. She's just been informed that Simon Cardale plans to go to the tabloids with a story about the Foundation abusing its position as a charity. The source of my information? Lady Cardale and Ms Phillips.

"Yes, I agree that such a story would have a shocking effect on donations . . . absolutely. Miss Cardale is most distressed that any words of hers, uttered in confidence, should be distorted to harm her father's Foundation. She's concerned that when the journalists start to dig around they may uncover a rumour that's been flying around . . ."

"What rumour? I don't believe it, of course, but is it true that someone's nephew got preferential treatment? . . . No, that's not slander. Putting a question is not slander. I agree it could do a great deal of damage if the press heard . . .You can't understand why Simon would want to bring the Foundation into disrepute? In my opinion, it's a question of sour grapes. He expected to inherit Eden Hall and didn't. Perhaps he hasn't thought the matter through and thinks that he can damage Miss Cardale this way, although I'm afraid the end result would be merely to harm the Foundation.

"As Sir Micah's executor, you'll undoubtedly have Miss Cardale's best interests at heart. Impressive, isn't she? Shrewd. Honest. Tenacious. An asset to the Hall and the village. Her plans for both are imaginative and practical, don't you think? . . .Yes, you really must have a chat with her about them soon.

"You don't see how anyone can stop Simon talking to the press? Of course he's every right to say what he likes, provided it isn't slanderous. He'll have to watch that angle though, because he's threatened in the past to smear Miss Cardale by linking her romantically to her cousin . . . something which both Miss Cardale and her cousin deny. My client has put up with a lot from Simon for the sake of the family, but if her name is dragged in the mud, she might well lose patience with him and sue . . .

"No, I quite understand . . . Indeed. Thank you, yes. You can reach me at this number till six o'clock.

"Oh, there's just one other thing. I have to declare a conflict of interest. Miss Cardale and I are engaged to be married . . . yes, before Christmas, I should think. No doubt she will ask you to give her away . . . yes, yes. I look forward to hearing from you."

Minty thought, *Oughtn't it to be my uncle giving me away? Not that I want him to.* She wanted to screech with laughter because it really wasn't an appropriate thought at the moment.

Patrick put the phone down and grimaced. "Fifty-fifty on Lord Asher stopping the story, and if he fails with Simon, he'll have a word with someone he knows at the paper who might be able to squash the story anyway. He said he'd ring me as soon as he had any news, and I'll let you know what happens. If the press do get hold of it, you'd better be prepared for the worst. It's best to say 'No comment' and refer them to me. Don't talk to any of them, however sympathetic they may sound. The story might make headlines if nothing else more interesting happens today, but it's not scandalous enough to run for long. Even if the worst comes to the worst, it'll all be over within a week. Just sit tight."

"I feel so helpless. And guilty. My wretched tongue!"

He smiled, "Remember: 'For evil to prevail, all that is needed is for good men to do nothing.' You saw something was wrong and you tried to stop it. This is a direct result of your poking the devil in the eye. I'll ring you as soon as I hear anything. Go home and talk to Annie. She must be devastated."

His internal phone rang. He listened and said, "I'm nearly through ..."

The door sprang open and in stalked the parrot-faced woman Minty had seen outside. "Well! A fine thing, being kept waiting ..."

Patrick had risen. "Lady Silchester, may I introduce Araminta Cardale, your goddaughter? Minty, this is your godmother, Lady Silchester."

Lady Silchester gave Minty a look of dislike. "My granddaughter has spoken of you. Gone to your head, getting the Hall, has it? Well, you'll soon learn what's what ... and now, young man, my appointment was for eleven, and it's nearly half past!"

"An emergency." Patrick drew out a chair for her.

"Emergencies," pronounced Lady Silchester, "often seem to be blonde and blue-eyed."

Minty tried not to giggle while making her way to the door. How on earth did Patrick put up with such rudeness? She tried not to bang the door behind her. Well, she didn't try very hard, perhaps. A small revenge in the face of looming catastrophe.

Reggie put her back into the car. "You look as if you need a quiet time out, miss."

"Yes, Reggie. I do."

He drove her out to a country pub which had a garden sloping down to a shallow, rippling river. There were picnic tables set out on the lawn, and some white fan-tailed doves pecked at the turf and cooed in the branches of a nearby tree. The sky was cloudy, but there was a hum of bees in the air. She sat beside a huge purple buddleia which was attracting swarms of butterflies. Reggie ordered halves of shandy and some ham sandwiches for them. He would have retired to a distant table, but she asked him to sit with her.

"Your father loved this place," he said, sitting down opposite her. "Now and then he'd say to me, 'Take me somewhere quiet, Reggie, 'cos I need to think.' Sometimes he'd sit in the back of the car with his eyes closed, and I'd read the papers. Sometimes we'd go to a pub and have a meal. It doesn't seem right that he's gone, and him not much older'n me."

Minty blinked. "I grieve for him, too. Dear Reggie, I think you loved my father, didn't you?"

"Dunno about love, miss," said Reggie, who had the inarticulate man's distrust of the word "love". "I *liked* him, and I think he liked me. He was that glad he got to know you before the end. I'll be sorry to go in some ways . . ."

"Go? Why?"

"Simon said I'd to leave because of the Americans coming in. Even if they don't, you won't need a full-time chauffeur. Plus Chef wants my place because it's bigger'n his and he's got these women . . . beg pardon, miss . . . two of the restaurant staff wish to spend time with him. It's all right. I've started to pack up my tools already."

Minty tried not to think about what might be happening in London. "Your tools?"

"I've always liked fiddling, making things work. Especially clocks. They make a room feel homely. Your father used to drop in of an evening sometimes, and I'd show him what I was up to. He said it rested his mind." He ran a hand down over his face and tried to look cheerful.

She was distressed. "I didn't realise you wanted to leave."

"Now don't you worry about me. I've a little house in South London which Sir Micah bought for me years back. My sister runs it for me as a bed-and-breakfast and I've always got my room there. He left me a year's wages too, remember. I'll soon find something else, never you fret." He sniffed. "Truth to tell, I'll never know why he kept me on so long. There's plenty can drive as well as me, that can speak the foreign lingos, too. As for being his bodyguard, I let that something Miles attack you. I was too slow to stop him."

She took a deep breath. Even if Patrick got her some money for her shares, the money situation was still far from clear, and what she was about to do would mean an extra call on her resources and an even bigger bank loan. "I don't want you to go, Reggie, unless you feel you have to. I don't need a regular driver as my father did, but you were more than that to him. You were a loyal friend. Suppose I could find the money, would you consider working for me, too?"

"Me? But what would you want me to do? I'm not your college-educated type. I wouldn't know what to do with accounts and books and office stuff."

"The Houseman's job is vacant. Couldn't you apply for that? I have plans for the Hall, but if I want to move even a table here or a picture there, I need help. My father's rooms are perfect in their way but they don't feel like home yet. I'd like to go into the attics and rescue some family pieces, put them around the place. Also, I need you to find me a reliable workaday car, cheap.

"Then about the clocks. There are some clocks in the Hall, but not one appears to be working. Some may be too valuable for you to touch, but couldn't you find out how much it would cost to restore them? I suspect some just need winding. If we could get them working, it would be like restoring the heart to the Hall. So if I can find the money, will you stay?"

Reggie put his hand out for her to shake. "Will I? You bet."

On the journey back to the Hall Minty kept taking out her mobile to make sure it was switched on. She envied Patrick having work to do. Meanwhile, she must talk to Annie.

According to the map in the office, the entrance to Annie's flat was through an unobtrusive door between the restaurant and the gift shop. In passing Minty again noted that though the house and gardens were open, neither restaurant nor shop were busy. She'd have to do something about both soon.

Annie's flat was in the loft over the restaurant, with pale oak exposed beams rising to the roof. It was charmingly furnished in cool creams and pale blues. The floors had been stripped and left uncarpeted, save for a few silky Chinese rugs. Annie was sitting in an armchair by an unlit fire, gazing into space.

Minty had never seen Annie doing nothing before, and it shocked her. She sank to her knees at Annie's side. "Annie, I'm so sorry!"

Annie tried to smile, but it wasn't much of an effort. "So am I. I had no idea that Simon would take that line. And Lady Cardale went a lot further than I expected. Well," she said in a lifeless voice, "it's done now. All over. Finished. Nearly twenty-one years of my life . . . wiped out, just like that."

"No, it isn't," said Minty. "Patrick got Lord Asher on the phone and maybe—just maybe—he can stop Simon."

Annie blinked. "Patrick Sands? Approached Lord Asher? He doesn't know him, does he?"

Minty said, "That didn't stop Patrick. You should have heard him! He was brilliant, shifting the blame from me to those who tattled, and then onto Simon. The point is not who started this, but how to stop Simon. Lord Asher is going to see what he can do, and Patrick will ring me if he succeeds. If he doesn't and it all comes out . . . well . . . we'll survive."

Annie looked grey and shrunken. "You might. The Foundation won't. Who would want to give money to a corrupt organisation?"

Minty said, "How many schools has that man built for you?"

"Only that one."

"Well, then. The Foundation acknowledges its error, corrects it and carries on as before. It'll cost something to put right, but it'll be worth it, won't it?"

"If you'd only kept your mouth shut!"

Minty grimaced. "Does it do any good to cover up a mistake? Didn't anybody check on what the architect had done before? Was it sensible to appoint an architect whose uncle was contracted to build the school? How did my father miss it?"

"He hasn't been well for some years . . . we were abroad so much."

"What would he have done if he'd spotted the collusion? Heads would've rolled, wouldn't they?"

"Not collusion. It was . . . convenient, that's all. There's nothing wrong with keeping it in the family."

"Provided everything's above board. This wasn't. I'm sorry I didn't take my worry to you first. I tried Sir James . . ."

Annie was magnanimous. "You trusted him on our recommendation."

"Sir James thinks I'm a naive, brainless bimbo. I suppose it was he who tattled to Simon. I don't think Lord Asher would have."

Annie looked at Minty, without curiosity. "You're going to marry Patrick Sands, aren't you? Your father said you would, in spite of everything."

"Yes," said Minty, blushing. "Oh, yes."

"I wish you well," said Annie, still in that dead voice.

Minty spotted some papers on the rug and tilted her head to see better. They were particulars of houses for sale locally.

"You're moving?" The idea was disturbing.

"Micah was always urging me to find a place of my own, but my flat here is so comfortable and I thought you'd need me to ease you into running the Foundation. You've no interest in it, have you? In any case, by tomorrow morning there won't be any Foundation to serve."

"Dear Annie, don't be so gloomy. Maybe Patrick will pull it off. You've seen what I'm like. I'm not cut out for big business. As I see it, the Hall's a full-time job. My job. Why, even Lady C had to pass the job on when she got interested in charity work."

"Lady Cardale did perhaps exaggerate this morning. She was wrong to say we could influence what the bank will lend you. I'll help you work out a business plan, if you like. What's more, I'll ask Lord Asher to come down soon, so that we can discuss your plans for the future and see how best we can disburse the trust fund."

"That would be good," said Minty, and refrained from mentioning that Patrick had already spoken to Lord Asher about it.

Annie plucked at her skirt. Her eyes moved to a black-and-white photograph on the mantelpiece. Sir Micah, looking relaxed and jovial in casual clothes. "I still find it difficult to believe he's gone."

"So do I." Greatly daring, Minty reached across and put her hand on Annie's. "I know I can't replace my father, but if you're at a loose end and looking for something to take your mind off things . . . well, you're the nearest thing I've had to a mother since I was five years old. Of course I'll understand if you want to leave, but won't you reconsider? I need help with the Hall, too."

Annie sighed. "I don't think so. But thank you for offering."

Annie's phone trilled, and she reached for it with a languid hand. Then sat upright. "Yes, Lord Asher? . . . Well, yes, if there's to be an emergency meeting of trustees, I suppose I could come up to London straight away, but . . ."

She glanced at Minty. "Yes, she's here with me at the moment, but . . . Patrick Sands suggested . . . what!"

Minty's mobile rang and she took it over to the window to answer it. Patrick, of course.

"Minty, Lord Asher's just been on the phone. They've got Simon to promise not to go to the press for the moment and they want you and Annie to attend an emergency meeting up in London this afternoon. How do you feel about it?"

"Lord Asher's on the phone to Annie now. I don't want to go. They'll be frightened for the future of the Foundation. They'll want to ignore the real problem and focus on my telling tales. The easy way out for them is to round on me, get me to resign. Lady C's already suggested it. Do you think I should?"

"Definitely not. I've been trying to understand what Simon's hoping to get out of this. Lady C might just want you disgraced, but I think Simon's playing a different game. I think he's after money. Much as it annoys me to see Simon benefit, I've suggested to Lord Asher that the trustees might like to come to an—er—agreement with Simon. In short, to pay him off."

Minty spurted into laughter. "That's brilliant."

"It's unethical," he said in a stern voice. "I'll deny I suggested it if anyone asks, but it might work. Now if you don't go to the meeting, there's a risk they'll turn on you anyway. Is Annie going? If so, give her your proxy vote."

"You are a truly remarkable man, Patrick."

"Am I not?" he said, and disconnected.

Annie was looking flustered. "They want us up in Town, now. I don't understand why we should pay Simon off. It seems wrong. If only Micah were still alive! I've sat at his side and followed his lead all these years. We've never had this sort of thing come up before."

"You never had Simon on the Board before. Annie, you voted to elect him, and now you've got to deal with him. You're a player in the big game now, whether you like it or not. I'm not coming with you, but I am going to give you my proxy vote. Make them see that to keep the Foundation going, they've got to meet Simon's terms. For the moment. Then quietly but quickly set up some kind of appraisal of what's been going on, and allocate money to put it right. Simon can only hurt the Foundation by going to the press before an investigation starts. Once it's under way, the news will have lost its shock value."

Annie stared. "That might have been your father talking. Why won't you come with me?"

"I've invited some people to tea. Best of luck, Annie."

Chapter Thirteen

On her way through the tower office, Minty was captivated by the view from the window. There's a special blue and gold brightness about a sunny October day. The trees in the Park were rapidly turning golden, and leaves were coming adrift and lying in circles on the greensward below. Hodge was making heavy weather of trying to start the mowing machine. She wondered if Reggie could get it going.

Iris came in wearing her cat-like smile. "Mrs Wootton from the Manor, Mrs Collins and Mrs Chickward have arrived. I showed them into your sitting room and asked Serafina to serve tea, but I must warn you there's an atmosphere. Mrs Chickward has scheduled one of her famous At Homes for the same evening that Mrs Collins has called a committee meeting, and Mrs Wootton is invited to both. Would you like me to take notes?"

"Please. And ask Barr to join us."

"Barr left a message for you. The wages were due yesterday, and there's not enough in the bank to pay them. What is he to tell everyone?"

Minty pressed her hands to her forehead. "Tell them I'll arrange things with the bank tomorrow. Now I've got to tell the ladies there's no money for Christmas trees."

She passed through her own empty office into the green sitting room, where the three women occupied a brocaded sofa or chair each. The atmosphere was, as Iris had said, unfriendly. Mrs Chickward and Mrs Collins were shooting hostile glances at one another while Venetia Wootton looked flushed and guilty.

The coffee table bore a silver tea service and fine china displaying home-made sandwiches, cakes and biscuits.

Venetia Wootton sprang to her feet and rushed to embrace Minty. "My dear, I am so sorry. I only told one person in the strictest confidence about your plan for a Christmas tree season, and I know you wanted to tell Mrs Collins and Mrs Chickward yourself, but it appears they'd already heard."

Mrs Collins was an "off-comer", that is, someone who hadn't been born locally. She was accepted to a point by the village because she put a lot of energy into running local organisations. A lady of substance in every respect, she was wearing a black dress patterned with lilac flowers, and the plate in front of her was piled with sandwiches and cakes. Speaking with her mouth full she said, "My dear Miss Cardale . . ."

Her rival for local influence was Mrs Chickward; of county stock, she was as tall and thin as Mrs Collins was shortish and stout. Mrs Chickward was drinking tea with lemon and had nothing on her plate but one small biscuit. "Araminta," she said, inclining her head to welcome her hostess.

The two women relished an endless game of one-upmanship. Mrs Chickward had scored a point here by using Minty's proper Christian name.

"I poured for you," said Venetia, looking unwontedly chastened. "Hope you don't mind."

"Not at all," said Minty. "I'm asking the Administrator to join us, to advise on finance. You know how new I am to this job. I'm afraid I tend to jump into things without thinking them through, and that's why I needed to ask your advice. I thought it would have been a splendid idea to have a Christmas season, with each room decorated by a different group of flower arrangers. It would have been too late to attract visitors this year, but if we had had some decorations in place we could have got them photographed and had a brochure printed to bring in extra visitors next year."

Barr appeared with Iris at his side. "Ladies, will you permit me to join you?"

Minty checked. He was sober and could obviously turn on the charm when necessary. Minty poured out tea for him. Iris shook her head at Minty's offer of tea and took a seat by the window.

Mrs Chickward announced—her thoughts were always announced, rather than spoken—"I welcome the idea in principle. When I heard about it—and I must admit that I was a little hurt that you hadn't thought fit to consult me at the beginning—I contacted some of my flower-arranging team and we worked out a budget."

She produced a sheaf of papers from a handbag so large it might almost be called a briefcase. "We worked on the assumption that you would want the Great Hall, the main reception rooms and the Long Gallery decorated."

She handed over a typed estimate. The total made Minty goggle.

Mrs Chickward took a nibble from her biscuit. "You can't expect a flower-arranging club to decorate a room for nothing. We're usually allowed about a hundred pounds per arrangement. In this case, we'd be supplying Christmas trees, lights and decorations as well. It couldn't possibly be done under a couple of hundred pounds a room, and in the case of the Great Hall and the Long Gallery, treble that amount."

Minty threw up her hands. "Mrs Chickward, you're a marvel. How I wish we could do it this year, but the coffers are empty and until probate is granted, I'm living on money advanced by the bank."

Mrs Collins licked her fingers and wiped them on a linen serviette. "Dear Mrs Chickward is, of course, a superb flower arranger, but perhaps not the most practical of mortals when it comes to making ends meet."

Mrs Chickward's back became even more upright, and Minty wondered what financial miscalculation Mrs Collins might be referring to. A fifty-pence piece gone missing at a Women's Institute meeting?

"However," said Mrs Collins, ladling sugar into her milky tea, "finance is a particular talent of mine. I think we're all agreed that what's good for the Hall is good for the village. Yes? So the question is, can we cut our cloth to provide a suitable coat? Doesn't the Hall have a plantation of Christmas trees? I know they're usually sold off in the market, but in this case might we not have first pick?"

Hodge! thought Minty. *Is he selling Hall produce on the side? I wouldn't put it past him.* She shot a glance at Barr, who looked self-conscious. Yes, Barr knew about it, too.

It cost Mrs Chickward something to agree with her rival. "Well . . . yes, I suppose if we had the trees for free . . . though my ladies would still need funds to light and decorate them." She held up a bony hand to prevent Mrs Collins from interrupting. "Lo! I have an idea!"

Minty suppressed a giggle. Could the rivalry between the two ladies work to the Hall's advantage?

Mrs Chickward waved a graceful hand in front of her closed eyes. "I have it!" She opened her eyes again. "We must go for splendour in the Great Hall, but perhaps we could ask our ladies to use their ingenuity elsewhere to decorate rooms on a limited amount of money . . . say for under a hundred pounds a room. One room could be decorated with brightly coloured shapes cut from plastic sheeting, another with seed pods dipped in gold or silver. And so on. If we publicised this angle, people would come to copy our ideas."

Minty was impressed. "Mrs Chickward, that's brilliant."

Mrs Collins patted cake crumbs from her ample bosom. "I've an even better idea. Sponsorship. We ask the village shops to sponsor a tree, or a room . . . or whatever they can afford. We would of course give them a mention in the programme."

Venetia was getting excited. "Hugh and I would like to sponsor the Red Room. I've always liked that best. Oh, my stewards will be so thrilled!"

"The village shops," decreed Mrs Chickward, "must have programmes or fliers on their counters, to direct visitors to the Hall."

"Television coverage? Advertisements in the local papers? A mention on local radio?" Mrs Collins took another scone. "Where's Gemma? Shouldn't she be in on this?"

Iris spoke up from the window. "I tried phoning her, but there's no reply. Her car's out."

Minty looked at Barr. "What do you say, Barr? If we could get sufficient sponsorship, should we go ahead? I do have someone in mind to take photographs and bring out a brochure, perhaps even set up a Web site. Is it too late in the year?"

Barr looked uneasy. "We've never had sponsorship for anything before."

Minty looked at Mrs Collins. "Would you be responsible for getting in as much sponsorship as you can? Yes? And Mrs Chickward, would you organise your ladies? Venetia, I need to speak to the stewards. Would you arrange that?"

Mrs Chickward was consulting her diary. "We could open in six weeks' time, perhaps even on November 5th, the anniversary of Guy Fawkes' infamous attempt to blow up Parliament. It amuses the locals to put an effigy of someone unpopular on the bonfire. I wonder who it will be this year?"

"It was an effigy of Miles last year," said Venetia. "There wasn't half a row about that. Both Simon and Miles were furious."

Mrs Chickward did not permit herself to smile. "In any event, it's a yearly charitable event in aid of the Royal Society for the Protection of Birds."

Barr grimaced. "Mrs Chickward, I've some bad news. I know this is one of Lady Cardale's pet projects and that you've managed it for her for some years, but Simon cancelled the order for the fireworks."

"What!"

Iris put the events folder into Minty's hands. The second piece of paper was a flier for A Giant Fireworks Display in aid of the Royal Society for the Protection of Birds, November 5th at Eden Hall.

Minty said, "I don't understand. Surely the charity provides the fireworks?"

"No," said Mrs Collins, looking thoughtful. "Lady Cardale supplies the premises, the refreshments and the fireworks for free. The charity sells tickets at thirty-five pounds a head and makes a killing."

Mrs Chickward had gone white. "You mean there aren't going to be any fireworks? But I've sold four hundred tickets and . . . no, I can't believe it. There must be some mistake. Simon wouldn't!"

"Simon would," said Venetia, grimly. "You remember all that fuss last year when he dragged out payment for the fireworks, and for the string quartet? They had to send him solicitors' letters before he paid up."

Mrs Collins spilt her tea. "You can't mean he's cancelled the string quartet for my Musical Evening? But . . ."

Mrs Chickward evened the score. "Your first venture into the field of culture, isn't it, dear? And how many tickets have you sold?"

Mrs Collins mopped up her tea with a trembling hand.

"This is terrible," said Minty. "Barr, how much do the fireworks cost?"

"Upwards of ten thousand pounds for a good display. As for the string quartet, Simon asked me to sign a blank cheque for them on the General Account and I know it's been cashed."

"The question is, who cashed it?" asked Venetia.

Iris said, "I'll check." She left the room.

Minty skimmed through the file. "I only had a quick glance at this file the other day, and it did occur to me that it was short on detail. I thought perhaps Gemma must have the real file, because there's no mention here of how much the charities pay the Hall to cover costs, refreshments, electricity and so on."

Mrs Chickward said weakly, "We all knew Lady Cardale had money. I assumed this was her way of giving something back to the community."

Barr said, "I'm sorry to disabuse you, ladies, but neither she nor Simon paid a penny towards these events, and that's one of the reasons why the Hall's in such a bad way financially."

There was a silence full of unspoken thoughts, most of them unpleasant.

"What are we going to do?" asked Mrs Chickward. "Araminta, you can't see your way to . . . ? No. I suppose there's no reason why you should take on your stepmother's debts of honour, but . . ."

"There's nothing in the bank to pay for these things."

"We'll have to cancel," said Mrs Collins, faintly. "There's nothing else for it."

Iris came back in. "The secretary of the string quartet says that as they'd had so much trouble getting the money out of Simon last year, they'd asked for their fee up front. She hasn't received it yet. She says that if she doesn't get it by this weekend, they're pulling out."

Gloomy silence.

Minty thought about Annie speeding up to London, and the row that might even now be going on at the Foundation. Had Simon contacted the press yet? Would Patrick's intervention save the day? Patrick . . .

She made an effort to concentrate on the matter in hand. "There's a possible way out. I don't like it much and I don't suppose you'll like it, either. I'm prepared to go cap in hand to the bank with a business plan and borrow some money for these two events, provided I'm reimbursed by the charities afterwards. But we must have a proper accounting in future. Rent, services, refreshments, whatever. If Gemma can take this on . . ."

Both women shook their heads. Even Venetia looked doubtful.

". . . then Iris will cope, won't you, Iris? The immediate problem is how to make those first two events pay, while still raising money for charity."

"It can't be done," said Mrs Chickward. "We must resign ourselves to running the event at a loss. The plan for the Fireworks Evening was to have a champagne reception in the Great Hall, followed by a move to the south-facing rooms overlooking the lake. The fireworks are set up on the other side of the lake, so that they reflect in the water. If the weather's fine, we go out onto the terrace to see the display. I can't pack any more people into those rooms."

Iris said, "Might I make a suggestion? Throw the grounds open to the public at a fiver a head, children under five for free. Chef to provide food for an outdoor stall, where the stewards can sell hot dogs and hot soup to the crowd. People'd come from miles around to see a really good display, even if it rains. You'd need extra stewards to hold the crowd back, of course, and ropes, but . . ."

"Leave that to me," cried Mrs Collins, once more in her element.

"Bring in outside caterers if Chef can't cope," said Iris, "and a team to clear up afterwards."

"Iris, you're brilliant," said Minty. "Would it work, Mrs Chickward?"

"Undoubtedly. But what about poor dear Mrs Collins and her soirée?"

"I can't pack any more into the Great Hall, I'm afraid."

Minty said, "How about moving the event to the Long Gallery? Erect a small stage in the middle and have your audience on either side? That way you could double or even treble the number of seats."

Iris raised a finger. "Will Mrs Collins let me know who is to sponsor decorations for the Christmas tree event, so that I can start putting a programme together?"

Mrs Chickward and Mrs Collins dead-heated. "I'll be responsible for the Great Hall . . ."

"I wouldn't mind sponsoring . . ."

Minty suppressed a giggle. "It's a very large room. Perhaps one of you should sponsor for the Great Hall and the other the Long Gallery?"

"To be honest," said Mrs Chickward at her most stately, "the previous arrangements did give me some twinges of conscience. Araminta, I think you should employ a good accountant to ensure this situation never arises again."

"Agreed," said Minty, who was well aware that Mrs Chickward's much-loved nephew was an accountant, and a good one, too. On the other hand, Neville was rather too fond of Minty, so . . . And could she afford him? Could she afford not to?

She rose to her feet and took a deep breath. "One more thing. I'm sorry you got to hear about the Christmas trees from other people. I want you to be the first to know that Patrick Sands and I are to be married before Christmas. The announcement will be in *The Times* tomorrow."

"Splendid. Congratulations!" Venetia enveloped Minty in a hug.

"Wonderful news," enthused Mrs Collins.

"I thought as much," said Mrs Chickward, bestowing a stately air-kiss near Minty's cheek. "I'll send you an invitation to my At Home next week. Dear Mrs Collins had arranged a committee meeting for that evening but I'm sure she'll postpone it, won't you, dear?"

Mrs Collins conceded defeat. "Of course, dear. Especially if you've saved an invitation for me, too."

Mrs Chickward smiled with her teeth. "Of course."

Minty mentally recorded a drawn match.

Barr shook her hand. "This calls for a jar of something." He caught Minty's eye and added, "After work, naturally." He stuffed cake into his mouth.

Serafina trundled a trolley into the room, as a signal that the party was over. Iris held the door open for Mrs Chickward and Mrs Collins, but Venetia and Barr hung back.

Venetia said, "I'm so glad Felicity Chickward's going to sponsor you in society, since Lady Cardale will hardly be helpful that way. Everyone who is anyone goes to Felicity's At Homes." She swept out, and Serafina started clearing the table.

Minty said, "Be glad for me, Serafina."

"Another man to look after! I told Annie how it would be but she wouldn't listen. Oh, and that funny little man Jonah's brought over Ruby's sewing machine and she's set it up in the spare bedroom to alter your clothes. Says she's tired of being on her feet all day long at the shop and would rather work here."

Minty fell into a chair, said "Ouch!" because it dug into her back in the wrong place. She told herself to relax, limb by limb. She wondered what was happening in London, what her stepmother would say about the new arrangements for events, thought of her beautiful wedding dress, and Patrick. Patrick . . .

She took her hand away from her mobile phone with an effort.

Money. Would the sale of her shares bring in enough money to see the Hall through? How much must she ask the bank to lend her? How much information did you put in a business plan?

Barr picked up the untidy bundle of papers he'd dropped on the floor, and helped himself to some more cake from Serafina's trolley. "Thought you might like to see the Building and Maintenance Fund ledger. Absolutely no mention of the three million. I've got the cheque stub here. See? Nearly three million to 'F & F'. There's something at the back of my mind . . ." He shook his head. "I can't find a receipt of any kind. Are they bookmakers, do you think? 'Fast & Furious'?" He crammed cake into his mouth and looked at Minty with the trusting gaze of a spaniel relying on his mistress to dig him out of a hole.

Minty tried to make a joke of it. "Perhaps a nightclub. Gambling debts. 'Fast women and Fickle Friends'? What do you think, Iris?"

"Paying off the debt on his aeroplane? 'Flights without Fear'."

"Wages," said Barr, softly persistent.

Minty nodded. "I'll see the bank manager tomorrow. And Barr, I realise the books aren't complete, but can you let me have a list of items bought over the last couple of years for the Hall? I'm particularly interested in the furniture in Lady C's rooms."

"Which really belong to the Hall, eh?" Barr started laughing and choked on a crumb. Minty patted him on his back, and Serafina handed him a glass of water. "Nothing stronger?" he asked.

"Not till you're off duty," said Minty.

What next? No message yet from Patrick. Keep busy.

Minty went down the stairs, crossed the courtyard and made her way through a door marked "Private" into the modern kitchen presided over by that amazing cook, Florence Thornby. The kitchen was bright with white tiles and good lighting, filled with delicious scents of baking and the cheerful sound of popular music from a radio.

Florence—like Mrs Collins—was also an off-comer, having married into the Thornby farming family some twenty years ago. Like Mrs Collins, she enjoyed good food and was efficient in everything she undertook. For some years she'd been cooking for Lady Cardale and her family five days a week, leaving a well-stocked freezer for them to dip into at weekends. Simon's plan to lease the Hall to an American company would have meant the end of her job and that of her teenage daughter Gloria, who had the family's heavy build and worked—rather desultorily—in the restaurant across the way.

The Thornby family had been the first to befriend Minty on her return, and she was very fond of them. "Dear Florence, congratulate me! I'm marrying Patrick Sands as soon as we can make the arrangements."

Florence gave Minty a hug. "I'm that pleased. Have you had tea? There's fresh scones on the cooling tray and I'll make a cuppa in a minute."

"Just a cuppa. You'll make the wedding cake?"

"Four tiers; bottom one fruit, next chocolate, third plain sponge and the fourth to be kept against the first christening. I've the tins looked out already. Now don't you get cross with her, but Ruby showed me your wedding dress this afternoon. It's perfect. Ruby's just taking it up at the shoulders a trifle, and she's asked Jonah to do your bouquet."

Minty blinked. "Jonah? But—well, I know he does arrange flowers beautifully, but . . . you're all going too fast for me. I haven't even got a ring on my finger yet."

"The sooner the better. It'll be a good day for the Hall when you bring Patrick Sands here. Clear out the musty old ways. And don't you worry about me. When Lady C and Simon go and the electricians come in to do the re-wiring in this wing, I'll treat myself to a nice holiday abroad somewhere, and the landlady at the Plough has already asked me to drop in and talk to her about a job. If I can only get Gloria in there, too, I'll be well satisfied."

Minty looked across the courtyard. Not many people were in the restaurant. The displays of food looked tired and Gloria Thornby was drooping around the place, not exactly helping to make customers feel wanted.

"Florence, I need to ask you a 'suppose' question, and you don't have to answer now. Suppose I wasn't happy about the way the restaurant is run here and . . . ?"

"Yes," said Florence, polishing her stainless steel sinks. "Of course I'd be prepared to take over the restaurant and turn the place round. Forget about opening in the evenings; nobody wants that around here. Pensioners' lunches, now. They'd go down a treat."

Minty grinned. "Now, then. It was only a 'suppose' question. Chef may be happy to take my worries on board and start producing good food . . ."

"And pigs might fly. He's never done a proper hand's turn all the time I've been here, and as for the goings-on in his quarters with those two girls, and trying to turn Reggie out so's he can spread himself around . . . but you won't want to know about that!"

Minty nodded. Reggie had already hinted as much.

"As for the special events, he orders pre-cooked meals from town and takes a cut. I could turn out something at half the price and tastier, too."

Minty grimaced. It was even worse than she'd suspected. "He's got a cast-iron contract, and I can't afford to buy him off."

"You'll find a way. I'll start on some costings for you when I get home tonight."

Faint but pursuing, Minty said, "Christmas menus from mid-November?"

"Of course. With a vegetarian option. I've heard you're cooking for Patrick tonight. Do you want to dip into my freezer for something?"

"I give up," said Minty. "The grapevine wins, OK. No, thanks, Florence. I'll pick up something in the village on my way up the hill . . . and if you're anything to go by, I shall be fending off questions about flower girls . . ."

"No flower girls. Gemma as the only bridesmaid—though she doesn't deserve it, the silly chit."

"Patrick will hate it if we make it too formal."

"Patrick will do more than dress up in tails for you, you know that. Now who's giving you away?"

This was a question fraught with awkward possibilities. "I wish I could ask your father-in-law," said Minty, and meant it. "Or Hugh

Wootton. They've both been so kind to me. But Patrick has already asked Lord Asher, my father's executor."

Florence peeled off her rubber gloves. "I don't deny my father-in-law would have been pleased, but your man's got hold of the right end of the stick, and you'll find a way of making my father-in-law feel right about it."

On her way out Minty saw Chef in the courtyard, smoking under a sign which said "No Smoking". He was a lanky, black-haired man with a pronounced cleft in his chin and bold eyes that seemed to see through her clothing.

She pointed to the sign and said, "Oh, Chef! You're setting a bad example."

He lifted his upper lip, defying her. She flushed, told herself that she wasn't ready to deal with him yet and went on her way.

Chapter Fourteen

She took her time walking up through the village, doing some shopping and stopping for a chat here and there.

Patrick's secretary gave her keys to his rooms and said he was running late, surprise!

His kitchen was modern, full of light and peaceful, a hundred times better than the dark and dingy room in which she'd spent most of her time back in the city. She thought of her uncle and aunt, and pulled a face. What should she do about their demands for money and attention?

By six o'clock she'd joints of hare braising in the oven, with onions, herbs and spices, and a twist of lemon peel. She prepared the vegetables, then set about making a blackberry and apple crumble for pudding. She used Patrick's heavy silverware and cut-glass tumblers to lay the table in the adjoining dining room, and set white Wedgwood plates rimmed with gold to warm above the stove. She put a bowl of sweet peas on the polished mahogany of the table, and adjusted the leather-seated, high-backed chairs around it.

She checked to make sure Patrick's car was still in its parking place at the bottom of his garden. It was. Patrick loved his garden, which was bright with red-berried shrubs set around a sundial on a paved area. He'd planted something for every season of the year. At the moment there were Japanese anemones and helianthemums in full flower, and he'd cut back the buddleias and stands of fennel earlier so that both were still giving colour. What would he make of the flowerless grounds at the Hall?

She turned her back on his garden and considered his sitting room, which occupied the width of the house. You could learn a lot about a person by looking at the way he lived. His furniture was of different periods but blended into a harmonious whole. Two armchairs and an enormous Chippendale settee were grouped round the fireplace, comfortable as well as easy on the eye. The occasional tables were of the right height. His own chair would be the leather one beside the revolving Canterbury, which held a helter-skelter pile of books. More books crowded bookcases nearby. Lighting was by courtesy of Chinese-style table lamps, crowned with fringed lampshades.

Over the marble mantelpiece was a large gilt-framed mirror, a trifle foxed but still carrying its original beautiful glass, and underneath were a couple of Art Nouveau bronze figurines, some Satsuma vases and a silver-framed portrait of a woman, presumably his mother.

The walls were wainscoted but painted a light cream. The wide old floorboards glistened and a large rug in front of the fireplace was a dark red, probably Turkish, with an indecipherable pattern. For pictures he'd hung a couple of old, sepia-toned architectural prints.

Her verdict: he appreciated beautiful furniture, but it had to be both comfortable and practical.

She contrasted Patrick's home with her own luxurious but uncomfortable quarters and sighed. He wasn't going to like giving up this comfortable nest, was he?

Still he had not come, so she set about ironing some shirts of his which had been left in a basket in the kitchen, silky grey-striped shirts and severe business-like whites that needed cuff-links.

She felt a little shy, wondering if she'd know what to do when he came.

His footsteps were light on the stair, but she heard him coming. "Late again!"

"A truly wifely greeting! Can I smell home cooking?"

She was putting the ironing board away when he came into the kitchen. He stopped at arm's length, looking at her. She felt her colour rise.

He was smiling. "I'd kiss you, but the way I feel now, I haven't strong enough brakes."

She brushed her hair back from her face. "So how did you happen to break your rule this morning?"

"Necessity. I'd have fallen apart if I hadn't stopped you."

"So all I have to do to make you kiss me is . . . break off our engagement?"

"No, you don't, you baggage. You stay right there. I need a shower and a clean shirt before I can cope with you. I feel as if I've been paddling in murky water all day."

She handed him his clean shirts. "And was justice done?"

"Justice?" He looked wary. "No, I don't suppose it was justice to let Simon get away with it, but . . ."

He shrugged and set off for the stairs to the top storey, when his phone rang.

He draped his shirts over a chair and answered it. "Yes . . ." He looked at Minty, mouthed the words, "Lord Asher."

"Yes, I understand . . . yes, of course. Yes, I suppose there would have been some . . . hm . . . No, I should think she'll be satisfied, if not entirely pleased . . . Am I up in Town next week at all? Yes, I suppose I could . . . Thursday? I'd have to check, but . . . ah. Right. Well, yes, I might well be interested, but . . . right, we'll speak again."

He rang off. "Simon's been bought off. Nobody's particularly pleased about it. And Lord Asher would like to see me next week. He says he's been asking around about me, thinks I might be an asset if I were interested in going on the Board of Trustees." He punched the air. "Yes!"

Patrick went on up the stairs and she dashed back to the kitchen to put the vegetables on.

Patrick always had a hidden agenda. Look at how much he'd kept from her before they got engaged, never letting her suspect that she was to inherit the Hall.

Yes, he loved her, and yes, he'd be a lot more use on the Board of Trustees than she ever would. But why did he want it? He was just a country solicitor, without ambition. Or was he? Had she misread his character? That was an uncomfortable thought, but one that needed looking at.

Had he been using her love in order to get himself on the Board of the Foundation? And if so, why? Because he hated Simon and could continue their vendetta there?

She felt slightly sick.

He was cleverer than her, of course, and more worldly wise. She'd always known that he was devious, but this . . .

Would she ever be able to trust him, fully, completely? She could not, must not go any further into this relationship until she could answer that question.

Dear Jesus. Let him be the man I thought him— And suspected he was not.

He'd forgotten his clean shirts. She took them up to the top floor. She could hear him in the shower, humming, behind the bathroom door. The next door hung open but didn't lead to the master bedroom. This was a room which might once have been a dressing room. A plain, white painted cell. A single bed. There was a high-backed Windsor chair and a bedside table with a Bible and some Bible-reading notes on it. A bedside light, a clock alarm. No mirror, no pictures . . . but a palm cross had been tacked onto the wall opposite the bed, where he could see it when he opened his eyes in the morning. No curtains. The bed linen was neither fashionable nor new. No carpet, just a small mat on the floorboards.

He would keep his clothes . . . where? In a cupboard in another room? This room was for sleeping in and for praying. It was the room of a man without vanity. It was almost a monk's cell.

"Whoops!" he appeared in the doorway, bare-chested in jeans. His feet were bare. "Straying into dangerous territory here, Minty."

"This is where you come to pray. You speak the truth here."

He heard the ragged note in her voice and stilled. "I can pray anywhere."

"Tell me the truth. No more secrets. I want to know the sort of man I'm marrying and at the moment, I don't think I know you at all. Why do you want to go on the Board of the Foundation?"

He flushed. "Don't look at me like that." He spread his hands wide and shrugged. "You know why I want it. Revenge. And why not?"

"You still hate Simon so much?"

He let out a shuddering sigh. "Yes, I do. What he's done to me—to us—to our family . . . the years of watching my father turn grey and my mother die. I love you as I've never loved anyone else, but of course I saw that making you love me would be another way of defeating Simon."

"And now you're using my love for you to get onto the Board of the Foundation? I can't let you do that. You have to let it go, Patrick."

He laughed, short and sharp. "You don't know what you're asking!"

She thought, *He doesn't love me enough!* "If you love me . . . and God . . . more than you hate Simon, then you can do it!"

His mouth twisted into an ugly shape. "And you? Aren't you still carrying a burden of hate around for your uncle and aunt? For your father and your stepmother?"

She blazed up. "How dare you! I forgave my father before he died, once I understood something of him . . . and my uncle, too! But . . ." She faltered. "Perhaps not my aunt. Not really. I've tried to, but . . . why should I forgive my stepmother anything?"

"Two emotional cripples, that's us."

She stared at him and he stared back. She thought, *This could kill our love . . . if we let it.*

He took a half step towards her, crying out, "No, Minty . . . !"

At the same moment she stepped towards him. "Oh, Patrick, I'm sorry!"

He held her close and her arms went around him. He smelt of good soap. His skin was still slightly damp, but warm. His body against hers was lean and strong. "Minty, forgive me."

"Patrick, don't ever . . . you're right, of course."

"You're right, too. If I tell Lord Asher to get lost, will you still marry me?"

"We nearly quarrelled . . ."

"It's easy to speak words of love and mean them, but there's a lot we've got to sort out between us, isn't there?"

She drew back a little. "We can do it, I know we can."

His rather hard expression softened. "Yes, we can, but . . . let's take it step by step, shall we? This is our first evening together as two people who love one another. Let's put the problem areas aside for the moment. Give ourselves space to be easy with one another. When I came home and found you here, it was like a dream come true . . . and then I nearly threw it all away, didn't I?"

"I'm scared. It was so easy for us to quarrel."

He ran his finger down her nose. "Give me one of those shirts, woman, and let's eat. I'm hungry."

As she took the food to the table, he said, "Looks good. Smells marvellous. Shall we get a licence and marry tomorrow?"

"The village would never forgive us. Besides . . ."

"We wouldn't feel properly married if we didn't do it before God and in our community. I agree. So, you fancy hearing the banns being read in the church here? Shall we make an appointment to see the Reverend Cecil? Will you have to ask your uncle to officiate . . . ? Mm. This is good. Who's responsible for this delectable dish, Florence or Serafina?"

"I was, you idiot!"

"I'm amazed. Did your aunt teach you to cook?"

She grinned. "No, she's a terrible cook. It became my job to peel potatoes and prepare vegetables as soon as I could stand on a stool to reach the kitchen sink. When I was old enough to be a Brownie, my aunt sent me off to do some badges, to keep me out from under her feet. I was supposed to start with Housework but when I got there to enrol, the class was full. I loved my first Sunday School teacher and I knew she taught the Guides basic cookery, so I asked her to let me join her class even though I was much too young, really. She knew my circumstances and let me in. She even gave me extra lessons . . ."

The words caught in her throat, remembering how it was only a week since her father's funeral, and how much he'd enjoyed hearing her tell tales of her childhood. Well, in future it was going to be Patrick she could talk to.

"She had recipes dating back to her mother's childhood; the old country favourites that are tasty but don't cost much. She let me copy her recipes and after a while I started doing them in the vicarage . . . and you'll never guess what! Neither my aunt nor my uncle ever thanked me for taking over the cooking. In all those years. It amused me to try different recipes, and it made the housekeeping go further."

What's going to happen to my skills now I haven't a kitchen of my own?

He took another mouthful. "Well, at least that's something to look forward to when we get married . . . apart from the view from the bedroom."

She giggled. "Inside the bedroom, or from it? Do you fancy a four-poster bed?"

"Will I have to wear an old-fashioned night shirt and night cap while you chase me round the bed with a warming pan?"

"A striped night shirt, definitely. Not sure about the night cap."

"A pity. I've always wanted a night cap. A floppy one finishing in a tassel. What will you be wearing, I wonder?"

She blushed and ladled more onto his plate. He was eating as if he hadn't had a square meal for days. Come to think of it, he probably hadn't.

He said, quietly, "Are we rushing things? I suppose we are, but . . ."

"I couldn't marry anyone but you."

"And I couldn't marry anyone but you. There's a lot to discuss, though. I've always thought of myself as a patient, quiet sort of man . . ."

She laughed.

He looked wounded. "I'm the very mildest of men. You bring out the best—or the worst—in me."

"I've always had a temper. But you know that. All my aunt's training hasn't beaten it out of me."

"Suppose . . ." He fidgeted with his watch and took it off. "Suppose I rented an office somewhere else in the village, and we had the use of the whole of this house . . . ?"

"That's for our old age, Patrick. When we retire from public life and leave our children and grandchildren to do what they like with the Hall."

"I can't wriggle out of it, can I? I've got to go and live with you in a four-poster bed and be cosseted by Serafina. I suppose there are worse fates."

"Do you fancy blackberry and apple crumble to follow?"

"*Many* worse fates. With cream? Perhaps you can cook for me on Serafina's day off."

He insisted on making the coffee because he had an old machine that could be temperamental. "And now," he said, "to business. I want you to sit here, under this big side lamp." He led her to one end of the big settee and, as she had guessed he would, he sat opposite her beside the pile of books on the Canterbury.

He smiled as she pushed her hair back from her neck, and curled up on the deep cushions. Oh, how comfortable it was.

He said, "I often used to imagine you sitting there with the light from the lamp turning your hair all different shades of fair, with your legs tucked up under you. Don't move, will you, or you might vanish."

"I won't move," she said, also smiling. "I love you, Patrick Sands."

"Mm. I thought I couldn't love you any more—till I tasted your cooking. Now . . . ah! I've got it." He reached out a long arm and plucked a slender volume from among the books beside him. "This is it. 'How do I love thee? Let me count the ways . . .'"

"Elizabeth Barrett Browning. I'll give you another one. First Corinthians, chapter thirteen."

He reached for a Bible on the top of the pile. "Now why didn't I think of that first? 'Love is patient, love is kind. It does not envy, it does not boast, it is not proud. It is not self-seeking, it is not easily angered, it keeps no record of wrongs. It always protects, always trusts, always hopes, always perseveres.' Do you really love me like that, Minty?"

"Not always, but I'll do my best."

"I know another one. From the Song of Solomon . . ." He hesitated. "Or should I keep that till we're married?"

She laughed, remembering some of the lines. "'My beloved is near . . .'?"

There was a wicker work-basket lying open beside her, with a shirt on top lacking a button. An old cardboard box beneath held an assortment of buttons.

"Would you mind if I sewed on a button for you?"

"No, that's too much! I don't expect you to . . . that's not in my dreams." He turned his head away, putting his hand over his eyes. He was not a man to weep for grief, but happiness caught him unawares.

She picked out a button and sewed it on in silence. Presently he took his hand away from his eyes to watch her. "I'm building a storehouse of new dreams."

"If I picked up a duster or peeled a potato at the Hall, I'd have Serafina on my back. It's amazing how quickly you get used to being waited on. I leap out of bed and never think to make it, nowadays. How my aunt would scold. There, all done. You have something to pay me with?"

He put his right hand in his pocket, and then took it out again. He got up, restlessly moving things on the mantelpiece to left and then right.

"Well, it's like this. I didn't know where you were till I took over the practice from my father. I thought you'd probably forgotten me, but then again I thought you might have remembered, so on your eighteenth birthday I tried to gatecrash your party in the church hall . . ."

"And my aunt turned you away."

"Well, I'd bought a little ring for you. Nothing expensive, because I'd only just started earning, but I thought you might like it."

She stared at him. He'd bought her a ring, all those years ago?

He upended one of the Chinese jars on the mantelpiece until a jeweller's box fell out. He threw it to her; she caught it and opened it. Inside was a graceful Victorian ring, with an enamelled pansy on it. Now it was her turn to brush tears away. "Oh, Patrick! It's lovely."

"No, don't put it on yet. I can't think why I kept it. It's only a trifle. When it came to your twenty-first birthday, I thought you might like something a little more grown-up, so . . ."

He upended the second of the jars and threw her another box. This one contained a dark blue sapphire, surrounded by diamonds. Again, it was another old ring, set in gold. She held it in both hands, looking up at him. "You know me well. It's what I would have chosen for myself. Will you put it on?"

"We . . . ll, no. Actually, it's not really like you, now." This time he brought a box out from his right-hand pocket, and handed it to her. Inside was a modern gold ring, set with just one large stone. Was it a diamond? It flashed blue.

"It's a blue diamond. I had quite a job to find one, but that's how I see you now. When you look at me, that's what your eyes are like."

She held the rings up one by one. "The pansy ring is how I was when I first came back to the village, unsure of myself, aching for love. The sapphire is how I've been since I learned to love you, and been loved by my father. The diamond is for the woman you want me to become."

"As I see it, you're half way between what you were and what you will be. I suppose you could wear whichever one suits your mood at the time."

She took a couple of light side combs from her handbag and stood up. Looking in the mirror, she drew back her hair from her face on either side, and put in the combs. The little girl lost had gone. A grown woman stared back at her from the mirror.

"Is this right, Patrick?"

"Yes." He sounded breathless. "That's how I dream of you, sometimes. But whatever you wear, whatever you do, whatever you choose—that's all right by me."

He put the pansy ring on her little finger, the sapphire on the third finger of her right hand and the blue diamond on the ring finger of her left hand.

"So now I'm engaged three times over?"

"It's best to make sure," he said, seriously.

Chapter Fifteen

"Iris, will you make an appointment for me to see the bank manager this morning?"

Iris looked up from her copy of *The Times*. "The announcement of your engagement's in. That'll bring some more phone calls. Yes, I'll make the appointment at the bank for you, but first you've a meeting with the Heads of Department—and I've heard that both Mrs Kitchen and Chef are going to be awkward."

The tower room was barely large enough to accommodate everyone. Barr seated himself at the coffee table, stretched out long legs and reached for a biscuit. Mrs Kitchen, the housekeeper, sat opposite him, flexing her neck and squaring her elbows.

Tim—the newly appointed Estate Manager—took a chair against the wall, dropping his pen on the floor. Dark-chinned Chef lounged in Iris' swivel chair, looking at once bored and threatening, while Doris from the gift shop perched on the edge of her chair, as nervous as Tim but handling it better. Venetia Wootton arrived late and took the last of the comfortable chairs round the coffee table.

Hodge the gardener failed to attend.

Minty had never taken a meeting before and wasn't sure how to handle it. She fingered her sapphire and diamond ring, put her trembling hands behind her and perched on the edge of Iris' desk.

"Good morning. Sorry I haven't got round to seeing everyone yet, but I hope to do so soon . . ." On second thoughts, it hadn't been a good idea to start with an apology. "Barr, may we have your report?"

Barr said that the fabric of the Hall was in pretty good shape, visitor figures slightly down as were the takings from the restaurant and the gift shop. Owing to financial constraints, they might have to defer scheduled maintenance work on the north wing for a year, but that wasn't a great problem. A specialist firm had been contacted about putting the fountain back in order. Miss Cardale had assured him their wages would be paid within the next few days.

Mrs Kitchen pinched in her lips. "How does Miss Cardale propose to keep the Hall going if we're heading for bankruptcy, which I can see we are?"

"The bank is prepared to cover our costs until probate is granted. My father also left money in trust for the Hall and . . ."

"I understood," said Mrs Kitchen, "that the trustees don't want you fribbling the money away on unnecessary expenditures, like this strange notion of keeping the house open with childish decorations." Had she been listening to Lady Cardale on the subject?

Minty said, "My father also left me a lot of money which is not in trust, and which I'll be able to access when probate is granted. Plus I do have other resources. You've all heard about the Christmas tree project? Good. Even with sponsorship it may not break even this year but will be self-supporting in the future, and bring in a lot more visitors."

"If we stay open till Christmas—which I'm against, mind," said Mrs Kitchen, "then I'll need another cleaner. An old friend of mine, Mrs Guinness, has expressed a wish to . . ."

"Mrs Guinness?" Minty could hardly believe her ears. "I had dealings with her when I was supervising the holiday cottages and I don't think she's quite right for a job here." That was an understatement. Mrs Guinness was a slovenly creature whose ideas of "thine" and "mine" were hazy. Minty cringed at the thought of her being let loose on the Hall.

"Indeed!" said Mrs Kitchen, with a face like vinegar. "Who employs the cleaning staff, may I ask? You, or me?"

Minty stopped being conciliatory. "You do, of course; but as long as I pay your wages you'd be wise to take my advice."

"I understood you've no money of your own till probate is granted . . . *if* it's granted." She had definitely been listening to Lady Cardale. The others looked uneasy, avoiding Minty's eye.

Minty began to get angry. "Mrs Kitchen, Eden Hall has come down to me through generations of Edens. It's in my blood. I do have resources which you don't know about, and even if I do have to take out a loan from the bank to tide us over, then that's what I'll do."

Minty swept them with her eyes. "I'm new and will make mistakes, but it's up to you—all of you—to help me keep this place going. If you want to leave, fine. If you stay, you'll have a proper written contract. Is that clear?"

Most of them approved, but Chef hid a contemptuous laugh, thinking he was safe whatever Minty said or did. Tim fumbled with his pen, dropped it again and picked it up.

"Yes, Tim?" said Minty.

"Glad to hear about the p–pay and you're spot on about c–contracts. I've been t–trying to work out from Miles' figures, how much the estate c–costs, but it's c–complicated. No proper records. One thing: we need another Ranger soonest, for the Park. Boundary walls have tumbled down, branches of trees have died and might fall on anyone trespassing. We might get sued if they hurt themselves.

"The estate owns a couple of farms, but the rent hardly covers our office telephone bill. I'll need more time to get the whole picture, but there's one thing we could do, and that's sell off the holiday cottages. Do that, and we fund the Ranger's salary."

"An easy option," said Minty, briskly. "But a long-term disaster. Selling off property means less income in future. I'm hoping the trustees will approve a programme to revamp the cottages so we can let them out at a better rate. We should recoup the expenditure within a couple of years."

Barr put up a finger. "The garden and lawns round the house. Mr Hodge sends his apologies and has given me a quote for a new mower and for replanting the formal garden."

"Why isn't he here?"

There was some mumbling at the back. Someone said, "Market day, isn't it?" A concealed titter ran around the room. Minty made a mental note to find out why.

Chef lifted his eyes from contemplation of Minty's ankles. "Forget Christmas catering. The makeover of the restaurant's due to start in three weeks' time. That's when we close for the season and I take my annual leave."

"I cancelled the makeover," said Minty. "Far too expensive and out of keeping with our country house image. The design team are coming down to see me next week, when we'll discuss doing a quick paint job to freshen the place up without breaking the bank."

"You can't cancel it. Simon said . . ."

"Simon paid the designers in promises. Forget about opening in the evenings. Think pensioners' lunches. Oh, and by the way—Gloria stays, right?" Gloria Thornby did work at a snail's pace, and she was buxom rather than trendily thin, but she was a good-hearted girl, she was Florence's daughter and Minty didn't like the thought of her being sacked just because Chef liked his girls anorexic.

Chef stood. "You can't do that!"

"It's done. And now, Doris— "

"I know my rights!" said Chef. "Take a look at my contract and— "

"I have," said Minty. "There's nothing in it about a makeover, or opening in the evenings. Doris, are you happy to keep the shop going till Christmas?"

Chef shouted, "We'll see about that!" And strode out of the room.

Minty breathed out, slowly. "Well, now . . . Doris?"

Doris fluttered. "Well, yes, but . . . what happens if Chef walks out? He's temperamental, I know, but all chefs are, aren't they?"

"Leave Chef to me," said Minty. "Now, Doris?"

"Opening till Christmas with new stock? Yes, of course. That is, what sort of budget? I shall have to go to a trade discount warehouse. Goodness knows it's late in the season to . . . but yes, of course. It's a wonderful idea."

"Finally," said Minty, "has everyone brought a suggestion as to how we can improve facilities at the Hall?"

Pieces of paper arrived from every quarter. Some had two or three suggestions on them.

Venetia stood up. "Before we go, I think we'd all like to congratulate Miss Cardale on her engagement to Mr Sands. Won't it be lovely to have a wedding at the Hall? Let's all wish Miss Cardale the very best for the future."

There was a reasonably enthusiastic response.

As Iris was showing the others out, Venetia said hurriedly to Minty, "Toby's thrilled about the job. He finishes his present contract this week and will be with us Monday or Tuesday. Isn't that great?" She was glowing with excitement.

"We certainly need him," said Minty. *But can we afford him?*

After they'd gone Minty sank into a chair and lifted the heavy hair from her neck. *Phew! Was I nervous! Did I wind Chef up enough? If only he'd walk off the job!*

The phone rang. Patrick. "Minty, have you enough money to cover the wages this month? If not, I'll transfer some funds."

Minty gasped. "But . . . !"

"Think of it as a loan, if you must. Are you with Lloyds Bank? Yes? Consider it done. Now, about the money Simon took. Did you find out where it's gone?"

"Debts, he said. All we know for sure is that most went to some people called 'F & F'. 'Fribbles and Fancy'? 'Facts and Figures'?"

"Furlong & Foster."

"Never heard of them."

"Yes, you have. They're your father's solicitors, your solicitors now. You met old Mr Furlong when the will was read."

"I was in a daze that day. I remember Lord Asher read the will, but . . ."

"As your father's executor, yes. Old Mr Foster had lost his voice. Why don't you give them a ring, see if they know anything about the missing millions?" He put the phone down.

A vista of possibilities opened up in Minty's mind. Something Gemma had said . . . ?

The phone rang again, and Iris answered it. "That was Lady Cardale, back from London. She's got guests for lunch and wishes you to join her."

"Hm? What guests? Is Gemma around?"

Iris was staring out of the west window. That was the beauty of the tower room; it had windows which faced east, south over the lake, and west over the entrance to the Great Hall.

Minty went to look, too. Two expensive cars had drawn up on the semi-circular sweep of gravel below. No cars were usually allowed to park there, but that had never stopped Simon in the past and it wasn't stopping him now. He hopped out of his Porsche, sun glinting on designer sunglasses. A chauffeur opened the door of the second car and two tall, well-dressed men got out and looked around as if they owned the place. One of them carried a briefcase. Simon shook hands, laughing with them.

Iris' pretty mouth took on an ugly shape. "You Christians preach that one should forgive. I can't accept that."

"Forgiveness isn't easy," said Minty, "but . . ."

"I don't suppose you've ever felt towards anyone as I feel towards Simon."

Minty was silent, for Patrick had shown her that she still hated those who'd wronged her. "Who are those people? Simon's practically licking their boots."

Serafina had come in and was peering over their shoulders. "Those clothes aren't British. Americans?"

Minty guessed. "The people who want to turn the Hall into a health farm?" Simon and his mother were all for it, and would have been directors of the company that was to run it, but she'd told the Americans she wasn't interested, so why were they here?

Minty's mobile rang again. It was Patrick. "Money transferred, so you can pay the wages. Also, the Reverend Cecil says he can fit us in about half past four. All right? The best person to speak to at Furlong & Foster is 'young' Mr Foster. Frank. He's a friend of mine but I can't approach him about this."

"Patrick, some Americans have arrived, acting as if they own the place. Lady C's invited me to have lunch with them. What do I do?"

"Speak to Frank before you speak to them. Be wise as the serpent and as mild as a dove." Patrick's voice sharpened. "I've got another client. See you at four thirty."

He disconnected. Iris and Serafina were looking at Minty for orders and she didn't know what orders to give.

The men had disappeared inside.

She leaned back against the wall. Simon couldn't force her to sign. Eden Hall was hers. It belonged to her by right of law and through her ancestors. She didn't know what tricks he had up his sleeve, but she was not, repeat not, going to let him bully or cheat her out of it. The very stones under her hands seemed to agree. They seemed warm to the touch, acknowledging her right to defend them.

Dear Lord, tell me what to do. Simon has done so much damage to so many people . . . even to his sister . . . It would be wonderful to have a sister I could love, but I can't trust Gemma.

Perhaps there's a way to appease the Americans, though. Suppose . . . ?

"Iris, I need to speak to Mr Frank Foster, of Furlong & Foster. He's our family solicitor, apparently."

"Didn't I give you a message from a Mr Foster, who wanted to make an appointment with you? I'm sorry, I ought to have realised who he was."

"I didn't recognise the name either," said Minty, "so I didn't bother to ring him back . . . which may turn out to have been a mistake."

Iris looked up the number, punched it in, spoke, listened and turned back to Minty. "He's got a client with him, whom he's taking out to lunch. He may not be available till mid-afternoon. Shall I ask him to ring you back?"

Minty nodded. What other way was there to get at the truth? "Will you give my apologies to Lady Cardale? Say I'm unable to join her and her guests for lunch, but they'd be welcome to come up here afterwards for coffee. Then get Barr back up here with the accounts. I want to know if Simon has made any payments to an estate agent within the last three months. Yes, I said estate agent. Hurry, it's urgent. Serafina, is Gemma back yet?"

"Florence said she came back early this morning and has crashed out."

Minty raced through her rooms to the far tower and down the stairs to Gemma's. She pounded on the door and called Gemma's name. No reply.

She got out her bunch of keys and found the one that fitted. She shot through into Gemma's bedroom and found that Serafina had spoken the truth. Gemma was sprawled across the bed, half naked and unconscious. Minty shook her arm. No reaction. On the floor beside the bed were Gemma's two precious files, the one for a wedding that would not now take place and the other for . . .

"Peacock Place," said Minty, rescuing the details of the house Simon had been buying for Miles and Gemma. Was this where the three million had gone? Minty leafed through the details. The estate agents were . . . Eastwick and Briant.

Minty pulled the duvet over Gemma and fled back upstairs.

Barr was already there, looking through a mountain of cheque stubs with Iris. He smelled of sherry.

"Oh, Barr, I need you sober!"

"Only a slurp, my dear. Brain working OK, honest. You want the list of all the things Simon's paid for out of the different Hall accounts, right?"

"First I need to trace one or more payments to an estate agent called Eastwick & Briant. Give me some of those cheque stubs and I'll look, too."

Silence while they worked.

Iris shook her head. "Nothing in my lot."

"Not here, either. It has to be somewhere!" Minty paced the floor. Serafina hovered in the doorway, which made Minty think of something else that might help in the forthcoming interview. "Serafina, can you get hold of Reggie? I want him to collect my father's portrait from the library and hang it in the sitting room up here over the fireplace."

Barr said, "Nothing in mine, either."

Minty pushed her hair back from her face. "I must think crooked, like Simon. I know! Iris, here's the letterhead of the firm he was buying the house from. There's three partners—no, four. See if you can find an entry for any one of them. Eastwick, Briant, Purvey and Price."

Silence.

Then Iris said in a hushed voice. "Mr S Purvey. A cheque for twenty-five hundred made out to him personally, not to his firm."

Barr lifted a hand. "Wait a minute. Miles boasted that Simon was buying a house for him and Gemma? Is that where the three million went? 'F & F'. It rings a bell. No, I still can't place it."

"Furlong & Foster, solicitors," said Minty.

Barr slapped the desk. "Of course! We used to deal with old Mr Furlong but he's past it, and there's a new young chap come into the firm. Foster, that's it."

Minty glanced at the clock. How long would the Americans take to eat lunch? She pushed her hair back from her face. "Let's see if we can work it out. This summer my father was dying. Simon was in charge of everything, believed he'd inherit everything and had a tame accountant in tow. He'd run the Hall down so much that it no longer afforded him a good living, so he thought up a splendid plan: he'd lease it to the Americans while retaining a directorship of the company which was to run the place.

"Miles was Simon's best mate and engaged to Gemma, but Miles couldn't afford to buy a big house like Peacock Place on his own. Simon was planning to shovel responsibility for the Hall off onto the Americans and there was all that money sitting in the Buildings and Maintenance Fund. So he took it out to buy Peacock Place for Miles and Gemma, going through the Cardale family solicitors. At least, we hope that's what happened."

Iris frowned. "Why would he buy them such a big place?"

"Perhaps he planned to move to Peacock Place with them? Perhaps he planned to raise a mortgage on it, which would ease his cash-flow problem? Remember, buying it didn't cost him a penny."

Barr said, "Then you returned and Simon discovered that far from being the heir apparent, he wasn't going to be left enough even to cover his debts."

Minty nodded. "I refused to have anything to do with the Americans, so that lucrative deal fell through. Miles landed in prison and Gemma called off the wedding. Simon now had an expensive house on his hands, no income and a load of debt. Question: why didn't he raise a mortgage on Peacock Place? Answer: because the title deeds were in the name of the Hall, and not in his name. At least, I hope so. Gemma told me the other day that he'd put the house back on the market."

"It could all be above board," said Barr. "How could it benefit him, if the title deeds are in the Hall's name?"

"I don't know!" wailed Minty. "Except . . . wait a minute. He paid Mr Purvey at the estate agency something on the side when he bought the property. Why? Because Mr Purvey helped him get the property cheaply? Perhaps he's hoping Mr Purvey will juggle the figures for him again. Simon's not been straight with me about it, remember. When I asked him where the money had gone he said it was to pay his debts, and that stopped me investigating further. I think he's giving himself time to sell the property and rake off a nice little commission. I think the Hall does own the house and if so . . ."

Barr tapped his teeth with a pen. "What if we do? How does that help you in dealing with the Americans?"

Minty looked at the clock again. "Ring, Mr Foster, ring!" She began to pace the floor. "Perhaps there's another way to get at the truth.

Let's follow up that cheque to Mr Purvey. Iris, can you get one of the senior partners at the estate agents on the phone?"

"Mr Eastwick," said Iris, handing over the receiver.

It took Minty twenty minutes to find out all she needed to know and to give the senior partner all he needed to know. She put the phone down with a clatter. "Simon did buy Peacock Place, and the solicitors he used were Furlong & Foster. The house is worth far more than three million, but Mr Purvey persuaded the vendors to accept a lower price so that Simon could afford it—and took a nice little backhander for himself by way of services rendered. The house is now back on the market with a price tag of four million, which is what it's really worth!"

Barr and Iris gasped.

Minty grinned. "The disclosure that Simon paid Mr Purvey twenty-five hundred has caused his senior partner considerable alarm. Exit Mr Purvey."

Serafina came back into the room. "Reggie's fetching the portrait. I asked Florence to let me know when Lady Cardale's party would be on its way up. Ten minutes, she says."

Minty looked at the clock. "Come on, Mr Foster, ring! Whose name is on the title deeds? Simon's, or ours?"

Ruby appeared in the doorway, holding up the freshly laundered white silk blouse which Minty had worn to the opening ceremony of the school in London. "Minty, you're not going to an important meeting wearing a creased blouse."

"They're on their way," reported Serafina.

Still Mr Foster had not rung back. Minty quickly changed her blouse, then went through into the cool green sitting room, where Reggie had taken down the mirror and replaced it with her father's portrait. Minty put her hands on the mantelpiece and looked up into the eyes of the portrait.

Sir Micah seemed to be looking down on her with loving-kindness. She was his daughter, and it wouldn't do any harm to remind her visitors of that fact.

She flicked back her hair and exchanged her sapphire and diamond ring for the cool brilliance of the blue diamond. Simon walked in, alone.

"I thought I'd better set the scene." He put a bottle of champagne down on the coffee table. He had a camera slung around his neck. "Serafina, you old bag, find us some glasses."

"I don't know what you think you're doing," said Minty. "I've no intention of leasing the Hall to anyone."

"You haven't enough money to pay the wages. The bank won't lend you money to underwrite your fantasies, and when the electricity and council tax bills come in, you'll be bankrupt. So be a good sweet girl and listen to what the nice men have to offer."

In stalked Lady Cardale in a black suit with an asymmetric neckline. Behind her came two large Americans with watchful eyes, brilliant teeth and immaculate tailoring. Their tans were as good as Simon's, and their manners better.

"Jules. Derringer. My stepdaughter, Araminta."

The Americans acknowledged the introduction with grave smiles. They were both so large and so tall that Minty had to look up and up to meet their eyes. Eyes which told her nothing.

Simon put a glass of champagne in her hand and cried, "Watch the birdie!" His camera flashed, and Minty realised he'd caught her standing between the two Americans.

"Here's to us!" cried Simon. "And now, who's got the cheque?"

The bulkier American produced a cheque from his pocket and held it up above her shoulder, just as Simon let off his flash camera again.

"The moment of truth," said Lady Cardale, acid in her voice.

Minty could see how much the cheque was made out for. With that money she could keep the Hall afloat till probate was granted, save people's jobs, start all sorts of initiatives in the village. She could feel her heart thumping.

Simon looked triumphant. *Money can buy you anything!* Simon was mistaken.

Simon was grinning. "You can buy yourself a house in London, visit all the Paris fashion shows, spend half the year in Barbados, if you wish. Raise your glasses, everyone! To our future!"

They all drank but Minty, who asked the Americans, "You are paying Simon a commission on this?"

Derringer's eyes sharpened. Jules hadn't caught the warning signal and proceeded, "All taken care of. Good of you to think of your family, Miss Cardale."

"Goodness has nothing to do with it," said Minty.

Lady Cardale was looking up at the portrait of her husband. It seemed to disturb her. Simon busied himself taking photographs of the group. "Well, I suppose the time has come for the grand signing. Everyone got their pens ready?"

One of the Americans produced a sheaf of papers from his briefcase and laid them out on the table with a flourish. He stood over Minty and pointed to a space for her signature.

Simon was agog. Minty looked at her watch. When would Mr Foster ring? She must buy some time. She could pretend to go along with the charade for a while, couldn't she?

"Oh, but I have to read it first," she cried with girlish enthusiasm. "My solicitor told me never to sign anything without reading it through."

Everyone else smiled, though some of the smiles were a little thin. Minty took a seat and began to read the document through. It was a long document, and very detailed. Still Mr Foster didn't ring. Finally she threw the papers down and gave a trilling little laugh. "Oh, it's all gobbledegook to me! I've never been able to cope with legal terminology."

"Let's get it over with," cried Simon, losing patience. "Sign on the dotted line."

At that very moment Iris signalled to Minty from the doorway. Minty excused herself and rushed to take the phone in the tower room. It was—thank God—Mr Frank Foster returning her call, and very much at her service. Would she care to drop in one day soon? There was a great deal to discuss and . . .

"Yes, yes. I will. But in the meantime, I have a problem."

Five minutes later she put the phone down, punched the air to convey that it was good news to Iris and Barr and returned to her guests.

"You want me to sign something," said Minty, picking up the document. She slashed through the first mention of the Hall, and wrote in another name.

"Wha–a–t!" said Jules.

Minty produced a sunny, confiding smile. "Your solicitor's got the name wrong, silly man. You're leasing Peacock Place, not the Hall."

Simon turned to ice, eyes wide.

Derringer blinked. "Explain yourself, Miss Cardale."

"Miss Cardale," said Jules, "we know you're in trouble financially and willing to lease the Hall. You invited us here to . . ."

"I didn't invite you," said Minty. Then, "No, that's childish. Gentlemen, there's been a misunderstanding. The Hall is not available, no matter what Simon says."

"We were given to understand that—"

"Wishful thinking, I'm afraid. Didn't you get my letter, saying I had no intention of selling? Even if I were, you'd never get planning permission to convert the Hall to a health farm."

Jules reddened. "Then why have you played us along today?"

"I wanted to offer you something else, but had to get a legal point cleared up first. If you gentlemen are looking for a large country house which you can convert without too much trouble, I happen to own exactly what you want."

Simon drew in his breath but didn't protest.

Minty smiled. "Peacock Place is smaller than this but has eighteen bedrooms, six baths, reception rooms galore, and extensive outbuildings which can easily be converted to treatment rooms. Splendid Victorian conservatory, twenty acres of luxuriously wooded grounds. Vacant possession, all mains laid on. It's on the market for four million pounds but considering all the trouble you've been put to, I'm prepared to lease it to you on reasonable terms."

The larger of the Americans loomed over her. "You're not in financial trouble? Not on the verge of bankruptcy?"

"In your dreams!" said Minty, inelegantly.

The large American's eyes narrowed and he glanced at Simon, who'd turned as red as he'd been pale before. Lady Cardale drained her glass and dabbed at her upper lip.

Jules said, "Simon, what do you have to say?"

Simon raised his shoulders. Attempted a laugh. "She doesn't know what she wants two minutes together. Yesterday she was all for it. Today she's changed her mind. Tomorrow it'll be another story."

Minty decided to ignore that. "I think, Jules, that you should take a look at Peacock Place."

The large American swung round to look at Simon and Lady Cardale. And back to Minty. "This is all very . . ."

"Clever," said Derringer. "Very clever, Miss Cardale. It's been an experience, dealing with you. I assume, since you are such a very clever young lady, that Peacock Place is exactly as you describe it."

"Never set eyes on it," said Minty. "But I shall find it saleable, if it isn't what you want. I rather hope it is. It would be good to have such businesslike and pleasant neighbours." She showed him the details. "Just what you want."

Derringer bit back a hasty retort. He was on the verge of losing his temper, but controlled himself with an effort. Somewhat ungraciously he said, "Well, we'll talk again once we've seen the place. Jules, you agree?"

He shook her hand and to his enormous credit, didn't try to mangle it, though his far superior strength would have enabled him to do so. He looked up at the portrait of Sir Micah, then back at her. Almost, he smiled. "I knew your father. I'm sorry we can't get the Hall, but I remember him saying how fond he was of the place. Perhaps this is what he would have wished."

"Thank you. You are very kind. I'm really sorry you've been put to so much trouble."

She shook hands with Jules and pressed the papers on Peacock Place into his hands. Simon slid his fury under cover and said, "No great harm done, then?" They inclined their heads towards him and withdrew . . . closely followed by Lady Cardale, who had drunk several glasses of champagne while staring at the portrait of her dead husband . . . which had seemed, to Minty's eyes, to be staring back at her.

As soon as the door closed behind them, Simon turned on Minty with a growl. His arm swept round to hit her but she managed to avoid him by stumbling back into the settee. If he'd been a cat, he'd have spat at her. He caught hold of her arm, twisting it up . . .

. . . and released it because Serafina was holding the door open for him to leave.

He said, "We'll speak again." He left, his eyes promising revenge.

Minty shivered. The scene had cost her something in nervous energy. She wept a little, from relief and exhaustion.

But at least the Hall was safe for the time being.

Chapter Sixteen

At half past four she rang the bell at the vicarage, wondering if Patrick had arrived before her. At that moment he came up behind her, and his hands clasped her shoulders. She leaned back against him.

"My darling girl, you've been crying!"

No one else had noticed.

She put his hand to her cheek. "Relief from tension. The wages cheques have gone out and by the time they're presented, the money you've lent me will have been cleared. I don't know what I'd have done if . . . I suppose the bank might have agreed to . . . but as it is . . ."

"Think nothing of it. It was a fiendish plot to get you in my power. Did you speak to Frank Foster?"

"Yes, and I palmed the Americans off with Peacock Place. Simon—" she shuddered—"was not amused. I'm trying not to think about it. Do you think Cecil will want me to take the children for Sunday School this week?"

"I'm stewarding; that is, unless some child gets itself locked in, or a window pane is smashed and needs boarding over. These things do seem to happen on a Sunday morning."

She flicked lint from his lapel. "You'd rather do anything than stick to routine, wouldn't you? Will every meal have to wait while you do odd jobs for others?"

He fingered his chin. "Do I overdo it? Did you ring the bell? It sticks sometimes. Hark at me. Babbling. Must be nervous." He pressed the bell, harder. "Do you think Cecil will expect me to wear my heart on my sleeve?"

The door opened and the Reverend Cecil beckoned them in with apologies; he'd had to dash up to the old people's home, been kept longer than he'd expected, come through to the study, this way, mind the hole in the carpet. How good it had been of Minty to take the children last Sunday, though he was afraid it had upset their usual teacher, a fine woman, been teaching the children for twenty years. He'd promised to have a word with Minty about it, not wanting to create waves, you know, and perhaps Minty would like to take the children only when their usual teacher was away, he was sure she'd agree.

The Reverend Cecil was a shortish, skinny, youngish man, who'd once been curate to Minty's uncle. While Minty had never thought Cecil a great brain, he'd impressed her as a humble servant of God. Originally Cecil had tried to co-opt her as a parish worker and later asked her out. Minty reflected that this meeting could have tricky undercurrents.

In fact, Cecil did find their haste to be married somewhat surprising. Minty and Patrick answered all his questions calmly and correctly, but still Cecil hesitated. At last he said, "I'm not convinced ..."

Patrick broke in, impatience showing. "You don't have to be. It's our decision to marry in church, but if you don't wish to marry us we can always arrange a registry office wedding next week."

Cecil looked pleadingly at Minty. "Are you really sure?"

"Yes," said Minty. "I couldn't marry anyone else but Patrick and—let's make it easy for you, Patrick—he says he can't marry anyone but me."

"Is that true, Patrick?" Cecil asked.

"I suppose so." Patrick fidgeted with his wrist watch. "If Minty were to ask me to jump in the lake fully clad, I suppose I'd do it. Reserving the right to complain afterwards."

Cecil didn't like it, but he gave in. "So ... when ...?"

"Three Sundays to read the banns. We marry the following Saturday."

"Y–yes. Eleven o'clock? A great day for the village. Choir and organist? Yes. A rehearsal the night before? It's best. Any special readings ... hymns ... you haven't thought about it yet? May I suggest we have the usual ..."

"We'll let you know early next week."

"You'll want your uncle to take the service?"

"No," said Minty. "And Lord Asher will give me away."

Patrick rubbed his ear but didn't comment. Cecil, however, grew animated. "Your uncle, my dear Minty, I mean ... he will expect!"

"No," said Minty firmly. "My aunt is not well, and I doubt if either of them will make the service."

Once outside, she turned on Patrick, daring him to argue with her.

Patrick put up his hands. "Your decision, Minty."

Minty was abrupt. "It was you who asked Lord Asher to give me away, which I was thinking my uncle might do. I suppose you have to go back to work now, but will you come up to the Hall for supper and view your future living quarters? Serafina's cooking tonight."

"I'll be there."

Annie was drinking tea in the sitting room when Minty returned, while Serafina hovered in the background. Minty threw herself down into a chair, said "Ouch" because it didn't give. She forced her mind back to the Foundation.

"Dear Annie, am I still in disgrace? Tell me what happened in London."

Annie looked tired, and for the first time Minty speculated as to her age. Late fifties? Possibly even early sixties?

"I was sorry that you did not see fit to attend."

Minty threw up her hands. "I had to decide: Foundation or Hall. You know where my heart is, but that doesn't mean I'm not interested in what went on in London."

"The trustees were not happy. When all the shouting had died down—and most of that was directed at you, I'm sorry to say—they agreed that Simon be appointed a director of the building firm and receive an 'introduction' fee from the architect. Then we had to pacify the builder and the architect, so the trustees voted to award them the contract to build the next school for the Foundation."

Minty had thought she was too tired to get angry and discovered she'd been wrong. "That's disgraceful. You know the last school they built is a shambles!"

"The architect has received prizes for . . ."

"Has anyone asked the teachers? What about my suggestion that we run a survey on past projects? Buried, I suppose, to pacify Simon and his cronies!"

Minty raged about the room, not allowing her voice to rise, but clearly wanting to break something.

Annie closed her eyes for a minute. "My dear Araminta, you know nothing of such—"

"I know when I smell corruption."

"It was the price of your remaining on the Board. Remember, several of them want you to resign."

Minty stopped pacing the room and looked up at her father's portrait. What would he have done? He wouldn't have resigned. No. That would be the easy way out. He'd have stayed on, and worked from the inside . . . as Patrick would. She sat down opposite Annie. "I'm not resigning, and I'll do my best to attend all future meetings."

"It won't win you any prizes in the popularity stakes."

"I don't expect them. I may have been a green girl to start with, but I'm learning."

Annie put her cup down with a snap. "Throwing your weight about, more like. What's this I hear about a meeting with the Americans?"

Serafina had been talking? Carefully Minty explained what had been happening in Annie's absence. It turned out to be quite a lengthy report.

"You think the Americans will take Peacock Place? What will Gemma say?"

"If Gemma were sober for more than five minutes, we might be able to discuss it. As I see it, she's lost the house anyway. Yes, I do think the Americans will want it. It's far more suitable than this place for a health centre. But if they don't, it goes back on the open market and we look for another buyer."

"Serafina says the wages cheques have gone out. I assume you got a loan from the bank for that. Well, you don't seem to have managed too badly in my absence." A pale smile. "That is a very fine diamond you're wearing. I can't say I approve, but I suppose I'm not particularly surprised. Your engagement to a man without money or influence was, of course, a topic for discussion up in London today."

Without money or influence? Minty had seen Patrick at work and knew better, but she didn't argue. "We're getting married in just over three weeks' time." Minty took a deep breath. "Dear Annie, will you help us organise the wedding and reception? No one could do it better."

"Your aunt?"

Minty shook her head. "She's not well, and in any case I wouldn't ask her."

Serafina spoke from the doorway. "Florence has made a start on baking the cake, Ruby's asked Jonah to prepare the wedding bouquet, Mrs Chickward rang to say that she's prepared plans for the flowers in church and for the Long Gallery where the reception is to be held. And Reggie wants to know if he should order a white limousine to take you to the church, or will you go in your father's car."

"Gracious!" said Annie, faintly. "What about a wedding dress? Is there time to get one made?"

Serafina grinned. "Minty bought that in London."

Annie stared. "Before you met Sir James, or after?"

Minty looked self-conscious. "Before. I was determined to marry Patrick, no matter what. I just had to convince Patrick we were doing the right thing. So, Annie. Will you give us your blessing and help us arrange everything? I really can't ask my stepmother . . ."

"No, indeed," said Annie. "Is there time to do everything properly? The wedding invitations! Have you a list of who you want to invite? Does Lady Cardale know you're getting married? Who will do the catering? Who are to be the ushers? The best man? The ceremony . . . what hymns? Will your uncle take the service or—"

"Dear Annie, Patrick's coming to supper this evening. We'll discuss everything then."

Back to work. What next? Minty disentangled the brochure on Eden Hall from the papers on her desk. She read it through again, because on first reading she hadn't noticed any information about the Eden family. Possibly Lisa had thought it unimportant? Or perhaps there was another brochure somewhere which focused on them? While she was waiting for Patrick, Minty went down to have a look.

The last of the day's visitors had gone and the sky was clouding over. The dark panelling in the Great Hall encouraged shadows, but someone had created a stunning arrangement of autumn leaves on a pewter platter in the middle of the banqueting table. Was this some of Jonah's work? She must remember to thank him.

Minty scanned the brochures on the table and found just one crumpled leaflet referring to the Edens. As she did so, she heard a footfall on the staircase behind her.

Simon. She froze.

He came down the stairs with his forefinger pointing at her as if he were aiming a gun. He grinned, teeth gleaming. She shrank against the table, then stiffened her spine. Never show fear.

He tucked her hair behind her ear. Not smiling now. Eyes half closed.

"How did you manage to pay the wages, my pretty? Is the bank really going to tide you over?"

"None of your business." *Don't mention Patrick. There's too much bad blood between them already.*

"So what am I going to do with you, eh?" He grasped the back of her neck and shook her. She was jammed against the banqueting table. She couldn't move. If she screamed, no one would hear.

"I've been trying to think of a suitable punishment for you. I asked myself if it would amuse me to destroy your looks. But no, that would be crude. Don't worry, I'll think of something soon . . . something appropriate . . . and then I'll let you know what it is. It will be something for you to look forward to."

He flicked his fingers, and she started. He smiled. And left her.

She clung to the table, scolding herself for letting him frighten her. He was bluffing, of course. He hadn't really meant it.

Storm clouds were building up outside.

It was raining when Patrick rang the bell and Minty let him in. Thunder rolled away over the Park. *Giants moving furniture upstairs,* thought Minty, remembering childhood stories. "This way." She led him through the rooms which had until recently been occupied by the Foundation, and which were now empty, dusty, waiting to be rewired. From there they passed into the cloisters. Rain thudded down into the courtyard, but inside the cloisters they were dry.

"Hold on a minute." He considered the forlorn fountain in the middle and turned on his heel to look up at each of the wings in turn. "Do you come this way at night?"

"It's a bit spooky at the moment, I admit, but during the day there's people working in the Estate Offices, and Florence in the family's kitchen at the end."

"This place must be a nightmare to secure at night. How many people have keys?"

"Barr locks up last thing at night, I suppose. I haven't really thought about it."

"Isn't there an outside door directly into your tower?"

She shook her head. Trust Patrick to put his finger on a weak point. "I'll talk to Barr about security. How do you fancy living in a Gothic ruin?"

"I have my mind firmly fixed on the four-poster bed and Serafina's cooking."

He was being very positive about coming to live at the Hall. Somehow she must make their rooms comfortable—but how?

"Four poster first." She led him up the stairs to the first floor. "Tra-la!" she said, standing aside to let him see the great four poster.

"Wow!" He was impressed. He prowled all around it while she released the cords which held back the side curtains. She pulled off the plastic cover and climbed up onto the bed, inviting him to join her.

"This is something else! Oughtn't we to have taken off our shoes first? Ouch. I like a hard mattress, but this would be torture."

"If I get a new mattress and pillows, would it do?"

He stroked her cheek. "Don't be so defensive. It's fabulous. All we need is a bell pull within reach. I'll stretch out my arm and summon slaves to waft in our meals. I could work here, with my laptop and mobile. A power point for a couple of lights, a bookcase and a hostess trolley, and I need never leave this room as long as I live."

She thought of his bare, monk-like cell of a bedroom. "I know you need your own space. We'll have to find you a room where nobody else is allowed to go."

"Isn't the chapel somewhere above this?"

"Yes, but . . . well, there's a toilet of sorts next door in what used to be a powdering closet, but it's not very nice, and I think we'd better go upstairs for the bathroom. Come and see."

She took him up the stairs and through the door into her suite of rooms. The spare bedroom was occupied by Ruby and her sewing machine. Minty's own blue bedroom with its luxurious bathroom lay beyond. Serafina appeared to show him her own quarters which overlooked the Fountain Court, and then accompanied them through the starkness of the dining room into the stiffness of the sitting room beyond.

Annie joined them, smilingly proud of the décor of these rooms. "Sir Micah had a top designer create all this. It cost a bomb, but it was well worth it."

"Splendid," said Patrick, being civil. He inspected the sea and sky-scapes on the walls. "These are rather wonderful. I almost wish I'd known the man."

Annie's smile faded but Minty nodded. He'd got his point across. He hated the uncomfortable furniture but he liked the pictures. She showed him her father's office, bleak and businesslike, and the workaday tower office beyond.

"That's all," she said, "but I'm working on it."

Patrick nodded, on his best behaviour.

"These rooms were Sir Micah's favourites because of the view," said Annie.

Patrick inspected the view and agreed it was stunning. The rain had almost stopped, and a fine gauzy mist overhung the Park, fading the trees into the dusk.

Serafina and Annie were pleased with Patrick. Minty despaired. What could she possibly do to make the place more home-like? More like his own home?

Serafina served a delicious supper of leek soup, grilled trout with almonds, and a salad. Followed by a date and walnut pudding which caused Patrick to compliment her and have two helpings. Followed by coffee in the sitting room.

Minty sat twisting a lock of hair between her fingers, frowning as she considered the problem of their living quarters. Perhaps there was some comfortable furniture in store somewhere. She'd hardly had time to explore yet. Suppose she asked Reggie and Ruby to help her look ... but then, what would Serafina and Annie say? They thought the place was perfect as it stood.

Annie opened her laptop. "So let's talk about the wedding."

Minty tried to concentrate. "The date and the church are fixed, and I have my wedding dress. I'll ask Gemma to be bridesmaid and she can choose her own outfit. I'll talk to her about it as soon as she sobers up."

Patrick took up the tale. "The church is booked. Cecil's taking the service and Lord Asher is giving Minty away. If we can decide on the wording for the wedding invitations now, we can get them printed in a couple of days in town."

Annie nodded. "It's usual for the parents of the bride to issue the invitations, but I spoke to Lady Cardale and she said she'd be leaving the Hall that day and would not be present. Would the Reverend Reuben and Mrs Agnes Cardale be prepared to act as hosts, together with Mr Sands senior?"

Minty shook her head. "My aunt's not well and they couldn't cope." The excuse came glibly now. Annie raised an eyebrow but didn't object. Patrick gave her a sharp look which meant, "We'll discuss this later."

Patrick said, "It's not uncommon nowadays for the bride and groom to invite the guests, RSVP to the Hall. I've roughed something out . . ." He produced a couple of sheets of paper and laid them before Minty, who nodded and passed them on to Annie. "And my guest list." He produced another piece of paper and a floppy disc. "All the names and addresses are on the disc, and here's the name of a local printer who can be relied on to turn the order round in twenty-four hours. Ushers . . . these three should do, I think."

Minty opened her mouth, but he forestalled her. "Yes, of course Ian Thornby is to be one of them. My partner will be best man, as I was for him. A lot of these people Minty won't know, but they'll want to know her."

"But . . . !" Annie looked over the list. "The Lord Lieutenant, and also Lady . . . ? And I thought this man was a recluse . . ."

"A gentleman of the old school," said Patrick comfortably. "He collects vintage cars. Minty will like him and he'll like her. I was at school or university with some of these people. Then there's my godfather, and a few friends of my father's. They'll all want to come if they can manage it at such short notice."

Annie eyed him with respect for the first time. "How long have you had this all worked out?"

"I've had twenty years to think about it," said Patrick, "but I don't suppose Minty has given it a second's thought."

"Give me a chance. We must invite the Woottons, of course, and the Thornbys. My friend Carol Tinderman and her parents, from the city. Everyone in the village and everyone who works here at the Hall. Have I forgotten anyone important?"

"Yes," said Annie, with a grim smile. "The trustees of the Foundation."

"Yuk," said Minty. "Well, I promise to be polite. I do want all the children at church but no, I'm not having any flower girls or pages. I just want them to come and have a good time. We'll have a buffet spread down one side of the Long Gallery. Lots of fruit cup, some champagne for the toasts, I suppose. Tea and coffee. We get away by four o'clock so that nobody travels back in the dark. Is that all right?"

"The catering," said Annie, looking worried. "I hear that Chef is . . ."

"Being awkward, yes. I'll ask Florence if she can manage with whatever extra help she needs, or get caterers in."

"Service sheets for the church?"

"Patrick and I are discussing them this weekend."

Patrick grinned. "If you ask for 'Onward, Christian Soldiers', I'll object to the marriage."

Minty laughed. Annie looked scandalised, then frowned. And at last almost smiled.

Patrick said, "I'll make arrangements for the honeymoon. I can only manage a fortnight away at the moment. Have you got a passport, Minty?"

She shook her head.

"We might get one through in time. What else is there?"

"Photographer," said Annie, faint but pursuing.

Minty held up a finger. "I'm interviewing someone on Monday or Tuesday who wants to take over doing brochures, photographs, and so on for the Hall. If he's suitable, he can do the photographs."

Annie frowned. "It's all going to cost . . ."

"I'm paying," said Patrick. "Which reminds me, Minty, there's no need for you to borrow from the bank till probate's through. Let me know how much more you think you'll need and I'll transfer it into your account."

Annie gave a little cough. "It's very good of you to offer, Mr Sands, but I hardly think you realise the amount entailed."

Patrick treated her to a bland smile. "Oh, I rather think I do."

Minty shot him a look which said, "We'll discuss this later."

Patrick yawned, and looked out of the window at the rain. "I quite fancy a walk, but . . ."

Minty scrambled to her feet. "That's what the Long Gallery's for, taking exercise on wet days."

It was dark on the stairs, but she didn't fear Simon now that Patrick was with her. She switched on some of the lights nearest the door of the Long Gallery, striking glints of gold from the frames of the pictures but leaving the far end of the room in shadow.

Patrick took her in his arms. "Would madam care to dance? One, two, three . . ."

She began to laugh, following his lead.

They'd danced together at the charity ball, the night Sir Micah faded away. But this was different. This was just the two of them, swinging in great circles around the room, with Minty's laughter rising to the ceiling. As he twirled her around, Minty fancied that the portraits of her ancestors looked down on her with faint smiles on their painted lips. She imagined the people in the portraits dancing here down the years, minuets, waltzes, polkas, rag-time . . . dancing in and out of the shadows . . .

She leaned back in his arms. "Can you do the twiddly bits?"

"Like this?" He did some complicated steps which left her wrong-footed, so he picked her up and whirled her round and round till she cried for mercy.

They collapsed onto a window seat, to discuss the wedding and what hymns and readings they would like. He said, "I insist on 'See the Conquering Hero Comes . . .'"

"If you do, I shall have the Mendelssohn 'Wedding March' and get the choir to sing the version I learned in the Guides, 'Here comes the bride, Forty inches wide . . .'"

He talked about the friends he wanted to invite. "Most of them will be at Mrs Chickward's next week." He stroked her cheek. "Minty, you look tired. I'm concerned that your uncle . . ."

Drowsily she put her finger on his lips. "Not now."

"Have you contacted Frank Foster. What about the money . . . ?"

"Sorted. I'm a clever little girl, I am. I've been such a good girl today, pretending to be grown up and making important decisions.

Kiss me." She raised her face for a kiss, and got it. "Don't send me to bed yet. It's so nice, being here with you."

He opened his jacket and she crept inside its warmth. "You look no more than five years old. You'll be putting your thumb back in your mouth any minute."

She stared into space, remembering when she'd stopped sucking her thumb.

Partly to himself, Patrick said, "Who'd have thought it, this time last week? You and me here, together." He looked around the vast room, where dusk was beginning to blur pictures and furniture alike. "Shall we dance at our wedding?" He answered his own question. "No. Let's talk and meet people and laugh with the children. Do you want a foreign honeymoon to some far-flung place? Lakes, mountains, ancient monuments . . . you choose."

She shook her head, her eyelids closing. "Just you and me. Somewhere quiet."

"The ideal would be to stay in the four-poster bed upstairs, draw the curtains and let people bring us food and drink, only we can't because the Hall will still be open to the public. I'll find us somewhere quiet, shall I? A hotel in Scotland, perhaps? Up to bed, sleepyhead. Can you walk, or shall I carry you?"

"I can walk, if you give me a goodnight kiss."

Chapter Seventeen

Saturday morning. She jerked awake with the words "market day" running through her head. Was the gardener Hodge involved in something questionable on market days?

It wasn't yet seven o'clock and no one else was up, but people went off to market very early. Perhaps she could catch Hodge at . . . whatever it was he was doing. She was annoyed with Hodge because he hadn't done a thing about clearing the formal garden or mowing the lawns. As far as she could tell, he'd tinkered with the old mower a couple of times and then made himself scarce.

She pulled on jeans and a sweater, noticing that there was a pearly mist outside but that the sun was trying to break through.

After a few minutes in the chapel, she drank some fruit juice and seized a piece of bread on her way to the tower office. She wanted another look at the map of the outbuildings before she started blundering about trying to locate Hodge. Yes, his quarters were . . . there . . . behind the restaurant block in part of the old stables. His house was almost opposite the disused door into the walled garden.

The map showed a second entrance to the walled garden, from the visitor's car park.

She skittered down the stairs, ran across the Fountain Court and through the north wing to let herself out into the courtyard. No one else was about yet. Simon's windows on the top floor were firmly shut against the mist that had closed in around the house.

She turned into the Park, running lightly across the still straggly lawn to the visitors' car park. The wall of the garden rose ahead of her. Rounding a corner she came across large double doors which were standing open but were partially blocked by a white van. The van was half full of crates containing freshly harvested vegetables, leeks, carrots, potatoes. Waiting to be loaded were pails containing newly dug-up wallflower plants. As she watched, Hodge laboured up with a box of onions.

He saw her and nearly dropped his load. Far from being derelict, the walled garden looked to be well tended and productive.

A much younger man appeared, carrying boxes of dried flowers from a lean-to shed against an inner wall. When he saw Minty, he too nearly dropped what he was carrying.

A pale sun began to shine through the mist and reflected from a large greenhouse. Again, there appeared to be nothing dilapidated about it. Far from it. Minty could see ranks of cyclamen and azalea plants inside.

"Going to market?" said Minty.

Hodge just stared but his companion said, "What's it to you?"

Minty said, "Hodge, we need to talk. Your place or mine?"

The younger man took a step back. "Is she . . . is this . . . ?"

Hodge looked at Minty, but spoke to his assistant. "Make yourself scarce. There'll be no market for us today." And to Minty, "Best come to my place." He dumped the box of onions and led the way out of the garden and back to his house in the middle of the old stable block. "Cuppa?" he said.

She shook her head. The place hadn't been decorated for years, but the leather three-piece suite and the giant television looked new. Hodge was unshaven, graceless. Minty wondered if he'd been better groomed when he'd been courting Ruby. It was ludicrous to think of them together.

Minty took a seat and waited for his explanation, which seemed to unnerve him.

He said, "I'm sacked?"

"How long have you been stealing from the estate?"

"Stealing?" He didn't like the sound of that word. "It wasn't stealing. Simon cut my wages. He sacked my nephew—that's my sister's boy that helps me take the stuff to market. Simon didn't care that I'd worked here man and boy for thirty years. He said I could stay on if I liked, and could make up my wages by gardening for people in the village."

That sounded like Simon, all right. "So you arranged to rent the walled garden from him and used it to grow crops to sell in the market?"

"We–ell, not exactly rented it, no. But Simon knew, all right."

"If Simon had known, he'd have demanded a cut. So how much were you paying him?"

Silence.

Hodge was surly. "The land was crying out to be used and Chef didn't want my stuff. He gets everything sent in from town—and then takes a back-hander for it. No one was wronged by it."

"That's not how I see it. There's the sale of the Christmas trees, too . . ."

He shifted uncomfortably. "Well, I had to look to the future. I've no pension."

She sighed. She understood the temptation he'd been under, and she'd a sneaking respect for the old rogue. Perhaps she'd give him a chance to work his way out of trouble. "And how do you see the position now?"

He looked up. "You won't turn a blind eye?"

She shook her head. "First, everyone who works for me gets a proper contract, fair wages and decent accommodation. Second, I need every penny I can rake in to keep the Hall running and make improvements. Third, I need to talk to your nephew, see if there's any way I can employ him, too."

He looked glum. "We were doing all right as we were."

"Look on the bright side. As of this morning, you get a proper wage and we start up a farm shop, selling what you've grown. Drive your van round to the courtyard and set up a trestle table to serve as a stall outside the gift shop. I'll speak to Doris and she'll take the money for you . . . which means you'll be free to replant the urns on the terraces with some of the wallflowers you've grown, and then get on with clearing the formal garden. I'll ask Reggie to see if he can get your motor mower going again. Then I'm going to need Christmas trees of all sizes to decorate the Hall for the festive season, and what's left over we'll sell in the farm shop. Agreed?"

He winced, then nodded.

She knew she'd always have to keep an eye on him.

It was still early, so she spent time prowling around the outbuildings, trying to work out which had been adapted for housing, and who lived where. She thought Chef and Reggie probably occupied the houses on either side of Hodge, but there were other somewhat dilapidated outbuildings farther away which might be put to good use in future.

While she ate breakfast, she scribbled notes to Iris about a contract for Hodge and leafed through the latest stack of messages. One was from Lady Cardale, demanding Minty present herself at ten, as she had a wedding present for her.

Could this be true? It seemed most unlikely.

At nine she knocked on Gemma's door.

"Who's that?" Gemma was lying back in an armchair, dark glasses on and dressed in T-shirt and jeans. Her hair was wet from the shower and she looked ill but was functioning, more or less.

Minty said, "Do you feel well enough to talk?"

"You're going to turn me out with the rest of the family."

"I'd like you to stay, if you'll help me. What I really want to tell you is that I'm marrying Patrick Sands . . ."

Gemma laughed and clutched at her head. "It should have been me getting married, not you!"

Minty reddened, but persisted. "I'd like you to be my bridesmaid."

Gemma moaned. "You're joking!"

"One more thing. Simon bought Peacock Place with money from the Hall accounts so it belongs to the Hall. I'm hoping to lease it to the Americans. I know you dreamed of . . ."

"Get out before I lose my temper!' Gemma curled into a ball, sobbing into her arm.

"Throwing your toys out of your pram won't help. Grow up, Gemma!"

Gemma screamed and thrashed her arms about.

Minty hesitated. "I'll ask Florence to look in on you."

"I'm not having that cow anywhere near me! Do you hear?"

"I hear," said Minty. And left.

Lady Cardale opened the door to Minty. "Do you still dress from the charity shop?"

Minty was wearing her diamond, but was clad in jeans and a sweater with her hair loose around her shoulders.

By way of contrast, Lady Cardale was in one of her designer dresses and looked as if she'd just come from the beauty salon. "I've something to say before you meet my guest. Mrs Collins tells me you've interfered with the arrangements for my charity concert. As I told her, transferring to the Long Gallery will be a disaster. However, it's done now, and if a few of us have to sit in a roomful of empty seats, we'll know who to blame for it."

"There wouldn't have been any concert at all if I hadn't authorised payment to the musicians," said Minty.

"The whole point of these affairs is that they are exclusive. The right sort of people—the people who pay to come to these affairs—do not wish to rub shoulders with all and sundry. And let me make it absolutely clear that you are not invited to join the reception line. Understand?"

Minty produced her social smile. "It never occurred to me."

"Well, now that's settled, you may come and apologise to my old friend for being so rude to him."

A tall, distinguished-looking man with pewter-coloured hair rose at Minty's approach.

Lady Cardale said, "Guy, this is Araminta Cardale, my stepdaughter, who so unexpectedly inherited the Hall. Araminta, this is Guy Hertz, the international dealer in Fine Arts who's found so many wonderful things for Eden Hall. He's been trying to get in contact with you for some time. Finally he appealed to me, and I agreed to arrange this meeting."

Guy Hertz had a charismatic presence, was extremely tall, and looked down his nose at Minty with a charming smile. "My dear Miss Cardale—at last! I fell in love with Eden Hall when I first saw it, so many years ago. Lady Cardale tells me you know nothing about Fine Arts, and I look forward to guiding your footsteps in future."

Minty tried not to be irritated by his patronising tone. She murmured that it was early days yet.

"Of course." He bowed his splendid head. "But we must get our priorities right, mustn't we? The delay has meant missing two wonderful opportunities to enhance your collection. A tapestry that would have graced the Great Hall and a sedan chair. I left urgent messages with your secretary but you failed to respond so both have gone to America. Lost to this country for ever!"

Minty was intrigued. These did indeed sound like the sort of things which would fit in at Eden Hall. "A pity. But no doubt there will be other opportunities."

"Well, certainly." Again that toothy smile. "If you'll instruct your secretary to put me through immediately when I get wind of something interesting? The market is so competitive . . ." He waved his hands in the air.

"I understand."

He flicked a look of triumph at Lady Cardale. It was a something and a nothing, but Minty realised he was showing off to her stepmother, registering that he now had Minty where he wanted her. She narrowed her eyes, thinking that Mr Hertz might be a marvel in his way but that she preferred Carol's father, her old friend from the city who also dealt in antiques.

"Well, now that's settled," said Lady Cardale. "See what Guy has brought you for a wedding present."

Guy placed a shagreen case in Minty's hands. She opened it to disclose a miniature of a fair-haired gentleman in Regency dress.

"One of your famous ancestors, my dear. Sir Piers Eden, who fought under Wellington in the Peninsula War. I had the greatest difficulty in wresting it from a fellow collector, but as soon as I saw it, I knew I had to have it for you."

Minty took the miniature to the window. What did she know of Sir Piers? There'd been a mention of him in the leaflet on the family. Wasn't there a framed silhouette of him on the top corridor? A portly looking gent with side whiskers and plentiful hair brushed forwards in imitation of the Prince Regent? The young man in this miniature was thin, pale and going bald.

Also his eyes were a warm brown, instead of the Eden blue. It was of course possible that an Eden might have had brown eyes, if this and that were taken into consideration. But on the whole, not.

The miniature wasn't signed, dated or ascribed to any particular sitter. She took it off its hook to see if there was a name on the back, but there wasn't. Where the miniature had hung the silk beneath was lighter in colour, but the discoloured area didn't match the portrait, which meant it was not original to the case.

She put the miniature back onto its hook and shut the case up. "Mr Hertz, I'm grateful to you for thinking of me. The miniature is delightful though not, I'm afraid, of Piers Eden. I'm sure it's worth a great deal of money—far more than you should pay for a wedding gift. I do hope you can place it elsewhere."

"Araminta!" gasped Lady Cardale.

Guy's rather prominent eyes became hard. "This is a gift—from me, to you."

Minty shook her head, wondering if he'd deceived himself over the provenance of the miniature, or had tried to deceive her. "It's much too valuable for me to accept. As you probably know, Eden Hall has at present no funds to buy anything."

Lady Cardale was furious. "Your behaviour at the Foundation was bad enough, but this surpasses everything! You are a rude, ignorant little girl who knows nothing about . . . stop flashing that piece of glass in my face!"

One of the lights in the room had found Minty's diamond and made it sparkle.

Mr Hertz frowned. "May I see your ring?"

"It doesn't leave my hand," said Minty, not at all sure she wanted this man pawing her ring.

Lady Cardale made a contemptuous sound. "If it's worth a tenner, I'd be surprised."

Mr Hertz lifted Minty's hand to the light. Producing a lens, he scrutinised the ring. She could see him re-assess her value even as he examined it.

"A fine diamond." His tone was bleak. "And rare. My congratulations, Miss Cardale." For the first time he looked at her with something like respect. "As for the miniature, it's possible I made a mistake. I hope you'll allow me to give you something more suitable instead."

"Of course," said Minty, not meaning it, and ignoring Lady Cardale's bubbling indignation.

Once outside the door, Minty gave way to a fit of the giggles. What a stroke of luck that she'd been able to spot a fake. But—a nasty thought—had he in the past got Lady Cardale to buy pieces for Eden Hall which were not all that they ought to be? Were there frauds among the antiques?

Minty shook off the suspicion. No, of course not. A reputable dealer wouldn't be so stupid. Would he?

She glanced at her watch. Was that really the time? She was running late.

First she must speak to Doris—who was due at the shop any minute now—and tell her about Hodge and the stall in the courtyard. Doris would want to talk about extra Christmas stock for the shop. What sort of a budget ought she to have?

Then she must go on to the restaurant, see if it was looking as dreary as usual, have a word with Chef, see if he'd produced something better to eat than his usual poor-quality fare . . .

She supposed that some day soon things would calm down.

"Iris, why are you here? You're not supposed to work at weekends."

Iris swung away from the computer and handed Minty some papers. "I wouldn't miss this for anything. First, the Americans rang to say they like the look of Peacock Place and want you to take it off the open market pending a detailed survey."

Minty punched the air. "Yes! Tell the estate agents, will you?"

Iris grinned. "There's a pile of letters which need your attention, some congratulating you on your engagement but some begging letters, would you believe! Oh, and you might like to speak to Doris at the gift shop."

"I was there not half an hour ago."

"Since then, that funny little man Jonah who hangs around Ruby has pinched all the bunches of dried flowers that Hodge had given Doris for sale. She wants you to get them back."

Minty shook her head. "He's done a beautiful arrangement in the Great Hall and if he wants to do some more and put them around the house, that's all right by me."

"I'll tell her. Now your uncle rang again and someone called—Lucas—is that right? He sounded angry."

"He's my aunt's nephew, and a bully. Forget him."

"Next I had Alice Mount on the phone, the girl who cleans the holiday cottages. She wants to see you urgently, but before you vanish again would you look at these drafts for the wedding invitations? I've been ringing round some printers, and the one Patrick suggested is best. If you agree to the wording and type faces—I've given you several to choose from here—then I can fax them the invitation, they can set it up, fax me back a proof and if you agree to that, they'll print this evening and Reggie can pick them up first thing on Monday."

"Brilliant. I like the top one best. Can you fax a copy to Patrick to see if he agrees?"

Serafina came in with some good coffee while they were talking. The phone kept ringing and the answerphone kept clicking in.

Serafina said, "There's an angry young man here to see you. Says he's your cousin."

Lucas charged into the room rather like the young bull he so much resembled. Temper had darkened his complexion, and his straw-coloured hair was dishevelled. He made no apologies for breaking in on them. Lucas never thought he needed to apologise for anything.

"There you are! Do you realise I had to pay to leave my car in your car park!"

"Lucas, it's a pleasure to see you, too," said Minty. "Won't you sit down and tell me why you're here?"

"*Sit down?* I haven't time to sit down! I should be out showing customers around at this very minute, and you want me to *sit down*?"

Iris swung back to her machine, while Minty gently urged Lucas into the sitting room.

"Calm down and tell me what's wrong."

He wiped his forehead. "Your uncle's half out of his mind. He's been ringing you every hour on the hour. It's all very well you being so high and mighty with all this—" he gestured around him—"but in an emergency . . ."

Minty refused to react. "My aunt's fallen down the stairs again, I suppose? Well, I'm sorry, but as you can see, I do have other responsibilities. You must find someone to help her with the housework."

Lucas said, in a shaking voice, "I could wring your neck. She hasn't just fallen down the stairs. She's snapped a ligament in her leg and broken her left arm and she's in hospital."

Minty tried to sound sympathetic. "I'm sorry to hear it. I promised to pay for her knee operation to be done privately, but then things went haywire here and . . . well, you don't need to hear my troubles."

"*Your* troubles? Would I have hared across the country, missing a day's work, if that was all?" He made a big effort to control himself. "The thing is, Aunt Agnes has got a respiratory infection, so they can't operate or pin the bone till it's cleared up. She's in a National Health Service hospital. The hospital says she can't be moved, but Uncle Reuben says that if he got her moved to a private hospital she'd get better attention, and they'd operate straight away. He can't rest, tries phoning you every hour . . . but I've already said that. As a last resort he said I must fetch you, so you could arrange things with the hospital." He was running out of energy.

Minty looked into space. She didn't want to go. The hatred that she'd always felt for her aunt boiled up inside her, hitting the back of her throat.

She tried to keep calm, to pray for guidance.

God wouldn't want her to help her aunt. Would He?

She struggled with herself. Why should she answer their call for help, when they'd treated her so badly?

She'd far more important things to think about. To do. People to see. Busy, busy.

What would Patrick say? She hadn't the faintest idea. She wasn't going to tell him, anyway, because he was such a soft touch he might suggest she go.

"I don't know," she said to Lucas. "I've got so much on here."

Lucas exploded. "*Of course you know!* You've got to come with me!"

"I don't *have* to do anything. I'll ring my uncle and discuss it. I don't suppose anything can be done about getting her into another hospital over a weekend, anyway."

He said heavily, "Minty, this is not like you. You used to be so quick to help others. Your uncle said he thought the money had gone to your head but I said, no, you weren't like that. Perhaps he's right and wealth has corrupted you. When we were together . . ."

"We were never 'together', Lucas. We were engaged for a very short time, but that was more because my aunt wanted it, than because we wanted it ourselves. Be frank with me, Lucas. I'm not your type, am I? Even when you did take me out, you were always looking at other girls. I expect you've found someone far more suitable since I left."

"Yes, well. The new manageress is . . . that is, I think she might . . . but that's entirely beside the point."

Minty said, "There's another thing. My aunt and uncle are moving into sheltered accommodation soon, which means you'll lose your free board and lodging at the vicarage. Have you made plans for that?"

He rubbed the back of his neck. "Come on, now, Minty. You know very well that they're planning to move here, and of course I'll come with them. They couldn't manage without me now."

"What do you do for them? Shop and cook? Clean? Help with the bills? You don't do any of that, do you? And you couldn't commute to the city from here, could you? Sorry, Lucas. I'm not extending hospitality to them, or to you. I've plans for the Hall and can't afford to lose any part of it—especially to non-paying guests. Which reminds me. I'm strapped for cash at the moment. You wouldn't like to lend me some money, would you? Or pay for my aunt's operation? Or put a down-payment on a retirement flat for them?"

"You're mad! Why should I do that?"

Minty tried to keep her temper under control. "Out of gratitude, perhaps, for their having given you free board and lodging all these years? I see the suggestion is unwelcome. Lucas, you're right in one thing; I have changed, because inheriting the Hall means taking responsibility for all the people who work here. Do you have any idea how much it costs to run? What the wages bill is? I've said I'll ring my uncle this afternoon, and I will. Now if you don't mind, I've work to do."

She walked out and left him. Discovered she'd walked herself right through the other rooms to the chapel. Sat down. There was a great blowsy bowl full of red and yellow dahlias in front of the altar. She felt like kicking it over.

She sat down in the carved chair, the chair in which her mother had once sat to be painted . . . and remembered that she'd asked Barr to rescue her mother's portrait from store and put it up in the library. Had he done so? She must check.

Well, Lord? I'm right, aren't I?

Why don't you want to ask Patrick's advice?

Because he'd say . . . because he doesn't know all the facts.

I know all the facts.

And You still want me to go? Knowing everything that she did to me? Are you reminding me about "forgiving no matter how many times you've been sinned against"?

Silence.

All right, she'd tell Patrick. Once he knew all the facts, he'd tell her to forget her uncle and aunt for good.

Chapter Eighteen

By the end of the morning she'd run out of patience.

Serafina had interrupted Minty at her desk to demand that Mrs Kitchen be sacked for making slighting remarks about Minty. At which point Mrs Kitchen stormed in to request that Serafina not interfere with matters which were no concern of hers. Minty lost her temper and said she'd like to bang both their heads together because she needed both of them and couldn't imagine the Hall without either. Then she apologised for losing her temper.

She went down to talk to Chef about new menus, and was told she didn't know what she was talking about.

She started on a business plan for the bank, but didn't know what should go into it. Annie, who did know, wanted Minty to sit down and study a booklet on the duties of trustees. Iris wanted Minty to deal with correspondence, and the phone kept ringing and ringing . . .

Doris left the shop unattended (!) to ask Minty to go with her to the trade shop to buy baubles and . . . and . . . and . . . underneath all, Minty worried about her aunt.

Doggedly Minty tackled each problem, soothed some and jollied others along . . . returned phone calls, made appointments for the following week and was at snapping point when Patrick rang to say he couldn't take her out for lunch as planned. A drain had backed up in one of the cottages at the back of the church and of course everyone knew he had a set of rods for drains and could be relied on to help in an emergency. He'd been up to his armpits in muck for an hour, and would have to make up lost time that afternoon.

She was terse with him. "It's stopped raining. I'll bring something round and we can eat in your garden."

"Something's happened? Curses. I'm as bad-tempered as a bear at the moment. All right, I'll shower and change and try to be back in my right mind by the time you come."

She asked Serafina to rustle up some food, made a couple more phone calls and fielded a complaint from one of the stewards—not Venetia—that that odd little man Jonah was making a mess in the State Rooms, creating displays with his dried flowers, and what did she propose to do about it? Nothing, was the answer to that. She thought Jonah had the right idea, even if he hadn't asked permission. But then, it would never have occurred to Jonah that he needed permission.

She put a file of work in her picnic basket and trudged up the back lane to Patrick's garden. He came out of the house doing up his shirt buttons and smelling of soap, with his hair all tousled. After a kiss for her, he took the wet-weather covers off chairs and a table while she laid out their picnic.

He took a bite out of a monster sandwich. "Don't talk to me till I've eaten."

Her uncle had been the same. Aunt Agnes would say, "He's in a bad mood. Get him something to eat." Mind you, there wasn't anything else the two men had in common. Except perhaps a belief in God.

He took another big bite and said indistinctly, "I love you, and I love Serafina. I love hot water and people who actually remember to thank me for doing something for them. Do I still smell of drains?"

She handed him a mug of coffee from a thermos. "Would I care if you did?"

"Did Serafina need a building permit to erect this sandwich? It's almost too big to get in my mouth. Yum." He finished that sandwich and eyed another. "Right. I'm feeling half way to normal. So what's up?"

She tried to laugh at herself, tried to relax. "Oh, nothing. I just needed to get away from the Hall for a little while." She showed him the file she'd brought with her. "These are all suggestions for what to do at the Hall. New toilets, new kitchens, new parking . . . new quarters for the staff . . . tear down the old stabling . . . two new gardeners needed . . . a whole wing of the Hall to be devoted to a museum for toys . . . no, for costumes. I'm to run craft courses, and put in an adventure playground for children.

"Everyone wants their own particular department made more important. I feel like throwing the whole lot in the air and catching just one piece of paper as it comes down and maybe concentrating on that. But no. I must be grown up and sensible, mustn't I?" She caught a note of hysteria in her voice and made herself calm down.

"It wouldn't be so bad if it were a nine-to-five job, but of course it isn't. I'm surrounded by people and can't get away from them. The phones ring all the time. Ruby's taken root in my spare bedroom, and Serafina never seems to leave the Hall. I've tried to talk Chef into providing decent food, but he's relying on his cast-iron contract and just sneers at me."

She rubbed her forehead. "Lady Cardale is . . . difficult. I can't cope with Gemma. Simon frightens me. I rush into making decisions, and then wonder if I've got them right. My uncle's pressuring me to . . . well, never mind that."

"Have you made sense of the books yet?" He reached for another sandwich.

"No, and the accountant Simon used has thrown up the job. Half the transactions haven't been recorded properly, but maybe I can get enough from letting Peacock Place to see me through."

A fine line appeared between his eyebrows. "Let me give you . . ."

"No. I'm grateful for what you've done already, but I'm not borrowing any more from you. I'll cope, somehow . . . it's just that I'd like to go to bed and stay there for a week."

He drained his cup of coffee. "Well, why not? Pack an overnight bag and raid Serafina's fridge. I've got time between three and four when I was going to do some paperwork, so I'll pick you up in an hour and take you to my quiet place for the weekend. I'll come back here at night time or cadge a bed from my partner in town. You can sleep late tomorrow. After church I'll pick you up and we can go for a long walk in the country."

"I can't just walk away from all my responsibilities . . ."

"You're not walking. You're running. Or do I have to carry you to the car and lock you in while I buy you a toothbrush?"

"You're a bully."

"Uh-huh. Now, are you going to eat that last sandwich or may I have it?"

Patrick wouldn't let her take a notebook and even made her switch off her mobile phone. No messages, no phone calls. Serafina accepted the change of plan without comment. Minty told Iris she'd be away overnight, but she didn't tell Annie because Annie might have argued.

It had started to rain again by the time Patrick put Minty in his car. She tried to relax, muscle by muscle, closing her eyes. When she opened them again, Patrick had drawn up in a quiet country lane close to a thatched cottage.

He unlocked the front door and let her in. "Kitchen and bathroom straight ahead, stairs to the bedrooms to the left, living room to the right. I'll bump up the heating."

She stepped down into a large, oak-beamed living room. The walls were painted ochre, the windows were all shapes and sizes, there were alcoves and niches and window seats. There was an enormous fireplace with a bread oven to one side, and some fine antique furniture including a Welsh dresser holding a collection of blue and white china.

There were good rugs on the red-tiled floor, the easy chairs and settee looked as if they'd be comfortable, and the room was lit by brass lamps which had been converted to electricity. There were books everywhere, and a flurry of papers on the gate-legged table.

Patrick said, "Would you like a fire? It's only a simulated log fire run on gas, but it's comforting now the weather's turning colder." He lit the fire and she crouched in front of it, getting warm. He left her alone in the room and she could hear him on his mobile, arranging to stay overnight with his partner, advising someone that he'd brought his fiancée over for the night and would she keep an eye out for her.

When she was feeling warm enough, Minty looked around. There were no flowers, no cushions, no womanly touches.

"All arranged," said Patrick, reappearing. "Mrs Mimms next door has keys and can be summoned by knocking on the wall. I'll go back to work now, and you can have a rest. Would you like me to come back for supper, or not?"

"It would be a pity to turn you out of your own house," said Minty. "I thought you went to a bed-and-breakfast when you worked in town, but this place is yours, isn't it? This is where you come to be quiet."

"Not so quiet. Listen . . ."

He threw open a window, and a sound which she'd hardly been aware of grew louder.

"Running water," he said. "This is Mill Cottage. The old water mill is across the road. The stream runs under the road and down the valley. You can hear it all the time, sometimes soft, and sometimes loud—especially when it rains. Sometimes it's soothing, sometimes stimulating. It's never the same, two days running. Tomorrow you can sit on the bank and watch it sliding by."

He gave her a hug, kissed her ear, glanced at his watch, yelped and shot out of the door. She listened to his car till it faded into the distance. Listened to the music of the water outside. Sat down on the settee for a moment to rest, put her feet up . . . and went sound asleep.

The kitchen was well equipped. Serafina had put in all the ingredients for supper so Minty sorted out some soup, a game pie and some vegetables.

There was a large man's apron behind the back door, together with mud-caked wellington boots and an ancient anorak and hat. In the bathroom there was a man's white towelling bathrobe. The room at the front contained a double bed and some of Patrick's belongings.

He'd put her overnight bag in the bedroom at the back, which was spartan but clean. A single bed, with a white cotton cover on it. An old pine chest, hooks behind the door to hang up her clothes, a mirror on the wall and a text worked in cross-stitch which read, "Be still, and know that I am God."

And she was still.

For once he wasn't late for supper. They ate at the table once it had been cleared of his papers, and afterwards sat close together on the settee, he with his arm around her. The rain continued to fall, and the stream to trickle on by.

Eden Hall and its problems seemed very far away.

She said, sleepily, "Why don't I just make over the Hall and all the money to you? It would solve so many problems."

"Your problems are for you to deal with, not me."

"May I give you a new car, when the money comes through? A Porsche?"

"What do I want with a new car? My trusty steed has a good few years left in her." He kissed her ear, which happened to be within reach. "You really know what to do. If you don't, look it up in the Golden Rule book. Now, I must be off."

He extricated himself and stood up. Put his hands in his pockets. Took them out again. "It isn't that I don't want to stay."

She nodded. She recognised the softness in her body, wanting him, ready for him.

"You'll be all right here by yourself?"

She nodded again.

"If you need transport, you could get Reggie to come over for you. I'll try to be back by one o'clock tomorrow, and if it's stopped raining we'll go for that walk, right?"

All was quiet, except for the murmur of the stream and the music made by rain trickling into the gutters. She leaned on the window-sill, watching the rear lights of his car disappear. She drew the curtains against the dusk and regarded the lamps and the fire with pleasure. She dimly remembered that she had problems to deal with . . . but this was a place apart, a place in which to forget Eden Hall. A place in which to be quiet. She would have a long deep bath and go to bed.

She woke late, with a feeling of peace which had been absent from her life for some time. The rain had stopped, and there was hardly a sound to be heard. The murmuring of the stream had sunk to a whisper. A fine mist shrouded the view, but as the sun broke through, a rainbow formed.

Her problems still existed but no longer seemed to matter.

A bottle-blonde little lady in her late fifties tapped on the door, bringing fresh eggs.

"Mrs Mimms from next door. Mr Sands always has some of my daughter's eggs when he comes. Oh my! What have I said? You'll think me quite mad—it's my daughter that keeps hens, I mean. Up at the farm. Mr Sands asked me to look in, see if you had everything you wanted. He hasn't brought any other young ladies here and he did say you were special . . ."

"Yes, we're engaged."

"Will you be living here when you're wed, or will you be at his other place, 'beyond'?"

Minty shook her head. "I inherited a house, and we have to live there."

"Oh." Mrs Mimms looked disappointed. "Pity, that. We like having him here, though we know he's too busy to spare us much time. Did he tell you, I'd be out on the street by now, if it weren't for him? He bought all three of these cottages when the Manor house was sold. Else it would have been holidaymakers, and they'd turn us out and tart up our places till we wouldn't know ourselves."

"That's like him," said Minty, wondering how much it had cost Patrick to buy them in the teeth of competition from holidaymakers with money to burn.

She boiled herself a couple of eggs and ate them with some of Serafina's bread rolls, and only then realised with a start that it was Sunday morning and that, way back in the village, the Reverend Cecil would be reading the banns for her and Patrick. Was she too late to go to church here, instead?

She strolled down the lane. It was good to be anonymous for a change. No one pointed at her or accosted her, wanting a job or money.

It seemed to her that the Golden Rule book that he'd talked about must be the Bible. But which part? She located a tiny stone church. There was an outer door which had been netted over to keep birds out, and the inside door was on the latch. The morning service was over and the church was empty, smelling of damp but still full of prayers.

She went in, touching the carved ends of the pews, wondering how many centuries had passed since this church had been built, and if Patrick worshipped here when he was able to get away. There was an ancient brass lectern in the shape of an eagle, and a hand-pumped organ. The windows were nearly all of plain glass, except for a Victorian one behind the altar in blue and scarlet, with figures busy fishing in Lake Galilee.

She sat and prayed for a while. *Please, Lord, You've given me all this money and responsibility, and I don't know how to deal with it. The Hall isn't really mine, anyway. I thought it might be, but it isn't. I'm just temporarily in charge, keeping it together to pass on to future generations.*

The word "Concordance" popped into her head, and she reached for one of the Bibles at the end of the pew. What words might slide into her mind if she stopped praying and started to listen? "Stewardship"? No. "Talents"? A talent in the Bible was a very great deal of money, and not what people thought it meant nowadays. Though it could be that, too.

There it was. The Parable of the Talents. The master entrusted talents to three servants. Two servants put them to good use and doubled their stake. The third hid his in the ground, gained no interest . . . and was rebuked for it.

Three cheers for the Golden Rule book. Patrick was right, and the answer to her problem was indeed there. The money had to be put to work. She spent some more time looking up everything the Bible had to say about forgiveness, and mulling it over in her mind.

It was drizzling again by the time she got back to the cottage, but now she knew what she must do. She made some phone calls and investigated the remains of the food basket which Serafina had put up for them. Patrick arrived just as she was laying the table. He held her at arm's length. "All right now?"

"Thanks to you. Patrick, I know this was your special place. It must have cost you something to let me in."

He sniffed the air. "Not if you've got food laid on. I was going to give you a late lunch at the local pub, but this is better."

"Serafina likes men with a big appetite, so she packed up enough for six. Patrick, could we come here for our honeymoon?"

"Not go to some far-off, exotic place?"

"Later, maybe. Could we start off here?"

"Yes, that would be good. To be quiet, by ourselves. Not to have to spend time travelling."

"I missed hearing the banns read. What was it like?"

"I believe I blushed. Lady Cardale announced afterwards that she wouldn't be at the wedding and she doubted if anyone else would, either."

"She said that to me, too. I don't care."

He grinned. "They'll come out of curiosity, if for no other reason. Before I forget, it's Harvest Festival next weekend and the Sunday School children are to decorate one of the windows. Hardly any of them came today, but Becky waylaid me afterwards and said they'd all come next week, if you were going to be there."

She sighed. "Which will make their present Sunday School teacher hate me. I'll have to have a word with Cecil about it."

When they'd eaten she said, "Patrick, I know we planned to spend some time together this afternoon, but there's something I have to do. I've rung Reggie and asked him to drive me over to see my uncle and aunt in the city. Unfinished business. I won't stay overnight, but see them and my friend Carol and come back tonight."

"Shall I come with you?"

She shook her head. "I have to do this by myself."

A car horn blared outside. Minty exclaimed, "Reggie's early."

It wasn't Reggie. As Patrick and Minty opened the front door, Simon leaned out of his four by four with the tinted windows. There was someone in the passenger seat, but Minty couldn't see who it was. Chef, perhaps? Or . . . was it Tessa, the girl from the Estate Office who was so clearly besotted with him? And if so, what did that mean?

Simon was laughing, blowing them kisses. "So this is your love nest, is it?"

Minty didn't know how to respond but Patrick said, "Grow up, will you, Simon!"

Simon drove off, still laughing.

Patrick rubbed his ear. "I wonder how he found out about this place? Perhaps I ought to step up security."

Reggie drove her swiftly through the countryside. The windscreen wipers whispered, "For . . . give. For . . . give."

She struggled with herself, but couldn't.

Reggie said he'd found a nice little hatchback car for her, one previous owner, low mileage. He'd done a test drive and it looked all right to him. Should he have it driven round to the Hall for her to have a look at?

"Thank you, Reggie. That would be good."

The city streets glimmered in the rain. Car headlights, shop fronts, street lamps. Traffic signals. Intersections. Giant lorries. Cars, vans, buses. Noise.

Reggie drew up behind her uncle's car outside the vicarage.

She took several deep breaths and rang the bell.

"You've taken your time!" She was shocked to see how much older her uncle looked. Her father had been charismatic with a massive head on him, whereas Reuben was taller, bonier, and looked angry rather than powerful. Now Reuben looked as if he might disintegrate if he didn't hold himself together.

It was even drearier inside his study than she remembered it. Dust was everywhere, junk mail spilling onto the floor. There'd never been any central heating, and only one bar of the electric fire was on. A bulb was missing in the overhead light. The remains of two take-away meals were on her uncle's desk. The carpet was unswept, the curtains not drawn.

"How's Aunt Agnes? Who's looking after you while she's in hospital?"

He glanced at the clock, which had stopped. "I have to take an evening service soon and then return to the hospital for visiting hours. It's quite appalling, visitors charging around the place all the time, no one tells them to go when there's more than two beside the bed, no peace at all for my poor Agnes. I tried to see the specialist this morning, but there wasn't one on duty, can you believe? The young doctor—or it might have been a male nurse, you can never tell the difference nowadays—said we'd see an improvement when they got the infection under control."

Minty nodded.

"Well, at least something will be done now you're here. I've got details of the private hospital and if you order an ambulance, we can move her tomorrow."

"Will the doctors allow her to be moved while she's being treated for an infection?"

He stared. "What's that got to do with it? Your aunt needs to be moved."

"No," said Minty, wondering how she dared contradict him. She tried to soften her refusal. "It's not safe to move her while she's being treated for an infection. We must wait till that's cleared up, and then . . .

well, there are problems with finance, but I'll do what I can provided it doesn't cost too much."

He towered over her. "You dare quibble over a few pounds to improve the quality of Agnes' life?"

"My father left you some money. Why don't you use that?"

His breathing thickened. "You know I can't lay my hands on it till probate is granted." He wasn't stupid. At that moment he realised that Minty couldn't lay hands on her inheritance, either. "So what are you living on, eh? I don't recognise those clothes, and now I come to think of it, you'd better change into a skirt and put your hair up before we go to the hospital."

Minty had forgotten she was wearing jeans and that her hair was hanging loose. His reminder of Aunt Agnes' rules about dress dragged her back into the past. "You must take me as I am. Yes, I've had to borrow money from the bank and could, I suppose, borrow more to help you out. Suppose you pay the interest . . ."

"You ungrateful girl! Didn't we take you in and . . ."

"Abused me," she said, keeping her voice low with an effort. "I owe you nothing. Suppose I go down to the police station and tell them how Aunt Agnes beat me, how she destroyed the only toy I was allowed to bring away with me? Suppose I told them how you gave away the money my father sent for my keep? Money which was supposed to put me through private schooling and treat me to holidays abroad and good clothes? Wouldn't they want to question you about it, perhaps charge you with theft?"

He struck her across the face, and then looked appalled at his loss of control.

She put her hand to her cheek. She thought of Gemma, with her bruised face. She thought of Patrick. She thought of crying, and didn't. Big girls don't cry.

"I'm sorry," he said, with difficulty. "I didn't mean to do that. You provoked me with your insolence. Your ingratitude. You left here a Christian soul, knowing the difference between right and wrong, but you appear to have forgotten all I've ever taught you."

"You taught me to fear you. You trained me to be your maid of all work."

"We treated you as our own."

"No, you treated Lucas as your own."

He said nothing to that. He was an honest man in many ways, but like Lady Cardale, he believed he was always right, no matter how skewed his view of the world might be.

Minty didn't think she could ever change him, but she'd try. "It's cold in here. Shall I make us a cup of tea?"

He didn't reply, so she went through to the kitchen to put on the kettle. The kitchen was as dark as ever and now it smelt of mice, as well. Dirty plates filled the kitchen sink.

Her precious recipe books were still on the shelf. She put them on the table to take with her. Automatically she began to wash up, looking out over the rain-sodden garden. Every year she'd planted annuals in tubs at the end of the garden, but they'd been neglected and were now dead. However, under the boundary wall there was a great stand of fragile-seeming, papery honesty, now grey with city dirt and rain.

Minty loved honesty; it was a plant for all seasons, its purple flowers in the spring being followed by green "pennies" in the summer. When the outer leaves were stripped away by autumn rain and wind, the seeds dropped to earth and germinated, leaving the inner white "pennies" to dance on stiff stalks throughout the winter.

She thought it might be fun to give Hodge some of those seeds. While waiting for the kettle to boil, she slipped one of her aunt's heavy coats over her shoulders and darted out into the garden. She got wet, even gathering just a few stalks.

Her uncle was waiting for her in the hall on her return. "Stealing now, are you? How dare you take your aunt's coat?" He raised his hand to hit her again.

From somewhere deep inside her, she found the strength to defy him. "You dare!" She dropped the coat in the hall and leaving the kettle singing, walked out of the front door and through the rain to the car.

Reggie exclaimed she should have waited for him to bring her an umbrella. Only then did she realise she was still carrying the honesty. She put it on the back seat beside her, and gave him Carol's address.

Chapter Nineteen

The Tinderman family were always glad to see Minty. "Come on in! You must be chilled! Can you stay the night? We want to hear all about everything!"

Minty explained she could only stay for an hour, since she wanted to visit her aunt in hospital. Reggie said he'd get the car washed and come back for her.

Carol and Minty had been known as "Loud" and "Soft" at college. Carol's noisy warmth and shrewdness had enlivened Minty's college years, while Carol in turn appreciated Minty's quiet loving-kindness. Carol had always urged Minty to get away from the vicarage, and was unselfishly thrilled that her friend had inherited the Hall.

Over a rumbustious high tea surrounded by younger and older members of the family, Carol tried on Minty's rings. She knew something about jewellery, since her father had an antique shop in the city centre.

"What's this Patrick of yours like?" asked Carol, trying on the little pansy ring. "Are we invited to the wedding? Has mixing with lords and ladies gone to your head?"

"Charming," said Mr Tinderman dismissively, when the ring was passed to him.

"Of course you're invited," said Minty. "I've met a couple of lords and ladies but they're human, like the rest of us. What's Patrick like? Well, I can be a child with him, or a grown woman. He makes me laugh. He's a Christian. He's the rock on which I build my house."

"Wow!" said Carol. "I wish I could meet a man like that. How does it feel, inheriting a stately home?" She tilted the sapphire ring to make it catch the light.

Carol's father approved the sapphire ring with an indulgent smile. "Pretty." And passed it back to Minty.

Minty sighed and smiled. "Inheriting is both terrible and wonderful. Half the staff think I'm the Wicked Witch of the West, and the other half are flawed. My stepfamily is—difficult. My trustees are excellent people but doubtful that I can measure up to the job. I have ideas, lots of them, but the money situation is far from straight-forward. If it weren't for Patrick, I'd have sunk without trace by now, handed the lot over to the National Trust, or something."

Mr Tinderman took the blue diamond from Carol and reached for his glasses. "Ah."

Minty's eyes narrowed. "Worth a king's ransom?"

"Well . . . let's say a prince's ransom. A rare blue diamond, beautifully cut and set. Your Patrick has paid you something of a compliment with this. I see you keep your rings on a ribbon round your neck. Allow me to find you a chain instead."

Minty wondered again how much her "poor" country solicitor was worth.

"So what are your plans for Eden Hall?" asked Mr Tinderman.

"I want to 'humanise' it, increase the number of visitors and lengthen the season. The village could become a tourist attraction in its own right with a few more facilities such as a coffee shop. There are no antique shops, though you'd think they'd do well there. We have several vacant premises at the moment so if you come across someone wanting to expand . . . ?"

"I might wander over your way some time," said Carol's father, smiling. "I always said you'd got a head on your shoulders. I suppose you want my girl here to be one of your bridesmaids, eh?"

"Yes, I would. Very much," said Minty, recognising a bargain to be made. Carol was to be a bridesmaid so that she could meet the "lords and ladies", and Mr Tinderman would consider opening a shop in the village. Social climbing at its easiest. And why not? It would be good to have Carol as bridesmaid. She'd asked Gemma out of duty and been kicked in the teeth. Carol was really her only good friend.

"Will you, Carol? Come over some time next week and see my dress, and then choose something you'd like to wear for yourself—or perhaps my dear friend Ruby can run something up for you. She's a fantastic dressmaker."

"Whoopeee!" cried Carol.

It rained throughout the evening. It rained while she visited the hospital and during the long drive back to the Hall. On her return she went straight to bed.

Next morning early she took her coffee and chunk of bread into the chapel.

She spread her arms wide and bent her head. *Dear Lord, I'm beginning to understand what I have to do. Stewardship. Every penny must be made to work. I need You to show me how to get on with all these people, how to sort out the money. Please be with me in all my business today. And I suppose I must ask You to look after Aunt Agnes, although after yesterday . . .* She grimaced.

She didn't want to hear anything He might be wanting to say to her, so she didn't give Him time to say anything.

Mrs Kitchen demanded to see Minty, complaining, "That horrid little man Jonah's been messing around with his flower arrangements while the house is open to the public, and what's more, that Reggie who used to drive Sir Micah around has been fiddling with the clocks—the very idea!"

Minty could see that both Jonah and Reggie were adding to the value of the Hall, but realised she needed to be tactful. "Dear Mrs Kitchen, you're quite right. I ought to have asked you if Reggie might see if he can get the clocks working. I'm afraid I'm proving hard for you to train. As for Jonah . . ." She lifted her hands in a helpless gesture. Mrs Kitchen almost managed to smile.

"Well, well," she said. "I know the poor creature's a few pence short of a pound and truth to tell, his flowers do add a little something."

"You're brilliant, Mrs Kitchen."

Barr came to discuss contracts and ask whether they should cancel the maintenance work on the north wing. He said he didn't know about such things, but he'd heard there were grants available to help with the maintenance of houses which were open to the public, and perhaps charitable status would help. His attitude was that he did his job, and Minty found the money to keep the Hall going.

So how did stewardship apply here? She concluded it was a false economy to do without a good accountant. She really didn't want to ask Mrs Chickward's nephew Neville—suitable as he might be—because he was so clearly smitten with her. She would ask Lord Asher if he could recommend someone.

That morning she had her first meeting with "young" Mr Foster, her solicitor. He proved to be a pleasant enough man, though lacking Patrick's personality or charm. He was able to reassure her again as to the ownership of Peacock Place and gave her sound advice about borrowing from the bank. He understood and endorsed her decision to regard herself as a steward of her property.

She refused his invitation to lunch and shot back to the Hall for a meeting with Alice Mount, who appeared for once without her little daughter, Marie. Alice was looking businesslike, dressed in a trouser suit. "I got a friend to look after Marie this afternoon and I'll have her kids tomorrow. Now I've got Spring Cottage, I can do that."

"Good," said Minty, meaning it.

"You was right about Dwayne needing to respect me, too. Dwayne almost said so, only being a man, he couldn't. After you left, we sat in the garden, listening to the birds singing. Dwayne said it was like God reminding us how good the earth is, and all the things in it.

"He said he didn't like the thought of Marie being brought up without God in her life. So some day soon we'll have her christened up at the church. Dwayne says he was always going to suggest we get married. Dunno that he really would have. Anyway, I've to go to classes and be confirmed first. I hope the Reverend Cecil won't be too hard on me."

Minty clapped her hands. "He'll be thrilled."

Alice flushed. "Don't get me wrong. We're no angels. Dwayne's going to go on living with me at Spring Cottage . . . that is, if you don't object."

It wasn't ideal, but it was moving in that direction.

"Now, about the job . . ."

Minty explained that everything was hanging fire till probate was granted, or she came by funds in some other way—by which she meant if the Americans took Peacock Place off her hands. Which reminded her that Patrick had offered to give her some more money. Had he been serious? Surely he couldn't afford it?

"So, can you hang on a little longer, Alice? Just do the cleaning for the moment, but begin to make a list of what needs doing to each cottage? Keep a note of how much time you spend on it, and let me have your time sheets as usual."

It was a filthy evening, so Reggie drove her up to Patrick's house, promising to have her new car delivered the following day.

Patrick ushered her upstairs. "I got pizzas sent in, all right? Don't let's talk till we've eaten."

She nodded, reminding herself that he'd probably had a hard day, too. Food helped, and the warmth from his fire.

"Now tell me how you got on." He put a cup of good coffee at her elbow and retreated to his chair with a sigh, relaxing.

She eased off her shoes and tucked her legs beneath her. "Do you remember Yabbit?"

He frowned. "Rabbit," he said, making much of the *R*, "was my favourite toy till you pinched him and changed his name to Yabbit."

She scoffed. "What does a ten-year-old boy need with a toy rabbit?"

"I only let you have him because you needed a security blanket more than I did, and having Rabbit did make you stop sucking your thumb. I seem to remember you carting him around by one ear."

"Her. Yabbit was female." She looked into the fire. "When my mother died and I was sent away, Nanny said I didn't need to take any of my toys, but I managed to hold onto Yabbit. I realised straight away that my aunt and uncle didn't want me. They told me my mother was a bad woman and my father never wanted to see me again.

"Looking back, I see that if I'd been a quiet and obedient child, they'd have liked me more. I learned to be silent and keep out of their way eventually, but at the beginning I fought back . . . not with my fists, but by taking Yabbit everywhere with me and talking to her in front of them.

"I explained that you'd given her to me and that she wasn't a toy, but a real person. At first my aunt made jokes about how I loved Yabbit more than them. Then she got angry and began to hit me with her belt. My uncle never stopped her, though if she marked me he'd frown and say that was enough. There are still a couple of scars on the backs of my legs, which is why I like to wear jeans or long skirts."

Patrick seemed to have stopped breathing.

"Yabbit was my dearest friend, my only comfort. My aunt knew that. So one day she took the lid off the stove in the kitchen and thrust Yabbit inside. I burned my hands trying to rescue her. My aunt said it served me right. I didn't cry, but I learned how to hate. To give him his due, my uncle was distressed—a little. For my sixth birthday he bought me a nasty toy dog from a jumble sale. I put that in the stove, myself. I didn't cry. I can't cry for Yabbit even now."

Patrick passed his hand across his eyes. "I'm amazed you've got over it."

"I haven't. My aunt's in an NHS hospital now with a pulmonary infection. I visited my uncle yesterday. He wanted me to pay for her transfer to a private hospital. I tried to talk to him and failed. He hit me. Mind you, it's the first time he'd ever hit me. I walked out and went to the Tindermans' for tea."

Her face screwed up and she began to weep. "I don't know why I'm crying now."

He came over to tuck himself in beside her and hold her tight. "Go on. Cry it all out. Cry for Rabbit, and all the years without love."

"*You* were Yabbit. I missed you so much. They told me that if I was a good girl they'd love me. I did try to be good, but they still didn't love me."

She sobbed herself into silence, and only gradually became aware of the quality of . . . serenity? . . . that surrounded her.

"Are you praying, Patrick? Pray out loud."

"Too embarrassing. I'm praying you can accept what's happened and move on. I was thanking God for letting us find one another again. I was wondering how your uncle and aunt could treat you like that. Maybe . . . maybe they don't find it easy to love people? Now you are secure in God's love. You respond to everyone—not just me—with loving smiles and gestures. I wonder, are your uncle and aunt so secure in God's love? Do they love one another, as I love you?" Silence. "I think I'd better go back to my own chair."

She couldn't think why for a moment. She was so comfortable where she was, nestling in his arms. Then she understood, and giggled.

He got up, grimacing, and put another log on the fire. "Cecil preached about forgiveness on Sunday. He reminded us that revenge belongs to God, and that we must be big enough to forgive. In a way, I wish I could. Did you get to see your aunt?"

"Yes. She looked terrible. She's on a drip. She looked at me and said, 'Go away.' So I did. It was lucky I had Reggie, because I was too shaken up to drive myself."

He stared at her, then through her. "I can see why you hate her so much, but you don't hate Lady C, do you? Yet it was she who really started this whole train of events."

Minty thought about that. "I'm afraid of what Lady C might say about me, but I'm beginning to agree with Annie that she really believes the poison she spits out. Time is on my side, and I don't think she's going to have a happy old age cosseted by her son and daughter. I don't forgive her, exactly, but I don't feel the hatred for her that I do for my aunt. It's not possible for me to forgive Aunt Agnes. I'm not even going to try. And don't give me the 'Christians have to forgive' bit."

He smiled faintly. "Luke seventeen verse four. 'If your brother sins, rebuke him and if he repents, forgive him. If he sins against you seven times in a day, and seven times comes back to you and says, "I repent," forgive him.'"

"That's it!" she said, fiercely. "She hasn't repented and therefore I can't forgive."

There was a long silence which eventually became comfortable. She said, "I wish we could stay like this for ever. I wish we were getting married tomorrow."

"Nineteen days to go. Have you got a new mattress yet for the four poster?"

"It's ordered. I think. I'll check tomorrow."

Chapter Twenty

At noon the following day Minty took possession of the first car she'd ever owned. It wasn't anything out of the ordinary, being a second-hand workaday hatchback, but Minty was thrilled with it. Reggie said he thought he could tinker with the engine to give it a bit more power, and Iris arranged the tax and insurance with her usual efficiency.

Minty was dying to go out for a run in it, but first she had to interview Toby Wootton, Hugh and Venetia's son, as a potential publicity organiser. She arranged to see him in her father's office, because Iris was addressing wedding invitations in the tower room. Toby would be expensive to hire and she still hadn't any clear idea of her finances, but she kept saying "stewardship" to herself.

She needed him in order to get on with her projects, and if the worst came to the worst she'd borrow more from the bank to pay his wage. And refuse to let herself panic.

Something worried her about Toby's CV, though, and she wasn't experienced enough to decide whether it was important or not.

After some thought, she asked Annie to sit in on the interview. Annie flicked through his CV. "He's always worked in the travel industry . . . and IT . . . but he's not held down any job for long."

"That's what's worrying me. Also, Iris was really peculiar when she saw I'd pencilled him in for an interview. She asked if Patrick knew, then clammed up and wouldn't say another word. Perhaps I ought to have discussed it with you and Lord Asher first, but I'm dying to get on with things and if you're here to check me, it can't do any harm to see him, can it?"

Annie actually smiled. "You sound exactly like your father when he'd got an idea in his head. He always wanted everything done yesterday. I know what Lord Asher would say, which is that you should advertise such an important job."

"It would take months. Toby's from the Manor so I wouldn't have to explain much to him about the Hall, his parents asked if I'd give him a chance, he's had experience in all the areas we need and if he proves impossible at least he'll have got us started, and then we can advertise the job nationally."

Serafina brought Toby in, because he'd arrived via the staircase at the chapel end of the suite—and not through the tower room where Iris was working. Tall and fair like his father, the retired major, he had his mother's fine-boned, almost triangular face and narrow eyes. He wore casual but good clothes rather than office gear and had the air of an onlooker on life. His fingernails were bitten.

Minty noticed Serafina's eyes flicker to Toby's hands and away. Serafina was a shrewd judge of character. She looked hard at Minty but said nothing—and withdrew only to return with the tea tray.

Minty poured for them while describing what the position entailed.

Toby nodded. "Yes, I can do all that. A Winter Wonderland, that's what we could call it." And again, "A new brochure for the Hall? Fine. Advertising for the charity events? Of course."

Minty looked at Annie for guidance. Toby sounded just right for the job, and yet . . . those bitten fingernails indicated that something was going on under the confident-seeming surface, Serafina had been wary and . . . what was it that Iris had against him?

Annie said, "We're a little concerned that you've never stayed long in a job."

He relaxed, transferring his gaze to Annie. Minty wondered if he thought her too young for the job of running the Hall.

"I wanted to see the world, but I didn't want to follow my father into the army. Now I'm home for good and looking for an interesting job. I'll inherit the Manor some day, but I don't have an army pension like my father, so . . ."

Annie helped herself to one of Serafina's home-made biscuits. "Would you be happy to settle here, after travelling the world for so long?"

"That's what I want. I seem to have been on the go all my life. A soldier's family lives where he's posted, so I went to school in Germany, Ireland . . . wherever. Then boarding school, rejoining the family at holiday time. University and then . . . more travel. I was born here and I've always loved this place. It's what I think of when I think of England. No matter where I happen to be in the world, every few years I feel the need to come back."

Minty doodled on her pad. It had just occurred to her that Toby was the same age as Patrick, Simon, Miles—and Iris. "You did live at the Manor as a child, though?"

He shifted in his chair but retained his smile. "My father usually let the Manor while he was on a tour of duty, but there was one year when it was too dangerous for us to be with him, so yes, we stayed put."

"And you went to the village school?"

Tight-lipped. A nod. Then a conscious relaxation. "I think I remember you. Didn't you used to play with my little sister?"

Minty threw her pencil down and walked over to the window to open it, feel the wind on her face and close it again. Annie was asking Toby what he thought of the way the Hall was arranged at the moment, but Minty was remembering something Patrick had said when she first came back to the village. He'd been explaining why he hated Simon.

". . . I was small and clever, and didn't see the sense of fighting in the playground . . . there was all that talk about my father and your mother . . . I ended up in hospital with rope burns and concussion . . . my father closed the house and took us away . . ."

Had Toby played a part in that long-ago episode? An episode which had altered the course of Patrick's life? Another thought. *Iris knows something.*

Minty excused herself to the others and went through to the tower office. Iris half rose from her seat. "I was just going to bring you this note. The Americans are arranging for a detailed survey of Peacock Place to be done this week and . . . I think I ought to warn you about Toby . . ."

"Toby helped Simon to torture Patrick?"

"Patrick told you? It was I who ran for a teacher. I thought they'd killed him."

Minty closed her eyes and leaned against the wall. *Dear Lord, I can't bear it! Tell me what to do!*

Her instinct was to throw Toby out, to hit him, to hurt him. As Patrick had been hurt. But, Patrick had survived and Toby bit his nails. Were those bitten nails a sign of insecurity, or of guilt?

Perhaps it was worth finding out.

Minty said, "Iris, I'll leave the door ajar, so you can hear what he says."

She returned to her office and resumed her seat. "Toby, you must have known Simon and Miles in those days. Tell me about them."

He flexed his shoulders. "Well . . . Simon was King of the Castle, taller and stronger and better looking than any of us. Everyone wanted to be in his gang. Miles was a bit of a bully. You couldn't always be sure that he'd laugh if you made a joke."

"And Patrick Sands?"

"Poor little Patrick." He laughed, but there was no humour in his laughter. "Patrick was the first person to befriend me at school. He was clever in some ways but stupid about people. He refused to help Simon with his homework."

Minty blinked. Had the feud really started over something so trivial? "I heard there was a spot of trouble."

He rushed into an excuse. "Kids' play, that's all." He crossed and recrossed his legs. "Gossip." He shrugged. "Patrick's father was having an affair with someone and Patrick had boasted that . . ." He stopped.

"Go on."

He grimaced. "You know what kids are. Simon said we should show our disapproval by not having anything more to do with Patrick. So we didn't." He tried to smile. "I'd forgotten about it, tell the truth."

"Wasn't there some bullying?"

"Just, you know, playground stuff. You're not really interested in this, are you? It's so trivial. I mean, all it was, Simon said Patrick had been boasting he was going to marry you when he grew up. We were furious. How dared he? Simon said he'd get Patrick to eat his words. He told me to get Patrick to meet me at the far end of the playground after school, so of course I did. Patrick didn't want to come at first, but I persuaded him. Miles and Simon were waiting for us. Simon started pushing Patrick around, trying to make him promise never to marry you. I told you it was absurd, didn't I? Patrick tried to get away, but I . . ."

He ran the back of his hand across his upper lip and gave that hard laugh again. "What kids get up to!"

"Was it you who ran for a teacher?"

Toby went a dull red. "No, I . . . how did you know about . . . ?" He stood, pushing his chair back. He was trembling. "Look, I'm not proud of myself; in fact I still have the occasional nightmare about it." He got the words out with difficulty. "All right, I know I should have told Simon to get someone else to do his dirty work, but I didn't."

"What did you do?"

"I . . . I held Patrick's arms up so that . . . Oh, I c–can't . . . Miles had this rope and . . . there was this branch of the tree that overhangs the playground and . . . and Patrick looked at me. He just looked, and I realised what I'd done and tried to make them stop, but they wouldn't listen. So I dropped my end of the rope and I thought they'd let him go, but Simon kept hitting him, saying he'd got to promise he'd never marry you . . . it was laughable, really! Then Patrick sort of keeled over and Miles kicked his head. Then someone screamed. And I ran away."

Toby turned his back on them, his shoulders up to his ears.

"Yes?" said Minty, even more quietly. "Who did you tell?"

"No one. I ran all the way back up to the Manor. I knew I ought to tell someone, get someone to help Patrick, but I didn't. I just ran away and left him there. When I got home, everything seemed so normal that I thought it couldn't have happened. I told myself I must have dreamed it. My little sister wasn't feeling too good. She'd got a runny nose and was whining. My mother was busy with her. I didn't get out of bed next day. I said I'd got my sister's cold. I didn't tell anyone what had happened. I managed to stay away from school for a week. When I got back, it was as if nothing had ever happened. Patrick had gone. I thought he was dead. His house in the village was shut up and empty. Nobody talked about him. That autumn I went away to boarding school. And that's it. End of story."

"When did you find out that he wasn't dead?"

"Not for years. I came back occasionally because, as I said, I love this place. But I never spent much time here. Blocked it out. It wasn't till my sister Pearl grew up that I heard his name mentioned again. She went out with him for a while, you know, when she was at college. She wrote and told me—I was working in the States at the time—and well, I was surprised and relieved that he wasn't dead but I didn't want her to marry him, so I was pleased when they broke up. And that's it, really."

"So you haven't seen any of them since?"

He shook his head. He was trembling but trying to control it. He resumed his seat, tried to get another mouthful of tea out of an empty cup.

"Do you only bite your nails when you're back home?" asked Minty.

"You ask such questions." He was flushed, perspiring. "Don't look at me like that! I . . . well, I suppose you're right. Recently my father's been pressing me to come back home and I want to, I really do. But the nightmares have been coming back again. He said there was this job going. So I decided I'd better try for it, put the past behind me. I mean, with Patrick long gone, what did it matter?"

Minty leaned back in her chair, considering what he'd said. She thought he'd suffered enough from what he'd done, but this case wasn't hers to judge.

Annie stirred. "Toby, do you still want the job?"

"Yes, I do. After all, you know the worst of me now."

Minty said, "The job's yours, Toby . . . if Patrick and Iris agree."

He mouthed the words "Patrick? Iris?" He pushed his chair back. Rubbed a shaking hand over his eyes. "What's Patrick got to do with it? And Iris? You're having me on!"

"Patrick's grown into a very fine man, Toby. When you meet him again . . ."

"No, I couldn't!" He leaped to his feet, panic-stricken. "It was a mistake coming here. Sorry. Sorry to have troubled you. Which is the way out?" He almost ran from the room back the way he'd come . . . in the opposite direction to the tower room where Iris was.

The room was very quiet when he'd gone.

Iris walked in, as self-contained as ever.

Minty asked, "Well, Iris? Could you work with him, if Patrick agrees?"

"He was a nice boy, easily led," said Iris. "I suppose he's much the same now. It wouldn't bother me to have him around. I've read his CV.

He could do the job all right, but could Patrick bear it? They nearly killed him, you know."

Minty hugged herself. "I'll have to ask him. Thank you, Iris."

When Iris had gone, Minty began to pace the room. "It was all my stupid fault, saying I wanted to marry Patrick when I was four. He wouldn't have boasted about it, but my mother and Patrick's father heard me and thought it was funny. They probably told other people, making a joke of it and . . . look what happened! So many lives ruined!"

"It wasn't you who ruined them," said Serafina, coming in to remove the tea tray. "This all goes back to Lady C's lies."

"Even further back than that," said Minty. "It was my old nanny, Mrs Proud, who fed my stepmother and Simon with the idea that the Hall was theirs for the taking. Annie, Serafina, tell me what to do."

Annie tapped the table top. "Toby Wootton isn't the problem. Patrick Sands is. Now we know why he hits a glass ceiling. It's invisible to outsiders, but from experience he knows that if he crosses Simon, he'll suffer for it. There'll always be that fear at the back of his mind, stopping him from achieving his full potential."

"Yes and no," said Minty. "It would have been one of the factors when you tackled him about our engagement, but it wasn't the only one. Yes, he does doubt himself, but . . . look what he's achieved, in spite of that bad start. He's taken me off Simon, and it's Patrick who's going to end up King of the Castle at Eden Hall, not Simon. But just as Toby bites his nails whenever he's reminded of his Judas trick, Patrick pays a price each time he scores a point off Simon. Haven't you noticed how he fidgets with his watch strap all the time? There's no visible scar there, but every time he looks at me, that wrist must ache."

Serafina leaned against the wall, arms folded, black eyes flicking from one to the other. "Well, Minty? Does he love you more than he hates Simon?"

"Ah ha," said Annie. "I hadn't thought of that."

"It's a factor in the equation," said Minty, in a dry tone, "but not the whole answer." She picked up the outside phone, and dialled the Manor house, getting through to Hugh Wootton.

"Hugh, Toby's on his way back to you now in something of a state. Some childish ploy has just come up and hit him. I'll be ringing through about eight o'clock this evening to tell him if he's got the job or not, so will you hold him there till I phone? By force, if necessary . . . no, I can't tell you exactly what it was . . . perhaps he'll tell you himself . . . yes, I'll ring about eight."

She put the phone down and got through to Patrick. "Patrick, have you nearly finished for the day? Yes, I know it's only half past five and you're working in town, but it wouldn't take you long to get back here, would it? You probably haven't eaten since breakfast. Why don't you ditch the rest of the paperwork and join me for an early supper . . . in half an hour, say? I've something to show you . . . You will? Good. I'll have someone let you in."

Serafina was on her way. "I'll start supper."

Annie said, "You won't want me here," but didn't move from her seat, and Minty didn't suggest that she go. Perhaps Annie had the right to see this through.

Minty washed her hands and face and made sure she was wearing her diamond ring. Even looking at that gave her confidence. Iris was sent home, taking the wedding invitations with her to be posted on the way. Minty looked at the phone messages that Iris had taken for her and a pile of bills that had come in. Most of the bills she redirected to Simon and Lady Cardale.

She went into the chapel and sat there, thinking over what had happened, trying to banish vengeful thoughts of Toby. Trying to work out how she was going to deal with the situation, because what she did now was going to set the keynote for the rest of her life with Patrick. She bent her head, closing her eyes. Praying that He would grant her wisdom, give her the right words.

Serafina summoned Minty to the dining room. "He's here, and supper's ready."

"Those are the words I like to hear best," said Patrick, catching Serafina round her waist and kissing her cheek. "Which of your specials is it tonight?" He shed his car coat and put his arm round Minty, urging her to the table, too. "Don't talk to me till I've had two helpings at least, right? Chicken soup with bits in it? And hot rolls? I love you, Serafina."

Annie followed them into the dining room with some papers. She hovered till Minty said, "Do join us, Annie. This affects you as well."

"What does?" Patrick tore into a roll and dipped his spoon in the soup.

"Let him eat first," said Serafina, putting the butter within his reach.

Annie put Toby's CV on the table in front of him. Patrick got on with his soup and, not bothering to read the name at the top, flicked through it. "Sounds all right. Never spent long in one place, though." He took another spoonful. "Why the long faces?"

He checked the name at the top and put the spoon down with care.

No one moved.

Eventually Patrick looked up and met Minty's eyes. He looked at the others, too. Then he swivelled round in his chair, ignoring the food in front of him. He looked like a boxer, coming out of his corner at the beginning of a round. He was pale, his nostrils wide.

Minty said, "Toby came here today, looking for a job. He'd no idea you'd returned. He knows he betrayed you and he's unable to forget it or forgive himself. I said it was up to you whether he got the job or not, that I'd ring him about eight o'clock, to let him know. My guess is he won't wait, but will run away—again. And keep running for the rest of his life. Unless you break the cycle."

He half closed his eyes, looking again to Annie, and then to Serafina.

Minty said, "Annie's here because she wants to know how you'll react. Serafina's here because she wants you to win."

His eyes went back to Minty. "You want me to forgive him, pretend that nothing happened? That it was all a childish joke?"

"It wasn't a childish joke. It was a betrayal of friendship. That hurt more than what Simon and Miles did to you, didn't it?"

He shrugged. He had himself well under control now. Stone-faced. He picked up his spoon and took a mouthful. He said lightly, "All right. I forgive him."

Minty laced her fingers together so tightly that the skin turned white. "If you can find it in yourself to meet him again, to talk to him, to forgive him in such a way that he understands that he is forgiven ... then the Hall gets the right man for the job."

He put his spoon down. "And if I refuse?"

Here it came. Minty prayed, *Give me strength, Lord.* "Why . . . nothing. Toby goes back on his travels, I advertise the post and we get married as planned."

"But you'll think less of me?"

She braced herself. "No. I love you and admire you and look forward to the day we marry."

"Only, if I can somehow manage to meet him . . . if somehow I could manage to . . ." He stood up, dabbing at his mouth. His pallor was shocking. His hands trembled.

Serafina scrambled to open the inner door for him and showed him out to the bathroom.

Annie said nothing. Minty closed her eyes and prayed. *God, be with him. God, be with us all. Please, God, show him how to grow . . .*

One minute passed.

Two.

Minty paced the floor. *I shouldn't have told him. It's all my fault.*

At last he returned, looking fairly normal though his hair was wet and his pallor still noticeable. He picked up his car coat. "Well, I suppose I'd better do it now, before I lose my nerve." He held out his right hand, which still trembled. "Minty, will you drive? I don't think I can."

Serafina said, "I'll keep your supper hot for you."

As they reached the gates leading to the Manor, a car with Toby at the wheel came rocketing down the drive towards them. Minty stopped Patrick's car between the pillars, blocking Toby's escape.

She said, "I told Hugh I'd not be phoning till eight, but it's only six and Toby's already running away."

Patrick got out of the car and walked over to Toby's, pulling open the door and extending his hand to the driver. Toby got out with reluctance. The two men stood facing one another for what seemed a long time. Minty couldn't hear what they said, but then Patrick folded Toby in a bear hug, and Toby's head dropped onto Patrick's shoulder. With Patrick patting Toby's back, they made their way across the garden and disappeared round the corner of the house.

Minty left Patrick's car where it was and walked to the front door, which was open. Inside, Hugh Wootton stood in the hall, looking as if his world had collapsed around him.

"He told you?" Minty said.

"I–I . . . can't believe . . . ! How could he!"

"It's all over now."

"It explains why he never came back to live here, but . . . if he'd only said! I'd never have suggested he apply for the job if I'd known."

"It's a good thing you did, Hugh. Toby's the right person for the job, but Patrick has to agree."

"He's my son and of course I love him, but . . . how can you forgive him so easily? I'm so angry, I could . . ."

She pressed his arm. "It wasn't easy for me, or for Patrick. I don't suppose it will be easy for you, either, but you can do it. Now you must go and tell Venetia. Once she knows, we can start looking forward instead of back."

Eventually Patrick and Toby returned from the garden. Patrick was quiet, but Toby was ebullient, released from the shame and guilt that had dogged him for so many years. Venetia forgave her son more easily than Hugh, and wept more perhaps for the waste of the years between, than for what he'd done. Patrick encouraged Hugh to look to the future.

Toby was full of plans for the Hall. Minty and Patrick smiled and nodded. When Hugh said they must celebrate, Minty excused herself and Patrick, on the grounds that Serafina was keeping supper for them back at the Hall.

Minty got into the driving seat of Patrick's car, with Patrick sitting limply beside her. She reversed out of the gate into the lane, parked the car and put her head down on her arms on the steering wheel.

Patrick put his arm around her.

"It's all right," she said in a muffled voice. "I just need to howl for a bit."

He didn't speak but took her in his arms. She sobbed into his shoulder once, and then once more. After a while she felt him begin to relax, and she did, too.

She sat upright. "So sorry. Didn't mean to collapse like that. How are you coping?"

"I'm the walking dead. When I think how quiet my life was, before you returned to the village! I used to get up in the morning knowing roughly what the day would hold. Now I never know what's going to hit me."

"It was a lonely life, wasn't it? And bitter. Did you really manage to forgive Toby?"

"I believe I did. I prayed that God would help me, and somehow the impossible became not too difficult."

A car came past them and slowed down for a good look before speeding off again.

"Oops!" said Patrick. "My reputation's gone! Caught snogging in Lovers' Lane! It was Simon in that car, but who was it with him?"

"Couldn't see. A woman, I think. Possibly . . . do you think it could be Tessa?"

"A nasty thought. She doesn't exactly love me at the moment. Well, sufficient to the day . . . Did you say Serafina was keeping some food for us?"

Chapter Twenty-One

Later that evening she went to the chapel to pray and found Annie and Serafina there, sitting one on either side of the chair with the carved back. Minty sat between them. She looked at the cross and let herself be folded in the atmosphere of prayer that lived in this room, adding her own heartfelt "Thank You, Lord."

When she finally opened her eyes, she saw that the other two women were both looking at her. She took their hands in hers and they said the grace together. "May the grace of our Lord Jesus Christ, the love of God and the fellowship of the Holy Spirit be with us, now and always."

As they went out, Serafina said, "I've never seen a soul saved before you came, Minty. First you helped your father repent his sins before he died, and now you've saved young Wootton. Not that he won't need watching, if Simon gets hold of him again."

Minty grinned. "I thought of getting Iris to look after him."

Serafina laughed. "Set a tiger to watch over a mouse?"

Annie shook her head. "I'll never understand you two. Iris appears to me to be a nice girl, and extremely efficient. Tiger, indeed!"

Wednesday morning. Patrick rang as she was leaving the chapel after her morning prayers.

"Sorry to ring you so early."

She sat down on the stairs to take his call. "You were fantastic last night, Patrick."

"No, I wasn't. You've put me on a pedestal. Uncomfortable places, pedestals. I'm really not hero material, you know. When I think how I fell to pieces last night . . . I'm not much of a fighter, am I?"

"You, not a fighter?" She started to laugh, until she realised he was deadly serious. "Patrick, you're the bonniest fighter I've ever known. You could have made a life for yourself elsewhere but you chose to come back here, where the enemy thought he was safe. You put on the armour of God. You put on the belt of truth, and the lies told about your father died away. You put on the breastplate of righteousness and became respected for helping those in distress.

"When you returned, don't you think that was like thrusting a sword in the heart of those who'd driven you and your family away? Don't you think they felt it when you joined the church here and became such a vital part of it? Didn't they cringe when you blocked their wicked scheme to lease out the Hall? And if you hadn't gone out of your way to help me when I returned, perhaps Simon's plans would have succeeded. Instead, you rescued me from under his very nose. You fight in your own way, Patrick. God's way."

He let out a long breath. "I suppose it has been a battle of sorts, but I still fall to pieces occasionally. How can you love someone who throws up at the thought of confronting an old enemy?"

"King David had the same problem, didn't he? He cried out pitifully when surrounded by his enemies . . ."

Patrick attempted a laugh. "'Save me, O God, for the waters have come up to my neck.'"

"'Be my rock of refuge, to which I can always go.' Then you had to tear out all hatred from your heart and forgive Toby. That took a bit of doing."

"I wouldn't even have tried if you hadn't pushed me into it."

"Oh, I think you would."

"You are . . . amazing. I wish I could jump into the car and come over now and . . . but perhaps it's just as well that I can't. I've a full day over here. You haven't forgotten our introduction to society this evening at Mrs Chickward's? Will you call for me on your way up?"

Minty had invited Slim & Fawcett—who'd designed that incredible makeover for the restaurant—to meet her an hour before it was due to open. She was there early and prowled around, trying to see the place as a customer would.

The Thornbys arrived; while Florence bustled into the Hall, Gloria plodded into the restaurant and Minty asked her to prepare coffee for them all. Chef arrived with his two anorexic kitchen helpers. Minty, who didn't usually have such thoughts, wondered if he was sleeping with one or both of them. Chef seated himself with the two girls, one on either side of him.

Iris came and took a seat at the back, unobtrusively opening her laptop. Barr bustled in, carrying his usual untidy folder of papers.

Gloria dispensed coffee and lurked in the background, scowling. She knew her job was at risk since she was no anorexic blonde and therefore didn't fit in with the designers' ideas.

In stalked Slim & Fawcett, a brittle blonde in a trouser suit and a black man with a shaved head. The blonde said, "Is she going to be late, then?" in a penetrating voice.

"Do you mean me?" asked Minty, amused rather than annoyed. These people had been dealing with Simon until now. She had low expectations of them and imagined they reciprocated.

"Oh. Pleased to meet you. I'm Ms Fawcett, and my partner here is Slim." The blonde signed to her assistant to open up his portfolio. "Well, Miss Cardale, I know you've expressed some doubts about our plans, but when I've explained . . ."

"I know your brief was to attract a more upmarket clientele, but . . ."

"This place," said the blonde, "reminds me of a British Railway cafeteria from the nineteen fifties. No wonder it's losing money."

"I agree," said Minty.

Chef beamed, as did his two girls. Gloria looked out of the window.

Minty tasted her coffee, which was dreadful. "Let me tell you how I see the future of the Hall and its restaurant." She explained her plans for extending the opening season, and the knock-on effect this would have on the restaurant and shop.

"I want us to run Christmas dinner specials from mid-November through to Christmas. I want to put on cut-price pensioners' lunches one day a week. I want us to serve the community, but I don't think we should open in the evenings."

Chef thumped the table. "I don't agree to any of that. As far as I'm concerned, I finish end of October and return at the beginning of March. I already have a job lined up in London for the winter, and I'm not missing that. What's more, there's no possible way I'd demean myself by cooking chips for senior citizens!"

Minty smiled sweetly. "Not only chips. Bangers and mash with onions, liver and bacon, steak and kidney pie. Blackberry and apple tarts, sponge puddings. Turkey and plum puddings and mince pies. Cream teas. An imaginative salad bar, home-made bread rolls."

"What do you know about such things?" Chef's tone was offensive.

"I cooked for my uncle and aunt from the time I was ten. From the age of fifteen I helped cook for all major church events, and from eighteen on I was responsible for costings and ordering as well. So when I say we should concentrate on traditional British food, I know what I'm talking about."

"It would choke me to prepare such dishes!" said Chef, magnificently. "I was not born to cook sausage and mash. I resign!"

Minty tried to look worried. "You wouldn't!"

"Certainly," said Chef. "If you don't see things my way I walk off the job now, this minute, and pack my things. And what will you do for the rest of the season, I'd like to know?"

Minty said, "That would mean breaking your contract!"

"Try me!" Chef folded his arms and grinned, scenting victory. "Those are my terms: no makeover, no Chef. What's more, my girls go with me."

One of his girls looked worried at this, but the other nodded and drew even closer to Chef.

"You're prepared to leave us without any staff, with visitors wanting coffee within the hour?" said Minty, watching the girl who didn't seem too happy with the way things were going.

"You know my terms."

The girl who wasn't happy opened her mouth to object, frowned, shut it again. She probably wanted to stay but didn't know how to say so.

"So be it," said Minty, trying not to grin. "Barr, would you like to take Chef and his two assistants to the Estate Office and give them the money due to them. Don't stint on holiday pay. Get them to sign the usual disclaimers. If either of you girls changes your mind and wants to stay, then you may do so—with a new contract. Iris, will you fetch Reggie, and see that the three of them vacate their accommodation here, leaving it as we would wish to find it. Thank you."

When they'd gone, Minty turned to the two designers. "Now, Ms Fawcett, Mr Slim, I realise you've been put to a great deal of trouble, but through no fault of your own you've been badly briefed. The restaurant here does need a makeover, though not of the sort you'd envisaged. The question is, are you interested, or do I look for another firm of decorators?"

"What sort of makeover did you have in mind?" asked Ms Fawcett, looking worried.

"A quick paint job at a reasonable cost, using warm, bright colours to fit in with a rural background. I think I know where I can find some old prints to put on the walls. The job to be completed in a three-day period from a Monday morning to a Wednesday evening before the end of October."

They were not happy about it. They'd hardly touched their coffee, and Minty couldn't blame them for that.

Ms Fawcett said, "We really don't think we could. Our reputation has to be considered!"

"I quite understand," said Minty with a meek air, and saw them off to their car. She made a note to ask Iris to get a local firm on the job.

Then she went to see Florence. Gloria was already there, pouring out her news, of course. Minty helped herself to a cup of good coffee and said "Ah!" as the first mouthful removed the taste of the dreadful liquid Gloria had made earlier.

"Splendid," said Florence, her plump, competent hands popping some individual pies onto a baking sheet and thrusting them in the oven. "I knew you'd get rid of those design people quickly, but I thought you'd have more trouble with Chef. Of course I can take over. Let's see what food he's left us for today's lunches."

Once across the courtyard, Florence looked askance at Chef's kitchen. "I'll work from my own quarters till this place has been thoroughly cleaned, and I'll need a helping hand till I can get another girl or two in from the village."

"I'll help today," said Minty. That afternoon she and Ruby were meant to be rummaging through the "junk" rooms in search of family bits and pieces to make her rooms feel more like a home, but sacrificing one afternoon was a small price to pay for getting rid of Chef.

Florence gave her a sharp look. "Can you cook?"

"I cooked for my uncle and aunt, and for church suppers. Tell me what to do, and I'll do it."

"Good girl," said Florence, returning to her own kitchen to take her pies out of the oven, releasing the delicious scent of spicy apple and blackberry pies into the air. "It looks as though Chef intended to do packet soup followed by commercial quiches from the freezer, with a leaf of lettuce and a slice of tomato for salad. Humph! Gloria, get rid of his menu cards and chalk a new menu up on the blackboard. We'll do home-made mushroom soup and bread rolls, followed by sausage meat and vegetable pie. Then fresh fruit salad and home-made blackberry and apple pies with ice cream for afters."

Still talking, she started to make out a shopping list. "Minty, you fetch me these things from the village—you've got your own car now, haven't you?—and then you can be my vegetable chef for the day."

"Yes, Chef," said Minty, saluting.

"Gloria will serve, clear tables and help wash up."

"Oh, Mum! I can't do everything!"

"Now, Gloria, no sulking. You've got to buck up your ideas, if you're going to work for me."

"Mum!" said Gloria, going red.

"For tea I'll do fresh scones with cream and some of my home-made jam, and I can knock up a sandwich cake or two, while Minty takes over selling ice creams."

Gloria piped up. "I think one of Chef's girls, Fiona, will want to stay, because her people live in the village and anyway she reckons Chef's going off her."

"She could be useful if she doesn't try to give me lip about the way Chef used to do things. Tell her she's on probation for a week. Now, Minty, I'm supposed to be cooking for the family till the end of October, though I've told Gemma I'm not doing another hand's turn for her, the way she carries on. We'll manage fine if I put in a couple more hours per day, we get in a part-time girl and Fiona works out. I'll speak to Hodge about supplying me with vegetables in future—his onions are a treat this year, though his carrots are not much good—and I know several farms who can supply me with better quality stuff than Chef ever had. We'll have a session tomorrow about menus, shall we?"

"As usual, you're ahead of me," said Minty. "We must discuss new contracts for the three of you. But I must admit I'm worried about Gemma."

Florence folded her lips. "That one exists on liquid and we're not talking Adam's Ale. I'm not employed to clean up vomit or be sworn at, and so I've told her. Anyway, she's off in her car today, though whether she's fit to drive or not, I couldn't say."

When Minty returned with the fresh fruit and vegetables Florence needed, Iris met her and helped to carry boxes from the car into the kitchen.

"Chef and one of his assistants have cleared their quarters and left the Hall, but Fiona's reporting for duty to Florence."

Minty said, "Would you like Chef's accommodation, Iris? Is it suitable?"

"It needs a good clean," said Iris, "but yes, I'd love it."

Minty translated. "It's a tip, but you'll make the best of it. You certainly haven't time to clean it. Chef's kitchen needs a good clean, too. See if you can get hold of Alice Mount, and ask her to do both. As for furniture . . ."

Iris grimaced. "The mattress needs throwing out. I'll borrow some bedding from home and my parents will help me get sorted."

"Which reminds me," said Minty. "I need a new mattress for the blue four poster. Can you measure up and order a good one for me?"

Florence was tireless. She never seemed to hurry, but effortlessly produced delicious food while overseeing what Minty, Fiona and Gloria were doing. Customers were pleasantly surprised by the quality of the food, the aroma of good coffee enticed more and more people into the restaurant and Gloria began to get the idea of hard work. For the first time since she arrived, Minty felt the restaurant was giving value for money.

They closed at five, but Minty couldn't leave until everything had been cleaned to Florence's stringent standards.

Staggering up the stairs to her rooms at last, Minty collapsed onto a chair, only to have Ruby and Jonah bombard her with their news. Since she'd been tied up in the kitchens, they'd gone ahead and rummaged in the store-rooms without her.

"Look!" cried Ruby, holding up some bolts of blue damask. "I found this trunk full of material, which will make up a treat . . ."

"Look what I did," crowed Jonah, waving his hand towards the mantelpiece on which he'd arranged Minty's sprigs of honesty in a pair of Sevres vases.

"Dear Jonah," said Ruby, brushing dust from his clothes, "you're just like a will-o'-the-wisp, drifting in and out whether you're supposed to be there or not."

"You said I was useful!" Jonah seated himself cross-legged on the floor and began to play with a glass snowstorm he'd found, turning it over and letting the flakes settle to reveal a mountain scene, and then upending it again.

"I found these, too," said Ruby, holding up two large, down-filled cushions. "Would you like them on the settee? There. Doesn't that look better?"

Serafina came in, arms crossed, fingers tapping. "I don't like people interfering in my rooms. Can't you see Minty's worn out and needs a rest, not to mention she's due at Mrs Chickward's in an hour."

"So she is," said Ruby, vanishing with her rolls of material, while her voice floated back to them. "I'll just iron the blouse I've put by for her . . ."

Minty closed her eyes. She would have liked a shower and a short rest, but obviously it was not to be, for here came Iris and Toby, wanting her to approve the advertising for the Winter Wonderland.

Catching sight of the honesty out of the corner of her eye, Minty remembered her aunt and broke off to ring the hospital. "Mrs Cardale's holding her own," was the reply. Minty shrugged. She didn't know what else she could do about her uncle and aunt. The memory of her aunt telling her to go away still stung.

She was discussing how many large notice boards they could put up around the village to advertise forthcoming events when Ruby came in. "You really ought to get dressed, dear. You can't go like that."

"Is that really the time?" said Toby. "My mother made me promise to get back in time to change, too."

"All change!" Iris sang out, looking amused.

Patrick was actually ready for the party, running down the stairs to the ground floor as she arrived. She stopped thinking about the problems of the Hall and reflected how rare it was to find a slenderly built man who moved so gracefully.

"Am I late?" He kissed her and stood back to survey her outfit. He himself was wearing a new silky pullover in a cream and blue fleck over a cream polo-necked silk jumper and black trousers. He looked good enough to eat.

She said, "It's only a few drinks in the garden, isn't it? I was going to wear a white blouse and jeans, but Ruby insisted on my best black trousers and this blue silk blouse. I don't know where she got it from because I didn't buy it, and I'm sure it's too formal for the occasion."

"My beloved, that outfit is perfect. It hints at Edwardian splendour. Remember that nothing Mrs Chickward does is ever informal. Her At Homes are famous, not to mention her garden, which people come from miles around to see."

Minty began to panic. Did her hair look all right, drawn back with combs? Would it be better to wear it loose? What if she made a fool of herself before all those important people? She'd only just left the vicarage and was unused to society. Could she fake a headache? Make her excuses?

Patrick was soothing. "You've nothing to worry about. Mrs Chickward is no fool. She knows your stepmother is on her way out, and that you are the future. To sponsor you in society will be a feather in her cap, so this evening will probably turn into a not-so-informal engagement party for us."

Minty's panic was growing. "I won't know anyone."

"Of course you will. Mrs Collins has received an invitation, a first for her; she's been angling for one for years. Her nephew Neville will be there to remind you that you could do with the services of a good accountant—which you could, couldn't you? The Woottons will be invited because they own the Manor, and Toby to welcome him home. True, there'll be some who'll come to look you over and perhaps—if they're friendly with Lady Cardale—hope to prod you into saying something unwise."

Minty was silent. It had been the same in the parish. You mustn't ever criticise anyone to anyone because they might be related, or best friends. Suppose she said something stupid and let Patrick down?

Patrick fiddled with his watch strap and she remembered why it chafed his skin. She forgot her own nerves. She caught his wrist and put it to her cheek. The skin on the inner wrist was soft, and although there was no visible scar, she guessed the inner hurt was going to be difficult to heal. Well, that was her job now, healing him. She put her arms around him and held him close.

He attempted to laugh. "You were so sweet as a child. You used to reach up to put your arms around my neck and . . . you were my sweet heart." He made two words of it, "sweet" and "heart". "You *are* my sweet heart. Minty, are you sure you really want me? I'm not much to look at, and there'll be lots of eligible men at the party."

"Sweet heart," she said, making two words of it, too. "Darling. Beloved. My love. Which name do you like best?"

"Come on, we'll be late."

"I like sweet heart best," she said. "Or perhaps you'd prefer Poppet or Peaches?"

He let them out into the street. "Not in public, Araminta."

"Patrick Sands, are you ashamed to be seen in public with me?"

"You know it's not that." They walked up the road to the Green together. Looking away from her, he said, "Sweet heart. Yes. Always. Which reminds me that I looked at wedding rings yesterday but couldn't decide what you'd like."

"My friend Mr Tinderman's coming over this week to look at empty shops, see if he might open up here. He's a jeweller and antique dealer so I could ask him to bring some rings over with him. Will you wear one, too? Something fine in gold, possibly slightly old-fashioned?"

It took him two paces to realise she was referring to him as well as a ring.

"I'll give you old-fashioned!" He caught her up round her waist and kissed her.

"Oh, you love-birds!" Mrs Collins was clambering out of her car.

Minty gasped, for Mrs Collins had outdone herself in splendour. She was wearing a black and gold turban with fringed ends and a filmy black dress, embroidered all over with silver and gold. A choker of real pearls encompassed her neck, and she looked extremely pleased with herself.

Patrick said the right thing. "You look splendid, Mrs Collins."

Chapter Twenty-Two

It was as pleasant an evening as could be hoped for in October. The house—like Mrs Chickward—was built on early Georgian lines but with some modern touches in furniture and furnishings. Admiring an abstract tapestry, Minty reminded herself that she must never write Mrs Chickward off as behind the times.

That formidable lady was dressed in an understated but expensive navy and white Chanel two-piece, which contrasted sharply with Mrs Collins' extravagant attire. Minty was thankful that Ruby had given her the right thing to wear.

They stepped out into a large, manicured garden. Patrick said in her ear, "Don't drink the orange juice—it's laced with champagne." He got her some straight fruit juice, instead.

"The garden's beautiful!" said Minty, admiring the autumn colours. She caught her breath, for Lady Cardale and Simon were looking daggers at her. No Gemma.

Lady Cardale said in a loud voice, "Some people have no manners. What on earth possessed her to gatecrash?"

"Rise above it." Patrick put his arm round Minty and steered her to another group, which greeted them with smiles and loud chatter. "Meet my partner and his wife . . ." Minty forgot their names immediately, but kept her wits about her because, as Patrick had said, everyone wanted to know about the wedding and the Winter Wonderland.

A stout woman elbowed her way in. "Glad to meet you, Araminta. What everyone wants to know is, do you hunt?"

This was a poisoned chalice of a question. The country people were all for their traditional hunt, but many townsfolk had vowed to stop it. Patrick looked faintly anxious and Minty realised she must be careful not to offend either side.

She kept smiling. "I'm a city girl, just getting used to country ways. Ask me again in five years' time."

Patrick looked relieved and swept her on to another group. These were older people, men and women. A plump-faced man with the knowing eyes of a politician asked whether she was prepared to carry on the excellent work her stepmother had been doing for charity. A woman with a thin nose—not his wife?—bobbed along at his side, nodding.

Alarm bells rang in Minty's head. Did they want her to go on making the Hall available for free? "Give me a chance to settle in."

"I'm chair of the Society for . . ."

"Then we really must talk sometime. I haven't got my diary on me. Would you like to phone me?"

A large woman, wearing some kind of mayoral chain, intervened to ask about the wedding . . . and a familiar face loomed up, which she couldn't quite place until she realised she'd danced with the man at the charity ball.

"Why . . . hello! Little Minty, again! We must have lunch some day."

Patrick's hand at her waist took a firmer grasp but before he could speak Minty said, as sweetly as she could, "Do you know my fiancé, Patrick Sands?"

"What, engaged already! Stolen a march on us, have you, Patrick?"

In fact, Patrick seemed to know everybody, including the parrot-faced Lady Silchester, dressed in unbecoming electric blue. Lady Silchester was there with her granddaughter, lumpy Tessa from the Estate Office at the Hall. It amused Minty to work out that Tessa, who had such an unimportant job, was invited because of her family connections, whereas Annie Phillips, who was a millionairess but not local, wasn't.

"So, Araminta," said Lady Silchester in her most disagreeable voice. "I hear you've turned down Simon, the most eligible bachelor in the county, in favour of Patrick Sands. I wish you happy."

Patrick moved his hand from Minty's waist to put it on her shoulder.

Minty smiled at the old dragon. "He suits me."

"Perhaps you can make him see sense, then. I'm worn out, trying to get him to release money for my granddaughter." Lady Silchester moved on to where Tessa was hanging on Simon's every word.

More names, more faces. Someone taking photographs. When she had a chance to look around her, Minty saw dear Hugh Wootton jotting down the names of some of the plants. The maples were magnificent, yellow and apricot and flaming red and deep scarlet. She wondered if the Hall would ever be visited for its gardens.

Hugh thanked her once again for restoring Toby to them and giving him a job. He also wanted to talk to her about being co-opted onto the Parish Council. She just stopped herself in time from telling him about Mr Tinderman's forthcoming visit only to discover that he already knew about it, having heard about it from someone who'd been talking to young Tim in the Estate Office.

Minty could only say, "We mustn't count on Mr Tinderman taking a shop. Perhaps he won't like the place."

Venetia came up with the amusing Mr Lightowler, who had taken over the bookshop and was planning to start a music society in the village. He wanted Minty to join. It was interesting to see that Mr Lightowler, who was a very new off-comer, had been invited because ... well, because he was contributing so much to the village ... and ... and ... her mouth was stiff with smiling, and Patrick had been nobbled by a stately elderly gentleman with a full head of creamy white hair. She rather thought she'd been introduced to him earlier, but couldn't now remember his name.

She looked around and marvelled that Minty, the vicarage maid of all work, had found herself so many good friends. She looked at Toby, almost handsome in his new-found ease; at comfortably rounded Neville Chickward, the accountant, who was looking at her with spaniel's eyes and still showing every symptom of calf love for her. What a pity that was, because otherwise he'd be ideal as the Hall's accountant. She compared all the men she could see with her own true love: dark, saturnine, exactly right in every way ... and Patrick caught her eye and gave her that little half-smile which means so much between those who love one another.

Mrs Collins raised her glass and her voice in a toast. "To the lovebirds, God bless them!"

Minty blushed and Patrick said, "Why didn't we elope to Gretna Green!"

When they left the party, Patrick announced that he was hungry. "You charmed them all, as I knew you would. Shall we eat at the Pheasant Inn?"

The pub's extensive menu was chalked up on a blackboard, every surface shone with polish and the background music was not intrusive.

The landlady, Moira, was a large woman with carefully blonded hair, heavy gold rings on every finger and an authoritative manner. Her husband was even larger, smiling but mainly silent. Patrick ordered home-made carrot and coriander soup, followed by duck breast with mango and lime sauce, while Minty contented herself with a dish of monkfish tails.

They talked over the party, and Minty tried to put names to faces. The man with the cream-coloured hair was the sixth Earl of something, and the woman with the mayoral-type chain was District Chairman. The politician was up for re-election, and the woman with a thin nose was the wife of an industrialist whose only child was suffering from coeliac disease and who spent all her time raising money for research.

With the coffee, the landlady came to hover and enquire if everything had been to their satisfaction.

Minty realised Moira wanted to talk. "Please join us?"

"I heard you got rid of your old chef. Congratulations. Mrs Thornby will do you proud and what's more, she's bound to order locally, instead of sending to town like your old chef did. That'll be good for all of us. I hear someone's interested in the vacant shops by the Chinese restaurant?"

"There's nothing definite as yet," said Minty.

"Ah. You're right to be cagey, the way gossip flies around this place. Now this Winter Wonderland you're setting up; I told Mrs Collins I'd sponsor a tree if I could have an advert in the programme . . ."

Minty blinked. She hadn't got as far as advertisements in programmes yet. She looked across at Patrick but he was leaning back, looking amused. "I'll suggest it to Toby Wootton, who's in charge of PR."

"There's one other thing." Moira fiddled with her rings. "Simon—and Miles—used to keep tabs here. Ran up quite a bill. We've written off Miles' now he's in jail, and I've asked Simon to settle but he says he's out of funds. I wondered if Patrick might send him a solicitor's letter."

Patrick shook his head. "You'd be throwing good money after bad because the man's no assets to pay your bill. Perhaps you'd allow me to pay it for him—but don't tell him so. Right?"

Minty put her hand on Patrick's and pressed it. She was so proud of him.

Moira was happy, too. "I don't think he owes much else in the village, except an enormous bill for petrol. I understand Bill at the garage—he's my husband's cousin—will have the bailiffs on him if he doesn't pay up. Repossessing one of his cars will hurt Simon good and proper.

"Yes, the village is waking up, and we all know who to thank for that. Not everyone's pleased, of course. The charity shop will have to close its doors if Ruby sets up as a dressmaker—which reminds me, dear, that that blouse of yours is absolute heaven; did she make it for you? I wouldn't mind something like that for myself . . ."

When Moira had gone, Minty said, "It's scary how the news has got around. Suppose nothing comes of Mr Tinderman's visit?"

"Even if it doesn't, there's a spirit of optimism about the place and it will rub off. Those shops will be re-opened by next spring, if even half your plans go through."

"Patrick, a personal question. Those shares you gave me for my birthday. You didn't beggar yourself to give them to me, did you? And the diamond? You said your father was almost ruined by the scandal years ago."

"And I've always pleaded poverty to you. Yes. Well . . ." He fidgeted with his coffee spoon. "My father *was* reduced to comparative poverty, but first my mother and then her sister left me some money. Quite a lot of money. I kept quiet about it because the only girl I ever told started making plans to spend it in frivolous ways. I said I'd been joking about having money and she dropped me, so I didn't tell anyone else. My father advised me to invest in student property and garages, which are always at a premium. It meant I could reopen the house here and if I wanted to take pro bono work, I could."

"It didn't end there, did it? You bought those cottages on the edge of town to give yourself a quiet place, and you rented the others out. Then you saw the potential of that derelict farmhouse up at Eden Fields and realised it could be converted into much-needed housing . . ."

"And suggested to Hugh Wootton and old man Thornby that we form a company to develop it, yes. You thought I was giving you a magnificent gift when I passed the shares on to you, but to tell the truth I hardly felt it."

"I suspect there's more. Last week you lent me the money to pay the wages, and offered to pay for the wedding."

He looked uncomfortable. "Think nothing of it."

"Patrick, how much are you worth?"

"It sort of mounts up . . ."

"Patrick Sands!"

"Somewhere around ten, possibly twelve, I suppose. Mostly invested in property."

She gulped. "Twelve million? Why hide the truth?"

"Pathetic, isn't it! I wanted you to 'love me for myself'."

She said, softly, "Yes, I do. And you don't love me for Eden Hall, but because . . . ?"

"Because you are my own sweet heart."

Minty's early mornings had slipped into a routine. First a visit to the chapel. Then she'd check on work being done around the house and gardens, have breakfast, deal with correspondence with Iris, and touch base with Toby.

Waiting was hard. Waiting on the Americans . . . waiting for Lord Asher to find time to see her about the trust fund for the Hall . . . waiting for Mr Tinderman. He was coming over with Carol that afternoon. Tim from the Estate Office would take him round the shops, and then they'd come up for tea at the Hall.

Today she approved the newly planted urns on the terraces, which Hodge had filled with wallflowers and trailing vari-coloured ivies. Reggie had got the old lawnmower working again, so Hodge could set about one last cut of the lawns. To give him his due, Hodge was working hard at the moment.

She darted into the walled garden where Hodge's nephew was beginning to assemble a mobile tower from which to tackle the ragged Portuguese laurel hedge around the formal garden. Nothing had yet been done about removing the dying box plants, but give them time.

Back for breakfast and a quick look at the newspapers . . . and oh, scream! The Sevres vases and the big squashy cushions Ruby had found for her had disappeared. She really must have a word with Serafina about making the place more comfortable.

Which reminded her that Reggie had been trying to get the enormous Tompion clock in the Great Hall working again. She must check on that and then ... she hesitated ... had she time to explore one of the basement rooms in the north wing before seeing Iris? There were rooms there crammed to the door with old bits and pieces. Or perhaps she should check on the far outbuildings because Tim had reported tiles were beginning to slide off one of the roofs.

She must also check whether Gemma had returned or not and ring the hospital to see if her aunt was any better.

She looked at her watch. Mr Tinderman and Carol might well be driving out of the city now. If he would only take just one unit, it would help with the cash flow problem. One thing at a time.

Tiles sliding off a roof. That must be attended to before the winter storms. She ran down the stairs, across the Fountain Court and through Florence's kitchen into the outer courtyard ...

... where someone caught her by the wrist and rushed her off her feet and round the corner into the desolation of the formal garden.

Simon. The sky seemed to darken overhead.

"Enjoyed yourself last night, did you? Thought you'd been accepted by society? You and your slimy solicitor friend."

He was hurting her wrists. "Please let me go."

It had been a mistake to beg. He enjoyed hurting her. His grasp on her wrists tightened.

He was smiling. Not nicely.

She met his eyes, tried to breathe deeply, tried not to let him see how much he was hurting her.

There was no one else around on this side of the house at the moment. If Gemma had returned, she'd still be in bed. It was too early for the room stewards. Hodge was mowing the lawn on the far side of the house; his nephew was in the walled garden. Florence would arrive for work at any minute but her kitchen was round the corner of the house. She wouldn't hear even if Minty screamed.

Simon rocked her from side to side. With a thrust of fear, she realised she was as helpless as a doll in his hands. *Patrick*, she thought. But Patrick had returned to town last night, and was working there today.

Lord, help me! No one else would.

"Dear little not-quite sister," he said. "You must admit you've been a bad girl, haven't you?" Again he shook her. "You should have listened to me when you first came back, then I wouldn't have had all these problems. I've lost the money from the American deal because of you. It's you who's turning me out of my flat, you who've cut off my income and taken the money that rightfully belongs to me. You deserve to be punished, little sister, don't you? Answer me!"

The pain in her wrists brought tears to her eyes. She gritted her teeth. "No!"

He twisted her wrists up and forced her back and down pinning her to the ground.

"Get off me!" She turned her head from side to side. It seemed to her that the house, the garden, the trees, the sky even, were watching, listening, holding their breath . . . anxious for her. She was one with them, would not let herself feel him pressing her down. This would pass soon.

He was strong. He trapped both her wrists with one hand above her head, and with the other pulled up her sweater. She felt his touch on her skin—and screamed. Knowing it was useless but unable to prevent herself. She tried to heave him off and failed.

This isn't happening. It can't be.

His voice was breathy in her ear. "You like this, don't you?" Grinning, he took her chin in his free hand and brought his mouth down hard on hers.

She tried to bite him. And failed.

Then suddenly, amazingly, he released her.

He knelt, stood up and took a pace back. He was flushed, laughing. Triumphant. "Of course you like it. Have you heard of the *droit de seigneur*? It's the right of the Lord of the Manor to take village girls on their wedding night. I'm not going to take you now. I'm going to make you wait for it. You won't know when, or where. It might be at night when you're asleep. It might be this evening, or tomorrow . . . or two hours before you're supposed to walk up the aisle to marry Patrick. You can't stop me. I know this place better than you do, and I have a master key to open every door."

She scrambled backwards, reached the wall, used it to lever herself to her feet. Panting. Eyes switching from right to left. *This can't be happening!*

"So now you know what my revenge is going to be. Or . . . there is an alternative. Do you want to hear it? Say yes."

She managed to gasp out a yes.

"Call off the wedding. You might as well, because Patrick's not going to want you after I've finished with you, is he? With any luck, you'll be pregnant, as well. He'd never marry a woman who's carrying my child, would he? He's far too proud for that. And you're such a goody-goody Christian you wouldn't get rid of a child in your womb, so you'll have to carry it to term, and then my child would be your first-born and heir to the Hall."

The horror of it!

"Oh, and don't try telling the police I've threatened to rape you, because no one would believe you. They'd think you were fantasising. After all, who in their right minds would prefer sour-faced Patrick to me! For your information, one of my drinking pals is the son of the local Inspector of Police. He's always amused at the way women try to pick me up in bars. He knows they're all hot for me . . . as you are, my dear, much as you may try to deny it."

She turned, tried to escape. He caught her wrist and easily, contemptuously, threw her back against the wall. He knocked all the breath out of her . . . and her head clicked back to the stone . . . she slid down to the ground. Through a darkening world she saw him brush his hands one against the other and walk off saying something . . . his voice faded out.

The sky faded out.

Chapter Twenty-Three

She fought upwards through the dark and heard someone keen. She realised it was her.

She was looking at life through a zoom lens as her beautiful future, her lovely life with Patrick, decreased in size and moved rapidly away from her. Simon would rape her, and she would be destroyed. She would be so ashamed that she'd have to run away and hide, not let Patrick near her and . . . what was there left?

The sun had come up and was warm on her face. Her head hurt, as did her wrists. Her vision was fuzzy. Then it cleared. A spider was trying to climb a thread of gossamer . . . up and up and . . . whoops, down it went again.

She thought of Robert the Bruce, being encouraged by a spider to try, try, try again. Only this spider didn't bother. It sat on the ground, thinking about life in general and deciding it wasn't worth it.

She lay there. And didn't move. Nor pray. There was something wrong with her vision. She couldn't think straight.

It was the end of everything.

Iris found her.

"Minty? Did you fall from the terrace? Don't move. I'll get an ambulance."

Minty made an enormous effort and lifted her head. Then managed to sit upright. One part of her mind told her that she was in shock. Another part still lay there on the ground. Dead. She turned her head to look for the spider, and wished she hadn't. Her eyes crossed and uncrossed. Anyway, the spider had disappeared. Only the tiny filament of gossamer web still hung there in the autumn sunlight. Minty reached out to touch the thread. And missed it.

Iris knelt beside her. "What is it? What's happened to your wrists? Simon! Has he . . . has he . . . ?"

She whispered. “Raped? Not yet. He’s going to, though.” She leaned on the wall to get to her feet. Her head! She felt sick. What was she doing today? She couldn’t remember.

She understood now how abused women let themselves be beaten up. “Cancel . . . wedding?”

“Rubbish!” said Iris.

Minty saw she was standing on one of the dying box plants. She bent down and tugged. That hurt her head. She lost her balance. Staggered. Fell to her knees. It was easier to reach the plants now she was closer to the earth. She steadied herself with one hand on the ground. The plant came out of the ground easily. She’d asked Hodge to clear this garden, and he hadn’t got round to it yet. Well, that was something she could do, anyway. Clear the garden. She bent to pull up the plant next to it . . . and the next. She would make a big pile in the middle of the garden and set light to it. And not think of Patrick. Thinking of Patrick made her head spin. Patrick wouldn’t accept another man’s child as his.

“What are you doing?” asked Iris.

Minty didn’t reply. She continued to pull up plants, crawling along the row, trying not to fall on her face. She had a headache. Saw double. Stopped what she was doing. Her vision cleared. She bent down for the next plant. What was it exactly that Simon had said he’d do to her? Now she could remember. Now the words had gone.

She heard Iris on her mobile phone, telling Serafina that Minty had been delayed. Iris was cool, Iris had been through this before, Iris had been raped by Simon and run away. Iris had lost her own true love when he heard what Simon had done.

Minty bent and tugged and threw the dead and dying plants into a heap. After a while she saw that Iris was helping her. That made sense. Two women without a future.

It was going to be a hot day. There wasn’t a cloud in the sky. The sky tipped around her. She steadied herself.

Someone came down to ask what was wrong. Toby? Iris sent him away.

Serafina came down with a basket containing coffee and rolls. Iris poured coffee and put it in Minty’s hand. Minty knelt there, holding the coffee, unable to drink it. Unable to think. Iris put the cup to her lips, and Minty gagged. Threw up.

Serafina wiped her face; Iris helped her to sit down with her back to the terrace wall above.

"This is Simon's work," said Serafina. "Iris, you get Patrick on the phone."

Minty shook her head, and then wished she hadn't. It hurt. "No. He's busy. Let him have the day in peace. He's coming over. Tonight. Don't tell. Oh. He's got to know, hasn't he? Because we can't get married now. Can we?" She heard herself talking in a high voice, like a small child.

"You're not thinking straight," said Iris. "Tell us exactly what happened."

Minty stared at her. How had Iris survived and become so strong?

She told them. It was easy enough, because it had happened to someone else, not to her. Besides, none of this was real. Was it?

"Minty," said Iris, "Patrick would marry you if you had two heads and were carrying Siamese twins!"

"I couldn't ask him to, not if they were Simon's twins." Minty knew that at least. Of . . . that . . . she . . . was . . . sure. She thrust back her hair, which had fallen around her face. She thought she must look like a street urchin, streaked with tears and dirt. Her hands were grimy, with broken nails.

Serafina clapped her hands together, loudly. Why so loud? "Simon has to be stopped."

Minty said, "No one would believe me. Simon said one of his best friends is the Inspector's son."

Iris drew in her breath. "So? He's not the only policeman around here, is he? Patrick will know who we have to speak to. He said I ought not to have run away. He was right. If I'd gone to the police then, none of this would have happened. Minty, I'll come with you to the police and we'll tell them what he's done."

"Dear Lord above, what have I done to deserve this? Or Patrick?"

Minty saw Iris' lips move, but heard nothing. She began to shake. Shock. She couldn't stop. Iris and Serafina closed around her, holding her tightly, holding her together. They half carried her up the stairs to her room, dumped her in a hot bath.

She put on a dressing gown which smelt of Serafina, staggered a bit, took some aspirin, said she'd be all right in a minute. If she put her mind to it she could block out what had happened. Mr Tinderman was looking at properties in the village. It would be a good thing for the village if Mr Tinderman decided to take one of the vacant units. She must be strong, pretend that nothing was wrong. The village mustn't suffer because of what Simon had done. And what had he done, after all? A few threats shouldn't put her off, should they?

She drank some soup. Tried to eat a sandwich. Couldn't get it down. Tried to read some correspondence. Couldn't concentrate.

Iris came and went. *Shield-maiden,* thought Minty. *Iris is my shield, even if she's no longer a maiden. How did she survive?*

She stared at her image in the mirror, huge staring eyes in a white face. Ruby brought in a fine blue sweater and brand-new jeans for her to wear. The sweater had long sleeves covering her hands. The bruises on her wrists were beginning to colour up. Ruby was silent, her eyes anxious. *She knows! Who told her? Serafina, that's who.*

She fell on her bed and tried to sleep but the moment she dozed off, she woke with a start, imagining Simon tossing her around like a doll.

She wondered how Mr Tinderman and Carol were getting on. *Oh, Patrick, my sweet heart, my love.*

She got up after a while. Her head ached. They'd be here soon. She felt numb. Couldn't feel anything, even when she knocked her arm. She felt as if she'd gone deaf, as if she were moving through air that had suddenly gone dead and heavy.

"What a marvellous place!" Carol danced into the room ahead of her father and another woman. Carol's voice zinged around the room and Minty winced. Tim from the Estate Office brought up the rear, grinning broadly. Carol kissed Minty, punched the air and cried, "Eureka! I'm going to be your near neighbour, Minty, because . . ."

"Not so fast, Carol!" Mr Tinderman took Minty's hand and his jovial expression changed to one of concern. "Are you not well, my dear?"

Minty forced a smile. "I fell and banged my head. I'm all right, really." With an effort she turned to the diminutive lady with fuzzy grey-blue hair and piercing black eyes who had followed Mr Tinderman in: "I seem to remember . . . ?"

"Ms Prendergast, of course you remember her," said Carol. "She used to run the canteen at college but took early retirement when her insides played up and . . ."

"Carol!" said her father, only half amused. "Let Ms Prendergast speak for herself."

"I'm quite recovered now," said the little lady in a voice surprisingly deep for one of her size. "I've been looking for somewhere to open a small coffee shop with living accommodation above. The smaller of your two units will do me nicely if I may have a short lease with an option to renew. My initial outlay will be considerable, as I will have to install a proper kitchen and toilet downstairs. Hygiene requirements are rigorous and must be met with exactitude."

Carol was jigging up and down with impatience. "I'm going to have the flat above Dad's new shop and oversee the conversion and set up with a photo-copier and computer, doing freelance office work or something. And I've brought a couple of bridesmaid's dresses along for you to see. I can't wait to meet your lovely man, and oh, isn't this village just the loveliest place?"

Minty indicated they should all sit down. She'd be a lot happier sitting down, herself. *Dear Lord, help me not to break down. My head hurts and so do my wrists. The aspirins must be wearing off. I can hear and see again. I can hear the rustle of clothing, footsteps on the boards.*

"We came early," said Mr Tinderman. "Chatted to one or two shop keepers, looked at transport, car parking and so on. I need a larger workshop for repairs and storage than the one I have in the city, and one of your units has a yard with sheds at the back, so it might do. I could send stuff down here that I can't sell in the city, and perhaps trawl around the neighbourhood sales here, seeing what I could pick up to sell in Town. We've been thinking for some time that Carol ought to leave the nest, and as she's fallen in love with the place . . . well, why not?"

Minty tried to smile. She told herself she was feeling better and she thought she was, a bit. Mr Tinderman produced a case of pocket watches and they joked about which one Patrick would like. Carol tried on the dresses she'd brought with her, and Ruby said she could run up something better than that chain-store tat which had been very badly finished, just look at these seams!

Serafina served them tea and cakes in Minty's cool green sitting room, where Mr Tinderman admired the paintings and forebore to criticise the furniture. Minty tried to get comfortable on the settee, expecting to lean back against the cushions that Ruby had found and irritably wondering why they weren't there.

One minute she thought she wouldn't tell Patrick what had happened and the next she knew—in despair—that she must and that he would say they must think carefully about postponing the wedding.

Patrick—who was usually late—actually arrived early. He took one look at her and knew something had happened, but managed to greet the Tindermans and Ms Prendergast with his usual courtesy. As he accepted a cup of tea, he turned to Minty with a questioning look. "I half expected you to ring me today. Kept looking at my watch, wondering how you were."

He saw too much, knew her too well. She put on her brightest smile. She couldn't tell him in front of the Tindermans, so she tried for a diversion. "Look what Mr Tinderman's brought you."

Mr Tinderman opened his case. "Voila! My lady Araminta commanded me to bring you a selection of pocket watches along with the wedding rings. In fact, we have a little bet on, she and I, as to which you will choose. Ancient and modern here, all in perfect working order. Some chime the hours and minutes, some give the date and month and phases of the moon. If you wear a waistcoat, they will fit in your pocket. Otherwise you may need a short length of chain to attach to a buttonhole for safety."

Patrick blushed. Minty could see he was both surprised and pleased. "For me? Really?" He touched several, even taking them out of their cases to look at them and admire the workmanship. But again and again his eyes slid up to a severely plain, elegant watch. He took it out and cradled it in both hands, smiling. He flicked it open as if he'd done it a thousand times before and nodded in approval of the restrained, traditional interior. "I won't ask the price, as it's a gift. But I suspect I've chosen the best."

Mr Tinderman laughed. "My lady wins. She said you'd go for that one, and let me tell you, it is the gem of my collection. Now for wedding rings . . ." He drew out another case and Minty and Patrick chose identical plain gold rings, to be engraved inside with their initials and the wedding date.

The Tindermans and Ms Prendergast left in a flurry of goodwill and promises to meet again soon.

Patrick turned on Minty even as the door closed, drawing her to the light. "What's happened?"

Iris came into the room, looking anxious. Serafina arrived. And behind her came Ruby and Jonah. And Reggie.

Minty explained, trying not to shake with nerves, trying to smile. "You may want to postpone the wedding. Simon caught me in the garden and ..." She told the whole sorry story, hoping he'd understand, fearing he wouldn't.

He sat her down. "You called the police, and the doctor?"

"No, I ..."

Iris hurried to explain. "She said ..."

"Idiots! Can't you see she's concussed half out of her mind?" He took out his mobile phone and located a number. "Jill, are you on call this evening? I've got a client who's been assaulted. Concussed. Wrists badly bruised. Threatened with rape, but thankfully not ... yes, yes." He looked at his new watch. "Be there in twenty minutes, maybe half an hour."

He made another phone call. "Are you on duty tonight? I'm bringing in Miss Cardale, who's been assaulted and threatened with rape. About half an hour. Yes, I've alerted the doctor already and she'll be there. Can you get hold of ... ? Yes. Thanks. Yes, as quickly as we can."

He turned on Iris, Serafina and the others and without raising his voice spoke fluently for a full minute on the subject of their incompetence and lack of common sense. Minty rather enjoyed the performance, thinking that this was how Patrick would act as master of Eden Hall.

Patrick pointed his finger at Serafina. "Serafina, overnight bag. She'll probably be kept in. Iris, no arguments this time. You're coming with us to the police. Reggie, I'm not asking you to drive us. I've got another job for you. Get hold of Barr; find out if it's true that Simon's got a master key, which I rather doubt. In any event, get a locksmith out, pay him any overtime he asks for, and have locks and bolts put on the doors at either end of this suite of rooms. Iris, you'd better stay with your parents till we can get new locks on your accommodation, too. Any questions? I'm carrying Minty down now and leaving in five minutes. Right?"

Jill was the police surgeon, a middle-aged woman with an air of quiet competence. She examined Minty, asked sensible questions, took photographs of the bruises and made copious notes for the file. Minty said she was feeling better. Did she really have to go to hospital? And no, he hadn't raped her. Only promised to do so.

"Promises, promises," said Jill, filling in a prescription. "And yes, you do have to have a scan, see if there's any real damage apart from a lump on the back of your head which is going to give you headaches for a few days. They'll keep you in hospital overnight to make sure there's no other damage done. If all's well, they'll let you go tomorrow. I don't suppose it'll be at all necessary, and I'm sure Patrick will make sure you're fully protected from now on, but take these for a month. They'll ensure you can't get pregnant, whatever happens."

Birth control pills? Minty giggled. She hadn't thought she could laugh again, but it appeared she could. Jill smiled. "Yes, that will remove the worst fear, won't it? And there are people who can help you with self-defence. Now, do you feel strong enough to make a statement? You can leave it till tomorrow, if you like."

"I can do it."

By this time Iris had told her story to a sympathetic policewoman who'd been trained to deal with rape victims. Iris wept. Minty then told her story. And wept. It was the most enormous relief to see that the policewoman believed her story, even the bit about preferring sallow, long-nosed Patrick to the splendidly handsome Simon.

Patrick drove Minty to hospital and she was given a scan although her eyes were fast closing on her. Finally she was shown into the private room which Patrick had arranged for her, allowed to get into bed and sleep.

She was woken at intervals during the night to check on her vital signs and ensure that she hadn't slid into a coma. In the morning she sat up in bed. Her stomach was calm and her vision had cleared though her head ached abominably and the bruises on her wrists had caused them to stiffen.

"I'm all right now," she said to the nurse. "Can I leave?"

"Not till the doctor's been. Meantime, there's someone here to see you. He's been here all night. Five minutes only."

Patrick came in, unshaven, still wearing yesterday's clothes. He touched her cheek. "How are you? The scan showed no damage, thank God." Usually she could sense his nervous energy, but today he seemed serene.

"Fine, just aches and pains. What's happened to you?"

"Tell you later. It may not last. Now listen, Reggie will come to fetch you. Don't get into anyone else's car, right?"

"Kiss me."

He fingered his bristly chin, and then did so. It was the longest kiss she'd ever had from him. She tasted cigarettes and coffee, smelt his sweat, yesterday's clothes. *Delicious*, she thought. *Real. Now I know we can make it, no matter what happens.*

"Yes, I know. I've been smoking." He held her hands, touched her swollen, bruised wrists with gentle fingers. "Somewhere around three o'clock this morning, I thought you might die. Take it easy."

Patrick had said, "Take it easy." Easier said than done. But the doctor did discharge her, and Reggie did come to fetch her.

"Take your time, miss. You do look peaky. Everyone's in a terrible state, knowing that if you'd copped it, we'd all be in trouble. There's new locks and bolts on the doors to your rooms. Iris spent the night with her parents, but I'll get new locks on her doors and windows today. Simon's gone missing. If I could only get my hands on him . . ."

Minty closed her eyes. She'd thought she'd be all right when she left the hospital, but she had no energy at all and everything ached. It was ironic that Simon should now be on the run, because she didn't think he'd intended to put her in hospital. Only, if he hadn't done so, the police might never have taken her seriously.

Iris met Minty at the lift door. Minty held out her arms—or maybe Iris did. The two women embraced. "Thank you, Iris."

Iris shuddered. "I was so afraid, telling the police. You were so brave . . ."

Minty shook her head and said, "Ouch." She saw Toby's concerned face over Iris' shoulder and tried to smile. "I'm all right, really. Well, nearly all right, anyway." She held on to Iris' hand and took her through to the sitting room, where she almost fell onto the settee. "I just have to rest for a while. Iris, would you be my second bridesmaid, if Ruby can find you a dress?"

Iris smiled through her tears. "I'm no maid, but of course I accept . . . and I suppose you won't be surprised to hear that Ruby has already measured me up for a dress to match the one she's been making for Carol. Oh, and Jonah's arranging all the flowers that have been sent up for you."

Serafina and Ruby appeared, looking anxious, and behind them came an enormous bouquet of flowers with a pair of legs at the bottom which turned out to belong to Jonah.

"From me, and everyone," said Jonah. "Hodge has sent up a bouquet and Florence says there's more flowers coming up now from the village."

"Gracious!" said Minty, and began to laugh. Everyone else laughed too, rather carefully and not too loud, but allowing them to express their relief.

Minty rested while Serafina fussed around her, and Jonah mounted guard on a chair opposite, playing with his snowstorm. To her surprise, Minty fell fast asleep on that uncomfortable settee. When she woke up it was late afternoon and Iris said she'd cancelled the Heads of Department meeting that day.

Minty had to acknowledge she'd not have been up to it.

Chapter Twenty-Four

Minty slept all that afternoon, but managed to eat a light supper with Patrick. Afterwards, he held her in his arms on the settee and talked about his night at the hospital.

"I sat with your watch in my hand, watching the second hand jump. With concussion you can drift into a coma and never come out of it. I tried to bargain with God; I'd give up hating Simon if he let you live. But you can't bargain with God.

"I knew I couldn't stop hating Simon by my own strength, so I asked God to help me. And then . . . it was exhaustion setting in, I suppose . . . I didn't hate him any more. I kept probing for my hurt, like trying to get a reaction from a bad tooth. Nothing."

A rueful laugh. "I reminded God that Simon hasn't shown any sign of repentance, that he's going to go on destroying till he's stopped. I asked God who was going to stop Simon, if not me. The thought came into my mind that I was to stop Simon, but that vengeance was His. I don't know how that works. Perhaps I've already done what's needed, by getting you and Iris to make statements to the police. Personally, I want him locked up where he can do no more harm, but I don't feel vengeful any more. I feel—detached. You're tired. You don't want to hear this now."

Her eyes were closing. "No one can be whole if they carry hate around with them."

He shifted under her. "This settee . . ."

"I'll do something about it soon. I promise."

"The village is buzzing with all this. Becky stopped me in the car park where she's no business to be. Wanting to know how you were. She says you're helping the children decorate the church for Harvest tomorrow. Do you feel up to it? And is there any news of your aunt?"

"She's dying, I think." She blinked. "I didn't know I was going to say that. Iris rang the hospital for me this afternoon and they said she was holding her own. Of course she's not dying. I'll ring them again in the morning."

"Would you like me to come with you, next time you go back to see her?"

"Mm. Yes, please." She yawned.

"Off to bed with you, but before you go . . ." He produced a small object from his pocket. "It's mace spray. Carry it with you all the time and don't hesitate to use it. And you're not to go anywhere alone. Promise?"

She nodded, without really understanding what she'd promised to do.

He said, "Now I've got a date with Reggie and Barr to see if we can re-activate the alarm system in the Hall. There is one but according to Barr, Simon forgot the code one night and got so angry he deactivated it. Which means you probably haven't got any valid insurance if there's a fire or an accident."

She held up her face to be kissed. *Sixteen more days. Will we make it?*

In the morning she woke with a feeling of depression. Was it raining? No, it was a bright, sunny morning, with a light dew glistening over the Park.

Her head wasn't aching but she remembered she'd promised Patrick she wouldn't wander around alone. How was she to check on everything, if she couldn't go on her rounds?

The doors at either end of her rooms had been fitted with new locks, but that excluded access to the chapel. She thought of going there, anyway. Then she thought that Simon might return and hide behind the door, knowing she visited the place a couple of times a day and . . .

No, she mustn't take unnecessary risks. A vista of tiresome scenes opened before her. She must ring the hospital and maybe her uncle, as well. She got dressed, finding everything taking twice as long as usual.

Serafina knocked on her door. "I'll come with you to the chapel this morning, shall I?"

Minty was grateful. She was used to being there on her own, but she found she could pray as well, if not better, with Serafina there. First she gave thanks for her deliverance, for the love and care she'd received from everyone around her. Then, following Patrick's example, she prayed for her aunt and for herself.

Dear Lord, I'm offering up my hatred of my aunt for You to take care of. I can't get rid of it by myself. If I'm honest, there's a part of me that wants to hold on to it, that savours the thought of revenge. But I'm willing myself not to do so.

Are you sure?

No, but I feel it's the right thing to do. I don't want there to be any dark corners in my soul.

A golden silence filled the chapel.

It was Saturday, so the house would be open at noon.

Iris came in even though it was a weekend, and they dealt with some correspondence. Iris was very patient with her. Minty asked Iris to find someone to give a quick makeover to the restaurant . . . not Reggie, because he was too busy. How had they ever managed without that man? Barr rang to see how she was. He sounded really concerned for her. Dear Barr; he really was trying very hard.

The Reverend Cecil rang to ask how she was, and did she feel well enough to help the children prepare for Harvest that morning? Yes, she thought she could.

The Heads of Department meeting had been cancelled the day before, but Iris had spoken to everyone; they'd assured her that all was well and that they were much encouraged to hear that two of the village shops were being let.

Minty had planned to talk to the stewards that morning before the house was open, but instead Venetia came up to say not to bother, and how relieved they all were that she'd not been badly hurt. Minty tried to remember what she'd intended to say to the stewards.

"Oh, I know. Venetia, will you find out if it's all right by them if the house is open till Christmas? I'm going to ask Florence if she'll put on a free Christmas lunch for all the stewards one day when the house is closed. And if there's anyone who hasn't received an invitation to my wedding, will they let me know?"

Venetia said that was splendid, kissed Minty and told her to take it easy. Iris reported that acceptances to the wedding invitations were coming in fast.

As members of the public began to trickle into the house, Minty felt it safe to leave her rooms and walk up to the church. The sun shone, but the wind was keen. The walk seemed to clear her head, which was just as well because she found the children were hanging around in a huddle in the porch, looking as if they'd like to disappear, given half a chance.

Minty helped them create a window display of autumn leaves, fruits and flowers, and added a special feature with the aid of some green and yellow paper.

"Let's cut out shapes of apples or pears, one for each of us. We'll write on the back something we specially want to give God thanks for, and hang it on this twirly branch of a tree. No one else will see unless they look very closely, but you'll know and God will know what we're giving thanks for. Right?"

"Chocolate," said Becky, thoughtfully.

"Conkers," said the boy from the hill farm.

"Mum's sausages and mash," said the twins.

"I'll do one, too," said Minty. She wrote on hers, "My Sweet Heart". And hung it on the branch with the others.

On her way back she looked into the gift shop, where Doris was darting between the unpacking of new stock and taking money for Hodge's plants. "I need some more help, dear!" cried Doris. Minty said she'd see what she could do. Now who could she ask?

She had a word with Florence and peeped into the restaurant, where the aroma of good coffee was enticing more and more people to spend time and money. On round the corner into the formal garden, where Hodge stood, scratching his head.

After Simon's assault, Minty had started to pull up the dead and dying box plants, but someone had been busy since, for there was nothing there now but a cleared square of earth, with a charred stain showing where the diseased plants had been burned. Hodge's nephew had got his mobile tower in place and was trimming the raggedy laurels with an electric hedge-cutter.

"Hodge, this is amazing. It must have taken you hours."

"It wasn't so hard, once we got started. Florence made her daughter do half an hour, Toby Wootton did some and Jonah . . . though he flitted off after a while. Got the attention span of a gnat, that one. So what do you want done here, then?"

Down from the terrace came Toby, waving a piece of paper for Minty. "Florence told us you were back. Iris said you'd want this, urgent." Jonah drifted down after him, still clutching his glass snowstorm.

"Whoopee!" cried Minty. The Americans had had a survey done of Peacock Place and were willing to discuss either leasing it or—better still—buying it!

"Gentlemen," said Minty. "We're solvent again and can afford to replant. Can you spare a minute to help us with the plan, Toby? Hodge, this is all about stewardship. Every penny that I put into the Hall has to pay a dividend in some way. We've always had a formal garden here with plants laid out in a geometric pattern. I want to continue that idea, but instead of box, I want to use lavender bushes whose spikes can be harvested in summer for sale in the shop.

"I want you to buy two-year-old plants and have the garden ready for the wedding. I want it to be laid out like a daisy, with yellow chrysanthemums forming the centre."

The sun went behind a cloud.

Simon strolled into the garden, the blue of his shirt no bluer than his eyes.

Minty recoiled. Her instinct was to run, but she told herself Simon couldn't do anything in front of witnesses. "The police are looking for you, Simon."

"You may have fooled a lowly copper, my dear, but others are not so stupid. Some of them are quite cross with you for wasting their time. Well, Toby! This is a pleasant surprise! We must get together, have a drink. Come up to my rooms this evening after work, right?"

Toby looked searchingly at Simon. "I'd like that."

Oh no! thought Minty. *Simon's got Toby just where he wants him, all over again.*

Simon swung back to Minty. "I need a word with you in private. Toby, this is between my stepsister and me, so find something else to do, right? You, too, Hodge."

"They stay," said Minty, alarmed.

Simon grinned. "Very well. If you want to be shown up in front of the servants, so be it. Your attempt to blacken my character rebounded on you, my dear. Once I'd explained that you were trying to flirt with me . . ."

Minty gaped. "What?"

He sounded bored. "It happens all the time. We had a good laugh about that at the police station."

Minty held up her wrists. "And these bruises? My concussion?"

"I had to hold you off, didn't I? You fell and hurt your head. An accident, which you can't lay at my door. As for that slag Iris, well . . . everyone knows she used to spread her favours around when she was here before . . ."

"No one who knows her would believe that!"

"No one believes either of you, my dear. Because . . . I had a witness to your appalling behaviour."

Minty gasped. Her brain zigzagged through various possibilities and came up with the truth. "Tessa! You've been using her, promising her . . . I don't know what! You got her to lie for you?"

"What a devil I am, to be sure," said Simon, amused. Turning serious, "You shouldn't slander people. What will Tessa do when she finds out you've accused her of perjury? Sue you, I shouldn't wonder. Both Toby and Hodge heard you!"

Hodge banged his ear. "Can't hear nothing with that hedge-cutter making such a racket."

Simon gave Toby a charming smile. "Well, Toby? I can rely on you to tell the truth, can't I?"

Toby flushed but didn't say anything.

A champion arose from an unexpected quarter. Little Jonah shook his fist in Simon's face. "Liar, liar! Your coat's on fire! Shall *I* tell the police about the girls you've forced in the past, who've been too ashamed to say afterwards?"

Simon's handsome face lost all its beauty. He swung his arm back, brushing Jonah aside as if he'd been a yapping dog.

Jonah went flying, the snowstorm spinning in the air. Toby sprang forward in a sideways rugby tackle and managed to prevent Jonah crashing into the wall. The globe rolled to Minty's feet.

Simon said, "He's quite mad, should be locked up!"

Toby set Jonah on his feet and gave Simon a steady look. "You haven't changed, have you, Simon? Once a bully . . ."

Simon's eyes became muddy. Minty thought a devil looked out at them. Then his eyes went blue again and he shrugged. "You'll regret taking her part. There'll be no wedding, mark my words. Oh, and Minty, my mother wishes to see you. Now!" He sniggered and left.

Minty was trembling. Her head was aching. Jonah was visibly shaken. She made an effort, picked up the snowstorm and put it back into his hands.

Toby gave her a tentative smile.

Hodge shook his head. "Don't you pay him no account, Miss Minty. Nor that Tessa, neither."

Minty tried to control her heartbeat. "Thank you, Hodge. Thank you, Toby. And you, Jonah. You were all so brave! Let's go and find Ruby."

She had to admit she was scared. Simon had got round the police just as he'd said he would, and he was going to exact revenge for losing the Hall.

Minty breathed deeply, in and out, then tapped on her stepmother's door.

"Come!"

Lady Cardale was reading a newspaper, which she lowered to register Minty's presence.

"I'm surprised you dare show your face," said Lady Cardale. "Your attempt to smear my son's reputation was quite pathetic, since I'm aware you allowed your cousin Lucas so many favours." She indicated a telephone and address book beside her. "I'm phoning everyone to say what you're really like.

"As for your interference in the arrangements for the musical evening, you haven't the slightest idea how to run an exclusive event, and there'll be a mere handful of people rattling around in the Long Gallery. I'll make sure everyone knows who to blame for that, too. Don't expect people to come to your wedding because they won't.

Needless to say, I shan't be there, as I'm leaving the Hall that day. Close the door after you."

Minty kept her voice steady with an effort. "This may be the first time anyone has complained publicly about your son's attitude to women and he may have wriggled out of trouble in the past, but people will remember. Mud sticks. No one should know that better than you.

"The poison you spread about my mother may have distressed her, but it was your behaviour with my father which sent her fleeing from the Hall. It wasn't guilt but going into premature labour which caused her to swerve into the bridge and killed her. You alone are responsible for her death and the death of her unborn child."

Lady Cardale picked up her newspaper again. "I don't have to listen to this. Please go."

"I understand you wish to take some of this furniture with you. If you give me a list, I'll have it checked against the items bought by the estate for the Hall."

Lady Cardale lifted the newspaper to shield her from Minty and made no reply.

Minty said, "As for your portrait, the artist was paid out of Hall funds so it belongs here, but I don't wish to be vindictive. I'll have a copy made as soon as funds allow, and that will be sent on to you in London."

The newspaper remained as rigid as before.

Minty rubbed her forehead in an effort to ease her headache. "There's one last thing. The Hall can't afford to continue funding charity events for free, so I'll have to contact everyone to make new arrangements. I've asked Gemma to continue working on them and she'll keep you informed of what's happening."

Lady Cardale pulled down the newspaper and looked Minty full in the face. Minty recoiled. She'd never seen such naked hate before.

"Get out!"

Minty stiffened her knees and tried to walk slowly from the room. As she did so, she thought she saw a shadow move beside Lady Cardale. Simon? Probably.

Once out of the room she leaned on the door and breathed deeply. Then skittered up the stairs because she'd done exactly what Patrick had asked her not to do, which was wander around by herself.

When she arrived back in the tower office Iris came to meet her, looking worried. "Is your head aching? You've been overdoing it, haven't you? Sit down. I'll ask Serafina to get you a cup of tea."

Iris wasn't her usual calm self.

Minty said, "What's wrong now?"

"Your uncle's just phoned. Bad news, I'm afraid. Your aunt died last night."

Minty sat down with a bump. "Oh. I'm sorry." And she really was. "How's my uncle taking it?"

"He seemed calm. He didn't ask for you, just said you ought to know. He's going out now to make the funeral arrangements. I asked if there was anyone with him. He said his nephew was busy, removing furniture from the vicarage to go into his girl-friend's flat."

Minty looked at her watch. "I'll drive over, just for an hour. He may slam the door in my face, but . . ."

"You're not fit. Reggie will drive you, and no argument."

Minty bit her lip. Patrick had said he'd go with her next time she visited her aunt, but he was a busy man and surely she could manage this by herself? Only, her head ached and her wrists were still swollen. It would be best to let Reggie drive her, after all.

She should be relieved that Aunt Agnes would never again shout at her. So why did she feel like crying?

Shock, probably.

No, it was more than shock. This was "if only" time. If only her aunt had been kinder to her, Minty would have been able to love her. Lewis Carroll said "if only" were the saddest words in the language, and perhaps they were.

Her uncle must be devastated.

The vicarage looked as grim as ever. Her uncle came to the door, looking over her head, seeing her and not seeing her, chewing on his inner cheek, fingers twitching.

"Why have you come? After what you said . . ."

"I'm so sorry, Uncle." And she was. She ought to have been more tactful, found some kinder way of getting through to him.

"That's all very well, but . . . !" His anger died as quickly as it had arisen. He looked defeated. Old. "Oh, come on in."

Reggie said he'd snatch a bite and she could get him on his mobile when she wanted to return.

The vicarage was cold.

Her uncle led the way to his study. "I was with her at the end. I don't think she knew me, though." Nothing seemed to have been touched in his study since Minty was last there.

He sat in his usual chair by the empty fireplace, opposite the chair which her aunt had always used. "I can't bear people fussing around me. At least you don't fuss. The funeral's next Friday."

"Was Lucas there at the end, too?"

He shook his head. "He's moved out, you know. I asked him to come with me to the hospital last night but he had something else on. She didn't mean any harm in what she did to you. It was the way she was brought up. How long are you staying?"

"I have to get back tonight. Let's get you warm first." She put the fire on, made him a hot drink. He was apathetic. She sat beside him, put her warm hand on his cold one. "Have you thought about the future? You were going to move into sheltered accommodation."

He wiped his hand across his eyes. "Do you know how long we were married?"

She knew. "You haven't got a curate at the moment. Perhaps they could find someone to stand in for you, give you a break? Perhaps you could come to stay with me for a while?" She could have kicked herself for suggesting that, because where would he stay, and what would he do at Eden Hall? She was appalled at the prospect.

Luckily he shook his head. "The churchwardens are going to organise a rota, see to my meals and cleaning the house."

"Since I saw you, the money position's improved. If it had happened earlier, maybe I could have got her into a private hospital."

"I blamed you for not doing so, didn't I? The doctors said you were quite right and that she'd the best possible treatment where she was. If it was anybody's fault, it was mine. Her sense of balance had gone and she kept falling down. The doctors couldn't do anything about it. That's why we were going to move somewhere without stairs. I didn't get on to it quickly enough. If I had, she might still be with us."

"You did your best."

She stayed with him for a couple of hours. He didn't want her to do anything but sit with him, so that's what she did. Before she left she asked him if he'd mind her taking the ancient exercise books in which she'd written down recipes over the years.

"You don't need to ask that," he said, apparently forgetting his outburst over the stalks of honesty. When she was leaving he said, "You're all I have in the world now."

What a day! she thought, as Reggie drove her away. But at least it had taken her mind off Simon for a while.

Chapter Twenty-Five

She was tired when she got back. It occurred to her that the sitting room didn't look quite as it had done before. Ah, she had it! All the lovely flower arrangements had disappeared. It was distressing, but she was too worn out to do anything about it. She lay on the settee and closed her eyes . . . and there Iris found her.

Iris was subdued. "Are you OK? I've been thinking. After Simon, I went to a self-defence class. Would you like me to teach you a couple of tricks?"

"I would indeed. Thanks, Iris." Minty struggled to sit upright, once more vowing to do something about that uncomfortable settee. "What else has been happening?"

"Gemma appeared, demanding to speak to you. She calmed down when I explained. I suppose the Reverend Cardale is her uncle, too? She said she wouldn't mind a job, so I suggested she check over the mountain of acceptances to the wedding invitations but—" Iris tried to look guilty and failed—"she said it should have been her wedding not yours, and she—er—went off again."

"Oh, dear." Then, meeting Iris' eye, she giggled.

"It was tactless of me," said Iris, sternly. "Toby needs to talk to you about the Winter Wonderland first thing Monday, before Mrs Chickward and Mrs Collins descend on us. He's drafted some advertisements for you to approve, and some fliers to put in the shops. I've got them here. If you OK them, they can go to press on Monday."

"They look all right to me, except . . . the date's wrong on this one."

Iris nodded. "I'll see that's altered. Lady C rang to complain that she doesn't pay Florence to cook food for the wedding. Apparently Florence sent Gloria up with Lady C's lunch, instead of taking it up herself."

"Tough," said Minty. "Particularly since she doesn't pay Florence's wages in the first place. Anything else?"

"Ruby's on the warpath. She said the cushions you asked her to put in here have been dumped back in her sewing room, and all the flowers Jonah arranged for you in here . . . well, I'm not sure where they've all gone, but Serafina put some in my office and carried the rest downstairs."

Minty clutched her head, which was aching again. "Every time I try to put a personal touch in this room, Serafina throws it out. Sorry. Shouldn't grumble to you."

"One last thing. Simon put this envelope through the door for you."

Inside was a card, blank except for a picture of a dagger. Fourteen days to the wedding. Would they make it?

The sun was going down in a blaze of red and orange, so Patrick persuaded Minty to take a short walk in the Park after supper. She showed him the card Simon had sent and brought him up-to-date with her trip to the city. "I ought to have tried harder to get through to my aunt."

"Have you stopped hating her?"

"I really think I have. I hope she's at peace."

"Look at the sky. The God who created that sunset also created you and me, and watches over us every hour of the day. He knows all about pain and sorrow. He knows all about death. Your aunt believed in Him. She belongs to Him, and He will know how to look after her."

There was a slight frost that night. The leaves clung on to the trees, more turning gold every day, but hardly any yet prepared to drop to the ground. What did drop to the ground was a multitude of horse-chestnut seeds, their prickly cases falling apart and scattering the mahogany-coloured conkers underfoot. Minty gathered a pocketful on her way to church and added them to the children's window display.

Lady Cardale was alone in her front pew, ignoring everyone else as usual. The children piled in around Minty. The twins took it in turns to sit on her lap, and Becky refused to budge from Minty's side. Patrick was on duty again as sidesman, but he slipped into the end of her pew after the first hymn. Which felt right and proper.

When their banns were read, Minty and Patrick smiled at one another.

Becky whispered, "Can I be a flower girl?"

Minty whispered back, "I'm not having any children as bridesmaids or pages, but I want all the children to come to the wedding and on to the Hall afterwards. Would you like to arrange that?"

Her importance duly acknowledged, Becky nodded.

Serafina served up a splendid roast lunch in the dining room and afterwards Annie joined them for coffee . . . which was when Patrick dropped his bombshell. Leaning back in his chair, he produced a folded piece of paper and coughed to attract their attention.

"As the toy boy in this household, I believe I have the right to state my terms."

Annie's eyebrows shot up, while Minty looked apprehensive.

Serafina grinned. "I'm not missing this," she said, and took her time clearing the table.

Patrick said, "I require a heated, indoor, marble-lined sunken bath, a jacuzzi and sauna, complete with yellow celluloid duck. I want a heliport on the roof, a fives court and a racehorse. However, I am a reasonable man and open to negotiation on all of these things—except the celluloid duck."

Annie was making notes. ". . . a fives court . . . and a racehorse. Presumably one that is capable of winning races?"

Minty was watching Patrick. "What do you really want, Patrick?"

A look of innocence. "I told you. A celluloid duck. I had one once, called Donald. I loved that duck. Somehow it got lost when we left the village." He smiled at her. "You know what I want, Minty." He took out a pack of cigarettes and lit up.

Annie recoiled and Serafina said, "Tut!"

Patrick half closed his eyes, inhaling. "I'm under a great deal of stress."

Minty bit her lip. "This is emotional blackmail."

Annie was bewildered. "I don't understand. He's marrying money and the girl he loves. He's moving into one of the most beautiful houses in Britain. What more can he possibly want?"

Minty took a deep breath. "Let me explain. After years of grindingly hard work, Patrick has achieved a lifestyle that suits him. He enjoys his work. He's not interested in how much it cost to make these rooms look like a spread in a magazine. His home is full of valuable antiques, which are both comfortable and practical. He's surrounded himself with books that are not just for show, but are read. His dining room is for daily use, his bedroom is that of a monk . . ."

"Not for much longer, I hope," said Patrick. He blew an almost perfect smoke ring. Annoyed, he said, "Look at that! I'm out of practice."

Annie flushed with displeasure. "I don't see why he's making such a fuss. He can bring his books here, if he wants. I daresay you can find a corner for them." Her voice trailed away.

"Yes, Annie? Where?" said Patrick. "You remember my office, don't you? It has built-in Queen Anne break-front bookcases, crammed with books. Upstairs I have four—no, five—more bookcases. The library here is full of books which were bought by Edens over the generations but are never read now, as far as I can see. Shall we throw them all out and replace them with mine?"

Minty held out her hands to Annie and Serafina. "I thought at first it might be possible to turn this wing of the Hall back into a family home, but that's not going to work because so much of it is open to the public. Also we need the money the tourists bring in, to keep the place running. So I have to look at what is possible, and that means making changes up here. Only, you two are the nearest thing I've got to a family, and I don't want to upset you."

Patrick said, gently, "Annie, you and Serafina created this suite for Sir Micah, not for her. She can't bear the thought of hurting either of you, but she knows I don't want to live in a show house."

Annie was bewildered. "What do you want to change?"

Minty took a deep breath. "Almost everything, except the two offices. The sitting room and this dining room . . . everything is to go except the pictures, the carpet in the sitting room and one or two family items. All this modern furniture goes into store in the basement, and Patrick brings in as much of his own furniture as he likes. Of course things will still get changed around as time goes on, but at least we'll have somewhere to sit and be comfortable in the evenings."

Patrick flicked ash into the saucer of his coffee cup, and Serafina picked it up to take it out to the kitchen.

"Please sit down, Serafina," said Minty. "Do you know, I've never seen you sit down. Not ever. And that brings me to my second big change. Your kitchen at the back here is tiny. Two people can't possibly work in it. I want to cut an archway in the wall which divides this room from what's now my bedroom, and turn that into a family kitchen, somewhere we can all sit down and chat and have cups of coffee and work if we want to."

Serafina opened her eyes and mouth wide. For one awful moment Minty thought she was going to throw a tantrum, but no; Serafina stamped out to her kitchen to collect a magazine, which she thumped down on the table. "There!" she said, pointing to a picture. "That's the sort of kitchen I want. I want those units, those granite-top work surfaces and a large table that can seat the whole family, where the children can do their homework, and I can look out at the view over the lake. My present kitchen can be turned into a utility room for the washers and dryers. Right?"

She plumped herself down onto one of the dining room chairs, nodding.

"Oh, but . . . ," said Annie, faintly.

Patrick took another drag on his cigarette. "I like the idea, but it'll take some time to get permission to cut through that wall and alter the plumbing because this is a listed building. I'll get started on that, but meantime, where will we sleep, Minty?"

"We'll have to get a surveyor in to see if the floor will stand the weight, but I thought we'd move the Victorian four-poster bed up here and put it in the end bedroom, which Ruby's been using as a sewing room. I don't like the pink décor, so it will have to be redecorated. Luckily there's a bathroom already behind it. We could eventually spread out into the rooms along the east side over Gemma's suite because we need at least one guest bedroom and a sewing room, and . . . oh, I don't know what else we'll need, but . . ."

"Bedrooms for the children," said Serafina.

"Give us a chance," said Patrick.

Annie was coming out of shock. "I suppose we'd better try to get some quotes, get builders round, but all the best people will be tied up for months."

"This one's on me," said Patrick, grinding out his cigarette and producing his mobile phone. "I'll fund this, and I know a good builder and decorator."

Minty looked at him, disillusioned. "You planned this, didn't you? Have you got your own tame builder lined up, ready to start?"

"They're just finishing another job for me at the moment, but I did say I might need them here. That you, Harry? Jack back off holiday yet? We're going to need him as well. Eden Hall, first thing Monday morning. Yes, I know I'm usually in town then, but I'll be here, too. Eight o'clock ..." He listened for a while, laughed and said, "Right, I'll ask her."

He smiled at Minty. "Harry wants to know if you've got a job for his teenage daughter who's just left school ... perhaps helping Doris in the gift shop? And may he and his men eat in the restaurant, half price? Florence's reputation has gone before her."

Annie looked dazed. Minty wondered if Annie was going to be flexible enough to take the transition from everything she'd known and loved, to an uncertain future.

Annie said, "Mr Sands—Patrick—if I may? I would very much like to give you a celluloid duck as a wedding present."

They couldn't start work on the new kitchen, but they could redecorate completely. Workmen underfoot ... which colour ... do you want to keep ... Patrick being calm and orderly ... the workmen big and burly and jolly ... plans being drawn up ... colours chosen ... measurements taken.

Minty fled down to the shadowy length of the Long Gallery for a bit of peace and quiet. But it was a little too quiet there. The pictures on the wall seemed to be looking at her, warning her ... Simon!

Was he there? She kept forgetting she couldn't go anywhere by herself. She turned and ran back up the stairs to the safety of her office.

Toby with his fliers and adverts . . . Iris with her correspondence . . . Barr wanting her to look at a consignment of china which had arrived for Lady C but had not been ordered by him . . .

Her uncle ringing about the funeral arrangements. He said again, "You're all I have left in the world now." She felt the burden of him descend on her shoulders even as she promised to be with him on Thursday, and stay for the funeral the following day.

Her rooms were stripped; some of the furniture was taken down to the basement in the lift, where it was stacked in a cellar amid predictions of moth and damp from Mrs Kitchen. Minty's bed and chest of drawers ended up in her office, while Ruby—complaining volubly—was relocated in a hastily cleared junk room above Gemma's suite. The rooms echoed to the sounds of workmen. Serafina shut herself into her rooms and turned her television up high.

Minty looked at the disorder and arranged to hold all her meetings downstairs in the library in future. So on Monday morning Toby spread out his plans for the Winter Wonderland on the big mahogany desk, and was just explaining to Minty that several people wanted to sponsor the most popular rooms when Mrs Collins and Mrs Chickward arrived—early—and everyone started to talk at once. Minty pressed her hands to her forehead and said she'd have to go and lie down if they made so much noise. After that, compromises were reached and everyone agreed to the final plan.

Mrs Chickward said, "My Flower Club arrangers will need two clear days to set up for the wedding."

"They'll have to work around the tourists going through the house," said Minty. "We can't afford to lose two days' revenue."

Mrs Chickward pinched in her lips. "So be it. Now I see swags of greenery entwined with gold and white ribbons and gold bells. There will be stands of white flowers twined round with more gold baubles for the fireplaces, and horizontal arrangements for the long buffet, interspersed with several tall silver epergnes from which flowers will burst and float upon the air."

Minty subdued a giggle and said in all sincerity, "That sounds absolutely wonderful, Mrs Chickward, but could you make it silver bells and ribbons because the wedding dress is white and silver?"

"If you say so. Then after the wedding, we'll bring in a gold and white . . . no, pardon me . . . a silver and white Christmas tree, but retain the swags of greenery, which should last till the end of the season, with care. The lights, the silver ribbon and the baubles will then be put in store and brought out again the following year."

"It's a pity," said Mrs Collins, "that we can't decorate the Long Gallery for my Musical Evening. The tickets are selling well . . ."

Ah-ha, thought Minty. *So much for Lady C's forecast of doom.*

". . . but the room will seem a little bare, won't it?"

Minty scribbled a note to herself. "I'll ask Hodge if he can supply some flowering plants to go round the musicians' dais . . . which Reggie said he'd organise. I'd better check on that, too."

"There's always something," said Mrs Chickward, sympathetically. "And now, my dear, allow me to give you this small token of my regard." From a large beribboned box Minty withdrew a tapestry picture of a cornucopia of flowers. Very charming, and obviously old. Minty cried out loud with pleasure. "It will go in our bedroom!"

Mrs Collins handed over an envelope with a grimace, knowing she'd been upstaged by Mrs Chickward once again. "I couldn't think what you might need, so I got you gardening tokens, which are always welcome."

"Indeed. You're both so kind. I'm extremely lucky to have made such good friends!"

Time plays strange tricks on those who live in fear. Some days dragged, every tick of the clock seeming to take for ever. Other hours passed so quickly Minty couldn't be sure what she'd been doing in them.

Some moments stood out . . .

Toby passing her on the stairs, calling out that he was off with Reggie to put some notice boards for the Fireworks Display around the village . . .

Patrick looking anxious. "Never leave your rooms by yourself, understand?"

Iris, showing her how to render a man helpless . . .

Minty dissolving into giggles because her new solicitor wanted her and Patrick to sign a pre-nuptial agreement. Mr Foster obviously wasn't aware that Patrick was probably worth even more than she was, if you excluded the Hall, which was entailed, anyway . . .

She remembered receiving the Americans in the Great Hall and taking them through to the library, where Serafina was laying out a light lunch. The Americans had by now swallowed their chagrin at not getting Eden Hall, and handsomely admitted that Peacock Place would suit them better. They wished to buy—not rent—Peacock Place. Buy or rent? She was in two minds about which would be best for the Hall. Would she be better off retaining the Place and getting an annual rent—but paying bank charges on the money she had to borrow till probate was granted—or raking in a hefty sum on outright sale?

She would ask Patrick. There was only one thing. The Americans seemed to think they still owed Simon a place in their plans and were almost reproachful to Minty, hinting that she'd treated Simon shabbily.

Minty blinked. "There's a long history . . . ," she began, and then shook her head at herself. Would it be right to tell the Americans everything she knew and guessed about Simon, when she couldn't prove any of it?

The Americans were a little patronising to a young woman who was unused to high finance. They were sure they knew Simon better than she did.

She tried to put her reservations into words. "Simon didn't make a success of running Eden Hall."

The taller of the Americans continued to smile. "We think he did, and he's got the right connections for us in society. Lady Cardale doesn't wish to come on the Board that's going to run Peacock Place, but Simon will. We plan to appoint him our general manager, with accommodation thrown in. He'll oversee the alterations and run the place, though of course we'll be over several times a year to keep an eye on things."

Minty said no more. Perhaps this new career would help take Simon's mind off revenge.

Then one evening she and Patrick dined with his partner and his wife. It was marvellous to get away from the Hall for a few hours, yet this glimpse of life in another household had its downside. His partner's only child—Patrick's godchild—was a frail little thing. As Patrick drove them away at the end of the evening Minty said, "I don't envy them. Add to prayer list?"

He nodded.

Eleven days to go. Minty took Serafina to choose units, tiling and lighting for the new kitchen against the day when planning for it was approved.

The spare bedroom was now in the hands of the painters. Minty wanted a certain blue in her bedroom to contrast with the willow pattern of the curtains on the four poster. They mixed the blue paint for the walls three times before Minty was satisfied.

Another meeting in the library. Lord Asher arrived to talk to Minty and Annie about the future of the Hall. They were both concerned about Minty, saying that she still looked peaky. Annie was almost motherly, and Minty felt a great affection for both of them.

"I promise you, no permanent damage done. I still get headaches, but the doctor told me they'll gradually fade. Now, let me tell you what I've been planning . . ."

When she'd finished, Lord Asher exchanged glances with Annie. He said, "Annie's been keeping me up-to-date on all this, of course. In the main we approve, with one important proviso. We feel you should appoint another accountant as soon as possible. Annie has heard good reports of Neville Chickward, Mrs Chickward's nephew. He's a little young, but keen and experienced in charity work. What do you say?"

Minty banished the thought that Neville was rather too fond of her. "Frankly, I'd be relieved. Barr has performed wonders, but we neither of us know how to apply for grants, and Simon's book-keeping was at best scanty and at worst . . ." She shrugged.

Lord Asher nodded. "Now about the money your father left in trust for maintenance of the Hall: we're happy to cover the re-wiring and re-tiling of the north wing, attend to the holiday cottages and put the fountain back into working order."

"Thank you," said Minty, truly grateful.

"One last thing," said Lord Asher. "The Foundation. I've been chatting to one or two of the other trustees and we want to suggest a survey of past work at our next meeting. But we'll need you to be there, to argue the case."

Minty put her head in her hands. "Are you sure you need me?"

"I'm sure. Also, I've been making some enquiries about your husband-to-be. A bit of a dark horse, isn't he? I think he ought to come on the Board of Trustees, but he's playing hard to get. Can you tell me why?"

Minty hesitated. "I'll have a word with him about it."

Chapter Twenty-Six

Time shot forward to Wednesday evening. Minty signed the last letter and picked up her jacket, ready to leave. Patrick was returning from town that evening and she was longing to see him again.

"Wait for me!" cried Iris. "You're not going through the house by yourself." They went through to the tower office . . . and froze.

A crude stick figure had been drawn on the lift door with a felt-tip pen. The figure was dangling from a gallows.

The lift doors opened and Toby stepped out. "What's the matter with you two?"

Minty swallowed. "Toby, where have you been?"

"Down with Tim in the Estate Office. He's faffing because Tessa's gone missing . . ." Toby looked where they pointed and gaped. "That wasn't here when I left."

"Iris was with me in my office, so there was no one in here for a while."

Iris had gone white. "I'll scrub it off, Minty. Toby will see you to your car."

Minty shivered.

❧

She asked Patrick, "Is Simon a psychopath?"

"Borderline, I should think. What he's doing is called stalking. I did wonder about getting an injunction to ban him from the Hall, but he has to do something pretty terrible for us to get that. I've talked to the police, told them what he's putting you through, but he's been clever enough—plausible enough—to be given the benefit of the doubt so far."

She threw down her jacket. "If only I knew when he was going to pounce . . ."

"My bet is he'll wait till the very last minute, the night before the wedding. He wants you to be so frightened that if he even shouts at you, you'll cave in." He lifted her chin. "I wish I could whisk you away till after the wedding. You're going to your uncle's tomorrow and staying over for the funeral? Simon won't follow you there. Why don't you stay on a few more days?"

She forced a smile. "And miss the Musical Evening? Mrs Collins tells me you've got two tickets for us. I can't think why. Lady C's poured out poison on me every time we've met. What makes you think she'll let me attend one of her functions?"

"How can she stop you? Do you know the secret of a successful revolution? It's like kicking in a rotten door. This door is rotten. So kick it in."

She braced herself. "Talking of revolutions, are you ready now to take on the Foundation? Lord Asher wants you—and I think you should do it, too."

He shrugged. "There's a lot to think about at the moment."

The day before her aunt's funeral, Minty held a last-minute briefing for Iris since there were a couple of crises brewing.

"Florence—I must remember to call her Chef now—is coping magnificently, but she's doubtful about that girl Fiona, the one who stayed on. She may need extra help from the village. Gloria's working twice as hard as she used to and complaining like mad, but it's good for her. Venetia's on top of things with the stewards, but Doris at the gift shop isn't coping too well. Harry the builder wants his daughter to get a job here, but I don't know . . . do we need someone older? Tim in the Estate Office . . ." She paused, frowning.

Iris raised one exquisite eyebrow. "Not quite up to it?"

"You can't blame him for panicking. Between Miles and Simon, the estate books are in a mess, and Tim feels responsible for everything that goes wrong. He thinks he's found someone for the Ranger's post, and I said I'd interview the man when I get back. Now Tessa took herself off without a word to anyone . . ."

Iris frowned. "I thought I saw her in the courtyard just now. If it was her, she's gone blonde and had a perm."

"Yes, it was her. She's got a new wardrobe of black clothes which cling where her previous garments sagged. I'd like to get rid of her, but I think Tim would go to pieces completely if he didn't have someone to help him in the office, and I suppose if we keep an eye on her she can't do much harm."

Iris was making notes. "I'll see Reggie gets on with making the dais for Saturday, and Toby thinks he'll have the Web site up and running by the time you get back."

Minty clicked her fingers. "Barr. Will you keep an eye on him? He's been so good, not drinking on duty, but I think the strain's beginning to tell. The accounts are too much for him. I've written to Neville Chickward asking if he'd be interested in taking over our books . . . remind me to speak to him on the phone, see if he's interested."

Iris nodded.

Minty tried to remember what else was happening. "Mr Lightowler at the bookshop is holding the first of his recorded musical evenings tonight, but obviously I won't make it. Will you give my apologies? And see me down to my car?"

How strange it felt to be back at the vicarage. Her uncle was pacing the floor. Uncharacteristically, he held out his arms to her and she went into them, wondering if he'd ever before embraced her . . . knowing he hadn't.

She made sure he ate, began to pack up some of her aunt's clothing, fielded telephone calls. At least people from the parish were looking after him now.

He said Lucas had been round a couple of times to collect things he'd left behind, and that the house seemed very quiet without him.

Patrick rang to make sure she'd arrived safely. His partner's child had been whisked off to hospital that day and he was still in town, but he hoped to make the funeral tomorrow. She took the opportunity to ask him about Tessa. "Shall I sack her?"

"No. Lady Silchester claims Tessa needs her money to put into a new business venture. I suspect this 'new business venture' only exists in Simon's fertile brain, but I've said I'd be happy to consider a business proposal from her. It might keep her neutral for a while."

Her uncle actually asked Minty how she was coping at the Hall. "I couldn't help seeing how much more alive you look. What's this man of yours really like? Your aunt was so sure that he'd lead you astray."

Minty patted his hand. "Patrick's a Christian. They want him to become one of the trustees for the Foundation."

"I suppose that's all right, then." He rubbed his eyes. "I need my eyes tested again. Agnes always arranged that sort of thing."

She kissed him goodnight when she went up to bed. She was amazed at how easy it was now to kiss him.

Time jumped. Patrick arrived just as they were about to go into church. Her uncle extended his hand to Patrick as if they were old acquaintances, and Minty smiled on them both. A neighbouring minister came in to take the funeral service, which was plain but seemed to give her uncle consolation. No flowers, no choir. Lucas came in late.

Before he went back to work, Patrick said, "You do realise this is the third time I've come here looking for you? I came once when you were eighteen and once when you were twenty-one. Both times your aunt sent me away. I've still got to leave without you today."

She kissed him. "This time you know I'll follow."

Agnes Cardale had made a straightforward will, leaving everything she possessed in the house to her husband. She'd also held some shares, which were to be divided into three equal parts, between her husband, her nephew and Minty.

Lucas couldn't hide his greed. "You don't need any more money, Minty. Best let me put your shares in with mine."

Minty had been taken aback to find her aunt had left her anything at all. "No," she said thoughtfully, "I've got one or two ideas for charities myself. I want to give the village children a Christmas party for a start."

Her uncle patted her shoulder. "Agnes would have liked that."

It was a beautiful evening when she returned to the Hall. She stopped on the driveway to let a coach ramble past. The setting sun lit up the windows, the grass was newly cut, the horse-chestnut trees in the avenue were surrounded by children looking for fallen conkers. She dug Reggie out of his quarters to escort her up the stairs to her rooms.

"Welcome back," said Iris. "Your friend Carol Tinderman has been on the phone. She didn't know about your aunt dying and wanted to know if you were all right. She plans to come over early next week to see you, have a fitting for her bridesmaid's dress and get into the shop to take measurements for her father."

"Maybe I can even find time to help her measure up."

"Chance would be a fine thing. The Americans have been on the phone, wanting to attend the musical soiree tomorrow night. I tried to get tickets for them but there aren't any. Mrs Collins says she'll squeeze them in somehow if they're going to buy Peacock Place and she'll take them to Lady C's cocktail hour beforehand.

"Chef's had an argument with that silly girl Fiona who walked out, only to return an hour later. Chef's still going to need extra help in the restaurant tomorrow, as she's got quite a few parties booked in. She's trying to get another girl from the village, but I don't know if she'll succeed at such short notice, and—oh yes—you'll be pleased to hear the takings have more than doubled since the old chef left."

There were moments of serenity.

Patrick drove her to a quiet country pub for a meal. The pale blue sky gradually turned to pink as the sun set. The trees rustled, dry leaves falling. Dahlias blazed in gardens. Birds made sleepy sounds. Hawthorn bushes threw brilliant patches of red against the fading sky. A star appeared overhead.

Minty closed her eyes and relaxed. She was safe for a while. "Nine days. Do you think we'll make it?"

"I can do it in hours. I even did it in minutes today, with a calculator."

The food was good: steak and kidney pie, and wild rabbit with cherries, all cooked with beer. Over coffee, she noticed he was frowning. "So what have you been up to?"

He eased his shoulders, looked away from her. "Thinking I should have told you something before, something which might make a difference. You wanted me to help you with the Foundation. Lord Asher rang me today, and I said no. Don't frown. I know it looks as if I'm afraid to venture into the Great Big World, but it's not that.

"Do you remember St Paul once wanted to go up into Asia but the Holy Spirit wouldn't let him? All the time we were apart I planned to make a name for myself, so that I'd have something to offer you. There were plenty of opportunities and it wasn't that I didn't want to take them, because I did. Once I was on the point of catching a train to London for a vital interview . . . I could see myself as Lord Chief Justice . . ."

He inspected his fingernails. "That very morning I'd been asked to drop a note in to someone on my way to the station. He wasn't a friend. I didn't even like him very much. He was in a diabetic coma. I missed my train and the appointment. I was told I'd got my priorities wrong."

He looked her in the eye. "I'm a slow learner. It happened twice more: once a man's dog had been run over and I stayed to comfort him, and another time a woman had been receiving filthy anonymous letters and was on the verge of suicide. I stayed with her, too. Finally I understood that God wasn't impressed by my worldly ambitions. I could make money, yes, if I put it to good use. But forget worldly ambition. I thought He might let me have a go at the Foundation, but no. Between the time my secretary told me Lord Asher was on the line and my picking up the phone, the police rang asking me to get down to the station urgently. I thought about saying to God, 'Can't go, I've got a career opportunity to follow up.' I knew what He'd say to that. So when I got back to the office I rang Lord Asher and told him no."

He made a defeated gesture with his hands. "I'm never going to be anything but a country solicitor."

Minty stared into the future. Annie had warned her about his "glass ceiling," though she'd thought Simon was the cause of it. This proved it wasn't Simon that held Patrick back.

Minty thought of all the good things she knew Patrick had done, the people he'd helped, the times he'd put himself second and others first. She banished her dreams of him strutting his stuff in London. It cost her something, but she did it.

Goodbye fantasy. Welcome reality and a man for all seasons, a man of God. "Of course I'd have like to have married a High Court judge and been Lady Muck, but what we have is better, isn't it? Don't we complement one another in every way? By the way, I've a suggestion to make . . ."

She thought he might dismiss it out of hand, but he didn't. He looked long and hard at her and then nodded. "Well, why not? I'll announce it at the wedding."

The sky darkened to navy blue. More stars appeared. The moon rose and was reflected in a pond nearby. An owl swept past on heavy wings. Tiny pipistrelle bats swooped across the pond, hunting for night insects. They walked along the lanes for a while, holding hands.

Saturday morning, and the first of the day's problems surfaced. Fiona called in sick, they couldn't get anyone else to help in the restaurant and Reggie wasn't happy about the dais for the concert.

Minty tied back her hair, donned an apron and got Serafina to escort her as she went to help Florence in the restaurant. Hours later, just when they thought they were finished, a coach party arrived unexpectedly demanding cream teas and wanting to use the loos . . . one of which had stopped working. Minty prised Reggie away from the dais and got him to look at the loo, but when she got back to the kitchen she found the dishwasher had packed up and they hadn't enough clean cups and plates to feed the coach party . . .

An hour and a half later Florence saw Minty across the courtyard and into the Long Gallery, where Hodge and Reggie were having a shouting match about how to place the steps to the dais, and where to place the flowering plants. Barr was setting out chairs for the audience and yelling at both of them to shut up—which didn't work.

Minty thought she saw Simon hovering, but ignored him. She was too tired to react. She'd been on her feet for hours. She looked and felt like a bedraggled hen.

"Dear Reggie, what a wonderful job you've made of the dais! Now if we put these movable steps just here . . . at the side towards the back . . . that's splendid. And Hodge, what beautiful plants. Have we got a couple of old lead troughs we can put them into, do you think? Didn't I see some in the old kitchens downstairs? Reggie, do you think you could help Hodge look for them?"

"I said there wasn't enough plants . . ."

"He said the steps should go in the middle . . ."

"You're both wonderful people, especially when you let a woman have the last word."

At that they paused, glanced sideways at one another and laughed. As they left, Gemma floated in wearing a shiny black trouser suit which looked as if it had been painted on her.

"Florence has forgotten to take up the canapés for Mother's cocktail hour. Can you get them for her? I've got to get back to look after the musicians."

"Florence forgets nothing. Gloria's staying on to heat them up and serve them to the guests. Which reminds me, I'd better get dressed, too."

Gemma gasped. "Are you coming? Does Mother know?"

"Not to worry. Patrick and I will sit at the back and enjoy the concert. I just wish I felt up to it after a day working in the kitchens."

"Tell you what, I'll come and make you up. A touch of mascara here, some eye shadow . . . perhaps a hint of blusher? You won't know yourself."

"That's nice of you, Gemma. I appreciate it." She looked round for Barr, to escort her up to her rooms.

Gemma was predictably horrified by the crowded room which was currently serving Minty for office, living and sleeping space, but settled her half-sister on a chair and opened the make-up box she'd brought with her.

Ruby grumbled, "Do you really want to look like everyone else?"

"Of course she does!" Gemma skillfully used foundation, blusher, lilac eye shadow, powder, dark red lipstick, mascara and eyebrow pencil. "There! What do you think?"

Ruby had propped a long mirror against Minty's desk. Minty gaped at her new image, and Gemma was satisfied. "There, you see!"

Minty saw that she did indeed look different; almost like a film star. But did she look like herself? She wasn't sure. Minty met Ruby's eyes in the mirror and saw she was doubtful, too.

Gemma gave a little shriek. "Look at the time!" She fled.

Ruby had laid out the pale blue-grey dress with the floating scarf panel which they'd bought in London. Serafina slipped it over Minty's head and did up the zip. The dress fitted beautifully. Minty held back the curls from around her face, and then let them drop. She put on her high-heeled shoes and checked that she was wearing her diamond ring.

Patrick came up in the lift and knocked on the door. Serafina let him in. He was wearing evening dress with the chain of his new watch just showing, and was at his most darkly attractive.

Serafina said, "Doesn't she look marvellous?"

Patrick blinked, fingered his jaw. "Superb."

"No, I don't," said Minty, making up her mind. "Give me a minute . . ." She sped into the bathroom to cream off Gemma's careful handiwork. A dab of foundation across her nose, a trace of a pale rose lipstick. Enough. She lifted her hair back from her face, set in the side combs, and went back to her office.

"Is that better?"

Serafina was mute, but Ruby clapped her hands. Patrick's smile was enough to tell Minty she'd done the right thing. "You don't need that heavy make-up. When your colour comes and goes, and your eyes look at me so truthfully . . . you're way beyond being pretty. You're beautiful in a most unusual way. Here's something to complement the dress."

He handed her a worn jewellery case. "I expect you have Eden family jewels in plenty, but this was my grandmother's and I'd like you to have it."

Inside was a Victorian diamond brooch in a flower design. The stones were large and brilliant. He pinned the brooch on her dress, where it did indeed look exactly right.

"You give me so much."

The crease showed down his cheek. "I'm enjoying myself."

Minty kissed Serafina and Ruby and thanked them for looking after her so well. She put her hand within Patrick's arm and they went down in the lift to the first floor, to the balcony overlooking the Great Hall.

Below them Lady Cardale was at the head of the reception line, wearing her favourite black, glinting with sequins and a diamond necklet. The elderly Earl was on one side of her and a stately woman whom Minty thought she'd met at Mrs Chickward's on the other. Mrs Collins—in the gold and black outfit she'd worn the other night—completed the reception line. No Simon.

Minty drew back. "You want me to walk down those stairs and confront her? Are you sure this is a good idea, Patrick?"

"Trust me, there'll be no fireworks. The moment you appear, the old queen is dead. Long live the new. Walk down slowly. Wait in the reception line till she sees you. Incline your head. If the Earl and Mrs Perlman recognise you—which they should do—you touch their hands, murmur how lovely to see them, ditto to Mrs Collins and go through to the State Rooms. I'll be a half pace behind you."

"She'll kill me!"

"Not in front of witnesses."

That made her smile. She walked down the centre of the stairs, very slowly, aware that Patrick was shadowing her. "Do you know what I've been doing today? Acting kitchen maid."

"Mm," said Patrick. "It's always quicker to do it yourself than organise someone else to do it for you."

The guests all wore evening dress, some short, some long. A woman waiting in the reception line caught sight of them and tapped her husband on the arm. "Look, it's Araminta Cardale, the heiress."

The guests stood still, leaving a space for Minty to approach her stepmother. Lady Cardale's eyes promised vengeance. Minty quailed. But, conscious of Patrick at her elbow, she managed to keep smiling. She inclined her head and passed on to the Earl, whose bristling eyebrows shaded eyes as penetratingly blue as Minty's own.

"Lovely to see you," she said. She shook his hand because he seemed to expect it. He was smiling, covering her hand with both of his, passing her on to Mrs Perlman, who was wearing a hideous green dress. Mrs Perlman was also smiling, nodding to Minty, and even patting Patrick on the cheek in a friendly fashion. Mrs Collins looked as if she didn't know whether to smile or cry, so Minty kissed her cheek and passed on.

They walked into the Chinese room, where the word seemed to have spread, for groups of people were looking at the doorway, waiting for her to appear.

A woman came up, asking Patrick to introduce her to Minty . . . and a man and his wife whom she'd met at Mrs Chickward's. Then the two Americans, tall and courteous, pleased to find themselves accepted socially. Minty was surrounded by people all wanting to talk to her. Patrick extricated her to pass on to the Red Room, where Mrs Chickward—in plum-coloured velvet—brought over several more people to speak to them.

The Woottons were in the Library, and crowded around her. Venetia introduced her to the Deputy Chief Constable and the headmaster of a prestigious private school.

It was, bewilderingly, a triumphal progress.

They went through into the Long Gallery. Barr had laid out rows of seats in semicircles around the dais, which was now decked with troughs containing massed azaleas and cyclamens. The Deputy Chief Constable seemed to expect Minty and Patrick to take a seat in the front row which had been reserved for important people, but Patrick guided her to a seat at the back.

Gemma floated around looking marvellous, distributing programmes. If she'd only smiled, she'd have been the belle of the ball. Minty checked that all the blinds were down, which they were because the night was drawing in. She didn't want Patrick to see the new planting in the garden below until their wedding day.

Lady Cardale passed them by with the Earl on her arm, and the other dignitaries followed her. Everyone in that party—especially Mrs Collins—looked around to see where Minty was sitting.

Patrick murmured, "Those who take the best places are humiliated if they are asked to move down, while humble folk—like us—may find themselves elevated to great heights . . . yes, here we go. The Earl's coming back for you."

Sure enough, after a whispered conversation with Lady C, the Earl was indeed making his way back to where Minty sat.

Exercising charm, he said, "Miss Cardale, Patrick. Would you care to join us at the front, where you'll be able to see better?"

Minty was flustered. She rose to her feet, because that's what Patrick and the Earl seemed to expect. But then she froze. Lady C was not looking back at Minty, but straight ahead. Everyone else in her party was looking round at Minty.

Minty realised that her stepmother had been publicly humiliated by their turning to Minty. Lady C deserved it, of course.

But . . .

"It's kind of you to ask, but I'm quite happy where I am," said Minty, also exercising charm. "This is Lady Cardale's evening. She's worked hard to put it together, and she deserves all the thanks." She smiled brilliantly at the Earl, and resumed her seat.

The Earl retreated and Patrick put his hand over his eyes. "My darling, you never fail to surprise me. I planned that you should humiliate that woman in public . . ."

"Well, I'm sorry, but it wasn't fair to . . ."

". . . and you don't just humiliate her, you annihilate her. Of course you didn't mean it that way. What you did was far worse. You forgave her, publicly. Be sure that it will be all round the room in nano-seconds. She must be grinding her teeth in fury."

The musicians entered and swept up the steps onto the dais, settling their music stands, waiting for silence.

Minty had never thought she'd be sitting in a glorious room like this, wearing a beautiful dress and diamonds, to hear classical music. How great God was, to have put such marvellous music into the heads of composers, and then given musicians the ability to let it flow out through them to everyone else.

Patrick checked that she was enjoying herself. She smiled back at him. Music was going to be just one more link between them.

Chapter Twenty-Seven

Lady Cardale summoned Minty to her rooms early next day. Serafina escorted Minty and waited outside the door for her. Minty had put on one of her London outfits for church. The dress had a cowl neck and a longish skirt which swirled around her legs as she walked. She'd learned it paid to be properly dressed when she visited her stepmother.

The air in the spacious sitting room seemed grey and unused, the blinds half-drawn. Lady Cardale indicated a chair and Minty sat, warily. Lady C looked worn and, for the first time, bony.

Minty looked away, not wishing to triumph over the older woman's loss of beauty. There was something different about the room. Yes, she had it. Most of the yellow tickets had gone.

Lady Cardale said, "I've been told that if I'm still here for your wedding, I'll be expected to provide overnight accommodation for some of my oldest friends. That's quite out of the question. Therefore I'm arranging to leave here earlier than I intended. On Tuesday, in fact."

This was unexpectedly good news. "Barr hasn't yet finished collating the list of furniture and pictures bought for Eden Hall . . ."

Lady Cardale raised her hand. "The London flat is fully furnished, so I'll only be taking a few things with me. I trust you won't quibble about them."

The "few things" still ticketed were antiques, but if this was the price of getting rid of her stepmother before the wedding, Minty thought it was worth it. "Let me have a list for insurance purposes."

Lady Cardale inclined her head. "I'd originally planned to return to the Hall for my charity events, but I've decided to run them from the London flat instead. No doubt we'll meet occasionally on Foundation business, but apart from that, I see no reason why we should ever see one another again."

Minty nodded. "Is Simon going with you, or direct to Peacock Place?"

"He makes his own arrangements." Lady Cardale didn't elaborate and Minty wondered if at last the woman was beginning to realise what Simon was really like. She stood, ready to leave.

"One more thing." Lady Cardale produced a painful smile. "My portrait. Is it still in the house? Simon looked for it, but . . ."

Was that why Simon had invaded Minty's rooms the other day? He must have been horrified by the chaos, had failed to find the picture—which was now hidden at the back of Iris' desk—and in frustration left his hangman drawing on the lift door. "It's in a safe place." She hesitated with her hand on the door knob. "Tell me; did you ever really love my father?"

"I wanted him the moment I set eyes on him." Her mouth worked. "He only married me because Gemma was on the way, and he never touched me after your mother died."

"Thank you for telling me that."

Lady Cardale's face hardened. "All those years he let us believe Simon would inherit."

Minty's tone was gentle. "Nanny Proud thought up that idea and taught it to Simon. She's enormously proud of you. Will you see her before you go?"

Lady Cardale nodded. Was that a sheen of tears in her eyes? It was hard for her to ask anything of Minty, but she did it. "I can't take her with me. She's too old. I . . . I trust you to look after her."

Minty held back a sigh. "I'll do my best."

Lady Cardale didn't go to church that day. Neither did either of her children.

Minty sat with Patrick. There were hardly any children there, because the Reverend Cecil had said they must go back to their old Sunday School teacher.

"Six days," said Patrick as they walked back to the Hall afterwards. "Don't drop your guard for a minute, will you?"

Working with Reggie and Barr, Patrick and Minty took the four-poster bed apart and carried it upstairs. While Patrick and Reggie re-assembled the bed in the newly painted blue bedroom, Venetia arrived to help Minty turn the now empty room below into an old-fashioned nursery, using furniture and toys found in storage upstairs.

When the bed curtains had been re-hung, the new mattress hauled into place and the bed made up with fresh linen, it looked fabulous. Minty hung Mrs Chickward's tapestry on the wall, while the men manoeuvred in furniture rescued from storage. The room was now ready for occupation, with a couple of matching bedside cabinets, complete with side lamps, a large rosewood wardrobe, chest of drawers and pier glass mirror, all of which Ruby and Serafina set about polishing.

Patrick wondered, "Will all this luxury be bad for my character?"

❧

Gemma waylaid Minty, fiddling with her hair, looking embarrassed. "I really ought to be a bridesmaid, don't you think? I suppose that's all right?"

"Yes, indeed," said Minty, giving her a hug, but secretly wondering what Ruby would have to say about providing yet another dress at short notice.

"Strapless black, I thought," said Gemma, "with green orchids in my hair."

"You'll have to match the others," said Minty. "Let's ask Ruby what she can make up for you."

Tears spurted from Gemma's eyes. She wept beautifully but Minty, half irate and half sympathetic, would not give in. "I'm sorry, Gemma, but no can do."

"Oh, very well, then," said Gemma. "If you want me to look a frump!"

❧

Four days to go. It felt like forty. Minty woke on Tuesday feeling lethargic. It had been wonderful to go to bed in the four poster, but now . . . another day . . . same old problems. It was tiring, always having to think before she spoke, being nice to people, cajoling, trying to think ahead, worrying about money. Never being alone to think.

When she did get away from the Hall with Patrick, they usually had to visit other people . . . like the Thornbys up at Old Oak Farm. Lovely people, so happy for her, and happy, too, that something was going to be done at last about developing the derelict farm up by the station. But she always had to be on her best behaviour. Sometimes she wanted to kick and scream and even use a swear word or two. She didn't know what was the matter with her!

Pre-wedding nerves?

Minty tried to pray. *Dear Lord.* She didn't know how to continue. She repeated the words, *Dear Lord*, over and over. Reached for her Bible but didn't open it. Just held it in both hands. The tension was getting to her. She was losing weight. Patrick was looking fine-drawn, too.

He said, "Every time I see you safe, I give thanks . . ."

She'd slept badly, thinking she heard mice in the wainscoting. Mice! That was all they needed. She could hear Serafina in the shower. Would it be safe to go through to the chapel without an escort? Just this once? She opened the door and felt her throat close up on a scream, for there were jemmy marks near the new lock.

Not mice. Simon with a jemmy? She closed the door with care, her mouth dry. She knew that if he'd really been set on breaking in, he could have done it. He was telling her that he could get to her whenever he wanted.

Iris and Minty watched as a removal van drew up outside the entrance to the Great Hall, and three large men vanished into the house to bring out carefully wrapped bundles of antiques . . . racks of clothes . . . trunks and suitcases and boxes. Gemma was helping, carrying pot plants and precious bundles down to her mother's car. The removal men secured the back doors of their van, climbed in and drove away.

"No Simon," said Iris. "No one's seen him around today, either."

"I'm almost sorry for her," said Minty, watching the black-clad upright figure of her stepmother descend the steps to the gravel for the last time. "She didn't get much joy out of being Lady of the Hall, did she?"

Lady Cardale seemed to realise she was being watched, for she turned and looked up at the tower. She didn't wave but turned her head away and walked over to her car.

Iris wondered, "Will she kiss Gemma goodbye?"

No. She didn't. She didn't even touch her daughter, who was left looking forlornly after the car as it disappeared down the driveway.

As soon as Lady C had departed, Minty arranged to meet Mrs Kitchen and Barr in her stepmother's suite of rooms. It was more like a maisonette, with living accommodation on the first floor and bedrooms above.

There was still a trace of Lady C's scent in the air, but everything was clean and tidy. Not a scrap of paper had been left behind, not a tin of beans in the kitchen, not a crease in a cushion. But an antique mirror over the fireplace in the big sitting room had been smashed.

Mrs Kitchen said, "How could she!"

Minty said, "I'll see if I can find a replacement in the junk rooms. Now we have a lot of people staying overnight for the wedding. Mrs Kitchen, can you get the bedrooms ready in time for them?"

"Why smash the mirror?" said Barr.

"Because she can't bear to look at herself?" said Minty. "Now, what about Simon? He didn't go with his mother."

"His car's gone." Mrs Kitchen led the way to Simon's suite at the top of the north wing. The place was decorated with discarded clothing—both men's and women's—empty wine bottles, overflowing ashtrays, unpaid bills. It stank of stale wine, stale food and Simon's aftershave.

He'd left a note on the table.

Minty. I hate goodbyes. I'm going to stay with friends till I can move into Peacock Place, so we'll still be near neighbours. I'll let you know where to send my things. Simon.

It was too good to be true, wasn't it? Yet there was no sign of him, his Porsche had gone and the house seemed all the quieter for his absence.

Tessa went around looking smug, which meant . . . what? That she knew something everyone else didn't? That Simon hadn't disappeared for good? That he'd promised her . . . what? It was hard to believe Simon had given up all thoughts of revenge.

"He wants you to think he has," said Patrick. "So we'll take extra precautions."

The painters had finished in Minty's sitting room. Patrick had kept the green walls, had had the woodwork painted to match and the ceiling lightened from pale green to white with a hint of lime. The floorboards had been polished, the marble fireplace cleaned and the carpet re-laid. Soon Patrick's furniture would arrive, but for the moment Minty stood on a stool in the great bare room, so that Ruby could check the hem of her wedding dress. The door crashed open, and Jonah rushed in.

"Can't you see what we're doing, Jonah? Out!" said Ruby.

Jonah was furious, jerking his arms around. "Hodge says he's asked you to marry him. I asked you first, didn't I?"

Ruby knelt to check the hem of Minty's dress. "At least he's got a house to offer me."

"You've got a house!" shrieked Jonah.

Ruby sniffed, her eyebrows eloquent.

Minty tried to distract Jonah, a ploy which usually worked. "Where's your snowstorm, Jonah?"

Jonah stamped his foot at her. "I may be muddled in my head sometimes—yes, like that globe when you tip it up—but the snowstorm always clears in the end, doesn't it? My head wasn't clear for a long time, especially when Ruby kept saying I loved Hannah and had to get her back. My head's clear enough now. I don't love Hannah, and I never did. I do love Ruby, and I always did."

Ruby ignored him. "You can step down now, Minty. You'll make a beautiful bride and I'm sure you and Patrick will keep your wedding vows—unlike some!"

Jonah mumbled something. Minty stepped down to the floor. "What did you say, Jonah?"

Another mumble. Then, angrily, "Hannah broke them first! She didn't like . . . didn't want . . . said it was dirty. I did try. Over and over I tried but she was bigger than me . . ." He made a helpless gesture.

Ruby stared, but Minty managed to find her voice. "You mean she refused to sleep with you? That the marriage was never consummated?"

Jonah folded his arms and tried to look as if he didn't care. He nodded.

Ruby and Minty exchanged glances.

Minty said, "That means it was no marriage, Ruby. Jonah doesn't need a divorce, but an annulment."

Ruby sat down on the stool and fanned herself.

Telling Patrick about it afterwards, Minty said she hadn't known whether to laugh or cry. "But you'll help them sort it out, won't you?"

Minty felt that her real self had shrunk somewhere inside the Minty that everyone else could see. The real Minty was a child reduced to sucking her thumb, while the outside Minty smiled and said all the right things to people.

It was the day before the wedding.

Sitting in the chapel with Serafina, Minty tried to pray. And failed.

Time speeded up. So much to do. So little time left to do it in. Anything she'd forgotten by now, must remain undone.

Mrs Chickward and her flower-arranging ladies were busy in the Long Gallery, Florence had commanded extra help from the village, wedding presents had arrived, also another enquiry from a distant cousin as to whether they could be put up for the night . . .

Overnight guests began to arrive at the Hall. Annie was in her element, acting as hostess. Carol arrived from the city, looking unusually subdued for once; Iris made her welcome.

At five o'clock Reggie drove Minty and her three bridesmaids up the hill to the church for a rehearsal, while Serafina helped Florence to lay out a buffet supper in the Great Hall for those staying the night. The Woottons would be looking after other guests—including Patrick's father—at the Manor while Patrick had arranged to take his best man and the ushers out for supper to a country pub.

The rehearsal in church was muted. Patrick's hand trembled as he took Minty's in his. When it was over he stood looking after her as she got back into the car with her bridesmaids to return to the Hall.

Time had no meaning. One minute Minty was helping Carol and Iris to lay out some wedding presents in the Great Hall, and the next she was greeting her uncle, who'd just arrived from the city with bumptious Lucas in tow . . . she was helping Annie show Lord Asher and his wife up to their room—Lady Cardale's old bedroom—and then Ruby was zipping up a cream brocade dress Minty had never worn before . . . and putting on the opal earrings which her father had given her mother.

She descended the staircase, with Gemma clattering along beside her in her high heels, wondering aloud how Minty was going to cope with her very first dinner party. Carol followed, taking everything in.

The hall looked splendid in the soft light of standard lamps set here and there, with candles in silver candelabra down the length of the table. The guests were to help themselves from a side table, supervised by Gloria and Ruby, who refused to be left out of things.

"What a bevy of beauty," said Lord Asher, who had brought his much younger wife. "A blonde bride with a red-head, a strawberry blonde and a brunette for company!"

Carol laughed and made sure she sat next to him at table. She knew a powerful man when she saw one. Carol's parents were also staying the night; her father's eyes were everywhere, assessing people and furniture, approving of what he saw.

Dear Jonah, who ought to have gone up to the Manor, had refused to go there without Ruby, so stayed at the Hall instead. Iris sat next to Jonah and made sure he didn't feel out of it. Barr sat beyond Iris, drinking perhaps a trifle too much.

Minty smiled and smiled. She saw that her guests had plenty to eat and drink, and listened while they talked at her . . . and the sound of their voices swelled and retreated . . .

Pre-wedding nerves, of course.

Would the evening never end?

The next time she sat at this table for a dinner party, Patrick would be sitting at the other end. If they made it.

"A wonderful evening, my dear." They were having coffee in the library, that splendid room in which Simon had once tempted her with a proposal of marriage, in which her father's will had been read, in which Simon's faithful companion Miles had tried to kill her, the room in which she'd entertained the Americans and talked of the Winter Wonderland.

Gloria had come in to clear away the coffee things.

"Bless you, my dear. See you tomorrow."

Her horrible cousin Lucas was pricing everything in sight, but her uncle was looking fragile. Minty took his arm and, together with Annie, walked with him and the other guests back through the beautiful rooms, into the hall and up the stairs to the guest suite. Annie stayed behind for a word with the Ashers while Minty saw the others settled.

She lingered at the top of the stairs, looking down, looking back down the years to the moment when she'd stood there as a small child, with people scurrying around below, crying out that her mother was dead . . . while her father turned to stone.

"Minty! Oh, there you are!"

There was only one lamp left alight in the hall now. The sideboard had been cleared, the table re-polished. Every trace of the feast had been cleared away.

Gemma was distressed. "It's Barr. Oh, do come, quickly! I was just checking that the library was clear and he stumbled in, giving me such a fright! He's been drinking again. Everyone else seems to have gone to bed or gone home. Can you help me steer him back to his rooms?"

Minty put her hand to the base of her throat. "In the library, you say?" Her voice rang out clearly in the Great Hall. A door closed softly upstairs.

The great house lay quiet about them. Waiting. Watchful.

"Of course I'll come."

They passed swiftly back through the silent rooms, with Gemma switching off lights as they went.

The library had been lit by several standard lamps during the evening, but now only one lamp was alight on a side table.

The shadows stole down from the ceiling and darkened the corners of the room.

Barr wasn't there. But Simon was.

Chapter Twenty-Eight

Simon was all in black. His fair hair shimmered. His hands opened and closed. He was grinning like a Halloween lantern.

Tessa was leaning against the far door. She was grinning, too, pleased to show that Simon could rely on her.

Gemma giggled as she set her own back against the door by which they'd entered.

"Shut up, Gemma," said Simon.

"Oh, I can't. Oh, Simon, you mustn't. Really, you mustn't. I can't bear to watch. Don't hurt her too much, will you?"

"What makes you think I'm going to hurt her?"

"Well . . . don't mark her face, then."

"It's not her face I'm interested in." And to Minty, "Here it comes, little sister. At long, long last."

Minty was surprised how cool she felt. There were no pockets in this dress, so she hadn't got her mace spray with her. She balanced on her toes. "The odds are in your favour. Three against one. Do you really mean to rape me with them looking on?"

"Who said anything about rape? You're going to come to me willingly, my lovely girl. I suppose you'll put up a token defence, but we both know that's just for show. Don't fight too hard, or I may well have to mark your face. I'm going to teach you enough so you won't want to marry anyone but me . . ."

He lunged at her, and she darted around the desk.

She felt her self-control slip and screamed. There was a listening silence. Nothing happened, except that Gemma began to bite her nails.

Simon hesitated and then laughed. "There's no one here but you and me . . . stand still, little one!"

He darted around the desk and caught her as she fled, catching her up from behind. "Stop struggling, you little fool!"

She stopped. He was holding her fast from behind, with both arms clamped to her side. She breathed rapidly, trying to snatch back at her self-control. She was helpless. She couldn't do anything to save herself.

"There, now! You see, it's all going to be so easy."

He bent his head and kissed her in the angle of her neck and shoulder. She closed her eyes, trying to think, to remember what Iris had told her to do. She forced herself to relax her muscles one by one. Slowing her breathing right down. He set her back on her feet.

As he did so, she lunged forward, trying to break his hold on her. And failed.

But she had thrust her left hand down and down . . . and now she grasped the inside of his leg through his trousers, nipped and twisted . . . hard. As Iris had taught her to do.

He screamed with pain and released her. As he did so, she drove her high heel down onto his instep.

There was a confused struggle at both doors and Gemma was thrust into the room, yelping. Tessa, too, stumbled forward.

Iris shot into the room in a swish of silk. Simon turned, mouth agape, and tried to swipe her out of his way.

Iris side-stepped, caught Simon's arm and throwing all her weight onto it, whirled him up and over . . .

He thudded to the floor, knocking all the breath out of his body.

"I wouldn't have missed that for anything," said Patrick, strolling in ahead of Annie, with Reggie grinning behind. "Better than any stag party."

Tessa made a stumbling run at Patrick with fingernails reaching for his eyes. Reggie caught her with ease.

Toby and Barr appeared behind Gemma, who was whimpering, fingers in her mouth. "But how . . . there wasn't anyone there . . . ?"

Minty said, "Ever since Simon threatened me, I've been watched every minute of the day. Annie was on duty this evening, but the others were all within call. Patrick guessed Simon would try something tonight, so he saw his guests settled at the pub and came straight back. Meanwhile Reggie was watching the courtyard to see when Simon returned and met up with Tessa. When Simon arrived, Reggie told Gloria, and Gloria gave me the message when we were all at table. We hoped

Gemma wouldn't get involved, though it was always on the cards that she would."

Gemma wailed, "He said that if I got you to the library, he'd tear up the letter I signed, making over all my money to him."

"Did you really believe he would?"

Gemma collapsed in tears.

Minty and Iris shook hands. Minty said, "You'll have to teach me some more tricks some time, Iris. I enjoyed that."

Patrick took out his mobile phone. "We have more than enough on Simon now to convince the police."

"N–no . . . Simon!" Tessa was struggling to reach Simon, who was showing signs of recovery.

He sat up, looking dazed. He pulled himself slowly to his feet, hanging onto the desk. Slowly he straightened up, staring wide-eyed not at Minty, but at Patrick.

He mouthed the words. "If it's the last thing I do . . ."

He gathered himself together, his face contorted.

He made a sudden headlong rush for Patrick, head bent low and arms flailing.

. . . and Patrick coolly, seemingly in slow motion, stepped aside . . .

Simon couldn't stop.

He crashed into the lintel of the doorway. There was a dull crack as his head met wood. He slid down to the carpet while Tessa began to scream, "His face! Oh, his face!"

Patrick used his mobile to ring for an ambulance as well as the police.

Her wedding morning. She'd asked Serafina and Ruby to dress her, but somehow Carol and Iris came too.

Gemma knocked on the door, holding out her make-up box. "I know you won't want to see me, but I thought you might like to use this?"

Minty hesitated. She didn't want any make-up, and she really didn't know if she could forgive Gemma, who had betrayed her after all that Minty had tried to do for her.

Gemma's face broke up. "I'm so, so sorry."

Minty held out her arms and Gemma rushed into them. "There, there," said Minty, thinking that if the girl really was sorry, perhaps there was hope for her.

Iris and Carol disapproved, but dear Ruby took Gemma away to put on her bridesmaid's dress.

Minty gave her rings to Iris to look after. Annie arrived with a diamond tiara which had been made for Minty's grandmother . . . Jonah arrived with a large box of bouquets, posies and headdresses . . . the three bridesmaids shimmered in blue damask dresses created by Ruby out of the bolts of material they'd found in the junk rooms. Gemma asked if she could be chief bridesmaid, but Minty said that honour must go to her oldest friend.

She looked in the mirror and saw herself as Araminta, and no longer as Minty.

Then the room was empty but for Lord Asher, come to take her to church . . . to help her into her father's car, beribboned and posied for the short journey . . . with Reggie grinning in the driving seat.

Many of the shops in the village were decorated with white ribbons and silver bells, displaying notices saying they were closed for two hours . . . children were running up the hill to the church, and groups stood outside with cameras ready.

A susurrus of silk and an indrawn breath from a full church, with everyone that she knew and many that she didn't all turning to look at her as she walked up the aisle on Lord Asher's arm.

Patrick, standing tall and grave . . .

Had the time really come?

His presence steadied her, as always, his eyes holding hers.

The hymn rolled out . . .

Take my life, and let it be
Consecrated, Lord, to thee:
Take my moments and my days,
Let them flow in ceaseless praise . . .

They'd found room for all the children in the choir pews, with Becky keeping them more or less in order, and blowing a kiss to Minty during the sermon.

The age-old words of commitment and promise. Patrick's voice was steady, but his hand was icy cold as he put the ring on her finger, and as she did the same for him.

Signing the register. The blessing.

The last hymn . . .

> *One more step along the world I go,*
> *. . . And it's from the old I travel to the new*
> *Keep me travelling along with you . . .*

The bells pealed out above them, as they made their way back down the church.

In the porch Patrick picked her up and whirled her round. "We made it!"

She clung to him as cameras whirled. Confetti . . .

She'd told Toby there were to be only a couple of photographs in the porch, and she wasn't sure they even had two, because Patrick was carrying her into the car, with Reggie laughing and holding open the door . . . and they were away down the hill, still clinging to one another.

They'd said the reception line was to be very informal, so that people could get to the food quickly. As soon as was decent she tugged Patrick through into the Long Gallery, so anxious was she to show him her special gift, the formal garden laid out in the form of a daisy.

Patrick twined his fingers in hers, and smiled . . . remembering . . .

Toby caught that image, too.

Minty was so happy she wanted to kiss everyone, and did manage to touch and caress most people, especially Carol, Iris and Toby . . . the Woottons, dear Annie and Serafina . . . Florence and the rest of the Thornby family . . .

She'd said, "No speeches, please!" But Patrick had to make one announcement just before the cake was cut.

". . . as from today, I'm adding my wife's name to mine. In future, I shall be Patrick Cardale Sands . . ."

When everyone had overcome their surprise, most said they were pleased.

"It was Sir Micah who rescued Eden Hall . . ."

Then whirling away to change into casual clothes, and running down to throw the bouquet high into the air . . . causing laughter when it landed in dear Ruby's hands . . .

Dashing out to Reggie, who was taking them—everyone supposed—to the airport, but in fact he only took them to a quiet back road where Patrick had left his car . . . and for the first time they could be on their own as man and wife.

Happiness suited Patrick. The sometimes severe lines of his face had softened, and he'd even put on a little weight.

Now he settled himself more comfortably in the bed with his arm around her. "I am, as you know, a man of few words . . ."

Minty yawned. How much sleep had they had last night? "A few thousand words . . . ?"

". . . but I feel that I must register a complaint about all those who have written on the subject of marriage. They didn't warn me that no matter how quickly I got out of bed, you'd get to the bathroom before me, or that you'd pinch my toothpaste . . ."

She giggled. "It was a mistake. You took me by surprise."

". . . or about the sweetness of waking up to find you so twined around me that I have trouble working out which leg is whose. I can't get used to the way you look up and smile at me with your eyes when I come into a room. Or what that does to me. Or the fact that you're forcing me to eat so much more than usual that I'll soon be a fat, bloated old man . . ."

She knew what had brought this on. At precisely one-thirty that afternoon they'd been working together in the kitchen. She'd been dishing up a late lunch, while he'd been tightening up loose screws on a cupboard door. He'd dropped the thread of whatever nonsense he'd been talking, put his hand in his pocket and taken out his mobile phone. Then put it back again. Had he been thinking of ringing his partner to ask for extra time? As if he'd transferred his thoughts to her, she'd suddenly remembered her responsibilities at the Hall.

So after a fortnight's seclusion—most of it spent in bed—he was preparing her for the fact that the honeymoon was drawing to a close.

She sighed. "Yes, I know we've got to go back. We did say we'd only be away for a fortnight, and today's the day of the Fireworks Party. It rained last night. Suppose people don't come, and the event's a write-off?"

"I love fireworks," said Patrick. "Let's get there in time to see the display."

They arrived at the top of the village and found nowhere to park. Coaches, mini-buses, cars, motorcycles crammed the sides of the road. A harassed policeman told them there was no point trying to take the car farther because every parking space within miles was occupied. Minty rang Reggie on her mobile phone.

"It's a sellout, Minty!" Reggie yelled. "Mrs Sands, I should say! There's thousands out front, and we're only letting the top brass with tickets for the house into the car park. That's full, too. But we knew you was coming back tonight, so I put some cones just off the avenue, half way down the drive on the bend. There's a steward on duty there, and he knows to save the space for you, right?"

They found the space and pulled off the avenue under the trees where they could see everything without being seen. The ground-floor rooms of the Hall were all lit up, and through the windows they could see expensively dressed people moving around with champagne glasses in their hands. Floodlights illumined a great crowd of people on the lawns leading down to the lake below.

Minty bit her lip. "We're not dressed for the party inside, and anyway I think Mrs Chickward should act as hostess tonight."

"I've got some heavy sweaters in the boot. Let's mingle incognito with the crowd outside. They're probably having more fun, anyway."

There was pop music blaring out from loudspeakers, the aroma of frying onions and sausages, hot dog stands, chicken tikka stands, candy-floss stands. People carrying children on their shoulders. People carrying makeshift lanterns and torches. Laughter.

Patrick hugged her. "All your doing."

Minty was amazed. "I didn't think we'd get anywhere near as many people."

A loudspeaker announcement: "The display is about to begin." The music faded, floodlights were switched off and the crowd fell silent.

A large area on the far side of the lake had been cordoned off for the display.

"Ooooh!" The first set of rockets were off, and everyone lifted their heads to the sky. "Look at that!"

Patrick stood behind Minty and put his arms about her. She leaned back against him. They were both smiling.

It seemed like only a few minutes, but Patrick told her afterwards that it was nearly an hour before the last flight of rockets lit up the sky and the last display spelt out "Good night". The floodlights and the music were switched back on, and people surged around the food outlets. Minty spotted Florence and Gloria serving hot soup and rolls. An enormous bonfire was lit half way up the slope, with a huge doll dressed in black with a yellow wig perched on top.

Minty gasped. "Is that meant to be Simon?"

Patrick laughed. "I bet Hodge thought that up. Want a hot dog?"

The bonfire was brilliant. The food hot and tasty.

After a while parents with young children began to trickle home, and expensive cars crept down the avenue, taking the guests away. The bonfire died down; the music and the floodlights were switched off. There was a general movement of the crowd towards the drive.

Everyone seemed in high good humour.

"Look, Mummy!" A child's piercing voice halted the crowd.

Patrick and Minty turned to see that every single window of Eden Hall was being lit with candles from within.

"What's that for?" asked someone. "Party's over, innit?"

Minty was transfixed. What a beautiful sight!

Patrick put his arm around her. "Your cue, Minty. The house is always lit up to welcome its mistress home."

"Are we living in a dream?"

"Perhaps it is. Perhaps when I wake up neither you nor the Hall will be there."

Minty wondered if his scars would ever heal properly, if he would ever quite lose the memory of what had been done to him.

Dear Lord, be with us. When we step back into the Hall, it's the real start of our life together. And yes, there will be problems, because there are always problems in this world.

He said, "You lead the way."

She said, "No, we go together. 'From the old, we travel to the new'. Remember?"

He nodded. "With God's help, we can do it."

We want to hear from you. Please send your comments about this book to us in care of zreview@zondervan.com. Thank you.

ZONDERVAN™

GRAND RAPIDS, MICHIGAN 49530 USA

WWW.ZONDERVAN.COM